FREDDY VS. ASH

FREDDY VS. ASH

A NOVEL BY

A. S. Eggleston

ISBN: 1507611463
ISBN 13: 9781507611463

Prologue

CAMP CRYSTAL, 2003. ABOVE THE night sky was a sense of calm and peacefulness. The black night was illuminated by the light of the stars, and the full, silver, moon. It was a vision of pure, and absolute beauty.

Below, was a battle between two raging behemoths, monsters of both the real and supernatural worlds. While it was only one-against-one in the fight, it was certainly a battle for the ages. One: A towering, unstoppable killing machine. A sick, twisted full-filler of vengeance. His name...Jason Voorhees. The other: A manipulator of nightmares, a dream demon, the ultimate seeker of revenge. The bastard son of a hundred maniacs.

His name...Freddy Krueger.

Somewhere, deep inside the torturous pit of Hell, these two wretched beings found each other. Freddy, despite the dark powers that enabled him to invade the dreams of children and murder them, had one weakness: If the children of Elm Street can forget about him, they can't fear him. If they no longer fear him, they can't dream about him. He can't return if nobody's afraid. Sure, being dead wasn't a problem, but being forgotten...now that's a bitch.

He needed someone, someone who'd make them remember. Someone dumb, easily manipulated, like that giant psycho-momma's boy, Jason. Freddy may have been able to get in Jason's head, and read him like a book, but he definitely underestimated his strength. No matter what his victims did, or tried to do, Jason always came back, and came for them.

Their final battle took place at Crystal Lake, or Camp Blood, as those who lived to tell had called it. It was Jason's home. It was where he consumed the lives of his victims.

Each had their own weapon of choice. For Jason, it was his machete: a blunt instrument used for decapitation, disemboweling, and impalement. For Freddy: It was a weapon he had constructed in the dark basement of the boiler room where he had worked. It was a copper-plated welding glove, with steel knives on each finger. It was perfect for torturing the little boys and girls he lured down there, and after he died...killing them in their dreams.

The bright light of the moon reflected upon their weapons as Freddy and Jason raised them to the sky and hurled them at each other. They viciously stabbed and swung their blades as they fought on the dock of Crystal Lake.

With each stab, with each puncture, with each flat-out punch and kick they hurled at one another, not only did they bleed profusely, but they were killing each other.

Everywhere the two went, there was blood. The whole camp was stained with blood and guts. It was a vision of pure carnage. Freddy stabbed Jason in the eyes with his knives. Jason ripped Freddy's arm right out of its socket. Freddy would use Jason's own machete to slash him, stab him, and pierce it straight through Jason's black heart. Jason used his brutal force to jam his arm right through Freddy stomach. They were both soaked and dripping with each other's blood.

Suddenly, the calm, black, waters of Crystal Lake was consumed by fire. The sheer force of the blast knocked Freddy and Jason off their feet and hurled them into the lake to be eaten by the flames. The fire rose, higher and higher as their bodies burned above the lake, and eventually drowned below. The black night was lighted by the bright, orange, glow of the fire. The flames were alive, as if they were dancing in celebration of the deaths of the two monsters.

Jason: Drowned as a boy, and left for dead into the cold, dark, waters of the lake.

Freddy: Burned alive at the hands of innocents for the sake of retribution.

As they were in life, so shall they be in death.

At least...That's what everyone had hoped for.

Yes, they were dead...for now. Freddy and Jason's souls are being tormented in Hell. Just like they were, numerous times before. And just like before, something will bring them back. Jason will rise again with a couple of new scars as a memento, ready to strike the next batch of young camp counselors who dare step foot on his territory.

As for Freddy... this time, he's not satisfied with just coming back for a while, killing a new crop of suburban brats, only to have some clever bitch send him back to Hell where he came from.

No, not this time. He's the Springwood Slasher, after all. He lured countless children into his murderous lair, did foul and unspeakable things to them, and killed them. All the parents in the neighborhood gathered around the power plant and lit the whole building on fire. His sanctuary, his hiding place, his dungeon, was awash with flames. Krueger thought his time had come, when three Dream Demons appeared before him, and allowed him the opportunity to live in the nightmares of his victims. He lived off their fear and fed off their souls. But that was nothing compared to what he has in store this time.

Since his plan with Jason had failed, Freddy devised a plot to go to the ultimate source of his evil power, and claim it for himself. It may take a while, but when he does, Freddy's going to find a way to be truly...eternal.

His name is Ash, and he is the Chosen One–at least–that's what he's been told. Back in the day, Ashley J. Williams was just like any other guy. He had a medium-wage job as a stock boy, drove an old, broken down piece of machinery, and had a beautiful girlfriend, Linda.

One night, Ash and Linda drove to a cabin in the mountains for the weekend.

That was where his average, everyday, life had ceased.

Beforehand, an archaeologist by the name of Professor Raymond Knowby had stayed there, in the cabin, to study his latest finds.

Inside the ruins of the castle of Kandar, among his discoveries was the Necronomicon Ex-Mortis. Roughly translated: Book of the Dead. The book served as a passageway to the evil worlds beyond. Bound in human flesh, and inked in blood, this ancient Sumerian text contains bizarre burial rites, funerary incantations, and demon resurrection passages. It was never meant for the world of the living.

Since finding the damned book, Ash has had every horrible and torturous thing imaginable done to him. Everyone around him had been possessed by the foul things that live inside the book. He's been forced to murder his loved ones, dismember their corpses, and bury them in shallow graves.

The bastards even came for him. It got into his hand and it went bad, so he lopped it off at the wrist with a chainsaw. Even when Ash thought he had rid himself of the evil things, he was sent back in time to the Middle Ages, leading a war against an Army of Darkness. He managed to return to his own time, but not without a price. He left as normal, young, man, and came back as a hero. Chosen by destiny, and screwed by fate.

After all this time, he now knows things that others cannot even comprehend. He knows that there is a living evil, a presence that lives not in the space that we live in, but beyond it. In the dark. In the night. And he cannot escape them. He tried to. Time and again, he tried to live as much of a normal life as he could. But wherever Ash goes, the Evil Dead follows. The spirits, or Deadites, as one would call them, are everywhere. They Eggleston / Freddy vs. Ash / 6 harbor all kinds of demons, and they're the stuff nightmares are made of. They fester in the dark bowers of man's domain, waiting to be set free.

Waiting to consume the souls of the living.

Waiting...for someone to let them out.

Chapter 1

Ash found himself in the heart of the desolate woods. He didn't know exactly where he was. He didn't know how he even got there. Then again, considering all of the head injuries he had sustained over the years, it was a wonder he could remember his name.

This was just like any other night for Ash: come home from work, hear from the locals about some poor sap going missing, and find himself in a place like this, to make sure the Deadite plague doesn't spread any further. This has been his life for the past thirty years. *It's a noble job and everything to protect the innocent and all...* Ash would often say to himself. *but I wonder sometimes what life would have been like for me if I'd never gone to that blasted cabin. Linda and I were serious. Who knows? Maybe we would have gotten married, had a few kids, and lived happily ever after.* But any prospects of that were dead and gone. Literally.

Nowadays, Ash doesn't really have time for an exciting love life. Even if he did, he couldn't risk it. It seemed like everyone he ever cared about, everyone he was close to, died around him. He didn't want to risk getting his heart broken again. *Again, very flattering to be the guy to rid the world of Deadites, but it still sucked sometimes.*

As he walked through the woods, Ash noticed something about his surroundings. Something about where he was...it just didn't seem normal. Of course, being miles away from town, looking for some possessed monster to hack off with a chainsaw wasn't very normal in the first place, but seemed like something was off. Ash looked up at the moon. It was full and glowing red. That was never good. A thick cover of fog surrounded him as he walked deeper into the woods. Even if the guy was here, Ash wouldn't be able to see him unless he was extremely close. And the trees...the trees just looked as if they were...staring right at him. As if they were monitoring and surveying him. The long, leafy branches looked like they were ready to completely engulf him.

He slowly, and cautiously, walked past the thick tree trunks. He glided his hand against the bark, getting a feel for where he was going. He felt blinded by the dense fog around him. While the glow of the moon provided a somewhat ethereal ambience, it did nothing in terms of leading his path. As he walked past the trees, he heard a sound, like someone was walking beside him. He whipped his head to the side, waving the fog from in front of him. He didn't see anyone and continued walking. But, in the back of his mind, Ash could have sworn he saw something with red and green stripes hiding behind the tree a few yards away from him.

Ash had been walking for quite some time now, ever since sundown it felt like. He was exhausted. Carrying a chainsaw on your right hand, and a double-barreled shotgun on your left was harder that it looked. Ash was tired of these games. They always hid in the corner, waiting to sneak up on him. Ash wanted them to just show up so they could die already. He put his shotgun back in his holster, and leaned back against the tree trunk behind him. He took just a few moments to relax, rest, and try to figure out where this demon could possibly be. Ash was breathing pretty heavily. Hunting down Deadites and sawing their limbs off was harder than it used to be. He wiped the sweat off his brow and mumbled, "Damn it, where are y– *Ack!*"

Before he could finish, he felt a pair of cold, grimy hands around his throat. They squeezed tighter and tighter, muffling Ash's screams. The hands belonged to a set of large and muscular arms, pushing Ash flat on the ground.

It was him. The undead bastard waited for the perfect opportunity to rip through the fog and attack Ash as soon as he let his guard down. But the ugly, decayed, giant didn't account for one thing...

Ash was the one with the chainsaw.

As the demon chanted, "Join usssss! Join usssss!" Ash wasted no time reaching over and starting up his favorite weapon. He couldn't afford to goof around, as he was losing air fast. That's right, he didn't need reload a chainsaw. He pulled the recoil as hard as he could.

rrrrrrr... Nothing. He pulled it once more.

rrrrrrr... Nothing, again.

He did, however, need to refuel a chainsaw.

Well, this is just great. Ash was slowly losing consciousness, he was being choked out by some rotted demon who weighed about two tons. He tried one last time. "Come on!" he said, his voice was scratchy.

RRRRRRRRRRrrrrrrrrrrRRRRRRRRRRrrrrrrrrrrRRRRRRRRRR!!!

Finally! Ash grinned from ear to ear. He directed his attention to the living undead hovering over him. "Hey buddy," he said, his voice still raspy. "Your insides could use some arranging!" He rammed his chainsaw right into the guy's stomach and though his spine, shredding his guts away. The living corpse shook and convulsed as the chainsaw cut through his stomach and chest. Blood sprayed in every direction, causing Ash's face and body to be covered in thick, gooey, redness. "Who's laughing now, huh?! Ha ha ha ha ha!"

Once the monster was completely disemboweled, Ash threw him off and got back on his feet. He studied him for a second, already smelling the rotting guts that were now exposed to the air. He looked at all of the blood and intestines that spilled over the creature. Ash would be lying if he said he didn't take a little pride in his work. He pulled out his shotgun and aimed it at the guy's head. If there's one thing he knew about Deadites, it's that they always like to come back for one last scare. The creature's eyes were blank white, looking and nothing and everything at the same time. He was still...for a minute.

He jerked his head up and reached for Ash, when his entire head suddenly exploded from the impact of the shotgun blast. He was finally dead. Grey smoke rose from the barrel. Ash nonchalantly blew it away, spun the gun once with his thumb, and placed it back in the holster.

Ash turned and walked away. Now, he could return back home, and grab a cold beer that had his name on it.

Snap!

What was that? Ash looked around. There was no one there. *Must have been a squirrel or something.* He carried on and continued walking, wiping the blood off his face. He didn't want to drive back to town covered in blood, and carrying an arsenal of weapons. *Probably best not to cause any suspicion.*

Snap! Snap!

Just keep walking. Ash couldn't let his paranoia control him. Besides, he was almost to his car: A 1973 Delta 88 Oldsmobile. The Classic, as he liked to call it. Even though it had been wrecked a few dozen times, it still managed to take him where he needed to go. He opened up the trunk, and unlocked his chainsaw from his arm, and set it inside. He slammed the trunk closed, and headed for the door.

Almost there.

"Aaaaaaaaah! Hhhhha ha ha ha ha! Ashhhhhhh! Join usssssssss!"

He whipped around and saw bodies coming from everywhere. Rising from the dirt, emerging from within the woods, they were even up high, hiding in the branches of the trees. They were disgusting and decrepit. Their faces were locked in permanent, demented smiles. Ash quickly reached for his shotgun and opened up the barrel to reload. He grabbed two shells from his shirt pocket. Several hands rose from the dirt, grabbing Ash by the ankles and knocking him down.

They all surrounded him in a circle, hovering over him, and reached down to scratch his flesh. He could hear their demonic chant, "Join usssss! Join usssss!" This had never happened before. Ash was completely powerless, there were too many of them. He did all he could, he tried to break away, but they kept pulling him back. He saw that his shotgun had landed next to him. He managed to grab it, replace the shells, and cock it in a matter of seconds.

BOOM!

One down.

He then aimed for one that was about to reach over to his leg, and take a bite of his flesh.

BOOM!

Another one down. But they still swarmed, and he was out of bullets. All he could do was just punch and kick the living hell out of them. "Get off of me!" he yelled. They just kept coming for him, holding him down so he couldn't move. "When will you stop torturing me like this?!" he howled. Suddenly, mere inches from his face, was another disfigured creature.

It was small, female, with little blonde pigtails. *This horrible monster used to be a sweet, little girl.* Her face showed nothing but evil, and a lust for blood. She spoke to him, replying to his cries of terror, "We will not stop until you set him free!" She opened her mouth wide, revealing a set of sharp fangs for teeth. Black blood came pouring out of her mouth, she stuck out her tongue. It was long, green, and absolutely disgusting. She laughed. Her voice quickly changed from that of a little girl, to something low, guttural, and evil. "Haaa ha ha ha ha ha ha ha ha ha!" Her face and body morphed. Her skin was no longer pale and smooth. It appeared to be burned, with scars everywhere and fleshy sinews hanging from her face. She no longer looked like herself. It was now someone completely different. It was a man. The same man wearing the red and green stripes on his shirt from before.

Ash shouted at the disfigured man. "Who the hell are you?!"

He quickly lunged towards Ash, wearing what looked like knives on his fingers…

Ash screamed at the top of his lungs. He feared for his life. "No! No!"

The four blades were now inches from his eyes.

"Aaaaaah! Aaaaaah!" Ash screamed until he gasped for breath. He found himself sitting up, back in his own bed. *It was all just a dream.* "I'm fine now." he said, reassuring himself. "It was just a bad dream,"

He felt a sharp pain run across his right arm. He looked at it. There were scratch marks on it. Some of them had blood seeping from the wounds. He was now unsure of himself. "or maybe it wasn't."

Ever since he came to Springwood, things just got even stranger. He figured, "I'll get out of Michigan for a while, rent a house for cheap, rid this town of its Deadites, do my heroic job, move on somewhere else. Like I always do." But something wasn't right about this house. He couldn't believe he got something this nice for so cheap: Two stories, three bedrooms, huge kitchen. It even had a basement to keep all of his gear in. Of course, he assumed something bad had to have happened at 1428 Elm Street, but it's not like Ash wasn't equipped to handle a haunted house. But still, something about this place just gave him a bad feeling.

Ash laid back down, but he certainly didn't go back to sleep.

Chapter 2

ASH NEVER EVEN SO MUCH as rested his eyes for the rest of the night. It was completely illogical to stay awake for an entire night just because some bad dreams, and he knew it, but they felt real so him. He could feel that huge, bulking, Deadite's blood gushing all over his body. He could feel the claws scratching and breaking his skin open. He could even smell the foul stench of that guy's rotting intestines exposed to the night air. Ash still couldn't explain to himself how those scratch marks appeared on his arms.

Maybe I did that in my sleep. he thought.

It didn't make sense, but that was the only reasonable answer he could come up with. He muttered to himself. "These damn nightmares are killing me." He sat in the middle of his couch in the living room, slumped over and completely ragged. For the rest of the night, he kept himself busy by flipping through various infomercials on TV, and drinking his coffee straight from the pot.

"Who needs a mug?" he said, justifying himself. It was apparent to Ash that he was going to need a lot this stuff, and a tiny little mug that reminded him how much he hates Mondays wasn't going to cut it. He took a small drink, grimaced, and spit it back out. *Coffee that's bitter and tastes like dirt isn't going to cut it either.* Ash grabbed a handful of sugar packets and ripped them open, pouring them in the pot. "Yeah, how 'bout a little sugar, baby?" he muttered to himself, shaking the packets to make sure every last grain went into the coffee.

His hair was a mess. It was ragged, and hadn't been washed in days. He'd accumulated puffy bags under his eyes. Ash was exhausted, dazed, and had caffeine running through his system. It didn't sit well him. The hazy look in his eyes, and his hand twitching as he lifted the coffee pot to his face showed it.

Morning had finally come, and if Ash hadn't already chugged an entire pot of coffee by now, this was usually the time of day when he'd start his first cup. When he drank it down to the last drop, he slammed the pot down and turned off the television. The sunlight broke through the curtains in the living room. The light illuminated on the wall clock just across the room. 7:23 AM, it was time for Ash to detach himself from the couch cushions and get ready for work. Before he got up, he quickly decided to take one last packet of sugar, tear it open, and hope those four grams would give him enough of a sugar high to get through the day. He tossed the empty packet on top of the pile already scattered across the coffee table.

He took a much needed shower, and put on fresh clothes. Ash went into the bedroom, quickly picked up a comb, and ran it across his head a few times. Before he left, he grabbed his name tag that read, "Ashley J. Williams - Housewares Dept." and pinned onto his shirt. He shuffled his feet back downstairs, grabbed his black leather jacket from the coat hanger by the front door, and he was off.

He stepped outside and squinted at the sight of the morning sun. He shielded his eyes with his metal hand and walked over to his Delta 88. He opened up the trunk. It was a mess. There were empty liters of soda, a couple issues of *Fangoria,* boxes of shotgun shells, and a chemistry textbook inside. Not much has changed, except now Ash had stuck a note on the top of the trunk. It read, "The words: Klaatu Verada Niktu" scribbled in pencil. There was some eraser marks on "Niktu", indicating he wrote down a few other words and realized that they didn't belong. He always had some trouble remembering that one. He took the note, and put it in his front pocket. "I'm gonna find that damn book, and when I do, I'm gonna make sure you guys never come after me again." he promised to himself. He promptly slammed the trunk.

He came in at work about half an hour early, which didn't bother him in the slightest.

Anything to stay awake, right? He strode through the pneumatic doors of the Springwood S-Mart, and took off his jacket. He paced his way to the Housewares department, casually waving at the other clerks he passed by.

Ash was lucky he had found an S-Mart in this town. His first job was a stock boy in Dearborn, Michigan, back when he was in high school. It was pretty much the only thing he knew how to do that was marketable. Of course, Ash didn't plan on staying here for very long. He'd heard this town had a bad history. There were a lot of murders, mostly children, but no one would go into detail beyond that. *Maybe that had something to do with my dream...The little girl...Maybe this town has a bunch of Deadite kids running around. Eh, I've been through worse.*

Among the clerks Ash passed by, were two kids that worked the check-out counter. Their names were Evelyn Marshall and Cooper Reynolds, two eighteen year-olds who had their whole lives ahead of them. They were a couple, and seeing them together made Ash sick to his stomach. There they were, these happy kids without any cares beyond whether or not they'll be able to pay their rent payment. Meanwhile Ash is condemned to a life of demon slaying. But he didn't mind catching a glimpse of Evelyn now and then. She was a pretty girl. She had big, beautiful, green eyes that would stop anyone dead in their tracks when she looked at them, and had jet black hair that stopped at her waist.

She leaned over at the check-out counter, looking very bored. The store wasn't going to open for another thirty minutes. She saw Ash waving at her as he walked away, so she smiled at him and waved back.

Cooper was standing next to her, he noticed the exchange between them.

He leaned over towards her. "You know he's got to be twice your age, right?" he said with a smirk on his face. Evelyn stood up and playfully punched him in the arm. Cooper raised his hands in defeat and stood up straight. He was really tall, and lanky. He was six foot three, so when he stood up, he towered over Evelyn. "Hey, I'm just saying," he said with a laugh, "I didn't know you had a thing for the Elvis impersonator type."

"I was only being nice." she said. "Besides, I don't. I have a thing for you." she wrapped her arms around his waist.

He put his arms around her waist as well. "Yeah, I know. I was just teasing you." he said with a loving smile. "Hey, Evelyn." he asked, his smile getting wider. "Guess what?"

She matched his smile. "What?"

He leaned in and whispered. "Chicken butt."

Evelyn snickered and smacked the side of his arm. "That's not funny anymore!" She ran her fingers through his shaggy, dark blonde hair before walking away, laughing.

Cooper put on a dramatic face pointed at her. "You lie!" he shouted.

The clock read 9:05 AM in the office of Lieutenant Harold Moore at the Springwood Police Department. Moore was a striking individual, six-foot-four, broad shoulders, blonde hair, and a beard on his square jaw. Moore was in his sixties, and had joined the police academy a few years after Fred Krueger's arrest back in 1968. He had never heard of a man so sick and vile. The things that he did to those innocent children made Moore sick just from the thought of it.

Before Moore had joined the force, his predecessor, Lt. Donald Thompson, did everything he could to make sure Krueger was put behind bars. But, they made the mistake of searching his home without a warrant. There was nothing they could do. So they rounded up the parents of Elm Street to torch the bastard. Moore watched from afar as the parents gathered to take justice into their own hands. He hated the concept of murder, that's why he despised Krueger and what he did to those little boys and girls, but when that Molotov cocktail burst through the glass window and sent the whole building on fire, he felt a wash of relief over him. Relief that Krueger was dead, and the children of Elm Street were safe in their own beds.

That is...until the killings started again in 1981. Moore, the entire police department, nor the parents knew how, but Fred Krueger started killing again. This time, in their children's nightmares. Children started to die by Krueger's blades in their sleep. Children were murdered by him more than they ever did when he was alive. They didn't know how to stop it. It was only until Lt. Thompson's daughter, Nancy, an intern at Westin Hills psychiatric hospital, had prescribed the children Hypnocil. It was a dream suppressant. It was perfect. It was a way to stop the dreaming. Several years ago, the entire town had concocted a plan to keep Freddy away from their children. Anyone who had even made mention of a man with burnt skin and razor fingers in their dreams was hauled off to Westin Hills with no access to the outside world. It worked...for a while. Eventually, the town's plan had been interfered when another killer had entered their once peaceful town. Luckily, Jason Voorhees had been driven out of Springwood before the whole town could be infected with fear. It was always the fear that drove Freddy.

By now, the town's plan had been altered to a lesser degree. Anyone eighteen or younger would be given Hypnocil, under the guise of pain medication or everyday vitamins. Moore felt that this was a more humane way to keep the problem under control, rather than forcibly admitting them to a psychiatric hospital.

It worked for several years. There was no more nightmare-ish activity in the town for ten years after the plan had taken effect. But recently, a few weeks ago to be exact, a few unexplained murders had taken place just outside of town. He was befuddled by the occurrences. Even more so, he was worried.

Moore was sorting through murder records when Officer Nathan Harris opened the door to his office. He was in his early thirties, with a semi-strong build. He had spiky, black hair, with thin glasses settling on the bridge of his nose. He had only been on the force for a few years, and was still learning the ropes. But, after living in Springwood for most of his adult life, he became acquainted with the town's history.

He poked his head out of the door and knocked on the wall. "Lieutenant?" he asked. "Is this a bad time?"

Moore's gaze peeled away from the papers and looked up at Harris, who stood at the far side of the room. He replied, "No, Harris." he waved his fingers, instructing him to come in. "But, make it short. What is it now?"

Nathan walked in, carrying a folder in his hand. Moore assumed it was more crime scene photos. "I'm just very confused about what's been going on around here lately, sir."

"I assume you mean the murders?" he said bluntly.

"Yes sir." answered Harris.

Harold leaned back in his chair and tried to rub the gruesome visions of the crime scene photos from his eyes. He had seen enough for one day. "What exactly is there to be confused about?" he asked, almost remorsefully. "For a long time, the distribution of Hypnocil to every home in the town worked. But, you know as well as I do, in this town, these plans only work for so long."

"No, no." rebutted Nathan. "It's not that. At least, I don't think it is." He laid the folder down in Moore's desk and showed him the pictures and reports. "Take a look at these records, sir. This is isn't like the usual murders done by Krueger. I don't think he's even involved in these."

"Why do you say that?"

"Well, just compare the two." he said. "Usually, the murders done by Krueger are in places where there are children: schools, homes, yada yada. And the victims, nine times out of ten, are kids." He spread the pictures all over his desk. "But in these, most of the victims are twenty-five or older, and occur in the outskirts of town. Most of the bodies we find are in the woods, sir."

He looked at the pictures. "You may have a point there, Nathan." he said. "But these murders look very brutal. How can you be sure it wasn't him? Maybe he changed his methods."

"Look at the pattern, here." he pointed to the picture showing a man who had his limbs sawed off, and his head shot. "Whenever Freddy killed someone, he always left four, continuous, slash marks all over their bodies. In this one, this man's arms and legs had been cut off with some sort of saw. And we found traces of shotgun shells in his skull. This man was murdered, but not by Freddy."

"So what we another maniac on the loose." he concluded. "Great."

He put the papers back in the folder. "But that's not it, sir. It's very strange, and I can't really explain it."

"What is it?" asked Moore.

Harris searched for the right words, but it was just so odd, that it felt weird even talking about it. "It's just that..." He closed the folder and leaned down, putting his hands on the desk. "I talked to the medical examiner today. And she said that the bodies were already decomposing hours before their pronounced time of death. And their blood, she said...that...they had different colors of blood in their bodies: red, green, black. And their eyes, they had no pupils. They were just...white. Doesn't that strike you as kind of...well, creepy, sir?"

Harold leered at him, disgusted by the visual images that came with what Harris had just told him. "My God, that *is* disgusting." he said. "Are you absolutely sure about that?"

"Positive." confirmed Nathan. "And I've done some research, and there were bodies like this found in other towns all across the country. What do you think we should do about this? Or is there anything we *can* do?"

Moore put his elbows on his desk, and rubbed his temples in an attempt to subside his headache. "I don't know what we can do about these people just yet." he said. "But, we do know that each of them were murdered. And I can tell from the use of a shotgun and whatever type of saw, that it's being done by the same guy. So, first things first, I want you track down our murderer, then we'll find out whatever the hell was going on with these people at the time."

"Okay," Harris nodded as he secured the folders in his hand, and walked away. "I'll get right on it." He quietly shut the door behind him as he left.

By noon, everyone had gone to lunch. Ash had traded his coffee for a 20 oz. energy drink. He knocked it back like he was drinking tequila out of a shot glass. His routine seemed to work, he didn't feel any compulsion to go to sleep at all. *Not...at...all.*

In the Garden department, Cooper and Evelyn were both lying in a hammock that was on display, swinging side to side.

He looked into her eyes. "You're beautiful." he said.

Evelyn smiled, revealing her pearly, white teeth. "You're handsome." she replied.

Cooper leaned in, closer to her face. "Not as handsome as you!"

Evelyn laughed. Her gaze trailed off and noticed Ash from across the way.

Cooper noticed her looking at him. "So what's this Ash guy all about?" he inquired. "Where's he from?"

"I don't know." Evelyn added. "I heard he got transferred from the store in Dearborn."

"Where's that at?" he asked.

"It's in Michigan."

Cooper watched as Ash crushed the can with his metal, semi-robotic hand, and threw it in the trash.

“He seems like a fuckin’ psychopath to me.”

Evelyn smiled a little bit. “Well, he *is* from Michigan.”

“Hey!” he protested. “I’m from Michigan.”

“My point exactly.” she said with a smile.

They laughed quietly, hoping Ash wouldn’t hear them. Cooper noticed Ash walking away, not towards them, but he was getting close. As he walked past, Ash looked over at Evelyn, cocked his eyebrows, and gave her a sly smile.

Evelyn shrugged it off, but Cooper wasn’t going to let it go that easily. What Evelyn saw as a cheesy, but innocent flirtation, Cooper translated as “I want to bang your girlfriend.” Cooper simply watched him the entire time he walked, burning a hole in the back of his head with his eyes.

Chapter 3

ASH STRODE ACROSS THE STORE, making a beeline towards the door that led outside. He needed some fresh air to clear his head. He zig-zagged his way past the crowd of people in front of him. He was almost out.

He zoomed by Buck, the janitor, who was talking to Anthony, the nerdy guy who worked in the Electronics department. Actually, it was more like Buck was listening to Anthony as he droned on and on. Buck was bored out of his mind, feeling like his story would never end.

Ugh...Lord, kill me now. he thought to himself.

"So I said to the guy," Anthony continued. He took his thick-rimmed glasses off, breathed on them, cleaned them on his button-up shirt, and put them back on. "I said, 'If you don't watch the first movie, you'll be totally lost. I mean–yeah, the second one is far superior, but if you have to watch them all in chronological order in order to get it.' Right? And he was just like–"

Buck was on the verge of slipping into a coma when he noticed that peculiar guy with the metal hand and the big chin walking by. He'd heard about him, rumors and such. Buck wanted to talk to him face to face. That, and it was a good excuse to get out of hearing Anthony run his mouth. He whipped around, cutting Anthony off in mid-sentence.

He stopped leaning against the mop handle, and stood up straight. His voice was deep and gruff. "Hey, you!" he called.

Ash stopped and slowly turned around. He saw this big, husky guy with a beard and a trucker hat staring at him. "...Yeah?" he said, hesitantly.

"What's your name?" he asked.

Ash glared at him for a second. *What does this guy want?* "Name's Ash. Housewares."

"Ash." he said, memorizing his name. "You're the one who lives in that house. 1428 Elm, right?"

He looked at Buck inquisitively. *How's that his business?* Ash took a step forward and held his head up high. "Yeah. How'd you know?"

"It's a small town. Word gets around pretty quickly."

"Well, what about it?"

Buck scratched his dark, scruffy beard, trying to find the right words to say. He was about to say something when Anthony beat him to the punch.

"That place is a murder house, man. Every time someone moves in there, it turns into a crime scene." he blurted.

"I think what my socially awkward friend here means," Buck added. "is that house isn't exactly..." Buck searched for the right word. "...safe." He continued questioning Ash. "You got kids?"

He answered firmly. "No."

"How long have you been living here?" he asked.

"About a week, or so." he said. "Just passing by, actually."

Buck hesitated for a moment before asking him the next question. "And in that week, 'or so'," he said sternly. "Have you had any nightmares?"

"Look, I didn't come here for a head-shrinking. Okay?" Ash said, annoyed. "So, just drop the questions."

He prepared to turn and walk away, when Anthony came forward. "Wait–wait–wait! Ash, wait a minute!" Anthony stopped him.

Ash whipped around and looked down at Anthony, glaring at him. He terrified him, but he still kept going. "Look, Ash." he said weakly. "There's something that you should probably hear. And you should hear it from us, because no one else in this town ever wants to speak about it–a–at least, not in great detail."

Ash was unfazed. He continued to give Anthony the evil eye. "I'm listening."

"A few years ago," he said. "something bad happened here."

"Look Anthony, we're not around a campfire, so cut it out with the ghost stories and start explaining. Chop, chop."

"Well–uh," Anthony was a bit intimidated at this point. He was about to spit out the town's dirty little secret to some stranger.

"Sometime today, maybe?" Ash said.

Buck rolled his eyes. *Now he's at a loss for words?*

Anthony cleared his throat. "You see, a few kids were, uh–slaughtered–a while back." his voice was hushed.

"...'A few'?" Buck cut in. "Try forty-two! Plus ten more kids back when that big guy waltzed his way in here–"

"Shut the hell up, man!" Anthony turned to Buck, his voice still hushed.

Ash was growing impatient, so he walked over to Buck. "Alright. You," he pointed to him. "I want some answers. Now."

He stood still, leaning on the mop handle. "About ten years ago, there were a string of murders that spread from here all the way to Crystal Lake in New Jersey. Over a dozen kids and one cop were slashed to death. They were stabbed, disemboweled, and chopped to death with some kind of blade. And the first murder," he paused. "was in that house."

Boy, I know how to pick 'em, don't I? Ash thought. "Okay." he said. "So, who did it? Was it like a–uh–" Ash was trying to find a word to describe "Deadite" without actually saying it.

"The police never caught him." Anthony joined in. "But they thought it was some copycat killer of–uh–somebody else. I can't remember who it was." he said, lying.

"So one kid gets killed in that house, and you're trying to tell me that it's haunted?" he asked. Ash wasn't denying the existence of supernatural forces, but he's seen scarier things than ghosts.

He threw their dead bodies in the furnace to be burned, leaving no evidence. Just in case.

Krueger was plotting his next move when the parents of Springwood joined together and set the whole plant on fire. They stood together, taking justice into their own hands as they watched it burn to the ground. Fred Krueger was dead.

But that wasn't the whole story.

Ash felt as if he'd heard enough. He'd seen disgusting excuses for human beings, but this story made him gag. Buck and Anthony continued to tell him that, yes, Fred Krueger was dead, but only for a short time. Ash kept waiting to hear that he came back from his grave to swallow people's souls, and unfortunately no one had a shotgun on hand, but he never did.

Many years after his "death", children were reportedly dying in their sleep. They would have such horrific nightmares, they claimed, that they were afraid to go to sleep, believing that they would die. These kids have reported seeing a man in their nightmares, with burnt skin, razors for fingers, and went by the name "Freddy".

What Buck and Anthony couldn't explain, however, was exactly how this Freddy guy would appear in a bunch of teenagers' nightmares and kill them in their sleep. So, with their long and sordid tale at an end, Ash left them and carried on, less confused, but more afraid.

Ash's shift was over at 5:00 pm, and normally he'd return home, relax for a bit, and move on to his night job of demon slaying, but something more important had caused him to make a change of plans.

He high-tailed it out of the parking lot and got on the road. As he drove, Ash took one hand off the wheel and dug in his shirt pocket. He pulled out the note that read "The words: Klaatu Verada Niktu" just to remind himself one last time. Because this time, he planned on doing it right.

"Alright, I think I got you know." he said to himself.

Ash drove off into the sunset with one destination in mind: The old, demolished, power plant on the edge of town.

Chapter 4

THE ROAD STRETCHED OUT FOR miles, winding from left to right on the outskirts of Springwood. This part of town was pretty much desolate. It had no homes or schools, even most of the trees were decayed and barren. Even so, the tallness of the trees on both sides of the road enveloped the pathway. The rickety branches creepily loomed over, as if forming a tunnel high above the road. This was a sight all too familiar to Ash.

As he slowly drove down the narrow road, he examined the nature, or lack thereof, surrounding him. He had a gut feeling that the Necronomicon had to be hidden somewhere in this isolated area.

The further Ash drove, he could see a small figure in the distance. He figured it must have been the old power plant. He cruised his way out of the trench of woods, and into the open trail that led to the plant. It was completely deserted and there was not shred of plant life to be seen. A strange feeling washed over his entire body, like his conscience letting him know this was a bad place to be.

Before he knew it, he ran over a dip in the road, which caught him off guard. The sudden rise and fall of the car caused him to slam on the brakes, stopping the car to a screeching halt, nearly causing him to bang his head on the steering wheel. He looked up and noticed he was right in front of the power plant.

"I got to stop daydreaming." Ash said to himself.

He stepped outside of his car and walked up to the building, surveying it. It was about fifty feet tall and appeared to be 5,200 square feet. It was quite a large facility. Although, most of the building's structure had been demolished. The plant was condemned shortly after Freddy was murdered, so the building eventually decayed over time. The ground was laden with bricks, pipes, and other kinds of debris. The twin smokestacks still held up. The one on the left was covered in grime and soot, while the right had been cut off in the middle, the rim was cracked and pointed like a crown. The sun had set behind the power plant, forming a silhouette all around the building and contrasting the orange-pink coloration of the sky with the utter blackness that surrounded the plant.

Ash walked around to the left wing of the building and saw the lower level. It had rows of window openings on each side of the walls, but no glass. There was black soot that spread from the top of the windows and upward. Ash walked closer towards the lower level and heard a crunch at the base of his shoe. It was broken glass.

This must be where all the action happened. Ash pushed on the metal doors, but they wouldn't open. They were covered in too much rust.

Ash rammed it once with his shoulder.

Then twice.

When he banged on it for the third time, the door finally busted open. It made a horrible creaking noise at it swung open.

The whole area was pitch black. The only light that came through was from the door and the openings in the window panes. He tried turning on the light switch, but no go. Ash opted to just take the flashlight out of his coat pocket and navigate with that. The boiler level was so spacious and high. It was like a huge, rusted cave. If the book was here, how was he even going to find it?

He explored it for a while, tunneling his way through all of the boilers, water heaters, and the swarm of pipes that surrounded him. He explored every corridor of that twisted, metal maze. After a while, he was climbing up the metal stairs, nearing the top level. He glided his hand across the railing for support. They were cold and brown with rust. Ash looked down below to the ground and nearly got vertigo from the height. His head was spinning, so he figured it would be best if he just kept looking straight ahead. The grating creaked with each step he took.

Out of nowhere, Ash heard a loud squeal piercing his ear drums.

SQUEAK!

He jerked his head in the direction it was coming from, searching with his flashlight. So many questions raced through his mind in that fraction of a second.

What was that? Is this old, rickety grate giving out? Am I going to fall to my death from up here? Was that a person? Is there someone else with me? Does this Freddy guy still roam here? Why didn't I bring my Boomstick?

Following the squealing noise, was a loud *clunk*. A pipe broke loose and fell down behind him. Ash sighed in relief and laughed a little bit to calm himself. He pointed his finger at the pipe, as if it fell on purpose. "Yeah, real funny." He turned back around, stepped forward, and was immediately engulfed with chains hanging from the ceiling. He gasped in surprise. He could have sworn he didn't see those chains before. There were several wrapped around him, like boa constrictors. He examined them more closely. He grabbed one and held the flashlight above it. It was covered from top to bottom in dried blood. *Blood that belonged to a little boy or girl, most likely*. Ash let go of the chain in disgust and wiped hand on his pant leg. He unwrapped himself from the chains. "All right." Ash said. "Get it together." he assured himself and resumed down the stairs.

He was back down on the lowest level and ready to just give up and go back home. He walked closer to the exit, when the light from his flashlight spotted something that caught his attention. There was something on the floor, just slightly left of the double doors. He looked down to the floor and saw more dried, spotted blood, except it was in some sort of a trail. Ash veered away from the exit, and decided to follow the dark, red, line. He noticed a large furnace nearby and walked toward it. Maybe it's hidden in there. He opened up the furnace door, but didn't find the Necronomicon. All he saw was remnants of...tiny ribcages...little broken skulls...and other bones.

"Ugh..." he said in disgust. "Those two weren't lying."

He resumed following the trail. Finally, when it stopped, it ended on what appeared to be a cellar door on the floor. "Of course." Ash said, bitterly. "It's always gotta be in some Godforsaken cellar." He opened up the door and used his flashlight to search the entryway. It was pretty deep. Ash looked behind his shoulder and noticed that it was already dark outside. "Should I really be wasting my time like this on the possibility that it *might* be here?" he wondered. He looked back down into the cellar. "It probably won't take that long. Might as well." He went for it. He delved deep inside the earthen floors of the cellar. This was the part of the boiler room that was completely hidden and isolated. So, of course it was perfect for Freddy to hide, or to play fun, little, games with the children.

Ash found himself in the main corridor of the cellar. It was much like the rest of the whole boiler level, just smaller. He passed through all of the pipes and pressure valves and didn't find a thing. Trenching a little further, past all of the equipment, Ash found a tiny room no bigger than a walk-in closet. A feeling of strange uneasiness increased within him. The hairs on the back of his neck stood up and he instantly got goose bumps across his forearm.

It's here. Somewhere. I just have a feeling about it. There was a shovel in the far corner of the room. Without a second thought, he grabbed it and started digging the ground beneath him. He broke away the foundation with the shovel, digging deeper.

And deeper.

And deeper.

CLINK! Finally, at around four feet under, he stopped.

There it was. He could see it with his own eyes. Natorum Demonto. The Book of the Dead. It still looked faintly similar to how Ash remembered it. The book was wrinkled and rotted, and rightly so, since its front and back was constructed from human flesh. The front cover formed the shape of a disfigured and demented grimace, as if the book itself was being tortured. It was pretty much the same, except it had a little more wear and tear.

"My God." Ash gasped. "There it is." Ash threw the shovel aside, making a loud noise as it hit the floor. He dropped to his knees. He wiped the sweat from his forehead, and extended his arms, ready to grab the book. He stopped himself right before his fingers touched it. "Wait!" Ash said to himself. "The words, the words. Jeez, I almost forgot." He cleared his throat and sat up straight, preparing himself. He inhaled deeply and professed the words dramatically.

"Klaatu...!" he shouted. He paused for a moment to remember of that was correct.

"Verada...!" One more to go.

"Nosferatu– I mean, Niktu! Niktu!" Ash became nervous. Last time he screwed up like that, an entire army of the dead rose from their graves and came after him. He didn't want that to happen again. He said it one more time, this time a little quieter, more genuine.

"Klaatu. Verada. Niktu." Ash pulled the book out of the dirt, and held it close to his face. He smiled in content, regaining his breath from the overall adrenaline he put himself through to find it. Ash looked dead straight at the Necronomicon. "Finally." he said.

"Soon, you and I...are gonna be no more."

It was pitch black by the time Ash had left the building. His muscles were sore from having to excavate and dig to find that book. He stumbled his way to his Oldsmobile, popped the trunk open and threw the Necromicon inside. It landed smack-dab in the middle, between an issue of *Fangoria and an outdated chemistry textbook.*

He fiddled through his keys, finding the right ones for his car, and unlocked it. He opened the front door and immediately felt a long, clawed, hand grabbing him by the back of his collar, pulling him back. The figure yanking him back made a rasped, hissing noise. Ash knew it had to be a Deadite.

He elbowed the creature in the ribs, releasing its grasp. Then, he quickly whipped around. "Hyah!" Ash yelled as he kicked it hard in the chest, knocking the demon down.

While it was on the ground, Ash reached in the passenger seat for his Boomstick. He aimed at the Deadite and took the safety off. He looked at the creature for a moment, waiting for it to get back up. It appeared to be a woman. She had long, reddish hair. It may not have been red hair, it could have been blood-stained hair, it was too dark to tell. Her jaw line had been elongated and disfigured like a gargoyle, revealing a set of rotting, green teeth. Her skin was gray-ish and flaky, like it was peeling off of her. And her eyes. Her eyes were blank and bloodshot, with black circles under her eyes.

The she-demon leapt up, quick as a cat, and said to Ash in that distorted, monstrous voice, "You will never stop us! His time is coming! He will be free, and you shall die!"

"And who might that be?" Ash teased the Deadite, never breaking away from his target.

The demon jerked her neck back, forth, and left to right, making a gut-wrenching snapping noise as she did so. "Freddy." The demon laughed, sinisterly. "He will return, and you will be his servant in Hell!" She laughed, gleefully.

"Oh yeah?" Ash said, nonchalantly. "Tell him I said this."

He pulled the trigger, blasting the demon in the head.

BOOM!

Her head exploded into little bits, spraying blood and brains all across the dirt. Her eyeballs and chunks of her brains scattered everywhere, like pieces of popcorn strewn across the bloody ground. Ash was surprised.

Huh...I didn't think those Deadites had brains. She was just a body without a head now. Her neck gushed a wave of black blood across the ground. Her spine was partially exposed above the cut-off point in her neck. The rest of her body just laid there. Her legs were bent opposite directions, and her gray, decrepit arms were permanently locked upwards.

Ash placed his shotgun back in the car. He started up the engine, and left the abandoned power plant, his red tail lights shrank in the distance. He escaped the rusted tomb, leaving nothing but a trail of dust and a Deadite corpse behind.

Chapter 5

THE DARKNESS OF EARTHLY HELL surrounded him. He was trapped between two worlds. Between our own, and one much darker, much more sinister and destructive. Enveloped by the malign fires, with black smoke under his feet, Freddy Krueger stood tortured as he was being forever pulled between the spaces of the living and the dead.

This was the fine print in the part of the deal he made when he sold his soul to the Dream Demons. Shedding innocent blood and feeding off their young souls would keep him strong. But when the killing stopped, and he was banished back to the evil realms beyond, he was weakened. Freddy was back into the eternal darkness. The everlasting pain.

After what seemed like a hundred lifetimes caught inside the evil abyss, Freddy had an epiphany. No longer was he going to follow the law of the demons. Countless times, he had been defeated and stripped of his power. Freddy set his sights on a new target, the source of his power. The ultimate source of demonic evil.

The Necronomicon Ex-Mortis. Natorum Demonto. The Book of the Dead.

Whatever they called it, it is the foundation of supernatural evil. The evil that has spawned countless others to do its bidding. With it, Freddy would never be defeated again. He would be immortal. Eternal. Forever.

All he needed now was someone to get it for him.

He had the Necronomicon. After all these years. After all the torment and deaths he had suffered through, Ash had finally claimed the bane of his existence. And he finally did it the right way this time. It was his to destroy.

Then, why didn't it feel like a victory for him? Why did he feel this overwhelming sense of dread clouding his mind?

Ash pulled into the driveway, turned his key, and stepped out of his banged up, yellow, Oldsmobile. He slowly walked past the front of the car, and grazed his hand across the hood, feeling all of the dents. Every bump and scratch he felt brought back a different memory of adventures past. Most of those memories were grueling terror mixed in with a little medieval torture.

He opened the passenger door and took his Remington out of the car. Finally, he walked over to the trunk and popped it open. There it was, still in the same place. Right in the middle, just waiting for him.

There was a full moon out that night. The pearly light glimmered against the dark blue sky. The light of the moon spotlighted on the Book of the Dead.

Ash picked it up, and absorbed it for a moment.

"Alright, now what?" he wondered. He'd never made it this far without royally screwing something up. He looked down at his watch. It was getting pretty late. "I guess this can wait until tomorrow." He decided to put it back for now and slammed the trunk down, and walked over across the lawn and stood in front of the house. He stood and looked at the house for a long time.

He'd seen the front of that house every day for a while, but Ash had never really seen it for what it was until now. They were right, it was indeed a murder house. It was once the home of Freddy Krueger. A sick...perverted...bastard. All of the weird dreams, the nightmares, what did it all mean to him? He listened to what Buck and Anthony had to say, but Ash didn't believe in urban legends. He only believed in what he could see, touch, feel, and what was trying to kill him. And the foul things that lived in the book made no trouble making their presence known. For all he knew, Freddy Krueger was dead and rotting in the earth.

Ash walked up the front steps, and opened the front door. The door opened wide and made a low, creaking noise.

Every bone in his body ached in pain. His head was swimming, making Ash walk a little unbalanced. He took slow steps and tripped on himself a few times as he walked past the staircase in the front of the room, and on to the door that led to the basement. The door was adjacent to the living room. He opened it and was immediately met with a thin, closet size entry leading downstairs.

He made his way to the basement, which was lit by a single light bulb hanging from the wall. He grew accustomed to this particular setting. He walked across the spacious room to his workbench. He laid his double-barreled Remington next to his chainsaw in top left corner of the bench. Two other weapons of his were on the bench. A pump shotgun and a 9mm pistol. Both were taken apart to be cleaned at a later time. He just kept thinking about the rotten, leathery face of that book.

Calling...

Beckoning...

All Ash could think about was how to destroy the damned thing. The Book of the Dead had survived thousands of years, hundreds of natural disasters, dozens of plagues, and one average, everyday excuse for a Chosen One.

How would tonight be any different?

He'd accomplished enough in the last seven hours, so Ash decided to call it a night. He grabbed a rag off the side of the bench, and used it to wipe the sweat and the droplets of blood off his face. He could work on destroying the book tomorrow. Right now, he was tired.

Ash was so exhausted, he didn't even want to bother going upstairs to the bedroom. *The couch'll do just fine for now.* He planted a seat in the middle, grabbed the remote, and turned on the local news. That would usually put him out for the night.

The television turned on to channel 6, KRGR, the local news station. Ash fluttered his eyes, drifting in and out of consciousness as he listened to the soothing narration of the attractive, brunette, anchor woman.

"...the police have no further details on the disappearance of Audrey Hamilton, a teacher at Springwood High, and a mother of two."

The anchor woman was sitting behind a desk. In the far corner, was a reference picture of the missing woman. She was smiling, her hand on her cheek with her elbow propped on her desk. Her hair covered most of her face. Her hair was long, and...red.

Red hair...

Ash sat up straight and became more alert. It was her. It was the same woman who attacked him earlier–except her skin wasn't decayed and her jaw line wasn't deformed, making her look like some kind of gargoyle. She was just a normal woman in that picture. Happy, smiling, and full of life.

Oh, how things change so quickly.

The newscaster continued. "...on a related, more disturbing note: the bodies of other missing persons have been found, mostly outside of town, their limbs severed and–"

Ash turned the TV off. He didn't want to hear any more. He set the remote on the coffee table. He buried his head in his hands and took a long, deep breath. This was one of the more depressing parts of the job. Realizing that he'd just taken the life of what was once an innocent human being. Someone who never did anything at all to deserve this. Seeing their faces on the news and watching their friends and family mourn for them. Sometimes it was just too much for him. He rubbed his eyelids, trying to somehow wipe away the sadness from his face.

Click.

The TV turned back on. *But how?* Ash had put the remote away. His eyes went wide as he jerked his head up to look at the television.

"...their heads decapitated in some of our findings." There was the newscaster again. Her demeanor was somewhat different. Her serious face and genuinely caring tone was replaced with a coy smile, she sounded like she relished every word. "Their skin had been decayed far past their presumed time of death." When she began her next sentence, her voice changed. With each word, it had slowly gotten lower, like a man's. Although, even a normal man's voice wouldn't sound this guttural and wretched.

What's going on here?

"All of the bodies had what appeared to be fatal wounds with a type of saw, and shotgun blasts to the head." Her voice by now had gotten just downright evil.

Freddy.

"The police suspect that bastard, Ash Williams! We'll hunt that rotten son of a bitch down like a no-good, dirty, dog!"

Ash turned away from the television screen and locked his eyes on the remote. He had no idea what was going on, but he didn't want to suffer through anymore of this. The back round noise still echoed as Ash quickly grabbed the remote and searched for the power button.

"Yeah, you're 'Chosen', all right. Chosen to have your fuckin' skin ripped off! Aha-hahahahahahahahahaha!"

Ash turned the TV off again, and threw the remote to the edge of the living room.

"...What the...?" Ash mumbled. His eyes went in every direction, searching, waiting for something else to freak him out.

Nothing.

Ash exhaled deeply and leaned back on the couch cushion, trying to relax for a moment. He stared at the ceiling and watched the propellers on the fan slowly spin.

He watched him intensely. Sitting just on the edge of the couch next to Ash, Freddy stared at him with a foreboding gaze. He took pleasure in this part of the game. Ash was getting weaker. Debilitated.

Freddy watched his bloodshot eyes flutter, his skin had gotten paler, like he'd just seen a ghost. That part never got old. Poor Ash had tried to stay awake, but it was already too late.

Freddy cocked his head to the side, and wriggled his finger blades in anticipation.

Now, the torture could begin.

"Whoa!" Ash yelled. He jumped in his seat and whipped his head to the right. He could have sworn he heard the sound of knives clinking next to his ear. But, there was nothing there.

Ash breathed heavily. Whatever he saw, it sent shivers down his spine. The goose bumps on his arms reappeared. He had no clue what was going on, but he knew one thing: there was someone in the room, with him.

He looked around him, but there was no one there.

He figured it must have just been his imagination. Nothing more. He looked at the wall clock across the room. It was past 2:00 AM, he'd been awake more than seventeen hours, of course he'd be hallucinating. Seeing and hearing things that were not and should not have been there. Becoming nervous, and a little paranoid, from it all. He'd had a rough night and he was very fatigued. He needed rest.

Of course. he thought. *Everything's fine, all I have to do is relax.*

Clunk.

Clunk.

Clunk.

Clunk.

Ash heard a noise coming from upstairs. "Huh–Wha–?" *What was that?* he thought. It sounded like footsteps. Slow, creeping, footsteps.

Is there someone upstairs? All of the windows were locked, there was no way someone could have broken in without him hearing something.

Eeeeeeeeeeeeeeer.

Eeeeeeeeeeeeeeer.

It was a different noise this time. It came from different parts of the house. It was a very loud, creaking noise, like the foundation settling. Ash turned in all different directions, trying to locate where the sound was coming from. But it came from everywhere. It was a multitude of various creaks and other kinds of racket.

Ash leapt from his seat and stood in the middle of the living room. He was alert and ready for whatever was going to happen next.

Without pause, the doorknobs on the front and back entrances started to rattle and shake violently. The doors themselves produced loud banging noises, like someone was beating on them from outside.

THUD! THUD! THUD! THUD! THUD! THUD! THUD! THUD! THUD!

Something bad was going on, and Ash knew it. He remembered that he had put away all of his gear in the basement. "Boomstick..." He leapt over the couch and raced towards the basement door. When he put his hand on the doorknob, he instantly felt a white-hot, stabbing pain across his palm. "Aaah!" Ash yelped. His left hand had been burnt, he quickly withdrew it. He looked at the doorknob.

It was glowing red from the heat. Ash figured he didn't have a lot of time, so he quickly used his metal hand to open the door and flung it open. He stepped forward to go down the stairs and felt as if he was going to fall. "Whoa!" He looked down and there were no stairs, just empty blackness. He re-adjusted his balance and stared down the bottomless chasm of darkness.

What was going on here? First there was a basement and now there wasn't. "What? Am I in "The Twilight Zone? What's going on here?"

Before Ash could begin to absorb the fact that his basement had just completely disappeared, the entry to what used to be the basement was immediately engulfed with flames. They rose from the bottom, up. Before Ash was about to become...well, ash...he quickly slammed the door shut. He needed a weapon. That much was certain.

He hastily scoured the living room for something he could use. Then he found it: the metal poker from the fireplace. He ran back to the living room and grabbed it. When he turned around, he noticed that all of the noise had ceased. It was completely quiet now. But still, Ash stood hunched over, ready to attack, his back to the fireplace, looking over the whole room. His eyes were wild, and he had sweat dripping from his forehead. What was going to happen next?

But still, Ash appeared confident on the outside, grinning and cocking his eyebrows, challenging whoever or whatever was pulling the strings here. "C'mon! C'mon, just try me!" he said, still catching his breath.

This poor bastard isn't giving up without a fight. Freddy thought. He had to admit, it was a little more fun messing with someone who had a little bit of personality. Someone who didn't just stand there, expressionless, like an idiot. And at least he fought back. Well, if one could call that "fighting". It was different than just some doe-eyed bitch in her nightgown, running and screaming for help. But still, this still bugged the living hell out of Freddy. *Why did it always have to be so difficult coming back from the dead?* he thought.

He watched him, huddled up and shaking like the poor sap that he was. He delighted in his torment. Freddy cracked an evil smile. He stood to Ash's left, though Ash couldn't see him. He wanted to kill him right then and there, slice his throat open maybe, but he was powerless without the Necronomicon. "Soon enough..." he said, while Ash was oblivious to his presence. "I'll have that book, and your soul along with it. But, I'll have to wait until you're weak enough to finish the job." He needed to weaken Ash, completely remove his strength and his will to survive. Then it would be the perfect time for Freddy to strike. "But until then..."

Freddy inched a little closer and reached out his glove hand, slowly. He flicked his index finger forward and tapped Ash on the shoulder.

(tap) (tap)

Ash felt a tap on his left shoulder. It felt sharp and pointed, like a knife. He whipped his head around, but there was nothing there. He felt like he was going insane. All of these strange and horrible things were happening to him at once, and there was no one in sight. What bothered Ash most, was not knowing who was doing these things to him. Things that didn't make sense. The banging on all the doors. The basement just disappearing. The roaring fire.

Feeling like there was someone standing right next to him the whole time...

His mind snapped. He gripped the fire poker until his knuckles ran white. His chest puffed in and out from breathing so heavily. If whoever wasn't going to show their ugly face, Ash was going to try to at least coax them out.

"C'mon! Show yourself!" his tone was infused with rage and desperation. "Come down here! I'll poke your goddamn eyes out!" he shouted. His eyes went everywhere. Looking up the stairs where he heard the footsteps. To the front and back doors where all of that noise started. To the basement door where he was met with a wall of flames. "Don't think I won't..." he muttered, fearfully. He took a few steps to his right, moving to the corner of the living room, his back still to the wall. His senses were raw and anticipating anything to happen at this point. He was ready to strike at any second.

The light bulb inside the floor lamp in the corner of the room flickered off and back on again. It was just for a split second.

Ash saw something out of the corner of his eye. He wasn't going to take any chances. In just a fraction of a second, Ash struck in the direction of the corner to his right. "Hyah!" Ash yelled as he swung the fire poker like a baseball bat at the floor lamp. It fell and knocked over to the wall shelf next to it, and the sweat from his hands caused him to lose grip of the poker. Ash felt like a total idiot. He bent over and reached for the poker.

When the lamp fell over and hit the shelf, it hit with such brute force that it dislocated one of the brackets propping it up. The shelf was bent at an angle, and the lantern that was on the corner of the shelf was now wobbling. It fell right off and landed on the top of Ash's head. He was knocked flat to the ground. He groaned in pain. He felt a knot in the back of his head throbbing as he slowly got back up, and put the fire poker back in his hands.

Ash heard a strange noise coming from the kitchen. He was still recuperating from his head injury, but decided to check it out anyway. The closer he walked towards the kitchen, the sound became clearer. It was like a low, hissing noise. Ash braced himself, and gripped the fire poker like a bat once again. He was now in the kitchen, following the noise. It lead him towards the refrigerator, where the cause of the sound was just a simple hiss. Ash lowered the metal poker and loosened his grip. He breathed a sigh of relief and turned back around to the living room. "It's alright. Relax, relax." he assured himself. He put the fire poker away and propped it on the corner, so he could wipe the sweat from his brow.

Ash stepped back into the living room. Meanwhile, the stereo in the back of the room turned on. A little blue light shown, indicating that the power had turned on. In an instant, the whole room was encapsulated with the brazen sound of shrieking death metal. The floor vibrated and Ash's ear drums pierced from the sound of that ungodly high volume the stereo produced. He put his hands up to his ears to try to muffle the sound, but it was much too loud and boisterous. "Aaaaah!" Ash screamed in pain. He fell to his knees and tried to plot a solution.

He looked around the room that saw that some of the furniture had...come alive. The little tassels on the curtains, the lamps, the books on the shelf, they were...dancing. They were bending and contorting to the rhythm of the music. It was disturbing and distracting. He had to make it stop. He crawled over and reached for the fire poker and decided to make good use out of it. Ash stood tall, raised it above head and swung at the stereo with brute force, smashing it.

"SHUT...!"

CRASH!

"THE...!"

CRASH!

"HELL...!"

CRASH!

"UP!"

CRASH!

The stereo had been smashed and broken into little pieces. The music had stopped. It was finally quiet. Ash dropped the poker to the ground and exhaled in relief. He was dripping sweat from the top of his head to the back of his neck, matting down his short, dark hair. He closed his eyes and paused for a moment to think and figure out what was going on here. This was all so surreal that it just didn't feel that it could really be happening. But it was real to him. Everything felt real. Just like the dream from last night. The scorching heat from the fire. The throbbing pain in the back of his head. The feeling that his ear drums were being torn apart from inside his head. *Could this all just be a dream?*

"Ha ha ha ha ha ha..."

There was that laugh again. It wasn't as loud as last time. It was quieter, guttural, echoing. Ash opened his eyes and looked straight forward.

Freddy was right in front of him.

He stood mere inches from Ash's face. He could see Freddy clearly now. But he wished he hadn't. Even though that old, brown, ratty fedora covered most of his face, what did show was simply repulsive. His skin was burned and disfigured. Little sinews of decayed flesh had been peeled off of him and hung across his face. Even whole chunks of his face had been missing, showing bloody muscle tissue. But he was smirking, showing hints of rotted fangs for teeth. Freddy quickly urged his face closer to Ash's and, with that low, echoing voice, said...

"Boo!"

Ash screamed at the top of his lungs, flailing his arms and legs. He flipped over, and landed face first on the hardwood floor. When he looked up, he saw the light of dawn showing through the curtains. Ash looked around and noticed he was lying right next to the couch. He had been sleeping the whole time. He pushed himself back up, sending a shockwave of pain across his bones. He muttered and groaned as he got back up. Ash had slept in his clothes from the day before. He noticed the dried up bloodstains on his shirt as he dusted himself off.

He felt a sharp, throbbing pain in his left hand. He held it up closer to examine it. As he looked at it, Ash noticed a large, red, burn mark on his palm. As Ash combed his hair back with his fingers, he realized that maybe it was time to start believing in urban legends.

Chapter 6

Ash looked up at the wall clock. He realized that it was time for him to get ready for work. He painfully pushed himself up, feeling the knot in the back of his head as he got back up on his feet.

Standing upright, Ash looked around him and examined the living room. If the injuries he sustained in his dreams were real, what about everything else he had broken?

Ash looked at the floor lamp. It stood perfectly straight, as if it had never toppled over. *How can that be?* Just a minute ago, it seemed, that lamp was broken and on the floor.

He directed his attention to the shelf on the wall next to it. The hinges were unbroken. The shelf was level, and everything on it was back in its usual spot.

Whipping his head in the opposite direction, Ash had prepared to see his stereo broken into a dozen pieces. On any other day, seeing his precious stereo that cost him nearly a month's pay, busted beyond recognition, would be last thing he would want to see. But, he hoped for some remaining fragment of the night before to make some kind of sense out of this. The stereo was unbroken with not a scratch to be found.

Come on, that's impossible! Ash thought.

Nothing was making sense anymore. He felt as if his sanity was being stripped away from him every minute. Something was obviously trying to come after him. He didn't have any definitive proof. What he saw was only a mere glimpse. But he knew. It was a persistent aching in the back of his mind. He knew who was trying to get to him. But he only saw him for half a second, how could he have known if it was really Freddy? Even if it *was* just for half a second, he was standing right in front of him. So close, he could feel the hot breath coming from his mouth. He remembered, it smelled like a rotting animal carcass, mixed with brimstone. Something awful, like that.

Mostly, he remembered that horrible, ugly face. The same face he saw the night before. Half of it had been covered by a dirty, brown hat, but the rest was...revolting. Skin charred to such a degree, that it would have killed any other living being. At the same time, it was raw and seeping blood in spots. The mere memory of his face disgusted Ash. Judging from what he'd heard before...and what he'd experienced just then...It seemed like Ash had just been the victim of a deathly nightmare. It was quite possible that maybe–if his assumptions were correct–Ash was Freddy Krueger's latest prey. His newest target.

But why? Didn't this Freddy guy always go after little kids, young girls and boys who were too weak to defend themselves? Why me? Why now?

Ash was going to be late if he spent any more time trying to figure this all out right now. He rushed up the stairs, hoping that a cold shower would set his mind right...and keep him awake longer.

The droplets of water shooting from the shower head felt like icy, cold, needles against Ash's skin. He shivered from underneath the shower head, feeling goose bumps rise from his shoulders as he clutched them for some small sense of warmth. As discomforting as it was standing underneath what felt like a hailstorm in the shower, it was still better that than going through what he had endured last night. Ash reached over and turned off the water, the knobs creaking as he did so.

He stepped out of the bathroom, leading straight into his bedroom. He promptly dried himself off, and put his work clothes on.

There was some blood on his shirt, specifically a large splatter on the right, near his ribcage. On his trousers, there were specs of coal and soot, along with dirt all across the bottom of his pant leg. He couldn't really do anything about that right now, so he reached for cleaner clothes in the closet. After buttoning his shirt, he turned slightly and reached over to the nightstand to grab his nametag. Spots of blood had accumulated over it as well. It seemed like a quick fix. He spit on the nametag, and wiped off the Deadite blood on his white shirt.

Before he left, he had a quick look of himself in the mirror, making sure that the slight dirt stains and cuts on his face would be "presentable" enough. With any luck, people wouldn't think he had entered the store after having just gone on a ravenous killing spree. Although, that accusation wouldn't have been too far from the truth. Ash felt he looked clean enough to show up for work.

Moving on from his wardrobe, Ash stepped up closer to the mirror, and studied his own face. He was aware that everybody gets older, and he wasn't excluded from that. When taking away the shotgun, the chainsaw, the leather holsters, and the blood stains that accompanied them, Ash looked just like any other man on the cusp of age fifty. He had crow's feet in the corners of his eyes. He wasn't as energetic and agile as he used to be. And frankly, he's starting to find people half his age to be a real pain in the ass.

But, some things remained the same. Over the years, he'd gained so many scars, it looked like a road map across his whole face. Thankfully, the mutton-chops across the lower half of his face covered most of them. On the bridge of his nose, he had just a small nick. On his forehead, right temple, and left cheek where fairly large scars, pink in coloration. His biggest one spread across from his upper to his lower lip.

Each scar was a memory of a different injury: being body-slammed into a tree by a demonic force, cut with a glass shard by an undead girlfriend, scratched across the face by a band of living skeletons. For most men, a face full of scarification and wounds wasn't considered classically handsome. But on Ash, considering how the placement of the scars was symmetrical with his bone structure, rather similar to that of The Tick, it gave him somewhat of a rouge charm.

Ash had also been lucky in the sense that he still had a full head of hair. He ran his fingers through his locks, and lingered on the wide, gray, streak of hair on the side of his head. Some have said it made him look distinguished, refined, and wiser; Ash viewed it as looking weak, and that he shouldn't be battling grotesque monsters anymore.

Deciding not to dwell on the subject any further, Ash turned away from the mirror, headed downstairs, and out the door he went.

Ash trudged his way to work around 9:00 AM that morning. He kept his black, leather jacket on him to conceal the small spots of blood that couldn't wash out. As far as the built-in dirt and grass stains on his pant leg, he'd just make up some story about how his car broke down in the middle of the road, and he was forced the push it back to the nearest auto shop. It wasn't that hard a story for people to believe.

Just like yesterday, he'd kept himself awake through massive amounts of coffee and energy drinks. But, unlike the day before, Ash wasn't able the get any kind of sugar high, or jolt, at all. He just felt depleted and diminished. At least when he was pumped up full of caffeine, he was able to get through the day just fine. Today, he didn't want to deal with whiny little brats and pencil-necked managers with clipboards all day, but it was better that than the nightmares.

Despite his high rank in the Housewares business, Ash had spent the better half of the morning stacking boxes of microwave ovens into a perfect, little pyramid. Apparently being "Senior Housewares Domestic Engineer" of S-Mart meant that he still had to stock shelves and price check this and that, but he got a shiny, new, nametag to boot. After thirty or so years, he thought he would at least get a clipboard of his own, and longer breaks at lunchtime.

Just as he stacked the last box at the very top, which stood as high as he did, just a little over six feet tall, Ash heard the squeaky footsteps of his nerdy co-worker, Anthony. He cringed at the sound of those rubber-soled loafers he always wore. With each wide step that Anthony took, the horrid squeaks got increasingly louder. Ash closed his eyes, and breathed a sigh of discontent. He really didn't have time for this right now.

Anthony stood but a few feet away from him now. Ash turned around to face him. He looked down at him, noticing his Beatle haircut that was parted perfectly down the middle. In fact, it was a little too perfect. He must have spent half an hour that morning making sure he was dressed in the height of nerdy fashion. "Hey, Ash?" he inquired as he pushed his thick, black, glasses back against the bridge of his nose.

"Hmm?" he replied.

Anthony looked into his bloodshot eyes. "You look like you haven't slept. I hope we didn't scare you yesterday."

"No." he answered quickly. "My, uh, car broke down on the way home. So, I had to walk here."

"Oh, okay." he said, relieved. "Say, uh, while I have your attention, do you know anything about home repair, do-it-yourself kinda stuff?"

It was kind of funny to Ash. The day before, he was telling horror stories to him, forewarning him about the dangers that may surface by living in a "murder house"; and here he is today, back to asking him dumb, meaningless, questions to get a little attention.

Ash leaned back against the stack, but not far enough to completely demolish the pyramid of suck-iza he had just completed. He was about to tell Anthony to bugger off in the nicest way he could think of, when out of the corner of his eye, he noticed a gorgeous blonde walking his way. She had shiny, red, lips, long legs, and was wearing a tight, blue T-shirt. It was time to bring out the old, Ash charm.

Speaking a little louder than normal, Ash kept switching eye contact between Anthony and the woman and said, "Well, I know my way around a screw." She was closer now, about to pass him by. Ash looked right at her and did his signature cocky smile. "Hi. How're you doing?" Their eyes met, and needless to say, she was not impressed. She scoffed and carried on without a second glance.

Oh, well. Ash thought. *Back to the pencil-neck.*

Anthony continued, ignoring his failed attempt at getting a lady. "Yeah...I was hoping I could get some advice about fixing the ceiling fans in my house." He made a propeller motion with his index finger, as if Ash didn't know what a fan was.

Arrogant little prick.

The guy wasn't really that bad. It was just that Ash felt absolutely drained, and didn't feel like putting up with anybody's crap today. He exhaled and rubbed his eyes intensely, trying to wipe away his sluggishness. "Look Anthony," he said, trying to be nice. "I, uh–I'm really not in the mood for this. I haven't slept in days, could you just leave me alone for one day?"

Anthony raised his hands, accepting defeat. "Fine. Whatever, Ash." He finally turned around and walked away, muttering various curses under his breath. "...like I didn't warn...don't blame me...your life becomes a living Hell..." Ash didn't hear a word, the loafers pretty much muted all Anthony said as he marched away.

What Anthony didn't know was that Ash's life was already a living Hell. It's been that way for as long as he could remember. Even as a child, Ash could just sense that danger was all around him. Maybe it was the bullies in middle school who teased him mercilessly. Or, it could have been the teachers who gave him bad vibes. It wasn't until that dreaded day he and Linda went to that cabin up in the mountains did all of those fears come to the surface. Even though he was just a normal guy, he was destined to be the one to defeat the foul scum of the earth for the rest of his days.

He'd had enough. Ash was determined to find out if his instincts were right. If it was truly Freddy coming after him all of a sudden, or if it was just a mixture of fleeting sanity and the power of suggestion.

But he wasn't going to find any answers with a crowd of people darting in and out of his way. *Maybe a little walk around the store will clear my head.*

Setting his price-marker aside, Ash left his post and paced up and down the aisles of the Springwood S-Mart. Springwood wasn't such a bad place on the surface. It was pretty much the standard, suburban, all-American, town. Colonial-style homes filled every block. The lawns were bright green and trimmed all year round, and the buildings were sans graffiti. Ash thought it was a nice place to live, so he didn't understand why he got the sinister urge that evil dwelled in this town. That was until he stayed here long enough. After adjusting to his nightly routine of hunting demons, Ash came to realize that evil can be found under the purest of guises.

As he walked, he constantly looked at the floor, muttering under his breath. "...gotta be some kind of...explanation...all of this...why did I...come here?" The lack of sleep was making him delirious.

Somehow, he found his way the Housewares department on the other side of the store. He casually looked around him: lamps, light sockets, nothing really interesting. At least he was safe. He was up and walking. Nothing could happen to him as long as he didn't fall asleep.

After Ash reassured his own security, he noticed the lighting had become slightly darker. One of the flourescant lights in the building had flickered off, and then back on again. Ash looked up at the faulty light. "Of course." Ash said to himself. Knowing the incompetent staff in this particular store, he knew he'd be the one who had to fix it. He continued walking, heading to the back of the building to find a ladder and a replacement bulb. "Ash, stock these shelves. Ash, stack these boxes. Ash, fix these damn lights." After walking a while, he realized something. He was all alone in the store. It was packed with people just a few minutes ago, but now it was barren.

Another light flickered.

Then another.

Soon, the entire building was almost pitch black. He looked up at them, "What the hell?" He took a step forward and slipped on something slick, nearly falling down in the process.

Alright, now what?

There was blood on the floor, a large, thick, deep, red puddle covered his boots. Ash lifted his head up and looked around him. He was no longer alone anymore. Surrounding him were the corpses of young children. Some were hung by a noose around their necks from the light fixtures. Others just laid down on the floor, their bodies had succumbed to rigor mortis, contorted in horrifying positions. A few had been impaled from the signs sticking up from the ground, stuck in the middle with their limbs reaching out. Each and every one of the children had been stabbed or cut in some way. Their skin was pale and their lips were blue.

He saw a little girl on the floor who'd had her throat sliced. Blood had poured down from her neck to the bottom of her frilly, pink, dress. She couldn't have been older than five years old. Over to his left, was a boy who was probably fourteen, impaled, and had his eyes stabbed out of the sockets. Streaks of dark blood ran from his eyes and the corners of his gaping mouth. Ash's eyes started to well up a bit, like he wanted to cry. He felt nauseous from the sight of it all. "God..."

Looking straight ahead, at the end of the trail of blood a few yards in front of him, was the cold, lifeless, body of another young girl laying in front of a full-length mirror. Her hair was short, blonde, and stained with blood. Her face was pale with hints of blue around her cheeks. She laid on the ground, facing Ash, staring at him. It looked like the wide trail of blood had come from her body. Her right arm was extended, like she was reaching out for help.

She spoke. Her voice was small and innocent. "Help me." In an instant, her body was jerked away, like something had grabbed her by her feet, and dragged her away. She had been pulled inside the mirror and vanished. She never made a sound. All that was left was Ash's reflection.

Without a second thought, Ash followed the trail and walked towards the mirror.

Chapter 7

He wondered how this possibly could have been happening to him. He never fell asleep. He barely even closed his eyes for more than a second. *How could I possibly be dreaming? Was I nodding off when Anthony was talking to me? Or did I even wake up at all today? What if the past twelve hours had all been just one, long dream?*

No, it can't have be. His normal workday up until now had been boring and monotonous, while these dreams were...something strange. Something surreal. They were apart from reality. He knew that he was inside the dream.

Cautiously, he walked towards the full-length mirror. Ash was completely defenseless, so he knew it was best to be alert. He tried his best not to overlook anything. He wasn't in his own world anymore. He was in someone else's, so he didn't know what kind of dirty trick might be played on him.

He walked closer, leaving a greater distance between himself and the dozens of young cadavers. The blood puddle sloshed quietly at he stepped, leaving dark stains on his work boots. He now stood at arm's length in front of the mirror. Ash didn't want to get too close to it. He knew what happened last time he came across a mirror that was obviously screwing with his mind. Maybe his reflection would come out and try to strangle him. Or possibly, it would smash to pieces, leaving little Ash's scattered everywhere and stab him in the ass with a fork.

This is where the little girl had been taken to. It must have led somewhere, a pathway of some sorts. It appeared normal, all he saw was himself and what was behind him: blood and darkness. Examining it closer, ever so slowly, he reached his hand out to tap the mirror. Pulling his index finger back, preparing to gently hit the glass, Ash looked at his reflection once more to make sure nothing bad would come of this.

No funny business, you got me?

His own reflection smiled back at him. Evilly. Slyly. His eyes had suddenly changed from a dark brown to a bright blue. He cocked his head to the side, and leaped out at Ash.

Ash gasped and stepped back. The other Ash's torso and arms were completely out the frame, still grinning at the sight of his fear. This other Ash was no longer a reflection anymore. He wasn't mimicking the real Ash at all. The real Ash was terrified, with a mask of fear across his face. Meanwhile, the other was showing an astounding level of confidence and a sadistic grin upon him. That kind of arrogance could only belong to Freddy Krueger. His mannerisms and approach were the same, the only thing that differed now was his voice and appearance.

Ash swallowed down a potential scream and asked him, "Wha-what do you want from me?"

He grinned even wider. Smiling a cocky smile not unlike the one Ash had just a few minutes ago. "I want you to let me out. You mindless, little stock boy!" he bellowed.

Ash's eyebrows scrunched together, as he felt a mix of confusion and anger. That was the last straw. For most of his life, Ash has had to deal with pea-brained Deadites demanding to be let out, possessing everybody he loves, and forcing him to hack them up with various gardening supplies. Ash wasn't that dumb. Considering all he'd been through in his life, he'd survived with only a few scratches...and only one missing appendage.

Ash's fear had completely washed over him, and was replaced with pure anger. First, this guy scares the living hell out of him, fucks with his mind for over a week, and now he wants Ash to free him? He was determined not to let this guy get to him.

"No way, buddy. Go find someone else to do your dirty work." Ash said, bitterly.

The arrogant smile that shown on the demented version of Ash's face was gone. These evil spirits, no matter who they were or where they came from, considering how many times Ash had cut them up or blown them to bits over the years, always loathed it when he wouldn't comply to their demands. But then again, out of all the souls to devour, his was going to be the hardest to acquire. He jumped forward, and grabbed Ash by his collar.

"Oh? A little slow, eh?" he teased.

Ash's confidence never left him. He grinned back, taunting him. "Yeah, enlighten me. Let you out, or what?" he dared.

Ash could hear a low chuckle come from beneath his throat. "Or..." he prepared.

Wait a minute. Ash thought. His voice had changed completely. At first, it was still Ash's voice talking to him. But now, it was lower, graveled, like he was actually speaking to him from the dark, bowers of Hell. It was the same sinister voice that had been taunting him in his nightmares. It was Freddy's voice.

Still grabbing him by the collar with his right hand, with his left, he grabbed his own face. Digging in with his fingernails, he tore the flesh from his face. Skin and muscle had peeled off of him like a thick, leathery band-aid. Blood poured out of the edges of his face. He ripped it off like a mask, revealing the retched face Ash saw in his nightmare last night. "...else!"

Ash had never seen that trick before. His eyes widened in surprise, but he expected Freddy to be involved in this. "Freddy!" Ash accused.

Freddy laughed derisively as he pushed Ash away, watching him fall and land right on top of a display table full of kitchen knives. "Haaa ha ha ha ha ha ha ha ha ha!"

Momentum caused Ash to topple right over it. He landed and hit his head on the checkered, marble tile. He rolled over on his back to see about a dozen sharp knives heading right for him. They each landed and struck the floor, missing him by a hair, like he'd been attached to the wheel of death in a magic show. But, the last blade was aimed right in the middle of his face. Luckily, Ash's reflexes kicked in right about then, as he prevented the knife from stabbing him between the eyes. He caught the kitchen knife by the blade with his metal hand.

When he looked up, he saw various S-Mart employees and shoppers circled around him. They stood there in disbelief, baffled at the fact that he didn't just get his face stabbed. Evelyn and Cooper were among the crowd. Evelyn stood with her hand covering her mouth. Even though she didn't know Ash that well, she was thankful he didn't get hurt. Cooper stood a few feet behind her, with his hands on her shoulders. He showed less concern for Ash than Evelyn did. Frankly, he was kind of disappointed that he didn't get not one scratch. In Cooper's mind, he would have deserved at least a slice on the arm.

Ash paused for a moment to breathe, dust himself off, and internally thank God that He let him not die a painful death just now. He was dumbfounded, he couldn't think of anything to say to justify himself. What could he do, say, "Sorry about that folks, I got sucked into a nightmare, and Freddy Krueger just tried to kill me...again. You all know Freddy, right? That little bastard's at it again."? The only rational thing he could think of was to laugh it off as Anthony helped him get back on his feet.

"What's going on with you, Ash?" he said, running his mouth at a hundred miles per hour. "You know you're not supposed to fall asleep on the job. You could have been killed!"

As Ash stood back up, he noticed that he was back beside the stack of boxes he finished earlier. It didn't make any sense. He remembered being way on the other side of the store. "Sorry." he apologized to Anthony. "It won't happen again."

Anthony, Evelyn, Cooper, and the rest of the onlookers left, and went about their own business. Ash was no longer in peril. *Show's over, nothing to see here anymore.*

Still looking at the pile of knives stuck on the floor, Ash kept thinking about how that could have been him. He waited until every last person had left him. "At least I hope it doesn't." he said quietly.

Sitting near the parking lot just outside of S-Mart, Cooper and Evelyn had just finished their shift, and were laughing. After the spectacle they had just witnessed, they had a lot to laugh about, at least Cooper did, anyway. Really, it was just good to be alone for a while. To be someplace quite. Someplace to get away from the crowd, all of the gasps and murmurs.

They sat on concrete step, Cooper had his arm wrapped around her shoulder. They exchanged pleasant conversation, and joked about what they saw earlier. Evelyn smirked as Cooper made fun of Ash falling asleep and tumbling over. "I mean, I feel bad for him and everything, but he's kind of weird, you know?" Cooper said.

Evelyn caught her breath, chuckled passively, but looked away the whole time. She did feel bad for Ash. She didn't know what was going on with him. She figured either he had a serious problem in his life, or he was just a major klutz. Evelyn rolled up the sleeves of her thermal green sweater until they were at elbow length. "That's not a nice thing to say about someone you don't know, Cooper." she said, criticizing him. "And, no, I don't think he's 'weird'." she said. "I just think maybe there's something wrong with him."

Cooper sat up a little straighter and smirked a little bit. He squinted his eyes at the glare of the sunset. "What, like he's mental, or something?" he joked.

"You know, that's what I really love about you, Evelyn. You never say anything bad about anybody, do you?" he said, not questioning, but assuming. "You're just...always really, really nice to *everybody*." He admired Evelyn in how kind and sweet she was to everyone. Even when it came to goofs like Ash, she always tried to see the good in them.

She turned and looked at him in the eye. "You know that's not true. Well...now that I think about it, yeah, I guess it is." she said with a timid smile. "It's just that," she prepared, searching for the right words. "It seems like he's got problems. Maybe his home like isn't that great. I know what that's like. I mean...You understand, right?"

He nodded in agreement. "Yeah, I understand. You had it pretty bad with your dad, way back when." he said. He turned to hug her tightly. "But you live with *me* now–well–you live across the hall from me now. Same difference."

Evelyn looked up at him, smiling and holding him.

Cooper looked into her eyes and grinned. "Don't look at me with that tone of voice."

"Stop judging me with your face."

Cooper laughed and continued hugging her.

Evelyn looked at the concrete below her. What they had just talked about had brought back some painful memories.

Her home life was, unsatisfying, to say the least. Having to grow up with an alcoholic father was difficult for Evelyn. It would have been difficult for any little kid. She was terrified of her own dad, the only thing she could do then was hide. Nightly, she would cower in her room, listening at her bedroom door, hearing her dad's drunken, heavy feet stagger around the house. Those bellowing footsteps would usually precede the vehement, angry shouting, always at her mother. Most of the time, to her, it just sounded like incoherent yelling, like he was shouting just to frighten everyone. But sometimes, she could make out a few words. It was always something profane. *Funny, how the only words I could hear clearly from him were the ones with four letters.*

Her mom didn't really do much, at least, not to Evelyn's knowledge. The only thing she would hear her do was try to stay out of his way, and remain calm even when she couldn't escape him. Not all the time, but every once and a while, during the nights when he would terrorize Evelyn's mom, she would be furious right back at him. Right after that, Evelyn would hear him punch her mom, following a great thudding noise. She always assumed that her mother had fell to the ground. Evelyn would lay there by the door, sobbing quietly for her dear mother, and stare at her bedroom window, fantasizing what it would be like to just pack everything up and run away. She was just nine years old at the time.

One night, things became really bad. The screams had gotten more boisterous, the smacks became louder, and the words had become more hurtful. She was afraid that if she didn't do anything, something horrible might happen to her mom. Evelyn got up the courage to race out of her room and into the living room, and yell at her dad, "Leave Mommy alone!". She saw him turn around and look at her with those cloudy, soulless eyes, and that grimaced face. He grabbed the back of her tiny head, and hit her face against the wall. She fell right onto the floor. She immediately felt her nose throbbing, and when she felt it run, she touched it and looked. A single streak of blood dripped from her nose. Little Evelyn immediately ran back to her room as fast as she could.

As soon as she graduated from Springwood High, she moved out on her own and made a living for herself. There weren't a lot of options for a girl who was fresh out of high school, so the only thing she could find was some low-paying job at S-Mart. She met Cooper there, which, somehow, made the drudgery of working day after day as a check-out girl a little bit easier. She loved him. And even though he was a wonderful boyfriend who promised to protect her at all costs, she knew that, if a time ever came where she was alone, she knew how to protect herself.

The memory of that night ran over and over again, like it was on a loop. What finally broke the cycle was when she heard the sound of Cooper's voice.

"Hey, there's a party over at Steven's tonight. You wanna go?" he asked.

She jolted slightly and turned her head around. Heavily distracted, she wasn't sure what he said at first. She was off into her own little world for a second.

"Sorry," she said. "I was daydreaming." She pondered. "Um…" She wasn't really in the partying mood. It was a Wednesday, after all. *Who has parties on a weekday?* She never started asking herself that question until she got a job. But, maybe she needed to have fun for once and go out. "Yeah, okay." she agreed.

Cooper beamed. "Yay." Before he left, he leaned over, below her chin. He asked. "Will you rub my hair real quick?"

Evelyn rolled her eyes and ran her fingers through his hair for the second time that day. She smiled as he looked up at her.

"You spoil me." he said.

"Yep." she agreed without a second thought. "Like a cat."

Cooper got off the concrete step, standing up straight. "Okay, I'll go warm up the car." He gave her a kiss and walked off over to the end of the lot where his car was.

Evelyn stood up and prepared to trail behind him when, out of the corner of her eye, she saw Ash not far from her, throwing yet another can in the trash. She stopped and turned around halfway. Ash was heading to his Oldsmobile, getting ready to leave. He seemed like a decent guy, but lately he appeared really upset and agitated. Evelyn wanted to at least find out what was wrong with him.

She quickly walked over towards him, he had opened the door and was about to get in. Evelyn waved her hand over to him. "Ash!" she called. "Do you have a minute?"

Gee, let me think...no. It was already sundown, soon it would be dark. Ash needed to get out soon before any Deadites started to show up in town. He saw her walking over to him. He thought he'd be quick enough to get in, slam the door, and pretend he didn't hear a word she said, but he had already made eye contact. "Damn it." he muttered under his breath. He didn't want to be a jerk, but if he didn't leave soon, something bad might happen. Ash kept his right leg inside the car. "I really don't have a lot of time–"

"I just wanted to say 'sorry'." she blurted, rushing the words from her mouth. "About what happened today." she still kept a sympathetic smile. "We should have helped you or done something, but we didn't. We just stood there, and I'm sorry about that."

He started to become anxious, like every second that went by might as well have been an hour. He began ducking into his car. "Yeah, kid. Don't worry about it."

Evelyn stepped up closer, so that the only thing between the two of them was the car door. "Is something wrong?" she asked before he sat down on the seat. "You seem very nervous about something." She looked past Ash and grazed her eyes over to the inside of his car. She saw what looked like a bunch of stuff covered by a dirty, white sheet.

What she didn't know was that "stuff" was his chainsaw and double-barreled shotgun, among other weapons and various dried-up blood stains in the back of his car. Ash noticed her peeking around, shifting her body away from him slightly. He mimicked her movement, blocking her view. He chuckled nervously, and said, "Listen, kid–"

"Evelyn." she interrupted. "My name is Evelyn."

"Evelyn," he repeated. "what *you* need to do is to stop looking around in other people's stuff, and what *I* need to do is to get the hell out of here, *capicse*?"

She was aghast for a moment. She was only trying to show some sympathy and be nice, and he just told her to scram. "Ash, I was just trying to be nice." she said.

Ash realized he wasn't going to get rid of her easily. He thought maybe he should have just slammed the door and kept driving when he had the chance. Being polite obviously wasn't getting him anywhere, maybe he should try another way. "Yeah, well, you need to scram, Evelyn."

As the minutes went by, they bickered at each other. Ash was losing daylight, literally. He didn't know what to do at this point, so he just kept shouting, hoping Evelyn would lose hope and walk away.

After some trial-and-error, Cooper finally got his car started. He drove a black, 1987 El Camino, and as the years went by, it took more and more attempts just the start the damn thing. After the fifth try, he had become a little irritated, his keys clinking with his many key chains. One of them was a logo from the band Slayer: red letters in front of a flaming pentagram. He kept the inside looking good, at least, he thought it was.

The tint on the windows had peeled off, making it look like a bad window cling. On the dash, there was an Iron Maiden "Eddie" bobble head in the far corner, shaking his angry, leathery face at him. He got out and looked around for Evelyn. He could hear voices coming from the other end of the lot. Looking across the way, he saw Ash yelling at her about something.

Immediately, he ran over to find out what was wrong...and beat the snot out of that Ash guy if need be.

Chapter 8

FROM ACROSS THE PARKING LOT, Cooper could see Evelyn and Ash bickering at each other. He couldn't make out any specific words, but he could see the tension on Evelyn's face, and the way Ash was pointing at her, it looked like he was blaming her for something. As he walked towards them, he could hear their voices more clearly. The angrier he heard Ash get, the faster he moved.

He couldn't help thinking that he must have done something to upset her. *Did he say something that offended her? Did he make another pass at her, and she finally had enough? Of course, with Ash, it was probably something weird and out of the blue.* The question he focused on the most was how was going to deal with him.

When Cooper caught up with them, he gently moved Evelyn away from Ash, allowing him to stand between them. "What's going on here?" he asked, leering at Ash.

Cooper hunched over to look her in the eyes, keeping his hands on her shoulders. "Evelyn, did he say something to you?" he asked her.

It all hit her at once. The yelling, the shouting, the arguing, why was she putting herself through this? She wondered why she didn't just walk away and leave him alone. Why did she just involve herself in some big scene like that? She felt so embarrassed, that she couldn't talk for a moment. "He–just–", she tried to justify herself. She became frustrated and tried to calm herself down. "he started yelling at me, and–I don't know, I guess I–"

Cooper cut her off, and whipped the other way around so that he faced Ash. "Have I not made it clear during the past week that I don't want you bothering her?" he said.

Ash remained calm, irritated, but calm. He looked at Cooper with resentment in his eyes. "Alright, I've had it up to here with your bullshit. Both of you!" he pointed at Evelyn.

He stood up straight, looking down at Ash. Cooper squinted his eyes, and turned his head to the side, inquisitively. "What the fuck is your problem? You don't talk to my girlfriend like that!" he said.

Evelyn grabbed him by the arm and pulled him down, so that she could speak in his ear. She was already furious, she didn't want to get Cooper involved. "Cooper, stop it, I can deal with this myself." she said, curtly.

"No," he said. He turned back to Ash. "I wanna know why this guy's always such a flake." He stepped closer to Ash, as he was talking he noticed him turn away a little bit.

His nostrils were still flared, and his eyebrows were still cocked, but Ash looked defensive. Cooper played on it. "Yeah," he said. "you know what I'm talking about, don't you?" he interrogated. "You always look like you're trying to hide something."

Evelyn paused for a moment to think about that. She *had* mentioned how Ash always seemed nervous for some reason. *Was* he keeping some kind of secret? She thought maybe Cooper was actually onto something. She looked at Ash and saw how nervous he looked. Even though he tried to hide it, he wasn't very good at it. She continued listening to Cooper.

"The constant coffee runs...the twitching, the spazzing. Do you stay out all night?" he asked. He smirked, and jutted his face in front of Ash. "What? Did you kill someone?"

Ash averted his eyes the other way, looking guilty.

It's more like hundreds, really... he thought.

Cooper's face dropped. Suddenly his smirk-y demeanor turned more serious. He stepped closer towards him. "W-wait? Did you?" he asked. He said, "Dude–"

Ash cut him off right then. He poked him on the chest with his index finger. "I'm not your 'dude'." he said sternly.

"Okay, sorry." Cooper looked at his metal hand, which was placed on the roof of his Oldsmobile. "Is that how you got the RoboCop hand?" turned back to Evelyn. "I knew it, Evelyn! I told you this guy was weird!" he said, cocking his thumb at Ash behind him.

Ash blew up with anger. Ash jerked his head up and stared straight at him. He pointed at him with his metal hand, threatening him. "Alright, listen, you little pipsqueak!" he barked.

Cooper intruded. "What are gonna do about it, 'Ash'-hole?!" he dared. Although, in Cooper's position, that wasn't a very bright thing to say. For all he knew, he could actually kill him right then and there.

For a quick second, Ash glanced up above the top of Cooper's head and saw the sunset slowly receding into the horizon ahead of him. It was going to get dark soon. Very soon. In fact, if he didn't leave right that very moment, all hell would break loose, literally. He had to think quick, so he directed his attention back to Cooper, and said, "I don't have time for this, I gotta get out of here. Now." he said, more to himself than to Cooper. He pushed him away, got in his car, slammed the door, and sped away.

Cooper and Evelyn listened to the sound of the tires squeal, and watched the red tail lights fade into the distance.

They had just barely made it to the street corner before the engine in Cooper's El Camino started to sputter and the stereo began go on and off. He put it in "Park", and proceeded to bang on the dashboard. "Oh, come on! Why?!" he muttered, hoping they wouldn't have to drive back home in silence. "This piece of crap's always got something wrong with it."

Evelyn had freed herself from the seatbelt, but still slumped in the cushions, watching Cooper hit the dash with the bottom of his palm. She knew why he so desperately wanted to fill the silence. She was really pissed at Cooper for interrogating Ash just a few hours ago. What he had said to him would have gotten Cooper a square punch in the face. She guessed he must have just been lucky.

The party was being held at Steven's house–well, technically, his parent's house. But, his parents were out of town, so all bets were off. It was a pretty nice house, too. Steven Gordon and his sister, Jill, lived in one of the more posh neighborhoods in Springwood. Of course, every neighborhood seems picturesque when compared to the crummy apartment building that Cooper and Evelyn lived in.

The house was two stories, painted olive green on the exterior. It had a garage, and square windows, one by the door, and three on the second story. From the windows, you could see strobe lights and high school kids passing by. The front door was off to the side, guided by a trail of various shrubbery and flowers. They had parked about a block away from the house. The rest of the street was lined with cars and high school kids.

Cooper leaned back in his seat, and turned to Evelyn. "Never mind." he said. "There's no point. You ready?" he asked.

Evelyn still stared at him with detest in her eyes. "Yeah..." she said passively. "I guess so." she pushed the clunky, metal door open and stepped out.

Evelyn slammed the door with a little more vigor than Cooper, which didn't settle well with him. It sounded like she was trying to shatter the windows. He flinched his eyes at the mere thought of it.

"I take it you're still mad at me?" he said, still flinching.

Evelyn put her hands on the roof of his car. "Yes, I'm still mad about what happened."

Cooper looked at the floor in shame. "I am so sorry, baby." he said, ashamed. "Please don't be mad." He raced over to the other side to meet with her. He took her hand in his. "I'm really sorry. I didn't mean to be disrespectful to you. It's just that, if I see someone getting in your face like that, I flip the fuck out."

"I know you do. And I appreciate it, but I can handle things by myself, alright?." said Evelyn. "And, it's not just you. I was mostly mad at Ash for acting like that. He just blew up for no reason." She playfully smacked him on the back of the head. "But you made it worse by almost getting in a fight with him."

"Ow!" said Cooper, rubbing his head. "Yeah, that's true. But I could've taken him, I'm like..." He put about half an inch of space between his index finger and thumb. "that much taller than him. So, no wonder he left, 'cause he was going to go down."

Both of them laughed. Cooper put her palm on the side of his face. He pouted his lip like a sad puppy. He said in a baby voice. "Sowwy. Do you forgive me?"

Evelyn exhaled deeply. She gave him a half-smile. "Okay, you're forgiven…this time."

"Yay!" he said and hugged her. "I love you."

"I love you, too."

They released themselves from their hug and walked on the concrete walkway leading to the front door.

They both had switched their S-Mart smocks for something more suited for a night out. Cooper had worn his gray and orange jacket. Evelyn wore a Black Sabbath jersey, with her freshly curled hair slightly covering the logo.

By time she reached the doorway, Cooper raced ahead of her to knock on the door. When he extended his arm to knock, the door had already flown open. Following was the sound of "Hey! Look who it is!" It was Steven, flailing his arms up, with a game controller in his left hand. It was amazing he could tell who it was, since Steven had dark emo hair covering most of his face. If it weren't for the bright, red, shirt and converse sneakers, he could easily be mistaken for a run-of-the-mill goth kid. "Come in!" he yelled over the music.

They edged themselves in, trying to avoid bumping into anybody. "Hi, Steven." Evelyn said, her voice almost fading in with the music.

"Hey, man!" Cooper yelled, nearly interrupting Evelyn. "What's up?!"

Evelyn stood between them, cramped and uncomfortable. She was starting to regret coming here in the first place. Steven stepped back and leaned over to Evelyn. "Jill's in the kitchen, I'll get her for ya!" He took a half-step to the side, poked his head out to the kitchen and yelled, "HEY JILL! EVELYN'S HERE!"

Well, jeez Evelyn thought. *I could have done that.*

She edged herself away and stood by the hallway, a few seconds later, she saw a beam of blonde hair darting in and out of the crowd. Jill ran up to her and hugged her. "Hey!" she said over the music. "I'm glad you made it!" Jill stepped back and Evelyn noticed her stars-and-stripes t-shirt, which had a few holes in it, and the sleeves were cut off. Jill was pretty much the standard blonde-haired, blue-eyed, pretty girl in high school. She had just turned eighteen a few months earlier, now making her two years older than her brother.

After the kind of day she'd been through, Evelyn needed some interaction with sane people. Evelyn and Jill had known each other ever since they were in high school, before she met Cooper. It was nice for her to know that no matter how difficult it was on her own, she had Jill to let her know things will be okay.

Steven turned Cooper, holding his controller up by his head. "Coop?" he said. "Do you hear it? Do you hear the call?" Steven asked.

Cooper squinted his eyes at him. "What call?" he asked him back.

Steven grinned and cocked his eyebrows. "The 'Call of Duty'!" he exclaimed.

Cooper put his hands close to his face and rubbed them together. He laughed evilly. "Ha ha ha ha!"

They both ran over to the living room and planted themselves on the couch, along with the rest of the gaming nerds. Cooper immediately picked up the controller that was laying on the coffee table and picked up where everyone had left off.

Jill nodded her head in disapproval. "Look at them. A bunch of five year olds..." She turned to Evelyn, smiling. She lead her into the kitchen. "Come on, I got food."

Evelyn and Jill walked over to the kitchen, the male, adolescent screams, and profanity slowly fading with each step. The kitchen was crowded with people, too, but it wasn't as bad. It least it was more quiet. They leaned back by the marble counter, watching the people zoom in and out. Jill grabbed a big bowl of chips and placed it between them. They each grabbed one and took a bite.

"So...how're things?" Jill asked between bites.

Evelyn looked at her derisively, mentally telling her that today had not been such a good day. "Pretty crappy." she began, "I mean, everything's fine now, but..." Evelyn grabbed another handful of chips. "I mean, I guess it was partly my fault. I kinda started a thing after work, but..." she said, her words muffled.

"But what?" Jill inquired.

Evelyn kept replaying the whole scene in her mind over again. The way Ash had been acting. How defensive he was about himself. His whole demeanor was strange, really. She kept trying to find a plausible explanation for it, but she just couldn't. It just made what Cooper said to him seem even weirder. Evelyn wasn't sure whether or not she wanted to show her face at work tomorrow and risk the chance of running into Ash again.

"I can't explain it." she said. "It's just–"

Before she could elaborate, their friend Faith Mori had walked in through the entryway and was now just a few feet from them. "Hi!" she yelled across the room, frantically waving her arm. Faith was a vision in 90's nostalgia. She wore a black tank top, with a red, flannel shirt tied around her waist, draping over her ripped up jeans, which were rolled up just above her knee. She looked like she had just been to a Pearl Jam concert. Her hair was short and auburn gently flowing against her pale skin. Her bangs just were above her eyes, making her look like her own anime character.

She walked up to them and sat on top of the table in front of them. "'Sup?" she asked casually.

Evelyn copied her remark. "'Sup?"

She answered. "Pretty good. Pretty good."

Jill turned to her. "Faith, where have you been?"

She looked around before answering, all the while smirking. "I may or may not have been out with your brother for the past hour."

She cocked an eyebrow. "Doing what?"

"Going to S-Mart, stealing one of their shopping carts, and then taking turns riding down a hill." She turned to Evelyn. "It was fun."

"I must've just missed you, then." said Evelyn.

"That was very strange, but I'm going to ignore that for now. Jill turned back to Evelyn. "So?" she said. "You were saying?"

Evelyn continued, "Oh, yeah." She paused for a moment, wondering how exactly to put it into words. "You remember that guy I work with?" she reminded them. "Big chin, kind of intense looking?"

"You mean the old guy?" Jill asked.

"Yeah."

"Oh, right." Faith remembered. "The guy with the–uh–" Faith raised her right hand and waved her fingers from left to right, mimicking Ash's semi-robotic hand. "Yeah, I know who you're talking about. What happened?"

Evelyn recalled her experience. "I was standing by the register, and I heard this crash. I went over there, and it was Ash. He..."

"...fucked up royally by the Housewares department today." Cooper said to Steven and the rest of his buddies. He didn't turn to face them as he spoke, as he was too busy shooting bad guys and dodging snipers. *Like a boss.* he thought. Cooper jerked and twitched his body from side to side, as if it would somehow affect his playing.

"What'd he do?" Steven asked as he took a drink of soda, his controller in the same hand.

"He fell over a table and nearly got himself stabbed by a bunch of knives." he said, switching eye contact between Steven and everyone else. Cooper smirked. "I mean it was...terrible...but, kinda funny."

Sitting next to him was Kyle. He was lean, with some stubble around his face, and had short, brown hair. He was wearing an "Avenged Sevenfold" t-shirt which had, over the course of the evening, accumulated food stains across it. He joined in the conversation. "Dude, why do you hate him so much?" he asked.

Cooper continued to stare at the television screen. He scoffed. "He's just such a..."

"...nice guy. Well, most of the time, he is." Evelyn answered her friends' question about Ash. "But today, when I wanted to see how he was doing, he was acting very strangely." she said.

"Strange how?" Jill asked.

"It was like he was in a hurry, you know? And he just acted really secretive." She elaborated. "And the more I asked about it, the angrier he got. Then Cooper got involved, they both started fighting, and it was just a big mess."

Neither Jill nor Faith really said anything for a while. They just nodded in passive sympathy.

"So," Faith said. "where do you think Mr. Big Chin guy was in such a hurry to go anyway?" She grabbed a can of Ready Whip and ate a palm-sized ball of whipped cream straight from the nozzle.

Evelyn stared at the ground for a while. She'd already been pondering that question for two hours now. If it didn't come to her then, she was sure the answer wasn't going to appear to her now. Evelyn simply shrugged.

Cooper lowered his elbows for the first time since he sat down to play the game. He rested the controller on his lap. Suddenly the sounds of gunfire and thematic score, along with the overlapping conversations from the crowd, and the techno music blaring from Steven's speakers, lulled in Cooper's ears. Everything just started to run together and fade away. "...Fucked if I know."

Chapter 9

THE TWIN HEADLIGHTS ILLUMINATED THE pathway as Ash cruised around town, hunting for demonic entities. He came across a long, stretched out overpass. Beside the moonlight settling on the indigo sky above him, the bright yellow lights coming from his Delta 88 were the only sources of light detouring him. He traveled so far that he was pretty sure he was about to reach city limits.

He hadn't seen a Deadite for the past few miles, he considered just turning to another street and heading to another side of Springwood. Ash looked around him, appreciating the quiet isolation around him, and the vast emptiness of Deadites so far. He traveled along a concrete road on the outskirts of town, above a railway that had been abandoned for over twenty years. Rusted boxcars and railroad fragments covered the ground. It was past midnight, so there weren't any people around to, hopefully, fall prey to the Deadites. He had felt this kind of isolation before, when he traveled to that cabin many years before, so Ash didn't feel so out of place here.

On each side of the road, there was a barrier of metal railings that stood beside him, acting as a wall. Where they to protect him, to keep him from the evil that lurks outside? Or, where they to seal him in and trap him? Ash decided not to revisit that thought, and instead focused on the road ahead.

It was the silence that calmed him. Ash never turned his radio on at night. If he did, he would likely become distracted and allow himself, or someone else, to be attacked. He had a feeling that tonight would be a slow night. At least, he was hoping tonight would be a slow night. He hoped that the Deadite population was slim to none by now. Ash had desperately wanted his run in Springwood to be over. He needed to be away from this town, and the delusional madness that came with it.

He prayed that it was just a delusion.

As the years have gone by, Ash had upped his artillery than just his trusty chainsaw and shotgun. Tonight, he brought with him yet another shotgun, this one manufactured by Beretta. This particular one was a pump action shotgun with a single eighteen-inch barrel, and a matte black finish. He had also kept a 9mm pistol in his shoulder strap, under his jacket. They were much sleeker than what he had been used to. Ash took his job seriously, which meant occasionally trading his bulky chainsaw for something lightweight.

His knuckles and his wrists grew numb from gripping the steering wheel for all that time. His back and neck became sore, and his eyes began to flutter from the sheer monotony of it all. Ash readjusted himself and wiggled his fingers to loosen himself up. Just then, it was only faintly, but Ash heard a low growl. It came from his left. His ear twitched at the sound of it. It sounded feral, but at the same time otherwordly.

He looked outside the windshield to see a tall, slender Deadite hiding near the gates beside the overpass. Even though it was dark outside, Ash's headlights permitted him to glance at his hideous facial features. The demon had a ripped and bloody T-shirt and jeans on. They were minor cuts, he'd probably gotten them from fighting off some other Deadite who had infected the poor man. He had long, ratty, black hair down to his elbows. The creases in his eyes were perversely deep and sunken, framing his dead, milky eyes. His jaw had elongated and hung open. Ash could see how his mouth had rotted from the inside out, his gums and tongue were black and slimy, while his teeth were yellow. His teeth were also large, misshapen, and stuck out in every direction, like a crocodile's.

Ash slowed his car down to about ten miles per hour. He quickly reached over to the passenger seat and grabbed his pump shotgun. He looked back to make sure the demon had not disappeared from view. He was still there, his gooey, salivating tongue sweeping side to side on the corners of his mouth, relishing the thought of eating Ash's soul, his pure and powerful soul. The undead menace sprinted forward towards Ash. With his right hand on the steering wheel, and the left holding the shotgun outside the window, the dark haired demon slayer pulled the trigger, and blasted a hole in the Deadite's head.

BLAM!

Blood, flesh, and brains shot out from the back of the demon's head like confetti. The demon's blood splattered in blotchy patches against the railing behind him. He instantly dropped to the ground, permanently dead.

His arm still outside the window, Ash grabbed his shotgun by the pump, shook it down, cocking it. A coy grin surfaced on his face. He laughed to himself. "That's what I'm talkin' about!" he yelled. As he drove further, Ash spotted two more Deadites ahead of him, one on his left, and the other on his right. The one on Ash's left was a woman, brunette, probably in her twenties. She wore a purple silk nightgown that cut off just above her knee. Her skin was dark and her hair had soft curls that came down to her shoulders. You could tell that she had been a beautiful woman before she came across whatever vicious Deadite that poisoned her. If she hadn't been possessed, she would have been the perfect woman for him.

Too bad the good ones are always taken...or possessed.

Her face, however, had been mangled. The corners of her mouth were contorted, curving upward into a bloody, demented smile. She had cuts that went vertically across her eyes. They sliced away her eyelids and caused her to bleed black and green blood from her sockets. She stared at Ash, twisting and stroking her hair, smiling her perverted smile. Her hands were dirty, and her nails were rotted and covered in dried blood.

Ash aimed his shotgun at the flirtatious Deadite. "Sorry, babe." he said as he drove closer towards the demon. "I'm not *that* desperate." Ash pulled the trigger.

BLAM!

The demon woman's smiling face had now been obliterated. Her meaty flesh, skeleton fragments, and everything that had been contained inside it, sprayed everywhere. The impact from the blast caused her to be knocked back. She flipped over the metal railings and fell thirty feet on a boxcar, ricocheting onto the rocky ground.

Next, was the Deadite on his right. This one had rotted significantly. His skin had a blue-ish coloration all over him. He had no mouth, only gums and bloody teeth. The right side of his face had somehow been ripped or bitten off, allowing Ash to see part of his skull. He also had a large chunk of flesh removed from the right side of his chest, leaving his ribcage and lung exposed. Ash observed his lung expanding and contracting as the demon snarled furiously at him. The demon hissed in a low voice. "Coming for you!" he snarled.

"Hey, ugly!" Ash yelled out to the demon.

The Deadite snarled at him again, daring him.

Ash reached for the 9mm pistol in holster under his jacket, and aimed straight at the hideous monster. Ash grinned and cocked his chin upward. "How 'bout a little superior firepower?" he said. Ash shot out the passenger window, putting a bullet hole in the Deadite's forehead.

BLAM!

The demon dropped down to his knees, and finally flat on his face, dead.

Ash sped up and put the gun back in its holster. He didn't bother with discarding the bodies. As soon as the sun would rise, the corpses would immediately disintegrate to mere dust. No one would ever think to look twice at the scene. At least these Deadites did *something* that made Ash's job a little easier.

He eventually took the exit off the overpass, and was about to head home when he spotted something illuminated from the far edge of his headlights. It looked like a body, or maybe two. Ash screeched his car to a halt and stared at the bodies. It was a woman hunched over the body of a man, who looked like he was dead. He couldn't see her face as her back was turned to him. As always, Ash expected the worse, so before he got out of the car, he made sure his 9mm was loaded and ready to go. He stepped out of the car, and slammed the door.

Ash walked slowly to the woman, his metal hand under his jacket ready to attack at any second. He could have been completely wrong.

Maybe these two are just innocent people. Ash thought. *And, maybe this guy fell victim to a violent crime...or worse, a Deadite.*

If that was the case, Ash needed to get the woman out of there quickly.

When he was just a few feet away from her, Ash stopped and planted his feet to the ground. He lowered his head, trying to catch a glimpse of her face, but she turned away whenever Ash looked at her. He tried to sound calm and reassuring for her. "Come on," he said, trying to lead her away from the dead body. "Miss, it's not safe for you to be out here. I know it's hard to leave him behind, but you have to get outta here before one of these things gets to you too."

Ash took another step forward and put his hand on her shoulder. He could now get a much better look at the young man. His eyes grazed past her and looked at the corpse. There wasn't a spot on him that wasn't covered in blood. His cadaver eyes looked up at the sky, lifeless and empty. His mouth was opened slightly, with streaks of his blood tracing from the corners. As Ash looked over to his midsection, he saw that the man's stomach and chest had been ripped open. His shredded flesh pointed up and out, like bark from a dead tree. His insides were empty, no bones, no lungs, and no heart. Ash was no stranger to this kind of image, but it still sometimes made his face stiffen in disgust. Ash was only human, after all.

The woman finally spoke, but her body stayed in the same crouched position. "I'm so glad that you found me." she said in a scared, timid voice. "I didn't know what I was going to do." Her hand moved slowly to meet Ash's, which still rested on her shoulder. Ash eyes darted at the woman's hand. He saw a gold band that resembled an engagement ring.

Yet another future ruined by those damned Deadites. Ash thought.

Ash felt a wetness on his hand. As he looked closer, he saw that the her hand was drenched in blood.

It was the man's blood.

The woman yelled in a scratchy, witch-like voice. "BECAUSE I'M HUNGRY FOR SECONDS!!!" She gripped Ash's hand tight like a vice and twisted it until the bone his wrist made a cracking noise. Ash screamed in pain. The woman whipped around and revealed her face to him. She was indeed a Deadite. Her skin was a sickly green color and her eyes were as white as ping-pong balls. She had stringy, blue, pulsating veins streaked across her entire face. Bright, crimson blood was dripping from her mouth down to the bottom of her shirt.

The sharp pain in his wrist caused him to fall to his knees. The twisting agony raced up and down his forearm. These demons have been known to possess the strength of ten men. The woman stood up straight. "You grow weak." she bellowed. "And as your strength slowly fades away, it only makes it easier for him to enter the world of the living." In the blink of an eye, the demonic entity hunched over Ash, making her close enough for him to smell the rotting flesh of her latest victim on her breath. "You are nothing but a vessel. A gateway!" she said. Blood spat out of her mouth as she spoke. "When the Dark One is free, the Chosen One..." she moaned at the thought of what she said next. "...shall DIE!"

Ash grimaced. He mentally blocked the stinging pain in his arm and reached for his gun with his metal hand. "Well, I got news for you, she-bitch." he said to the Deadite. "I don't go down without a fight." He pulled out the 9mm and shot the woman in the head. The impact from the bullet caused blood to spray out like a garden hose. Some of the blood splattered on Ash's face, on his jacket, and his white work shirt.

Ash stood back up and moved his wrist around. It still hurt, but he knew the pain would subside later on. He looked at the red spots on his shirt. He realized that maybe white wasn't a suitable color for Deadite slaying Ash turned around to go grab a rag in the car to wipe his face.

Suddenly, he felt something grab him by the ankle. Ash turned back around and saw that it was the young man who, only a minute ago, was cold and dead. The man howled, and in a chorus of voices said, "WE'LL SWALLOW YOUR SOUL!!"

"Yeah," Ash said as he pointed his gun at the Deadite. "like I haven't heard *that* before." Ash squeezed the trigger and...

BLAM!

It was "Game Over" for Steven when Cooper shot him to death during a "Call of Duty" multiplayer match. Steven was certain he was going to win that time. He had it all planned out. He was going to crouch beside the ruins of a broken down building and shoot an unsuspecting Cooper with a sniper, until he shot Steven in the back of the head before he could even hide.

Cooper raised his hands in victory. "Whoo!" he yelled at the top of his lungs. He stared at the television screen, completely oblivious to the dirty look Steven was giving him.

Steven threw his controller on the couch cushion beside him. "Dang it!" he said. His nostril's flared and his lips pursed like he had just eaten a lemon.

Cooper turned to his left to face Steven. "Ha ha!" he taunted him. "Got you *that* time, bitch!" Cooper started moving his hands, dancing on the couch. He started to sing to himself. "That's how I roll, that's how I get all the ladies. That's how I roll, that's how I get all the ladies..."

Evelyn, Jill, and Faith stood beside the entryway, watching the guys play their game, and look like idiots doing it. Evelyn nodded in disapproval as she watched Cooper taunt his friends. "Does he *ever* shut up?" Jill asked her.

"Not really, no." Evelyn said. She subtly pointed at Cooper, and said to both Jill and Faith. "You know, if this were a horror movie, he'd be the first one to die." The girls laughed at the thought of Cooper getting his comeuppance, all the while watching his victory dance.

Chapter 10

EVELYN AND JILL COULDN'T HELP but laugh the idiotic display of cheesy masculinity being shown before them. They both leaned back by the wall, acting as bystanders to the party going on around them. Evelyn kept her eyes locked on Cooper as he did his little dance.

Yeah, he's kind of hard to deal with sometimes. She thought, recalling back to the incident earlier that day. *But, I know he's just trying to look out for me.*

Evelyn looked over to Jill, who know was scrolling through messages on her phone.

I guess the entertainment around here didn't meet up to her standards. Evelyn thought.

As she turned to her right, Evelyn noticed that Faith was absent from the room.

That's funny. She thought. *She was here a minute ago.* She looked around, trying to spot her among the barrage of people. Evelyn looked around the living room, and she leaned over to peer in the hallway across from her. She had no such luck. Evelyn was about to lean over to Jill and ask where Faith might have gone, when she felt a slight push on her shoulder. Evelyn quickly looked back to her right and saw that Faith had already made her way past Evelyn, and strode towards the couch where Cooper was finishing up his victory song.

"That's how I roll, that's how I get all the ladies. That's how I roll, that's how I get all the ladies..." Cooper danced in his seat, waving his arms in front of him.

Steven had become frustrated at this point. He desperately wanted Cooper to lose just once. He brushed his brown, choppy hair back with his hands. "Shut up!" he yelled at Cooper. "This happens every time we play, man!"

Kyle sat up from the couch cushion. "You two take this stuff way too seriously, you know that? It's getting kind of old." He leaned over to his girlfriend. "Come on, Meg." They made their way out, and away from everyone else. They held hands as they walked through the hallway and up the stairs.

Faith now stood directly in front of them. She motioned her hands to Cooper and Steven, telling them to make a spot for her on the couch. "Move over, ladies!" she said, confidently. "Make room for someone who can play with dignity." Faith playfully grabbed the top of Cooper's head moved him out of the way. She landed on the cushion, while Steven handed her the controller.

The level started and they began to play. Cooper looked back and forth between Faith and the TV screen. "I'll have you know," he said, acting cocky. "that my record for beating someone is like two minutes and seventeen–" Cooper cut himself off when he felt his controller rattle. He saw a grin appear on Faith's lips. Cooper fell silent.

But, Cooper thought. *"Call of Duty" is* my *thing.*

"And, you're dead." Faith taunted him. She jumped up from the couch and stood up straight. She danced, mimicking Cooper. "That's how *I* roll, that's how *I* get all the ladies."

"Oh my God!" Steven exhaled. "Thank you for that! I thought he was gonna do that stupid dance all night." he said to Faith. He was impressed by Cooper's notable silence. Steven saw that Faith had extended her arm in front of Steven, offering the controller back to him. His fingers touched hers as he took it back.

"Anytime." Faith bent over to cup Steven's face in her hands and kissed him.

God, I love this woman. Steven thought.

The kiss lingered for a few seconds, until she quickly let go of him. "Hmm, I like putting men in their place." she said. She turned around to walk off. The flannel shirt tied around her waist twirled as she swayed her hips and joined Evelyn and Jill.

There was a moment of silence between Cooper and Steven. Cooper stared with widened eyes at his friend. He was a bit surprised at what he had just witnessed.

"Dude," Cooper marveled. "I still don't understand how you got her." *You're a nerd with emo hair, how did you do it?* He wanted to ask him that question, but quickly retreated.

Then he realized that Faith was a bit of a nerd, too. Unlike Steven, who was as shy as a stray kitten when it came to women, she was just confident...and apparently they liked that about each other.

He slowly turned his head to look at Cooper, his face still fixed in an expression of shock and excitement. "That's how *I* roll," Steven said. "...bitch." He quickly turned back to face the screen as if it never happened.

Ash flung the front door wide open. The bright red, mahogany door slammed against the wall as Ash leaned against it for support.

I'm so tired. Ash thought. *I can barely stand up.*

All of his weapons, his chainsaw, shotguns, and pistol, were hidden away in a duffel bag he had slung across his left shoulder. The bag was worn with various dirt and blood stains from adventures past.

He slugged across the room, dragging his feet on the floor as he headed for the basement. Ash turned the doorknob and opened the basement door. He slowly descended down the stairs, his feet slammed against the steps as if they were made of concrete. The words the demon had spoken to him had resonated with him. In fact, it more than resonated, his own thoughts were clouded from the Deadite's words swirling around his head. It was like an echoing tornado around his head. The thing that he hated the most, was that she was right. He couldn't deny the fact that he was getting weaker by the day, and he just couldn't explain how.

Ash stepped in front of the workbench and set the duffel bag in the center. He unzipped it and laid out his weapons to wipe the blood off them. He reached for the gun cleaner on the shelf above the bench, and grabbed a old washrag from the corner. He was about to clean the blood from his shotgun barrels when–

CREAK!

What was that? Ash thought to himself.

Ash whipped his head in the direction where he thought the sound came from. He turned around and surveyed the basement. His eyes went towards the old furnace next to the stairs, in the far right corner of the basement.

CREAK!

He heard it again. This time he was certain that it came from the furnace. He decided to move towards it and find out what was causing the furnace to moan all of a sudden. It was so laden with rust that it seemed impossible for the thing to function properly. For the entire time that he'd been living in the house, he never paid close attention to most of the rusted and dusty items in the basement. If it wasn't right in front of him and didn't serve a purpose, it might as well have never existed. Ash stood in front of the furnace and kneeled down to get a closer look at it. Cobwebs surrounded it from the bottom. Ash stared at its rusted iron gate for only a second when the gate flew open in front of him. He was taken aback.

How in the hell...? Ash thought.

Ash looked closer until he could see the old furnace's interior. Immediately he saw that it was covered in ash, dust, and more cobwebs. He noticed something else buried beneath the dust, as if it was meant to be hidden away. Ash reached his hand inside to pull it out and see what it was. He brushed through the debris until he felt something.

Ok, it's something wrapped in some kind of cloth. Ash thought.

Ash felt a sharp cut slice through his index finger. "Ow!" he exclaimed.

Is there a knife in here? He asked himself.

He brought it out so he could see it with his own eyes. Whatever it was, it had been rolled up tightly in an old, dirty, cloth. He unwrapped it as quick as a five-year-old tearing away the decorative paper on a Christmas present. What he had just revealed was an old welding glove with aged copper plating on the back and the fingers, and long, steel, blood-stained, razor blades on the tips of the fingers.

It was Freddy's glove.

He could feel it. The longer he held the glove in his hands, he started to feel dizzy and nauseated. Like the whole room was spinning around him.

It just laid in the palms of his hands, the copper plates clanking against each other as Ash's hands shook. He was now convinced. He knew know that there truly was another evil following him. A dark and shameless thing, weakening him, removing his sanity, trapping him.

Freddy was coming to get him.

Ash felt like he was about to vomit. "Oh...God..." Ash mumbled. He dropped the glove onto the ground, and tried to get back up. He slipped and stumbled in the process, but eventually managed to stand. As he tried to keep his balance, he walked back to the stairs. He knew what he had to do now.

"That damn book..." he said, trying to find something to balance himself with. "It's your fault! For EVERYTHING!" he said. Because of the Necronomicon, Ash's entire life had been ruined. He was destined to a life of Hell on Earth. He wasn't going to put if off any longer. If the book was destroyed, so would his tortuous life be as well. At the very least, there was bound to be some sort of incantation to trap the evil back again. Ash hoped that he would be able read it. Ash prepared to step up the stairs.

Ha ha ha ha ha ha...

Ash froze for a second and shifted his body to look around him. His foot stayed on that first step. He heard that low, sinister, laugh that had now become so familiar to him.

"You again." Ash realized. "You're here. But where?" Ash looked all around him, but found nothing. He slowly turned back, feeling the hairs on his neck spring up and he moved away.

Freddy stood beside Ash, watching him squirm. He smirked at the sight of his shaking hands, and the cold sweat appearing on his brow. He was weak, and the time to strike was now. Freddy had waited for this for so long. He had not just another chance to return from the dead, but to gain eternal life. A power he could have never imagined possessing before. All he had to do was wait for the imbecile to fall asleep, and then the fun could begin.

In his dreams, Ash would be vulnerable and susceptible to Freddy's powers, however weak they were at the time. But it would be just enough to enter his mind, read the incantations of the Necronomicon through Ash, and Freddy would be unstoppable.

"Your soul is mine." Freddy said, but his words went unheard to Ash. Much like Freddy, they were lost between the spaces of the living and the dead. Soon enough, the endless torture, being bound in a purgatorial state of entrapment, the desensitization of not being able to run his blades against the flesh of some ripe, screaming bitch, soon it will all be over. Freddy's patience was starting to wane. He had to wait for Ash to fall asleep before he could do anything. Until then, he just watched as Ash was becoming debilitated by the second.

Ash took it one step at a time as he reached up the stairs. "I'm going to take care of that book once and for all." he vowed. He leaned against the wall to keep from falling backwards. He felt like the ground was moving below him. Utter blackness formed out of the corners of his eyes. He knew he was probably going to pass out within the next two minutes, so he tried as best as he could to hurry to his car to get the Necronomicon. With it, maybe he could undo this whole mess.

I can't waste any time. Ash thought.

He was now at the top of the stairs, about to reach for the doorknob. He suddenly felt a chill race across his spine.

CLINK!

Ash paused for a moment. That noise...he had heard it before. It sounded like metal clanking against metal. He had heard it when he pulled that glove out from the furnace.

Freddy had flicked the fingers of his gloved hand apart, hovering his razor-sharp blades just above Ash's scalp. He couldn't wait until it was time to put those knives back to work again. Out of his frustration, of being restrained from the blood, violence, and violation, Freddy couldn't help but allow a smirk to emerge from the corner of his mouth in anticipation.

Ash pushed the door open, and fell down to his knees on his way out. In addition to his nausea and dizziness, his entire body stung in pain. He felt as if every square inch of his skin was being poked with needles. He managed to get back up, but with each step he took, he could feel the waking world slipping away from him. The pain quickly escalated. He knocked against a shelf in the wall he was leaning against, knocking over vases, books, and other knick-knacks he didn't really give a damn about in the first place.

Finally, he couldn't hold himself up anymore. Ash dropped to ground, holding himself halfway up by his elbows. He couldn't figure out which he was going to do first: pass out, throw up, or cry out in agony. The pain was excruciating, he wanted to die just so he wouldn't have to endure this vexation anymore.

He'd felt this kind of pain before, but not to this degree. This was such an exaggerated and raw discomfort, it was as if his skin had been peeled, leaving only his nerves to exposed to the harsh environment around him. The only time Ash had experienced this agony was when the forces of the Necronomicon had come to him, in an attempt to claim his soul.

God, that was horrible. Ash said to himself. As he recalled, he had only been possessed by the foul things only a few times. And a few times was enough. *But this...this is like a thousand times worse.*

Ash yelled in agony. "AAAAH!" He writhed around on the floor, begging for it to stop. Droplets of sweat raced down his forehead as he panted, feeling like he was losing oxygen. He looked up at the ceiling, everything he saw looked like it was moving around him like a merry-go-round. He wondered how many seconds he had left, and what would happen when his time was up.

"Not so tough now, are ya?" Freddy taunted Ash. He was kneeled over him, his head cocked to the side, marveling at the sight of this supposed "Chosen One" lying flat on the ground like any one of his own victims.

Freddy writhed and twitched the razor blades on his fingers around playfully. "Ha ha ha ha ha ha..." His laugh echoed through the spaces beyond. "Time for this 'hero' to step down and let the master take over." he said. Freddy flicked the blade on his index finger up.

With his left hand, he grabbed Ash by the throat, holding him down. Freddy could hear the pathetic excuse for a demon slayer gag and gasp for breath. "Now," His voice was lithe. "Let's see how strong you really are inside that weak, little brain of yours, huh?" He cocked his elbow up, aiming his razor blade dead center between Ash's eyes. Quick as a bullet, Freddy pierced through the base of Ash's skull.

Ash felt a sharp pain in his head. The phrase "splitting headache" didn't even begin to describe it. "AAAAAH!" He screamed again. He could feel it. It was happening again. Ash knew that, right at that very moment, something had taken control of him. Something that had come back from the dead.

And that something was none other than Freddy Krueger.

Ash felt his breath slow down to a pause, and everything just went...

Black.

Ash's lids opened, revealing a set of eyes that did not belong to him. They were pale blue, and black around the edges. Ash's face had been contorted and twisted until it resembled nothing like what he looked like before. He looked like pure evil. The lines of his mouth curved upwards, forming a sly smile. He had slight burn marks on the side of his face. This was no longer Ash Williams, mild-mannered stock boy destined to fight the evils of the world. This was the haunter of everyone's nightmares, the ultimate boogeyman, the bastard son of a hundred maniacs...Ash had become nothing but a vessel for Freddy Krueger at this point in time.

Freddy jerked upwards until he sat up. He stretched his arms and neck, getting used to the body now in his possession. He stood up, and slowly turned his head to the front door.

"Now," Freddy said to himself. "where's my book?"

He flung the door open wide, and strode across the lawn until he reached Ash's Oldsmobile. He stood, wide-legged, with his right shoulder slumped lower than the left. He was so used to having his trusty glove on him at all times, that he couldn't position himself any other way. Freddy felt around the pockets for the car keys. He opened the trunk, and there it was, right in the middle, calling and beckoning to him. Without a second thought, he grabbed the book and slammed the trunk.

He entered his home, and kicked the door closed behind him. Freddy paced to the kitchen counter, and set the Book of the Dead in front of him. He flipped through the pages, looking for the resurrection passage. Freddy ran his finger across the page. "Alright, let's see here." He searched for the passage that would bring him back from the dead. "Gotcha!" he said. He took a deep breath and began the phonetic pronunciations of the Necronomicon Ex-Mortis.

"Kanda–*ack!*" Out of the blue, Freddy felt a punch land squarely in his jaw. It was his own left hand.

Damn it! Freddy thought. *This moron wants to fight back!*

With his left hand, Ash took back control of his body, and landed another punch at Freddy in his abdomen. While it was his own body, and it hurt a great deal, he knew that Freddy was the one taking most of the damage. The punch caused him to double-over. Ash's voice had now taken over. "I'm not letting you read from that book, you undead bastard!" he said.

Freddy was back in control. "Looks like you don't have a choice, stubby!" he yelled. With Ash's metal hand, he grabbed him by the back of the head and slammed his head against the counter.

SLAM!

Over.

SLAM!

And over.

SLAM!

And over.

Ash pushed himself up. He wiped the blood from the corner of his mouth. "Is that all you've got, Freddy!?" he taunted. "I've done worse to myself!" Before he knew it, he felt himself reach for the Necronomicon.

Freddy didn't want to rush this, but he had no other choice. This was his only chance. "*Kanda. Estrata.*" he struggled to say the words. Suddenly, he felt Ash shove the book away and watched it drop to the floor.

"I'll be damned if I let you to live again!" Ash said.

Freddy retaliated. "Why can't you die like a good little piggy?!" He jumped over the kitchen counter and grabbed the Necronomicon off the floor. He panted as he recited the words. "*Demontos. Nosferatos.*" Soon after, Freddy felt Ash shift his body to the left and hit his knee straight into the counter. "Aaah!" Freddy screamed in pain. With his left foot, Ash stomped on his right foot, causing Freddy to scream in pain again. Freddy reached over and grabbed a butcher knife and held it to Ash's throat.

Before he could make contact, with his left hand, Ash blocked Freddy, pushing the knife away from him. He strained to keep Freddy from slicing his neck open. He felt the hand that Freddy was controlling begin to lower, and quickly slice across Ash's left forearm. It stung like hell, and Ash shouted in pain.

Freddy held the book to him, and resumed the passage.

From outside the house, deep in the darkness and in the night, the evil and powerful forces of the Necronomicon roamed the dark bowers of man's domain. It traveled faster than any man or beast. The entity emerged from the dark unknown, and into the seemingly peaceful area of suburbia. It entered Elm Street. It lived and followed the words of the Dark One, its master. It followed the words echoed by Freddy Krueger. "*Kanda.*" His words became louder. It knew exactly where to go. "*Demontos.*" At the very center of Elm Street, in front of the house addressed 1428, the entity shifted and came ever so close to the door.

Freddy reveled as he spoke the very last word of the resurrection passage. He spoke it wickedly. "*Kanda.*" he growled.

The entity burst through the door, like an explosion. The chorus of demonic voices howled and shrieked bloody murder. The forces of ancient evil met with its new leader and became one. Energy and light fused together and exploded like a flash of lightning. Freddy separated from the meek little vessel known as Ash Williams, and was now fully resurrected, charred skin, ugly sweater, and all.

Ash gained full control of himself. He felt worse than he did went he was possessed, but at least he was himself again. He heard a low breathing noise. Ash looked up, and saw that it was Freddy. He stood tall, asserting his power over the weakened and defeated Ash.

Freddy smirked and laughed softly. "Ha ha ha ha ha..." Freddy launched his razor glove straight at Ash's ribcage. Ash felt a smothering pain in his chest for a fraction of a second until...

He awoke.

Ash shot straight up. He realized what had just happened. There were four small puncture marks in his ribs, but they weren't fatal. He was still alive, but...he couldn't say the same for everyone else. "No." he said. He had find Evelyn and the rest of the kids.

Chapter 11

THE TWO EIGHTEEN-YEAR-OLDS, KYLE AND Meg, quietly shuffled up the stairs and searched the hallway for an unlocked room. The hall was ambient, lit only by the moonlight peeking through the window at the far end. Meg kept looking back, making sure no one was there to spot them. The turning of her head made her shoulder-length red hair flip left and right. Her heart had been pounding in her chest.

She had been with Kyle for over a year. She truly adored him and everything about him, from his short brown hair, to the tiny mole on the side of his right foot. In fact, she would even go so far as to say she loved him. He was always so nice to her, and treated her like fine china.

Meg and Kyle simply wanted to leave the crowd and be alone with him. They rarely ever had time by themselves. School kept them apart during the day. Friends and family kept them company in the evening. That night, they were done being around a crowd of their friends, and ready to just be with each other.

They entered the second door on the left at the very end. They were inside the master bedroom. None of the lights were turned on. It was completely dark. Kyle shut the door and pulled Meg in tightly. He leaned in and kissed her. Meg returned his kiss, she wrapped her arms around his neck.

Kyle pulled back. "Meg, are you sure you want to do this?" he said. "I mean, we can still go back to the party. I'm okay with that." The truth was, that he was just as nervous as Meg was. Meg was his first real girlfriend, and he had no idea what he was supposed to do. He felt like he was trying to skate on ice for the first time, nervous and afraid he was going to look like an idiot.

Meg looked up into his bright, blue eyes. She really did like him a lot. "Yeah." she said, feebly. "Don't worry about it." her voice started to crack. "I feel like we never get to be alone, we're always with someone else."

"Yeah." agreed Kyle. He looked down, appearing conflicted. "But, you sure about here? At Steven's house? I mean, it seems kinda cliché: going to a party at your friend's house, and sneaking off in their parents' bedroom. Right? What if someone walks in? Like Steven?"

"Kyle, we're never by ourselves. Ever. And now we are." She hugged him, burying her face in his chest. "I just want to be with you, without other people around bugging us for once." She turned and pointed at the doorknob. "And see? Look. There's a lock on the door. We'll have privacy, okay?"

Kyle hugged her back. "Okay." he agreed. "It does suck not seeing you all the time."

"I know." Meg said as she kissed him on the cheek. She gently pushed him away, leading him to the bed. "You just wait here," she put her hands on his shoulders and made him sit down on the bed. She spaced her words out. "I'm gonna go get something to drink." she said.

He smiled at her. "Okay."

And in a flash, she was out the door.

Kyle laid back, placing his arms behind his head, and stared at the ceiling. He sighed deeply.

Meg scurried quickly along the hall, muttering to herself. "It's okay to be nervous. It's okay to be nervous. It's normal, it's perfectly normal." She stepped back down the stairs and went into the kitchen to get a glass of water from the tap. She leaned her head back, taking a big drink. She set the empty cup down on the tile counter, and adjusted her black t-shirt, wiping away all of the lint that had accumulated on it.

His eyes began to flutter out of boredom, and from the fact that it was almost one in the morning. Kyle wondered how much longer he had to wait for Meg to come back. Finally, he closed his eyelids shut. In a matter of seconds, Kyle was asleep.

Oh, how sweet. Freddy thought, sarcastically. *Young love.* Freddy stood at the edge of the bed, watching Kyle sleep. *Makes me wanna slit their throats and watch 'em bleed.* He strode closer towards Kyle. This was his first opportunity to use whatever abilities the Necronomicon had to offer him.

Although Freddy now had the book, he still couldn't use it to its full advantage unless he created fear in the little town of Springwood yet again. He thought he'd have this technique down perfectly by now. But at least, with the Book of the Dead, he could speed up the process.

The knives on his metal glove stood straight up as he raised them up in front of his face. The corners of his mouth curved upward as he hovered closer to Kyle. He extended his arm towards him.

"I might not be strong enough yet." Freddy said.

SHIIING!

Freddy raised a single blade up and aimed it at Kyle. "But, this'll have to do for now." He laughed under his breath. "Time to spread the fear around."

While he was sleeping, Kyle felt as if he had been pulled under. He dreamt that he was falling back into an endless darkness. He couldn't see anything, he just felt that he was quickly descending into the unknown. It was terrifying. He wanted to scream for help, but he couldn't breathe.

On the outside, it appeared as if innocent, young Kyle was just sleeping normally. The movements he made were the lifting and lowering of his chest as he breathed, and his eyes twitching from under his lids as he dreamt. But past the seemingly calm exterior, Kyle's soul was in jeopardy.

When he thought that his suffering could not be reached any higher, he felt his entire body begin to burn. He sensed his skin melting off of him. *WHAT'S HAPPENING TO ME?!* He frantically wondered. *AM I DYING?! NO! PLEASE! I DON'T WANT TO DIE!!!*

Just as quickly as he felt himself burn, he was now overcome by petrifying cold. He was stiff, freezing, and numb. He was no different than a dead body. Just then, he felt the impact of his entire body hitting the surface.

Kyle was gone.

But his body had a new host.

His eyes opened wide. While poor Kyle was wasting away in the realm of the Deadites, Freddy was taking his body out for a test drive. Freddy stood up, flaring his nostrils, and twitching the corner of his mouth into a sinister smile.

Meg had just entered the hallway. She tousled her short hair and wiped off the excess chap stick from her lips. She grabbed the doorknob, and paused to take a deep breath in, and then out.

Freddy's eyes darted straight at the door as he heard the knob turn. He was instantly met with the sight of a beautiful, young, redhead. Her small, green eyes twinkled when she looked at him. She appeared nervous and innocent before him.

Just how I like them. Freddy thought.

Freddy quickly composed himself, getting rid of the grin on his face. He tried to look caring and overwhelmed by her. He wanted to lure her in close, because as of right then, she was his prey. He could have just put her against the wall and strangled her right then...

But, where's the fun in that?

"Could you lock the door?" he said.

Meg turned the lock on the doorknob. She walked over to who she thought was Kyle, and cupped his face with the palms of her hands. "Are you nervous, too?" she asked him.

He smiled and chuckled. "Yeah. But," Freddy pulled her in closer to him until she was sitting on his lap. "I'm not going to do anything you're not comfortable with."

"Promise?" she asked as she smiled.

"Promise." He opened his mouth and kissed her. He pulled her in so tight that there was no space between them. Freddy moved his mouth from hers, to her cheeks, down to her milk-white neck. He inhaled the scent of her perfume.

Meg felt his tongue run up and down the length of her neck. It was wet and slobbery. He moved back to her lips, her neck felt cold from the moisture of the saliva.

Freddy ran his hands over every part of her body he could grab, squeezing her hard and wretchedly. He stroked her legs and her breasts, gripping and groping them.

Even though she was surprised at his behavior, she smiled and giggled. "You really came around, didn't you?"

She felt his hot breath on her neck. He nodded in response. "Mmm hmm." He then resumed kissing her neck. He moved up slightly, biting her ear, growling quietly.

She felt his hand on her butt, and the other on her neck. Before she could react, he flipped her over on the bed. He was now on top of her. She smiled and said, "My God, Kyle, you've never acted like this." She laughed out of nervousness.

Since Freddy had possessed his body, the voice still belonged to Kyle, but sounded more guttural than normal. "You like it?"

Meg nodded and giggled. "Yeah."

"Good." said Freddy. "There's more where that came from." He lowered down and kissed her as Meg wrapped her hands around his neck. His tongue entered her mouth, swirling around hers. His hands grazed over her skin, groping every inch of her.

He then grabbed her thigh, and slowly spread her legs apart. His hand traced over her hip and lingered on her vagina. He groped her, probing her with his fingers.

Meg's eyes widened. She wanted him to stop. She muffled in protest. "Mmm mmm! Mmm mmm!" She pushed him away, separating his mouth from hers. "Okay, Kyle." she said, timidly and out of breath. "That's too much." He wouldn't let go. He just held her tighter.

He could feel her struggling. He loved it, he absolutely loved it. Freddy grabbed her legs and her arms tightly, so she couldn't get away. He smiled widely and breathed a little harder.

"Stop!" Meg said. She was so afraid, that she wanted to cry. "I said *stop* it!" She tried desperately to move.

He laid on top of her and grabbed both of her arms, crossing one wrist over the other, and pinned them down over her head.

Meg started to scream. Tears ran down both of her eyes. In between her cries, she pleaded, "No...please...no."

Meg's limbs were twitching and flailing, trying to force Freddy off of her. But, it wouldn't work. Her cries became louder. When she wasn't screaming for help, she was sobbing uncontrollably. She felt his hand cinch her shirt and then rip it apart, baring her lacy, blue bra. Meg screamed again. There was no one upstairs, and the music was too loud for anyone downstairs to hear her. She might as well have been in space.

Quickly and roughly, Freddy took off her jeans. Her frail body was writhing in fear against his. He couldn't help but laugh.

Freddy Krueger was truly a sick bastard.

He gripped her thigh and forced her legs apart. Meg's eyes welled up with more tears. She knew that she could not escape, and she knew the pain she was about to endure would be indescribable. All she did... all she could do...was cry.

As he looked at her, he took one hand away from her wrists and slid it down to the hem of her underwear. "Before we get to the main event," He quickly and roughly took her underwear off, leaving her exposed to him. "let's work on your opening!" He stuck his fingers inside of her, moving them around in a violent fashion.

Meg screamed. "Aaaaah!" Tears escaped her eyes as the sharp pain grew in intensity. "No! No!" she cried.

She acted quickly. Meg launched her knee at his groin and punched him in the nose, stopping him.

The impact was enough to knock Freddy back. As he looked back down, he saw Meg crawling away from him. His demented smile was replaced with a look of scorn. He grabbed a chuck of hair from the back of her head, and pulled her right back.

He hovered over her, snarling in anger. "You don't want to piss me off, bitch."

Although frightened, she managed to say, "Why not?" *Why is he doing this to me?* she thought. *I thought he loved me. What happened to him?*

In a quick, but smooth, transition, Kyle's sweet and innocent face was replaced by Freddy's. Kyle's "Avenged Sevenfold" shirt was replaced by Freddy's sweater. It was now him who appeared before her, ragged sweater and all.

In a flash, Freddy's image had left and Kyle's had returned.

Meg began to scream in horror. She felt suffocated from him being on top of her. Her breaths became shorter and shorter. The pinching and binding of having her wrists pinned down only made her feel that much more helpless.

Freddy hovered over her, no more than an inch from her teary face. His voice morphed and sunk lower, sounding more like himself. "Open wide..." he growled. "bitch."

And then she felt it.

The excruciating pain from between her legs shot through her like a bullet. She gasped. The pain from inside her only spread and escalated. She reacted the only way she could.

Meg screamed bloody murder from the top of her lungs. "Aaaaaa aaaaaaaaaaaaaaaaaaaaaaaaaaaaaaaah!!!" Before, she screamed in distress, hoping someone would find and save her. Now, she screamed out of hopelessness, out of pure, agonizing, torture. Her shouts had mixed with her crying. It became difficult to distinguish whether she was screaming, or sobbing.

Soon enough, blood began to stream down from her inner thighs. It quickly spread out and all around the base of her legs. Meg wanted to die. And she wasn't the only one who wanted that so badly.

Back downstairs, Steven and the rest of the gang were about to head upstairs. He had the same album playing in his stereo for the past two hours, and was getting tired of hearing "Born of Osiris" on Repeat. He felt the party needed to be livened up, and they were the only ones he trusted to go through his album collection.

"Steven, why did you put all of your albums in your room?" Evelyn pondered. "You could put them all next to your stereo, you know?"

"He's afraid someone's going to steal his White Zombie." Cooper countered.

Jill snorted. "Oh yeah, the one that has a typo on the sleeve, so it's a 'collector's item'." She mocked her brother with air quotes.

"Hey!" Steven intruded as he took the disk out. "You never know with some people!" He pointed to Cooper. "And it is a collector's item. I paid fifty dollars for it." He turned to open his door. He heard Cooper say,

Evelyn chimed in. "Exactly how does a typo automatically make it worth a lot of money?"

Steven snapped. "Don't judge me." He stopped before took the first step forward. He forgot to get drinks earlier. He turned back around. "Hey Faith, could you get me something to drink, please?"

She scrunched her eyebrows and crossed her arms in front of her. She leered at him. "And, why do you send the woman out to do things for you?" she asked. "Why not Cooper? I mean, he screams like a girl, but still..."

Steven's face dropped, and he instantly felt embarrassed. He really liked Faith, and he didn't want to do anything to make her reject him. "Oh–uh–" Steven tried to save himself. "I'm sorry," he said, sincerely. "I didn't mean to sound rude–"

"I'm messing with you." Faith smiled again and uncrossed her arms. "You know I like seeing that befuddled look on your face." She pat him gently on the side of his face. "It's cute." She walked into the kitchen.

Evelyn smiled at him. "You're so afraid of her." she noticed. "You're afraid of a lot of things, actually."

"Hey," Steven retaliated. "as long as I have this," he tugged the neck on his t-shirt and brought out a small, silver crucifix. "I have nothing to be afraid of." he placed it back under his shirt. "Come on." he said and placed his left foot on the step that led upstairs. "This time, I'll let *you* pick out the music." he said to Evelyn. "I know you like Black Sabb–"

"Aaaaaaaaaaaaaaaaaaaaaaaaaaaaaaaaaaaah!!!"

Everyone downstairs heard Meg's blood-curdling scream coming from the room at the end of the hall. They ran over as quickly as they could. The hallway was now crowded with kids. Steven tried to open the door, but it was locked. "Damn it, it's locked!" said Steven. "Cooper, help!"

Cooper stood next to Steven as they both tried to ram the door open.

Evelyn was behind them. Her hands shook and her eyes went wide. *Oh God, what's happening to her?* she thought.

Cooper and Steven listened on the other side. They could hear Meg sobbing and shrieking.

"That sounds like Meg." said Steven.

There was something else, too. It was quieter, but they could definitely sense it must have been whoever else was in the room with her. It sounded like heavy breathing and...

Laughing?

Meg's throat was dry and sore from all of her screaming. Her eyes were red and her vision was clouded from the tears. She couldn't bear it anymore. Her legs still convulsed from the pain, but otherwise, she felt numb all over.

And then she remembered. She kept a small pocket knife in her jeans. They were thrown in the far corner of the bed, which wasn't too far from her. Meg hoped she could slip away from his sweaty palms long enough to get the knife and stab him right in the eyes.

She twisted and fought as hard as she could. Finally, she was able to break away from his grip. Grabbing the pant leg, she quickly pulled it closer to her, and reached into the pocket.

Freddy smacked her in the face, causing her to whimper. "What do we have here?" he said maliciously. He yanked the small knife from her hand. "Oh..." he opened up the blade and breathed noxiously. "... perfect." he said.

He lowered his head and locked eyes with the beautiful girl he had just defiled, tortured beyond belief, and robbed of all innocence. He smiled from the power he had over her. Freddy held the knife over Meg's throat. "Was it good for you?" Freddy said contemptuously.

Meg screamed in fear. It would be her last. In mid-shriek, Freddy sliced her from ear to ear. Her howl had been mixed with the gurgling of her own fresh, blood. He jerked the knife away from her neck. The excess blood splattered on Freddy's face and chest. He felt a rush of adrenaline flow all through him. There was just something about the kill, feeling the warmth of his victim's spilt blood run down all over him, standing above the lifeless young bodies. Taking away the youth, that was what he loved the most. Eliminating those with a future, as it was something Freddy would never have.

Admiring her naked, bloody, body, Freddy held the knife tightly in his hands until his knuckles ran white with desire. Suddenly, he heard the door bust open.

Steven and Cooper had knocked the door right off its hinges. When they ran into the room, they saw a guy who looked a lot like Kyle, but acted nothing like him.

Freddy moved his shoulder back and turned his head to look behind him. *Oh, good.* he thought. *More.* His eyes had shifted from the pale blue that they once were, to a blank white all over. He lifted his leg and shifted himself away from Meg's dead body, allowing Steven, Cooper, and Evelyn to see her freshly mutilated and violated corpse, which had now been bathing in a pool of her own blood.

"Oh my God!" shouted Evelyn. She stepped away from view and placed her hand over her mouth, feeling like she wanted to throw up. Jill put both hands on her arm, leading her away.

Steven and Cooper's eyes both widened and their mouths gaped in shock and disgust. Cooper ran over to him and grabbed him by his shirt collar. "GET THE FUCK OFF OF HER!!!" he yelled. Cooper yanked him off the bed, but he quickly leapt back up. He grabbed Cooper's throat and strangled him. He gasped for breath.

Steven ran to his aid and punched Freddy in the jaw. The blow caused Freddy to let go of Cooper, and a drop of blood to shoot out of his mouth. He realized he still had the knife in his hand, so without a second thought, he struck the knife in Steven's shoulder.

"Aaaah!" yelled Steven as the blood poured down his shirt.

Freddy yanked the knife out, caused Steven's blood and some muscle tissue to pour out. His eyes looked, and then his head shifted to look out into the hallway. There were probably ten kids standing in shock. Evelyn was there, holding her cell phone, frantically dialing 911. Jill had already ran after Evelyn refused to move. He sprinted out the door, past Cooper and raised the knife.

Instead of shoving the teenagers out of his way, Freddy used the knife to stab them in the chest and slit their throats as he ran past. Some of them ran downstairs before he could get to them, but those not so lucky were stabbed once or twice in fatal areas before falling down, dead. Their pained screams filled the hall.

As Evelyn tried to run away, she spotted Freddy running towards her. Quickly, she headed towards the stairs. Cooper followed behind them. As they neared the balcony next to the stairs, Freddy started grabbing her arm and pieces of her shirt, hoping to catch her. "Stop!" Evelyn shouted. She jabbed him in the eye with her elbow, filling him with rage. Finally, Freddy leapt on top of her, which caused both of them to lean and fall over the railing on the balcony.

Cooper ran as fast as he could to save her. "EVELYN!!!" he shouted as he reached to grab her ankle before she could fall from the second story.

Downstairs, everyone else had witnessed what had happened. Most of the guests had fled the house, screaming. Faith and Jill were among the crowd. Both girls were petrified, they didn't want to leave them, but they were afraid of what might happen if they stayed. As soon as they saw "Kyle", waving a knife, with those pale, expressionless eyes of his, every last one of them, except Jill and Faith, had ran out of the house.

Freddy knew the impact of the fall would kill his host body, thus forcing him to leave the land of the living. He didn't want to go away without doing a little more damage, so before he plunged to the ground, he stabbed Evelyn in the Achilles' tendon with the knife. The next thing Freddy saw was the hard wood floor. He landed on his head, and the impact caused his neck to snap. The sound was sharp and gut-wrenching, like a celery stalk being broken in half.

Cooper held both of Evelyn's arms and pulled her back up. As soon as her foot touched the ground, she reacted with a groan of pain. She wanted to scream, but the kept her mouth tightly shut. Evelyn didn't want to be weak, she figured now wasn't the time to let her guard down. She sat down on the ground and tried to pull the knife out of her ankle, but she was so nervous that her hand was shaking. She didn't want to inflict anymore pain on herself. She was bleeding so much already.

Cooper moved her hand away from her foot. "No." he protested. "It's okay, you'll be fine. Just relax." he pulled the knife out of her quickly, like ripping off a band-aid. Evelyn held back another scream by covering both of her hands over her mouth.

Chapter 12

ASH'S SKULL THROBBED AS HE picked himself up from the floor. He staggered and stumbled, still reeling from the intensity of his latest encounter from Freddy. Ash mumbled, trying to verbalize and make sense of the whole situation, but it seemed impossible at that point.

When he stood up, and the pain subsided, Ash knew he had two options: He could skip town and let Freddy be the kids' problem as usual, or he could take matters into his own hands and send him to Hell permanently. As much as he had a pattern with screwing things up, endangering both him and the rest of the world, Ash also had a tendency to run away when it became too overwhelming, especially when he was younger.

He realized that it was time to stop running away. This problem with Krueger was a ticking time-bomb. If Ash didn't do anything to stop him, his reign of terror would only spread and get worse. The more powerful he became, the more control he would have over the Necronomicon, and he wouldn't have to wait for the children of Elm Street, or anywhere else for that matter, to fall asleep for him to collect their souls. Soon, he'll have dominion over the dream world, the waking world...and whatever else lies beyond.

The Necronomicon...

"Where is it?" mumbled Ash. *Maybe it's still here.* Ash didn't hesitate to move to the kitchen where Freddy had resurrected himself. *Maybe,* thought Ash. *just maybe I can fix this before it starts.* He rushed to the counter only to find it sans Book of the Dead. Ash slammed his fist on the counter. "Damn!" he exclaimed. "Krueger must've taken it with him."

Ash retreated from the kitchen and headed for the basement to pack up his weapons. "Let's see how you like a couple bullets in your skull, you bastard." said Ash.

Bloody duffel bag in hand, Ash emerged from the basement, and turned to walk to the front door.

KNOCK! KNOCK! KNOCK!

There was someone on the other side of the front door. Ash stepped forward, setting his bag full of guns, ammunition, and his chainsaw, to the corner of the entryway, just a few feet from the door. He lifted the curtain in front of window next to the door, and briefly peeked outside. He looked and saw that it was a cop. Not long afterward, Ash saw the blinking red and blue lights coming from the policeman's car, reflecting off the glass.

Ash composed himself, wiping off any excess blood that may have dried up on his face. He turned the doorknob and opened the door wide. "Hello, Officer." he greeted, nonchalantly. "What brings you here tonight?" Ash kept an ignorant smile on his face. He was no stranger to this kind of scene. All of the Deadite killings he had caused over the years...the screaming, the gunshots...they were bound to attract attention from the police. Somehow, he managed to smooth-talk his way out of every problem.

The officer stood at roughly the same height as Ash, but he was much younger. He adjusted his glasses before he spoke. "Officer Harris." he introduced himself. "Some of your neighbors called in, saying they heard a bunch of screaming coming from this house."

Ash pretended to look confused. He scrunched his eyebrows and darted his eyes at the houses in front of him. "Ummm..." he dragged on. "Are you sure you got the right house? 'Cause from what I hear, Mrs. Brady across the street likes to hit the sauce every now and then–"

Harris interrupted. "We got six calls specifically mentioning 1428 Elm Street, sir."

"Oh." said Ash. He leaned back, desperately looking for a viable excuse, in other words, a good lie. Ash smacked the middle of his forehead with his palm, as if he had just realized something. "You know what?" said Ash, still keeping the fake smile. "I bet that screaming you were talking about was my stereo. I had it on earlier."

Officer Harris looked at Ash skeptically.

"I'm into some heavy stuff." he defended. "I probably should have turned it down, huh? Sorry, I guess that was kind of a boo-boo on my part." he chuckled.

Officer Harris continued to stare him down, seeing if Ash would break down, but he didn't. "Uh-huh." he said. "And, what's your name, sir?"

"Ash Williams, Officer." he said.

"Alright, well–" Just then, the walkie-talkie on Nathan's belt went off. He listened until the signal cut-off.

Just a few minutes earlier, Freddy had begun to spread his mischief in the town of Springwood. After they had fled Steven's house, several of the kids, including some of the neighbors, had dialed 911. "I'll be right there." said Harris.

"What was that all about?" asked Ash.

He hesitated before answering him. "A bunch of kids were murdered a few blocks down from here."

"That's awful."

"Yes, well..." he said. "Mr. Williams, you have a good night, and," Officer Harris looked at his wristwatch. 1:56 AM. "try to get some sleep."

The cheeks on his face were growing sore from all the smiling. "Will do." said Ash.

Officer Harris turned around and quickly raced to his car. Ash shut the door behind him, watching through the small window on the front door, waiting for him to leave. "...Not." he added.

Ash watched in the direction that Nathan drove away. He had no doubt in his mind that Freddy had killed that woman. The squeal of the sirens, as well as the flashing lights from the hood of the car, faded as he left.

Ash picked up the duffel bag and stepped outside the house. He figured that wherever Officer Harris was headed, Freddy had to be there too. If he couldn't stop him right then, at the very least, he could prevent someone else from ending up dead.

2:14 AM. It had been raining. The street lamps above illuminated the concrete streets below. The roads glistened, reflecting the rusted gold coloration of the street lights. Even the sky seemed darker than usual. It was covered with wispy clouds, masking away the stars. Only the moon was visible. It glowed, giving off a strange presence. Ash's dented, yellow Oldsmobile barreled down the streets, zooming by one house after the other.

When Ash saw the swarm of police cars from the Springwood PD surrounding the two-story house in the middle of the street, he immediately stomped on the brakes. The car screeched to a halt. Without pause, Ash opened the door to his car, and stepped out.

A small crowd had gathered behind the yellow and black police tape that shielded the front of the house. The neighbors stared in shock as the coroners rolled out two gurneys, each containing a body bag, one with large patches of blood forming on the outside. Meg was under there.

Just outside the house, in the lawn, police officers were questioning several of the partygoers, the ones that didn't run off screaming, anyway. Among them was Officer Harris, who had arrived there about ten minutes earlier. Standing next to him was Lieutenant Moore. When he got the call, it seemed consistent with the types of murders done by Freddy.

But now, Lt. Moore wasn't so sure what was going on now. For so many years, Springwood had been so peaceful, and now, it's as if it was all unfolding again. Although, it wasn't Freddy's usual pattern of killing: Most of the murders usually began on Elm Street. This was just a few blocks down from there, but still. It usually happened to someone alone, after they had just fallen asleep. None of the kids were asleep. There was no alcohol in either of their systems, so they couldn't have passed out. And the first victim, she wasn't alone. Moore remembered something like this back in 1984 with the murder of fifteen-year-old Tina Grey. She was killed in bed and her boyfriend, Rod Lane, was convicted of murdering her. He "committed suicide" in his jail cell shortly thereafter. But, from what the surviving kids had told them, Kyle had exhibited behavior that was abnormal to his usual nature. *How does a timid young man turn into a lunatic killer with "white eyes" in an instant?* he wondered. All he could think about at that moment was how everything was running smoothly until this Ash Williams moved in a few days before. From what Harris had told him, he too had been exhibiting strange behavior. Lt. Moore briefly looked away from the kids and spotted Ash getting out of his car.

Ash slammed the door to his car shut, and made his way through until he had a front row view of the crime scene. He watched the bloody gurney that was following behind. The body bag apparently hadn't been zipped up all the way. Right before her body had been taken inside the black coroner's van, her arm, streaked with own blood, fell out and hung there, lifeless.

Ash quickly averted his eyes. *I was too late.* He thought. *Maybe if I showed up sooner, I...could've saved them.* He didn't see her face. He didn't know who was under that bag. It could have been anyone for all he knew. It could have been Evelyn that was slashed to death and lying in her own blood. He hoped that it wasn't.

He looked past the gurneys, and saw Evelyn emerging from the front door. She had her right arm slung over Cooper's shoulder. She was limping. Soon, Steven, Jill, Faith, followed behind them. Jill held her left arm, giving her extra support as they walked down the front pathway.

Ash was relieved when he saw that Evelyn and the rest of them were still alive. He ducked under the police tape and ran towards them. "Is everybody alright?" he asked, even though he knew the answer.

Evelyn looked up from the ground. "Ash?" she asked. *What are you doing here?* she wondered.

His voice was sullen, no longer angry. "Does this look 'alright' to you?" Cooper interjected, referring to the stab mark on Evelyn's ankle. "She got stabbed by one of our friends. At least, we thought he was. If you ask me, he was more like a maniac. So excuse us if we don't feel like conversing with another one." He had been through enough yelling in one night to waste anymore on Ash.

All five of them kept trying to get past him, but he put his hand in front of him to block them. "Listen to me!" he said, trying to get all of them to pay attention. "You're in danger, all of you!"

Evelyn stiffened and looked at Ash more intensely. Her voice became smooth and serious. "Ash, what are you talking about?"

He looked at Evelyn, as well as Cooper and the rest of them. He wanted to tell them everything, but couldn't. At least not there, where the police and a small portion of Springwood would overhear, and probably have him locked up. "It's just–" he tried to search for the right words. "You gotta believe me. You're not safe. None of you are. The real killer's still out there, and I want to tell you the whole story, but you *have* to come with me!"

"We're not going anywhere with you." Cooper said sharply.

All five of them began to walk away from Ash.

He didn't want to be responsible for any more deaths. Ash turned around and shouted, "If you don't, he'll slice you to death just like he did with them!"

Evelyn froze where she was. She couldn't help but think that maybe Ash was right. She had her doubts about him, sure, but she knew he wasn't a bad person. He wasn't evil by any means. Evelyn knew what evil was, and she knew when it festered inside of someone. So far, in her eighteen years, she had only seen what she thought was the height of evil two times. The first, was her father, after he drank to his heart's content. Seeing him slouched, but still towering over her young self. It horrified her. And the second, was tonight, when Kyle had raped and killed Meg. He was glad about it, like it gave him some kind of satisfaction to have her blood on his hands. She had never seen Kyle like that before. She didn't think he was capable of that. She didn't think anyone was. *And his eyes were different.* she recalled. *They were just...blank.*

Ash's words echoed in her mind. *The real killer's still out there!* She began to think whether or not it was possible that it *was* someone else. While she didn't fully know yet, she didn't want to take the chance of either of her friends winding up dead. "I think we should go." Evelyn said to all five of them.

Steven, Jill, and Faith protested, but Cooper words stood out amongst them. "Are you crazy?" said Cooper.

Evelyn let go of Cooper's shoulder and stood up without him. "No, Cooper," she said, trying to find her center of balance. "I'm not. I may have lost some blood, but not my sanity." her voice became shaky again from standing in the cold. "Look, he's right. It's too dangerous to be out by ourselves. And, I trust Ash. I say we all go with him."

Cooper tried to talk her out of it. "We need to get home, Evelyn." he pleaded.

"Well," Evelyn countered. "Jill and Steven's home is a crime scene right now, so they need us. Ash can drop us off, we'll all be together, and everything will be fine, okay?" Evelyn waited for a response. Cooper still didn't say anything. "Okay?!"

"Alright, alright!" said Cooper. "We'll do it." He turned his head and looked at Ash. He had been staring at him, waiting for him to say something. "Hey Ash?"

Ash raised his chin as a way of letting Cooper know he had his attention.

"Does that P.O.S. of yours seat six?" he asked.

He stepped closer to Cooper and, for some reason he couldn't explain why, he chuckled. "Nope."

⁂

All six of them crammed themselves in his Delta 88 like sardines, and quickly took off. Ash was planning to take them to the other side of town to Cooper and Evelyn's apartment like he agreed, with Cooper giving him directions from the passenger seat.

⁂

Lt. Moore and Officer Harris and just finished interviewing their share of witnesses when they saw Ash's beat up, yellow, car racing down the street. Harris caught a glimpse of the kids in the car, and who was driving it. They had wanted to bring them to the station for more questioning, and maybe find cause to place them in Westin Hills if need be, but that plan had just been ruined by the mysterious stranger with the metal hand and the large chin.

"Harris?" asked Lt. Moore.

"Yes, Lieutenant?" replied Officer Harris.

"What did you say that man's name was, again?"

"Uh–Ash. Williams." Officer Harris again replied.

"I want the whole department to keep a close watch on him." Moore said sternly. "If he's somehow involved in this, I want him and the whole lot of them sent up to Westin Hills. I'll be damned if this happens again."

"Yes, sir."

Chapter 13

IT WAS NEARING 2:30 AM. Evelyn, Jill, Faith, and Steven packed themselves in the backseat of Ash's Delta 88, while Cooper sat comfortably in the passenger seat. Ash had to drive all the way to the other side of town to get to their apartment. He had come to know Springwood well enough not to feel lost as Cooper shot out directions.

They had entered a long stretch of road, so there was no need for Cooper to tell him where to go at that point. After a period of silence, he decided to make use of the time he had.

"So, Ash," he began. "you claim to have a logical explanation to what just happened back there?" Cooper leered at him as he waited for him to respond. He was still skeptical as to how Ash was planning to explain himself.

Ash turned his head and looked at him for a second before returning his focus to the road. "I never said it was logical, kid."

"I didn't think it would be." Cooper retaliated. "Old man." he added.

At this point, Evelyn was fed up with their bickering. She poked her head out from the backseat, and told them, "Okay, you know what? This isn't the time for you two to fight like little kids." She turned to Ash. "Ash, just tell us what you know."

"*That* shouldn't take long." Cooper muttered under his breath.

Evelyn promptly smacked him in the shoulder. "Shut up." she said curtly, and leaned back in her seat.

Faith, sitting in the seat right behind Cooper, had been watching out the window as the telephone poles, the trees, and the road all sped past her. She stretched her legs as far as she could in the cramped space she was in. "And make it interesting." she joked. "I'm starting to fall asleep back here."

Ash briefly looked at her from his rearview mirror, scrunching his eyebrows. "That," he began. "oddly enough, brings me to my point."

"What do you mean?" asked Jill as she tucked her blonde hair behind her ear.

Ash leaned further back in his seat, gripping the wheel tighter. He tried to remember how Buck and Anthony had told him about Freddy, hoping to find a way to tell them without shocking them...or make them think he was deranged. "You guys know about what happened in this town, right?"

They all collectively shook their heads from side to side, meaning "No."

How could they have just kept these kids in the dark like that all these years? Ash thought. "Okayyy..." he said. *This is gonna be a long drive.* he thought. "From what I've heard, Elm Street's got a pretty bad reputation for, you know, getting hacked and slashed in your dreams by a guy named Freddy Krueger. Ring any bells?"

They just stared at him in disbelief.

Ash continued while he still had their attention. "He used to live here. He worked in the boiler level of this city's power plant. He killed thirty kids in this town. He was arrested, but the police didn't sign a search warrant in the right place, so he was let go. That night, the parents got together, covered the place in gasoline, and watched him burn."

"Oh, God." Evelyn said in disgust.

"It didn't stop there." Ash replied. "Ever since then, Freddy's been haunting people in their nightmares. The thing is," Ash hoped everyone wouldn't erupt in anger, or worse, laughter. "If he kills you in your dreams, you ain't comin' back."

"That's bullshit!" yelled Cooper.

"Wait–wait!" Evelyn cut in. "But, Kyle and Meg weren't asleep."

"Well," Ash said, a little bit ashamed. "That's kind of where *I* come in."

Evelyn, Faith, Jill, Steven, an even Cooper leaned in, anxious to hear what he had to say.

"You see, I," he stumbled around his words for the first time in hours. "I may have been the one who brought him back from the dead."

Cooper snickered. "Really?" he amused him. "How'd you do that? Voodoo?"

Ash loosened his grip on the steering wheel and steadied himself. He knew he had to tread lightly at this point with how he was going to explain himself. "I wasn't much older than you guys are right now." he said, almost sullenly. "My girlfriend and I went to a secluded cabin in the mountains where we found something...evil. It destroyed my life forever."

"What did you find?" asked Evelyn.

"The Necronomicon Ex-Mortis. Roughly translated: the Book of the Dead. I don't know how long it's been around. All I know is that it's home to evil, Kandarian spirits, and it has the power to resurrect the dead. And once they do, you're pretty much screwed."

"So you're telling us," said Cooper. "that this guy was possessed by a...Kandarian demon?" Cooper pointed his finger to the right. "Turn here." he directed him.

Ash turned the wheel. "Not necessarily."

Steven poked his head out from in-between Faith and Evelyn's shoulders. "Well then, what was it?"

"Freddy." Evelyn concluded.

"You got it." said Ash.

"I'm sorry, but," Cooper interjected. "are any of you buying this?"

"I'm not." Steven said.

"No." Jill joined him.

"Nope." Faith said.

"I'm sorry, Ash." Evelyn sympathized. "I want to believe you, but this just doesn't make sense."

"Yeah," Cooper agreed. "Freddy didn't kill those people."

Evelyn's mind flashed back to that moment when she saw Kyle hovered over Meg's body. She remembered how evil and sadistic he looked. *And his eyes...* "But," Evelyn countered. "There *was* something different about him." She turned to Steven. "Steven, you saw him up close."

Steven adjusted the bandage on his collar bone. "Yeah, don't remind me."

Ash, after being excluded from the conversation, decided to join in. He figured if he told them what he knows about the Deadites, maybe they wouldn't be so quick to dismiss him. "Let me guess." he said. "The guy had white eyes."

Almost simultaneously, everyone's faces had dropped. Their eyes darted at him.

He described further. "You know, all glassy and dead. He moved and jerked around, like he wasn't in his own body. And," he realized the similarity between Freddy and those Deadites when it came to this one. "he just smiled and laughed as he was trying to kill you."

"Yeah...how did you know that?" asked Steven.

"Because," Ash replied. "I've been fighting these things my whole life, that's how I know."

There was a moment of silence between everyone. They were astonished at how much he knew about what had happened.

Evelyn just stared at the floor, trying to piece everything together in her mind. The more she thought about it, certain things started to make sense. Seeing Ash at work desperately trying to stay awake. How he was always so secretive and paranoid. The murder at the party. It didn't really click for her until she remembered her and some other kids being questioned by the police earlier. She remembered them asking how Meg and Kyle had died, if any of them were asleep at the time, but mostly they kept asking about their dreams. *Have you been dreaming lately? What are they like? Do you see someone in your dreams at night?* Evelyn had a feeling Ash wasn't crazy or lying. But now, she felt worried about what might happen next.

"How do we know you're not lying?" Cooper asked Ash.

"He's not." Evelyn asserted. "I know he isn't."

Cooper turned over in his seat to face Evelyn. He looked at her, confused.

She read the expression on his face and explained. "Earlier, I heard the police questioning everyone. They asked me and a few others about our dreams."

"Yeah." Steven added. "One of them wanted to know if I've had any nightmares lately. I asked them, 'What the hell does that have to do with anything?' but they never gave me a straight answer."

"See?" said Evelyn.

Cooper turned back to Ash. "Okay." he agreed. "So, what do we do then?"

Ash had been thinking about that for a while. Even then, he still didn't know exactly what to do. "Freddy has the book." That much he was certain about. "If I can get it from him soon enough, I can stop him before..."

Ash had realized just how dangerous Freddy and the Necronomicon are together, and how little time he had. His mind brought him back to that cabin, how his life had been ruined just from reading the book. He remembered the hell he had gone through fighting an army because he misspoke a few words. Ash couldn't begin to imagine the horrors that would arise with the book in Freddy's possession.

"Before what, Ash?" asked Evelyn.

He spotted Evelyn from the reflection in his rear view mirror. "Before he becomes too powerful for me to do a damn thing about it." he said. "If a guy like Freddy can maneuver his way around the Necronomicon, he'll kill every last one of us, and let the dead walk the earth."

Everyone had stopped talking at that point. They simply laid back in their seats with worry on their faces. Cooper rested his elbow on the door, and set his head in his hand. Faith had gone back to staring out the window. Jill frantically picked at her fingernails, chipping away her nail polish. Evelyn sat with her arms crossed over each other. Steven brought out his silver crucifix and clutched it, hoping to give him comfort.

Ash looked at the watch that wrapped around his left wrist. It was 3:08 AM. He had now reached the apartment building and pulled over by the street.

The building was three stories tall, with concrete stairs that led to the front door. There wasn't anything particularly grand about it, except for the line of shrubbery surrounding the building. There was no light coming from it, not even the one above the front door. It was too late in the night.

Everyone had gotten out of Ash's Oldsmobile seconds after he stopped. All five of them walked over to him before he could drive away. Cooper leaned over to face him. Ash promptly rolled his window down. Cooper placed his hands on the door.

"So, O wise one," said Cooper.

Ash quickly turned to Cooper, his lips smirked and his eyebrows scrunched together. *Haven't heard that one in a while.*

"you sure Freddy's the one pulling the strings here?"

"Take my word for it, kid." he said.

"Okay." Cooper tried not to sound irritated from being called "kid" all the time. "Any words of advice before we meet our doom?"

"Yeah." The friendly smirk had left Ash's face. He was now utterly serious. "Don't. Fall. Asleep."

As soon as the words left his mouth, Ash put the car in gear and drove off.

Everyone had settled in Evelyn's apartment, which was just down the hall from Cooper's. They saw each other every day. Every morning, they would walk down the hall together as they left for work. Those thirteen months of her life had been perfect and happy, until now. Before, her biggest concern was paying rent and getting to work on time. Now, she just hoped that she and her friends weren't going to die.

The apartment was small and under-furnished. Everyone was forced to take refuge in the tiny living room. The walls were a warm beige color, and decorated with a few picture frames mounted above an old, ratty couch. A thick, fuzzy, blanket was draped along the right side of the couch. In front was the television that was held up by a small entertainment center that Cooper had helped her build when she first moved in. It didn't take very long to assemble it since most of the parts were made out of plastic. Most of that part of the wall had been covered with bookshelves. The room had been plastered with so many books that they almost served as decorations. In the corner, was a small stereo held up by a table. Various CD's were strewn around it: Avenged Sevenfold, Megadeth, and her favorite: Black Sabbath's first album.

Steven and Jill sat on the futon while Faith sat on the chair next to it. Cooper was too restless to stay still. He stood back behind the wall, occasionally pacing back and forth through the living room.

Jill had just finished filing down her nails after picking at them earlier. She worriedly touched her hair and looked at her own blood-shot eyes.

Steven waved his hand in front of her to get her attention. "Hellooo?" he teased. "What's wrong?"

"I think I'm losing my hair." she said. "You know, from the stress." She rubbed her eyes. "And look at my eyes, they're all red."

"Ah, you're fine." he assured her. He pointed at her face. "You just got that one ugly thing right there. What's that called? Oh right, your face!"

Jill slapped away his hand from her view. "Oh, real nice, bro!" she said. "Do I tell you that you look like a douche bag?"

"Yes!" Steven confirmed.

Jill laughed. "Okay, so at least I'm being accurate..."

Steven quickly put Jill in a headlock and started rubbing her hair.

"Quit it!" Jill put her hand on his face and tried to push him away.

"I'll knock the bleach right off your hair!" Steven said, muffled from Jill's hand smushing the side of his face.

"So, are we really doing this?" Faith asked after not speaking since being in the car. "Not sleeping? Just staying up for, what, days?"

"I guess we have to." Cooper answered.

"Well," Jill broke out of Steven's headlock. "I don't know if I can do that."

"Yeah," said Cooper. "me neither."

"We'll sleep in shifts." Faith proposed. "Just to be safe. If one of us looks like we're having a nightmare, we'll wake each other up."

Cooper realized that Evelyn had been in her room for a long time. He worried about her. "I'm gonna check on Evelyn." said Cooper.

She had changed out of her jeans and wore a pair of flannel shorts. She sat with her legs crossed, on her bed, reading from one of her books. It was one of her favorites, "The Raven" by Edgar Allen Poe. She needed to read something to calm her nerves. Evelyn wanted to find out first-hand if Freddy was real, but was worried about what might happen if she dived right in. *I need to know if Ash is telling the truth. If you* are *real, you'll show yourself to me tonight.*

KNOCK! KNOCK!

Evelyn raised her head. "Who is it?" she asked.

"Can I come in?" asked Cooper.

Evelyn set the book down, rushed to the door, and opened it.

"Are you okay?" he asked.

"Yeah, I'm fine. Why do you ask?"

"Well, you were gone for a while, I was just checking. What are you doing in here?" he asked.

"I was reading." Evelyn walked to grab her book and set down on the edge of the bed. Cooper sat beside her.

"Why'd you change?" he asked, regarding her clothes.

"Because the pants I *was* wearing are covered in blood."

"Right." he remembered, trying not to sound embarrassed. "What are you reading?"

"'The Raven' by Edgar Allen Poe."

He scrunched his eyebrows in confusion. "Why?"

"Seemed fitting, I guess." she explained. "Here, listen: Deep into that darkness peering, long I stood there wondering, fearing, Doubting, dreaming dreams no mortals ever dared to dream before; But the silence was unbroken, and the stillness gave no token, And the only word spoken was the whispered word, 'Lenore!' This I whispered, and an echo murmured back the word, 'Lenore!' Merely this and nothing more."

Cooper gazed at her, confused. "Are you *trying* to give yourself nightmares?"

"No." she lied. "I just...felt like I should read something to calm my nerves."

"Why'd you come here alone, then?"

"I wanted to get away from everyone for a few minutes." she answered. "With everything that's happened today...it's overwhelming."

"I know it is." Cooper began to inform her about the plan. He took her by the hand and gave her a comforting smile. "Speaking of which, we decided we're gonna sleep in shifts tonight."

"Yeah, that sounds like a good idea right now."

He helped her up to her feet and led her out of the door. "Come on. You need to be out here with everyone else. I know it sounds weird, but, if what Ash said had some truth to it, I feel like you need to be where I can see you. At all times."

She agreed. "I feel the same way."

Cooper grabbed the blanket from her couch. "Okay, guys." he announced. "Evelyn's going first. We'll wake her up in an hour, and move on to the next person."

As Evelyn laid down, Cooper gently covered her with the blanket. He pushed a string of her dark hair away from her face and smiled at her. "I'll wake you up in an hour." He kissed her forehead and walked off.

He turned off the lamp that was on the coffee table next to her before making his way into the kitchen. The room was now pitch black and everyone was quiet. She pulled the covers to her until they were up to her elbow. She stared at the ceiling for a moment before clasping her hands together, and closing her eyes. She whispered,

"And now I lay me down to sleep, I pray the Lord my soul to keep, and if I die before I wake, I pray the Lord my soul to take..."

Chapter 14

THE NEXT THING EVELYN KNEW, she was walking down the short, narrow, hallway in her apartment. She had no memory of how she got there. *How did I get here?* she asked. *This doesn't feel like a dream. It feels too real. But it has to be.* She could hear and feel everything as if it was actually there. She could feel the carpet fibers between her toes, the wood paneling on the walls as her hand grazed it, and her dark hair brushing against her arms. The room was completely silent, aside from the floorboards creaking with each step she made.

Emerging out of the hall and into the living area, Evelyn looked to her left, wondering if she would find Cooper and her friends all settled on the couch. She turned on the lamp, and there they were, in their chairs, asleep. She walked over to the chair that faced away from her. Evelyn swept her hands across the cushions until her fingers met Cooper's neck. He didn't move or flinch at all. She heard a creak coming from behind her. Her black hair flipped as she turned, only to find nothing there.

She muttered to herself. "Come on, I thought you were scarier than that." Stepping back, Evelyn looked all around her, the living room, the hall, the kitchen right across from her, even the ceiling. But, Freddy was not there.

Well, if he won't come to me. Evelyn decided to see if she could bring him out. She thought that, after all, if Freddy was as bad as she heard, the least he could do is prove that he was there. "FREDDY!" yelled Evelyn. "ARE YOU HERE?!"

Immediately, Evelyn felt a brush against her neck, and hot breath against her ear. In a deep, petrifying voice that could only be Freddy's, what he whispered to her echoed through the whole room. "I'm everywhere." he said to her.

Evelyn gasped and turned around to look behind her, but he was already gone. Freddy's words had sent a chill down her spine. Her eyes widened. She returned her gaze back to the floor. She felt her heart beating faster, the *thump*-ing of her heart echoed in her eardrums. When she turned, she noticed that the room was completely empty. Cooper was no longer sitting in the chair in front of her. Jill, Faith, and Steven were also gone.

Before Evelyn could calm herself, the floor began to shake, not violently, but enough for her to take notice. She quickly looked up, and no longer recognized her living room. The atmosphere had changed in an instant. All around her, the room was surrounded by dark lights mixing from red to green, to purple to blue, and back again.

She also heard a ferociously loud whirring noise. She couldn't tell where it came from, because it seemed to be traveling everywhere. It was horrible and screeching, like something trying to force its way into her world.

Evelyn felt something touching her feet and legs. Her eyes darted to the ground where she saw tendrils of black smoke covering the ground, and wrapping around her legs, like snakes. The tendrils planted her feet to the floor, trapping her.

The objects in her apartment: the lamp, her books, her CD's, her pictures, and the silverware in her kitchen, began to levitate high above the ground.

Evelyn braced herself as the objects began flying at her at high-speed. She protected her head by covering it under her arms. Even though she couldn't run, she was able to dodge away from most of them. From the corner of her eye, Evelyn saw a butcher knife from the kitchen flying towards her. She ducked down quickly enough for it to miss her and hit the wall by the front door instead. She gasped and short screams left her mouth as she avoided more. Finally, one of her own books from her bookshelf and hit her hard, knocking her to the ground. She looked at the book that hit her: *Something Wicked This Way Comes* by Ray Bradbury.

She could feel some blood running down from her nostril, but she didn't bother wiping it off. She saw the wisps of smoke crawling higher up her legs, past her knees, and closer up her thighs. Evelyn struggled to break out of its grip by shaking and jerking her legs. Suddenly, another hover of smoke shot up from the ground. This one had red and green stripes, with four long, silver, claw-like tendrils pointing at her. It smacked down and grabbed her left thigh. The tips of the claws left tiny puncture wounds on her leg. Evelyn screamed in pain, still fighting off her captor. She rapidly pushed and brushed the red and green cloud of smoke away from her. Eventually, the smoke had dissipated, and the ground was clear again.

Four little ribbons of blood streamed down her leg as she picked herself up from the ground. As she stood up, she heard a low, humming, growl.

From her hallway, the evil force, spawned from the Necronomicon, barreled down the narrow halls and closer to Evelyn. The force roared with an unholy growl, its voice growing louder and higher to closer it got to her.

The poor, young Evelyn, for a moment, was left breathless at the sight of it. Its appearance was inexplicable. She reached for the doorknob and swung the door open. As soon as she did, she saw that there was no outside beyond that door. There was only endless darkness.

She turned and saw that the entity was but a few feet from her. Without a second thought, Evelyn leapt into the dark void to fall for what she thought might last forever. *Just until I wake up.* she thought. *Hopefully, I'll wake up soon.*

It was a short fall that caused her to land right on top of a small bed in a dimly lit bedroom. She pushed herself up, recognizing the thick, patchy, quilt beneath her. She looked all around her as she slowly got up from the mattress. Evelyn remembered the floral wallpaper surrounding every wall, the old, mahogany, dresser on her right, and the open window next to it that allowed her to gaze outside when she was a child. She was in her old room. The very same one she used to run away to when she was afraid.

Of all the places Freddy could have taken her: on a boat surrounded by shark-infested waters, a desert filled with deranged axe murderers, or even Hell itself, this was someplace Evelyn never wanted to be. Not again. Because to her, this *was* Hell. For so many years, she was trapped here, left to cower in the corner. She would listen as her father's footsteps became louder, and her body would freeze as she feared that he was walking to her. *You bastard...*

Everything was exactly as she remembered it. Even the closet to her left contained the clothes she used to wear back in her elementary school years: Some blouses mixed with sports jerseys, jeans, two dresses shoved in the very back, and a pair of tennis shoes thrown on the floor.

Not long after she familiarized herself with where she was, the quiet atmosphere was soon filled with a faint noise. She listened attentively. She could hear it clearly now.

(crying...sniffling...whimpering.)

Evelyn walked to the end of the room, towards the door. She grabbed the doorknob and turned it, slowly and quietly. Opening the door by an inch or so, she peeked outside in the hall. It was dark, so she couldn't see much. She could only see what the shadows weren't hiding. Evelyn felt cold and nervous, not wanting to know what was on the other side, but she knew she had to in order to go further.

It looked like the silhouette of a man peeking out in the hall, but he was immersed in black shadow. His face was not visible, only the direction in which he moved. He stood in front of an open door in the hall just across from where Evelyn was standing. She remembered it. That was her parents' room.

After only a second, the man had turned to his right, and disappeared into the dark. When he turned away, the entry to the bedroom he had been standing in front of was now revealed to her eyes.

Feeling safe enough to go out, Evelyn opened the door just enough for her to slip through, and raced across to see what was on the other side. Her body stiffened and she stopped just a few feet from the door when she saw that, sitting in the middle of the bed, was her mother. "Mom?" Evelyn called to her in disbelief.

Her mother was like an older image of Evelyn. She had long, dark, hair, and had beautiful, full, red, lips like her daughter. The only difference was in the eyes. Evelyn's eyes were a glimmering emerald color. Her mother's eyes were a grayish blue color. Also, her mother's face had become sunken, with red lacerations across her forehead and cheeks.

She wore a white, silk, nightgown that reached to the bottom of her feet. She had been covered in bruises, all the way from the outer corners of her eyes to her arms, and probably more hidden underneath her gown. She sat there, stiffened, as tears ran down her face. The woman looked as if she was being held in place by an unseen captor. Her breath was short, like she was being suffocated. Evelyn's mom looked at her, smiling with false reassurance. "Don't worry, honey." she said in a light voice. "Mommy's fine. You're dad and I just had a little disagreement."

Evelyn took one step closer, nearing the entrance. "Mom, what did he do to you?" At this point, she herself wasn't sure if "he" meant her dad, or Freddy.

"Baby, it's nothing." her mother said. "You didn't have to leave home because of what happened."

Evelyn was shocked. "What?"

"How could you leave me, Evelyn?" Tears streamed down her mother's face. "Now I'm all alone. Why could you do that to me?"

Evelyn stepped back, horrified. "No. No." She shook her head. "This is a dream. You would never say that."

"You ran away. You left me here to die." In that instant, four large lash marks raced down from her left shoulder, diagonally to her stomach. Bright, crimson blood gushed from her body, covering her white gown in red. Soon after, stab marks appeared on her ribs and arms.

She screamed in terror as tears stung her eyes. "Aaaaaaaaaah!" Evelyn couldn't see who was doing this to her mom. She could only see cuts happening. Before she knew it, she door had been slammed shut, and the hall was quiet.

As she slowly stepped back, she hit something with her feet. Something made of glass that rolled and clinked against another glass object. She looked down at the floor and saw that it was strewn with glass containers of tequila, vodka, and beer. Her father's usual nightly drinks.

She covered her head with her hands. "This isn't real! This isn't happening!" she forced herself to say.

Suddenly, the echo was back again. It started as a whisper. "Evelyn." called Freddy. Then a quiet laugh. "Ha ha ha ha..." Finally, in a booming, graveled voice that reverberated both in her mind and in the hall. "Daddy's home..."

Her eyes widened. Her stomach dropped. She felt every bone in her body shake. The first thing she thought to do was run. She fled as fast as she could, racing down the hall, through the living room, and finally out the front door into the dark of night.

When she escaped out the door, she gazed across the porch, the lawn, and the houses in front of her. She didn't remember this place. She wasn't on her old street anymore. Evelyn stepped down the brick steps, and turned around the see the house she had been sent to in her dream.

The white paint, the green roof shingles, six windows on both stories, the bright red door, and the gold address plates to the right of it: 1428. Evelyn was in front of the house on Elm Street. The very same one dozens of other kids had lived in before. Where Freddy caught them in their dreams, and murdered them. The same one Freddy himself used to live in, and plan his next kill.

Her mouth gaped. She couldn't believe her eyes. But, now she knew. *He* is *real.*

"One, two, Freddy's coming for you..."

Evelyn turned around to see three little girls in white, frilly dresses, playing jump rope, and singing hypnotically.

"Three, four, better lock your door..."

The more she observed them, she realized something about them was strange, other than the fact that they were singing about Freddy coming to get her. Their voices sounded otherwordly, like they were ghosts of themselves. They moved and jumped slowly, as if in slow motion.

"Five, six, grab your crucifix..."

She walked closer to the little girls. She looked at their faces, determining that they couldn't have been older than eight years old. She made a conscious effort to keep a distance between her and the girls. This was a nightmare, after all. She didn't know what might happen next.

"Seven, eight, gonna stay up late..."

Their dresses, she thought. *they're all ripped and bloody.*

The ends of their dresses had been frayed, with speckles of blood. Some of that blood had dripped down on their white dress shoes. "Oh my God." she whispered. She felt like she wanted to cry. *Freddy did that to them.* she realized.

"Nine, ten, never sleep again..."

As soon as their song was over, out of nowhere, Evelyn saw Freddy's charred hand reach out from the shadows and grab the rope as it swung to the top, stopping it in mid-swing.

Evelyn felt her heart race again. She slowly backed away, but kept her eyes locked on him.

Freddy emerged from the shadows. First, the sleeve of his ratty red and green sweater came into view. He stepped forward, allowing

Evelyn to see his black work boots and greasy slacks. He didn't show his face at first. As he strode out from the darkness, he kept his head lowered slightly, his brown, wrinkled, fedora covering most of his face. He walked closer to Evelyn. He lifted his head, revealing his burnt face. With his left hand, he swiped the brim of his hat. It sat there, crooked, covering the top of his face and concealing one of Freddy's blue eyes while the other stared straight into hers.

Evelyn reacted in a mixture of fear and disgust from the sight of him. She watched him, petrified, as he got closer to her. She didn't know what to do. She could have ran away, but she was in Freddy's world now, it wouldn't have made a difference.

Freddy slung the rope over his shoulder and smiled at her. As he grinned, he revealed his teeth. They looked like...fangs. Sharp, pointed, bloody, fangs. He struck his glove in front of her and wiggled the knife blades around, as if he was waving "hi" to her.

She gasped, and began to step back as Freddy stepped forward. "It's true." said Evelyn. "You *are* real." But, she didn't want it to be true.

"Oh," said Freddy, disapprovingly. "Didn't your daddy ever tell you not to go lookin' for trouble?" he growled. "Or, was he too busy getting drunk?" Freddy grabbed the rope and held it end-to-end with both hands. He laughed maniacally. "Haa ha ha ha ha ha ha ha ha!"

Evelyn screamed and turned around to run away from him. For a second, she thought she was able to get away, until she felt the rope swing over her neck. She was pulled down to the ground, causing her to lose her breath.

Freddy wrapped the rope around her neck, constricting and strangling her. He used the last foot of rope to drag her across the lawn.

With each tug, Evelyn felt immense pain. She gagged and choked, but couldn't breathe. She stared up at the stars, listening to Freddy tell her in a sing-song voice,

"*I'm gon-na get you, I'm gon-na get you...*
Not another pe-ep, time to go to sle-ep!"

He stopped when they reached the base of a tree next to the house. Freddy unwrapped the rope around her neck. He grabbed the back of her head and slammed it against the tree.

SLAM!

SLAM!

SLAM!

She coughed up blood and spit it out on the ground. Her forehead was cut and bleeding. She cried as Freddy took the rope and tied her hands by the base of the tree trunk.

Evelyn laid on the grass, not able to move her arms. The more she tried, the more the rope would cut and scrape her wrists. Her eyes welled up with tears. She felt hopeless.

He kneeled beside her, admiring her scraped, helpless body, and her teary face. He flicked one of his razor fingers up, and used it to caress her face. *Her sweet, little face.* The blade stroked her softly, but he pressed hard enough to make little scratches where he touched her. Then her neck. He watched the sweat slide down her neck as he lingered his blade on her jugular vein. Finally, his razor blade traveled down to her chest. He breathed heavily on her.

Evelyn cried. She wanted proof that Freddy was real, and she got her wish. And now, she was going to die for it.

His blades trailed down her shirt. The razor-like edges cut through the thin cotton of her Black Sabbath jersey, shredding it. Her shirt now looked like strings across her chest, leaving only her black bra to cover her.

Freddy turned away from her, spread her legs apart, and kneeled over them. "Next time you see Ash," he growled. "tell him I have a message for him." Freddy started cutting her inner thigh with his blades.

Evelyn shrieked in agony. "Ah!" It felt like she was having surgery done on her without any anesthesia. She felt him slicing her left leg in quick, tiny cuts in different directions. She couldn't see what he was doing, but she could tell he must have been writing something on her leg.

She wanted to cry for someone to wake her. She didn't think it would work, but she had to try. "WAKE ME UP!!!" she screamed. "WAKE ME UP!!!" she screamed louder. "PLEASE!!!" She closed her eyes and sobbed.

She felt someone touching her shoulders, lightly pushing her. When Evelyn opened her eyes, she saw Cooper standing above her, looking frightened. "Evelyn?" he asked. "Are you okay?"

Everyone was kneeling at the edge of the couch. They all looked shocked, like they had just seen a ghost. When they heard her screaming, rushed over to her and woke her up as fast at they could. They all had seen her, shaking and convulsing on the cushions, screaming like she was being murdered.

Cooper was about to say something else when Evelyn wrapped her arms around him and hugged him tightly. She feared that she would never be able to do that again.

Her hands shook and her eyes were wide. "I saw him." said Evelyn. "I saw Freddy in my dream. He was there."

Cooper pulled back and looked at Evelyn in horror. When he saw her face, he didn't need to be convinced. "Evelyn," he warned her. "you've got bruises and cuts all over you."

She touched the wet patch on her head. When she looked at her fingers, she saw that it was blood.

"Can you walk?" Jill asked her.

Evelyn tried to get up, but gasped when she felt the stinging pain on her left thigh.

Cooper gently set her back down, and pulled the cover back. The sheets had patches of wet blood on them near Evelyn's legs.

Jill, Steven, and Faith moved in closer to look. They all reacted in horror when they saw it.

Evelyn propped herself up to look at what Freddy had written on her. Carved with his blades on her bloody inner thigh, wrote,

Freddy was here

Chapter 15

It was just after 5:00 AM. The sun had not yet come out. When Steven stood in the living room, looking through the blinds, he saw that the sky was only an indigo blue. The clouds filled the sky, hiding most of the stars. The tall, petrified trees formed black silhouettes in the back ground.

Looking into the horizon, he saw a red dot in the sky. For a moment, he thought it was the sun rising, but he was wrong. As Steven looked more carefully, he realized it was the moon. The moon itself had become red as blood. It didn't shock or frighten him any more than seeing Evelyn convulse on the couch, bleeding before his eyes. It only filled him with dread.

Steven turned away from the window and joined Cooper and Jill, where they stood by kitchen counter. They waited while Faith was in the bathroom, bandaging Evelyn's wounds.

Not all of them waited patiently. After nervously pacing back and forth through the room and biting his fingernails, Cooper leaned against the refrigerator, covering his face with his hands. His dark, blonde hair curtained around his fingers. He didn't want anyone to see that he was crying. He had almost lost his girlfriend that night. And at any moment, he could still lose her, and there was nothing he could do about it.

He felt a hand on his left shoulder, and Jill's voice shortly after. "Cooper?" she asked.

Cooper kept his face hidden. His voice was muffled through his hands. "What now, Jill?" he replied in a monotone.

"Evelyn's going to be fine." she reminded him for what he felt like was the hundredth time.

"It's just a few cuts and bruises." Steven added. "I mean, she's alive. That's what important."

Cooper dragged his hands down from his face, showing his red, teary eyes. He raised his voice this time. "Freddy carved her leg and used her as a punching bag." he told them. "He could've killed her."

Jill got in his face. "But, he didn't." she assured him. "So, why are you still focused on that?" she asked.

He took a deep breath to try to calm himself down. "I could've helped her."

"Oh, really?" Jill humored him. "How?"

He broke eye-contact with Jill and began pacing around the room again. "I don't know." he replied honestly. Since Evelyn woke up, he had gone through various scenarios in his mind on what he could have done to keep her from Freddy. He kept running them in his head on a loop, as punishment for not doing whatever it is he could have done. The truth was, there was nothing he could do. But, he still kept trying to find answers. "I should have watched her more carefully. Maybe then, I would have been able to see that she was having a nightmare and woken her up before Freddy got to her."

Jill interrupted him. "Cooper!"

Cooper stopped pacing and faced her. "What?"

"You can't control everything." she said.

"Yeah." Steven agreed. "It's beside the point, anyway."

"So what *is* the point then?" Cooper asked. "Tell me, Steve. What are we gonna do?"

"Well," said Steven. "if Evelyn survived Freddy in her nightmare, maybe we all can. Just long enough to find a way to get rid of him."

Cooper argued with him. "You heard Ash. Freddy's just gonna get more powerful, and who knows what else will happen. We can't stop him."

Steven stared down at the floor. "You sure are a big help." he said quietly. In a matter of hours, his and all of his friends' lives had changed. His biggest worry went from getting to school on time, to wondering if he'll be alive or dead by tomorrow. He felt hopeless. He was just glad that his sister was by his side. They were only a two years apart. Even though they bugged the hell out of each other, Steven and Jill were like best friends.

"Ash mentioned a book, right?" Jill asked Cooper. "The–uh–Necronomicon?"

"Yeah." answered Cooper. "So?"

"So...If the book is destroyed, wouldn't Freddy be, too?"

Cooper hunched over the table. "Yeah, but Freddy's the only one who has the book." he answered. "The only way to find it is to get to him, and there's no way I'm giving Freddy another chance to kill one of us." He stood up straight. "I say we leave town."

"I like that." Steven agreed. "I have seriously been considering that for the past couple of hours."

"Freddy only kills kids in Springwood." Cooper continued. "If we leave, he can't get to us."

Jill started to walk away. "I'm gonna go check on Evelyn while you two make travel arrangements."

She walked out of the kitchen, through the living room, and headed to the first door on her right, in the hall. The bathroom door was open by a few inches. Jill pushed it open, poking her head out the door. She saw Evelyn sitting on the edge of the bathtub with her leg propped in front of her, with a bloody towel under it. Faith sat beside her, wiping off the crusted blood and applying gauze.

Jill entered the room. She jumped up and sat on the counter next to the sink. "How do you feel?" she asked Evelyn.

Evelyn leaned her head against the tile. "Dizzy." she replied. The touched the dried patches of blood on the side of her head. "...and kind of gross." she added.

Faith turned to Jill, keeping the bandage on Evelyn's leg. "She's still bleeding." she said. "I'm hoping the bandage'll stop it."

The bloody patch on the side of Evelyn's head had dried up and felt crusty on her hair.

The streams of blood on her forehead and nose had also dried up and had gotten darker. She felt defeated. She just wanted to get bandaged, cleaned up, and move on. "Faith," she said weakly. "could you hand me that towel, please?"

Faith reached for the damp rag next to her and handed it to Evelyn.

"Thank you." she said weakly. She wiped off the crusted blood from her face, and then squeezed the excess water onto her scalp. It wasn't much of an improvement. The cuts were still visible and she still had some dark bruises on her, but she felt clean.

"So," Faith asked Evelyn. "what happened in your dream?"

Evelyn closed her eyes and took a deep breath. She didn't really want to relive the experience, but she figured she had to talk about it at some point. "Well," she pondered where to begin. "it felt...real. Like it was actually happening."

Faith lifted her leg up slightly to wrap the gauze around her thigh. She wrapped it around tightly, hoping to stop the bleeding.

"At first, I was here and everything just seemed normal. And then," Evelyn recalled seeing the entity from the Book of the Dead. "I saw this...*thing*...running towards me."

"Was it Freddy?" asked Jill.

"No," Evelyn answered. "it was something else. It was...like this... entity and it was coming right for me, so I ran. The next thing I knew, I was back in my old house."

Cooper and Steven had been standing by the door, listening. They entered the bathroom as Evelyn described her nightmare. Steven sat down on the floor so that he was next to Faith, and also by his sister. Cooper sat on the floor next to Evelyn.

"He knew all about me." she continued. "He knew *everything*." Her eyes became watery and she felt her bottom lip quiver from the images of her dream running over and over again in her head. "He took me to that old house on Elm Street. And there were these little girls, they looked like Freddy did something..." she didn't want to finish that sentence, because that meant she would have had to imagine what Freddy did to those girls. "They were singing." She repeated the song exactly as she remembered in her dream. *"One, two, Freddy's coming for you..."*

Listening to Evelyn recall her dream unnerved everyone. Jill would fold her arms, while Cooper would stare down at the floor.

After Faith had wrapped the bandage around Evelyn's leg, she clasped Steven's hand. Steven gazed at her brown eyes for only a second before she turned her head back in Evelyn's direction.

Her voice had become shaken and fearful. "And then I saw him. He wore this dirty, brown hat. He was horribly burned...all over...and on his right hand, he had...this glove...with razors for fingers." She began recalling what he did to her. "He strangled me, and dragged me across the ground...he hit me...and then he..." Out of embarrassment, Evelyn wiped a tear away from her eye. "I thought he was really going to kill me."

Faith gently set her leg down. "Well, you're all bandaged up now." she said gently. "Do you think you can walk?"

It already hurt her to walk with the stab wound on her right ankle. She set her feet on the tile and stood up. She winced slightly at the pain. "It stings a little bit, but I'll be okay."

Everyone had left the room, Evelyn followed. Cooper put her arm around his shoulder, leading her out the door. Evelyn unwrapped his arm from her, refusing his help. "No." she said. "It's fine, I can do it."

"Are you sure?"

Evelyn answered. "Yeah."

She sat down on a wooden chair beside her small table in the kitchen. She stared down at her bandage. Blood had already started to surface in tiny dots where Freddy carved her. She knew how deep he had cut her. Even after it heals, the words would still be scarred on her leg forever, constantly reminding her: *Freddy was here.* She heard Cooper's voice, breaking her thoughts.

"We should leave Springwood." he said. "Think about it. If we're not here, Freddy can't come after us."

Faith argued with him. "Oh, so you're okay with that asshole murdering *more* kids? 'Cause that's what I'm hearing from you."

"No!" he retorted. "It's better than Jill's idea."

Evelyn turned to Cooper. "Why?" she inquired. "What was her plan?"

He opened his mouth to speak, when Jill put her hand over it to silence him. She spoke for herself. "Remember when Ash said that Freddy used the Necronomicon to resurrect himself?"

Evelyn nodded.

"I'm thinking if we burn the book, or like, rip up the pages, Freddy's done for." Jill looked to Evelyn for agreement. "Right?" She detached her hand from Cooper's mouth.

Evelyn was unsure. She knew they all had to do something to stop him. But they couldn't do it by themselves, they needed to get someone to help them. *If we don't,* she thought. *we'll all die.*

Cooper pointed at Jill. "See?" He asked her, hoping she would agree. He summed up her plan in one word. "Dumb." He refuted it. "The only way to get to that book is through Freddy, and I'm not letting anyone go through that–" he pointed at the bandage on Evelyn's leg. "–again."

Evelyn stood up from her chair. "No, you're *both* wrong!" she said. She looked into Cooper's eyes. "We are not running away like cowards." and then to Faith. "And we're not gonna fight him by ourselves. We can't do this alone." She knew what she was going to say next was going to irritate everyone, especially Cooper. "We need Ash."

Everyone erupted at once.

"What?!" Faith yelled.

"Are you kidding me?!" said Cooper.

Then Jill, who flat-out said, "No!"

Steven was the only one who agreed with Evelyn. He spoke out amid everyone's shouting. "Hey! Everyone, SHUT UP!" he yelled.

And they all did. They turned around to look at Steven.

"She's right." he said. "I mean, it's stupid to do this by ourselves. I bet if we did, we wouldn't last another night. We barely did this time."

"Besides," said Evelyn. "Ash is the only one with experience in dealing with demons. He would how to kill Freddy." Even though she had grown to trust Ash, she remembered how much of a screw-up he was. "At least...I think he would."

Cooper walked up closer to her. "I'm sorry," he said, sarcastically. "but isn't Mr. Wonderful the reason WHY WE'RE FUCKING HERE?!"

Evelyn leered at him, pursing her lips and scrunching her brows. She prepared to say something when–

KNOCK! KNOCK! KNOCK!

Desperate to break the tension, Steven meekly raised his hand to volunteer. "I'll get it." he said.

He walked over the front door and looked through the peephole. He saw a tall man with dark hair and a little gray on the sides, and wearing a bloody shirt. The man looked up, allowing Steven to see the scars on his face. He knew it had to be–

"It's Ash." announced Steven.

Evelyn broke eye contact with Cooper ordered Steven from the distance. "Let him in."

Steven turned the latch, unlocking the door, and turned the knob.

Ash pushed the door open and immediately walked through. "Hey." he greeted Steven. He turned his gaze to the rest of the kids. "How's everyone holding up?"

Cooper shouted from across the room. "WE'RE COMPLETELY FUCKED!!!"

He walked away, allowing Ash to see Evelyn, bruised and covered in cuts and bandages. "Yeah, I think that speaks for itself." said Ash.

Evelyn stepped forward, making her way past Steven, Jill, and Faith. "Freddy told me he had a message for you."

"You mean threatening to skin me and making me as his own little puppet wasn't enough?" he said. "What did he say?"

"It was more of a visual, really." Evelyn led him to kitchen. She put one foot on the chair she was sitting on, and un-wrapped the gauze.

Ash saw the cuts Freddy left on Evelyn's leg with his finger knives. The letters were thin and crude, like someone had carved words into tree bark. Seeing what he did to her made his stomach drop, because Ash knew it was his fault that Freddy was free again. "Oh...God." he said. "Evelyn, I'm sorry."

"Save it." said Cooper.

Evelyn tightly wrapped her leg back up. After securing the bandage, she returned her gaze back at Ash. He avoided eye contact with anybody, staring at the floor, the furniture, the chipped paint on the walls–anything–to keep himself from feeling any more guilt for the damage he had caused. *Come on, Ash.* Evelyn wanted to say, but kept to herself. *Don't be a coward.*

Ash couldn't believe the mess he had gotten himself into this time. He didn't just put a few kids' lives in jeopardy, but he put the lives of every child in the world in the clawed hands of Freddy Krueger. *Boy,* Ash thought to himself. *I really screwed up...big time.*

Chapter 16

ASH LIFTED HIS GAZE FROM the floor and watched her circle the gauze around her leg. Even though he had felt guilty, responsible for what he had done, he kept thinking back to what he had warned them just a few hours before: *Don't. Fall. Asleep.* he told them. But did they do that? *No. These kids just go ahead and do whatever the hell they want.* he thought to himself.

Ash pointed at Evelyn. "What did I tell you, huh?" he said to her. "I told you not to fall asleep, and you guys turn around and let him slice you!"

Faith stepped forward and grabbed Ash's arm, turning him so that he faced her. "Hey!" she yelled. "I had a plan and it didn't work out, okay? So, don't blame her."

"Oh, you had a plan?" he said. "Nice goin' there, Sailor Moon."

Faith scoffed and leered at Ash for his cheap insult. "Sailor Moon's a ditzy blonde, you jackass."

He turned to Evelyn. "What was the plan, huh? Hang a dream-catcher above your head and hope Freddy doesn't get you?"

Evelyn interrupted them. "No." she said coldly. Her voice was now quiet and apologetic. She looked at Ash. "But, you're right. I shouldn't have done it."

Cooper walked up to him and stared him down. "We were just trying to find a way to manage. It seemed smart at the time, you know, considering it's your fault that we're now desperate to stay alive." he said in his irritated tone.

Jill leaned in close to her brother. "You know," she said in a quiet voice, but still loud enough for Ash to hear. "if it weren't for him, we'd be safe at home right now. We can't say anything to Mom and Dad about this."

"Hey, the car still has a full tank of gas, right?" Steven asked.

Jill nodded.

"We should all just load up and go until this whole thing blows over." he proposed. "I mean, it'll be tough convincing Evelyn to go with us 'cause she's all hell bent on this teaming-up-and-banding-together-with-Ash crap–"

Ash turned away from Evelyn. He studied everyone's faces. It was a bevy of emotions: guilt, fear, anger, and enmity (mostly intended for him). He prepared to lay down his own plan. Ash stood straight. He stepped away from Cooper and Evelyn. "All right, listen up you little knuckle-draggers!" he announced. "Here's how it's gonna go down." Ash turned his head and pointed directly at Jill and Steven. "No one's going anywhere." Ash noticed the surprised looks on their faces. "That's right. Some of you've been thinking about skipping town. But it's not gonna happen."

Cooper interjected. "Yeah? And why the hell not?"

Ash got in his face. "Because as long as Freddy has the book, he can go anywhere, not just Springwood." he said. "So, high-tailing it outta here won't do you any good. And it's not just Freddy." he told them. "It's those things out there: the Deadites. They live in the dark. Now all of you, listen carefully: They can get you when you least expect it. By then, it's too late for you. And now that they have a leader..." Ash muttered under his breath. "...again..." he returned back to his normal volume. "Well, let's just say it makes my job a hell of a lot harder now."

"So, basically you're saying we're screwed no matter where we go?" asked Cooper.

"Not exactly." he replied. "I can take Freddy down, but it's not gonna be easy."

"Maybe we can help." said Evelyn.

"No, it's too dangerous." Ash told her.

"So," Faith said. "what *are* you gonna do? Look for Freddy in the dream, ask him nicely for the book, and banish his ass?"

Ash leered at Faith for a moment. She, frankly all of them, was really starting to get on his nerves. The annoying part was that she pretty much had just summed up whatever plan he could think of in those few hours, aside from the "asking him nicely" part.

"Look," Ash said. "I have to get the book from Freddy. I haven't exactly worked out *how* I'm gonna do that, but it's all I got. That damn book has to be destroyed. Then, maybe Freddy...maybe this whole Deadite problem...will be over."

Jill nudged her brother on the shoulder and said to him in an "told-you-so" manner. "See? I'm not always wrong." she said.

Faith, who still stood close to Evelyn, glanced at her. She stared at the cuts and bruises on her. Faith felt so uneasy and disturbed every time she saw those slash marks. She was afraid that the bandages she hastily tied on her wouldn't be enough. "Ash," called Faith. "shouldn't we take Evelyn to the hospital or something? I mean..." she wanted to say *look at her,* but she figured Evelyn had been stared at enough already.

Ash answered her with a flat-out, "No." he elaborated. "If she goes, the doctor's gonna see where Freddy left his mark, and get suspicious. You can't let anybody know. You got me?"

Everyone begrudgingly nodded in agreement.

Ash continued. "The people here tend to hide Freddy away like he's their dirty laundry, or something. Judging from my little visit earlier today, I get the feeling the police are in on it, too. If they find out about this, they'll probably lock us up in the nuthouse."

"Westin Hills." Evelyn corrected him.

"What?" he asked.

"It's a psychiatric hospital. I've heard about some kids being taken there, but they never say what for. They're not allowed any contact with their family or their friends, and most of them never come back home." she said.

"All the more reason to shut up about it." said Ash. He looked across and saw the sun light peeking through the curtains in the living room. Seeing dawn was the most comforting thing in the world to him. It meant that, until later that night, he was safe from the Deadites. But now, if Ash makes the mistake of nodding off, he won't be safe during the day either. It's not just the Deadites he has to worry about anymore. It's Freddy as well. Ash was starting to wonder if he was even going to win this battle. Last time something like this happened, he had an entire army backing him up. *And what do I got now? A bunch of whiny kids?...I'm screwed.* "First things first," Ash said as he walked to the door. "I gotta get you guys home to your parents. It's dawn now, so they're probably wondering where you are." Ash opened the front door and let Jill, Faith, Steven, and Cooper go first.

Evelyn ran over and touched Ash on his shoulder. "I'll ride with you. I have to get the car back anyway." she referred to Cooper's El Camino.

"Fine." he said hesitantly.

The sun peeked through the clouds. The morning fog was starting to roll in, making it hard to see the road ahead. While it was still somewhat dark outside, the yellow sunlight that was visible over the horizon had brightened the sky a little bit. The red moon was gone, and wouldn't return for another twelve hours.

Ash parked his Delta 88 about a block away from Jill and Steven's house. He figured it'd be best if their parents didn't know that their kids were being chauffeured around by a guy with scars on his face and blood on his shirt.

He stared at the steering wheel while he listened to the kids say "Thanks, Ash." as they both got out of his car. Next, he heard the door slam, and the quiet shuffling of their feet as they walked home. Ash lifted his gaze from the wheel and watched Jill and Steven as they walked down to the end of the block, towards their parents, who were standing on the front steps, waiting for them.

They looked so relieved to see their children alive and unharmed. Jill wrapped her arms around her mother, tightly, while Steven hugged his father. After she kissed the top of her head, Jill's mother grabbed her face and looked at her worriedly.

Ash couldn't make out exactly what they were saying, but he was pretty sure it was along the lines of: "Where the hell were you?" "What were you thinking?" "Who were you with?" But, at least those kids had someone to care for them. They weren't completely alone. Not like–

"Thanks for the ride, Ash." said Evelyn, who sat in the passenger seat. "I appreciate it."

"Yeah, no problem." he responded. Ash looked at the scrapes on Evelyn's face as she unbuckled her seatbelt and reached to open the door. Even though she had washed the dried-up blood from her face, and changed from her torn jersey to a clean, purple tank top, black jacket, and jeans, she still looked a little roughed up due to the bruises on her forehead. It was funny when he thought about it: An undeserving kid getting beaten up by an evil force she had only recently found out about. Becoming the leader of her circle, and yet being stupid enough to put herself in harm's way when she was most vulnerable. The more he thought about it, Evelyn kind of reminded Ash of... himself.

Before she left him, he felt he had to ask her. "So, why'd you do it?" he said before she had the chance to open the door.

"What are you talking about?" asked Evelyn.

Ash smirked a little bit. "You know what I'm talking about. You expect me to believe after what I told you, you didn't think you'd run into ol' Dream Weaver? You knew what you were doing."

Evelyn slumped into her seat and sighed. She didn't look at Ash at first. She mostly gazed outside. "I wanted to find out for myself if Freddy was real." she finally looked him in the eye. "I didn't think anything bad would happen, because I knew someone was going to wake me up eventually." she exhaled. "It's a habit of mine." she said. "Going where I'm not supposed to."

"We have that in common."

"I'm sorry I doubted you." she said. She hesitated before asking him the next question. "So, um–"

Ash waited her to speak.

"why did this happen to you?"

Ash took a deep breath and wiggled his fingers on the steering wheel. "It wasn't always this way, you know. When I was younger, my life was normal. Then fate smacked me across the face like an angry girlfriend. Since then, I've had to watch everyone I've ever cared about die in front of me...it never ends. Take it from someone who's been there. In situations like these, be prepared to have people you love get taken away from you."

Evelyn couldn't speak at first. She just let his words soak in for a moment. "I'm really sorry." she said quietly. "I had no idea."

"I guess, after a while, I started to think that maybe this was how my life was supposed to go. That I was chosen to do this until–until I'm just not strong enough to fight the evil anymore."

Out of sympathy, Evelyn reached over and gave him a gentle pat on the shoulder. She was about to say something when Ash beat her to it. She figured it was for the best, since nothing she thought to say could have made much of an impact on the situation.

His voice became cryptic. "Sometimes, I think that day's coming sooner than I–"

"Ash!" she interrupted him. "Don't say that. We're gonna beat this thing, all right?"

Somehow, Evelyn was able to lift his spirits just enough for a tiny smile to appear across his face. "You really think so, huh?"

Evelyn nodded. "Yeah, I do."

"You got spunk, girly. I like that." he said.

She smiled in response.

Ash suddenly remembered. "One more thing." he reached over to the glove box to grab a pen and a small piece of paper. "If you, or any of your friends start seeing some ugly faces out there in the dark," he said as he scribbled his phone number on the paper. "let me know. And just a word of advice, keep an axe around handy, if you got one."

She took the paper with his number on it. She crumpled it up and put it in the front pocket of her jeans.

Ash leaned over to look out the window on Evelyn's side. He gazed across the street and noticed the black 1987 El Camino with chipped paint and cracked window tinting. All of the other vehicles on that block were practically new, and all were parked neatly in their driveways. Ash had a hunch it belonged to her.

"And people make fun of *my* car." he mocked her.

Evelyn couldn't help but laugh. It was the first laugh she'd had all day. It was comforting. "Yeah." she agreed. "But, it gets us around, so..." she grabbed the door handle and opened it by an inch.

"I guess I'll see you at work." said Ash.

"Well, it'll help me stay awake, right?"

"Yeah."

"And, Ash?" she asked.

He gazed back into her eyes as he turned the ignition.

She warned him. "Be careful." Evelyn stepped out and closed the door to Ash's Oldsmobile.

He watched her walk across the street and get into her car. Looking at his watch, he noticed it was almost 7:00 AM. His agenda for right now was to get home and change out of something less bloody. Ash figured the best way to stay awake right then was to get to work. At least he would be on his feet. And, he would have some time to conjure up a plan to get the Necronomicon from Freddy. Ash put his Delta 88 in gear and drove off, following the sunrise on the horizon.

Chapter 17

An entire workday had passed, and not once did Evelyn fall asleep. Not even for even a minute. It was difficult, since it was a slow workday. Not many people wanted to go out in the wake of last night's murder spree.

It was now 5:17 PM. Evelyn had unlocked her door and walked into her apartment, dropping her S-Mart smock and her purse on the floor. She immediately went into the kitchen and stopped in front of her coffee maker on the counter. Lifting the lid, she grabbed a bag of coffee grounds and poured it into the filter. She took a cup from the pantry and filled it with water from the tap. After pouring the water, she flipped the switch then prepare another batch of coffee.

When she wasn't waiting on customers at work, she had spent most of her day walking around the building, and consuming anything caffeinated she could get her hands on. And now that she was home, the trend would continue.

By the time sundown had arrived, she pulled her curtains back and watched the sun set as she nervously drank her coffee. It was still steaming hot and it burned her tongue, but she didn't care. She considered it as a sign that her senses were still alive.

As Evelyn stood there in the middle of her living room, with dark circles under her green eyes, and her mind racing with paranoid thoughts, she realized that she was acting exactly as Ash had been not too long ago. She, Cooper, and her friends used to joke about the way he frantically loaded himself up with coffee and energy drinks, always keeping himself guarded, like someone was after him. And now, Evelyn was in that same state of mind.

She so desperately wanted it to stop, to get away from where she was, even for just a few minutes. Even though she knew it was impossible, she wanted to go back to the way everything was before Ash and Freddy entered her life. She just wanted act like she and everyone else she loved wasn't in danger of dying by that bastard.

Evelyn took one final sip from her mug and set it down on her table in the living room. She wiped her pink, coffee-stained lips and headed towards the front door. She closed the door behind her and walked to the door just across from hers. Balling her hand up into a fist, she raised it and knocked on the door three times.

KNOCK!

KNOCK!

KNOCK!

She waited about ten seconds before she heard the latch unlock and saw the door open by about two feet.

Poking his head out from the front door was Cooper. He had his headset around his neck. Evelyn knew he must have been playing a game. His face lit up when he saw her. Cooper greeted her with a wide smile.

His voice was surprisingly cheery. "Hey!" he opened the door all the way. "Come to see me?" he assumed.

She tried to grin with the same enthusiasm as Cooper, but could only manage a timid half-smile. She nodded her head "yes."

"Well, don't be shy. Come in." he said. "I got a new game today, you wanna play?"

For the first time that day, her eyes glimmered and she smiled so wide, her teeth showed. "Yeah, I would."

Cooper stepped out of her way and extended his arm out, inviting her in. He was wearing a white, tattered, "Jimi Hendrix" t-shirt. The hem of his jeans rolled under his bare feet.

Evelyn walked into his apartment, which was identical to hers, except it wasn't as neatly kept. There was dirty laundry lazily thrown on the couch, and some on the floor. Instead of pictures, Cooper covered his wall with posters of his favorite games and movies. Above his sofa, right next to the door, was a poster for "Frankenstein Meets the Wolf Man" with rips and tears along the edges. On the opposite side of the room, above his TV where he had been playing, was a poster of favorite game, the original "Alone in the Dark" with the poster resembling the cover art of a boy holding a lantern up to a gothic mansion.

She immediately noticed all of the empty bottles of soda lying around on his table, one on the chair in his kitchen, and strewn across the counter. She squinted her eyes to focus on the bottle that was on the edge of Cooper's counter. The label read "No-Doze". *He's taking pills to stay awake.* she realized. *He's just as scared as I am.* This time when Evelyn looked up into Cooper's blue, bloodshot eyes, she started to doubt that it was from staring at his TV screen, but rather because he was frantically trying to keep himself awake.

"So," Cooper carried on. "it's this zombie survival game. There's a lot of stealth in it, so you can either sneak around them, or just blow their brains out. Personally, I prefer to–"

Cooper was about to say "blow their brains out" when Evelyn quickly pulled him in and hugged him tightly. He hugged her back.

Evelyn had her arms around him so tight, she could feel his heart beat against her ear. She nestled her head against his chest. "I don't want to lose you." she said nervously.

Cooper let go of her, and lowered himself so he was at eye-level with Evelyn. He rested his hands on her shoulders. He smiled in hopes to make her feel better. "I'm not going anywhere." he held both of her hands in his. "I would never leave you, okay?"

She mumbled so quietly, Cooper almost couldn't hear her. "Okay." she replied. "Come on, let's play. I'm sick of being sad."

He eagerly raised his arms up like a little kid. "Yay!" he said. "I'll get a controller for you." he ran over to the television stand to get Evelyn her own controller.

As Evelyn watched her boyfriend scramble to get a controller for her, she felt a smile turn on the corners of her mouth. She felt happy that, at least for a few hours, she could go back to the way everything was before.

They played on Cooper's brown, leather, sofa for nearly an hour. The orange sunset outside had now turned to dusk. All that lighted the apartment now was the television screen and the light coming from the kitchen not far from them.

Both sat in the same position: on the edge of the cushions, hunched over, with their forearms resting on their laps. Evelyn sat next to Cooper, on his right side.

At the moment, the game was set in an old, abandoned house with dark rooms and hallways.

"Oh, corridors!" warned Cooper. "That's never good."

Her eyes did not leave the screen. "Why's that?" she asked.

"It's always in the movies." he explained. "You go into a dark corner, and they load you with jump scares."

"Are you afraid of the dark?" she teased.

"Pbbt! No!" he said. "I'm afraid of the things *in* the dark."

"Well, good." she said. "Because I'm going outside."

"Alright, well then...I'll follow you...ladies first."

They escaped the empty house in the game and proceeded outside, where it too was dark and unnerving.

"I'm gonna go in the woods." Evelyn said.

"What?" Cooper said, almost laughing. "That's the worst place to go when there are zombies after you."

"Well, I'm bored. I wanna shoot something."

"No–no–no." Cooper protested. "Go in that ramshackle over there," Cooper pointed at the screen. "You can find some weapons there."

Evelyn squinted her eyes, searching. "I don't see anything in here."

"Well, in this game, you can use anything as a weapon." he explained. "Pick up that pan."

"I don't wanna use the pan. Why can't I use my gun?" she inquired.

"Fine, I'll use it." he said. "If you use the pan, you get to bash their head in–"

Just as Cooper was explaining, a decayed, gray-skinned zombie had snuck up right behind his character. It burst in the ramshackle with a loud hiss.

Cooper leapt in his seat and let out a loud scream. "Aaaaaaaaaaah!!!" he twitched his thumbs on his controller trying to run away. His words ran together. "Pickupthepanpickupthepanpickupthepanpickupthepan!"

Evelyn tilted her head up and laughed at Cooper's discomfort. "Ha ha ha ha ha ha ha!"

Cooper picked up the pan and whacked the undead monster in the head. "That's right! How do you like that?!" he threatened. "I'll smack the ugly out of you with my pan! Your name is Peter Pan now! You like it? You like your new name?"

Evelyn kept laughing to the point where she thought she couldn't breathe.

Apparently, his choice of weaponry was wasn't so wise. It wasn't long before he was cornered by zombies, and his character died instantly. Cooper threw his hands in the air. "Oh, fuck my ass!" he yelled.

Evelyn caught her breath and turned to Cooper. "Calm down!" she said, still smiling. "I'm taking a break." she got up and went into the kitchen.

"Okay." he said. "I'm gonna play something else." he fiddled with the controls and switched over to a different game.

"Good." Evelyn said from afar. "Maybe then, you'll calm down."

He put his headphones back on his head and began playing. Cooper sat back and slumped into the cushions, putting one foot over the coffee table.

This time, he had switched over to a very dark, gritty, 1st person survival game. His character had no weapons to protect himself. He was trapped in an underground torture chamber, and his only objective was to escape, or face the consequences.

Cooper had owned this game for a few years, so the graphics weren't as advanced as the game he and Evelyn had just played. His character walked through a long, stretched-out tunnel made out of brick with lanterns mounted on the wall.

He knew this game inside and out. He knew that after he passed this tunnel, he would enter a dungeon, where he would be chased by underground monsters. But something had changed. Cooper heard eerie music playing as he ventured further. "I don't remember this part having music." he muttered. He progressed anyway.

Suddenly, he heard a sharp, musical *sting!* coming from his game. It was especially loud hearing it from his headphones. "Ow!" Cooper said as he lifted the right side of his headphones to stop the ringing in his hears. He looked to his left to see Evelyn standing by the counter drinking a soda from the fridge. She didn't seem to notice him at all.

Cooper turned back to the screen, his headphones slightly askew now. His character left the tunnel, but wasn't in the area Cooper knew he was supposed to be in. As soon as he entered this place, the entire look of the game had changed. It didn't look like a video game at all. It looked so real. Cooper tilted the camera up and saw pipes and boilers everywhere. He pointed it down and saw he was walking on a grated, metal, walkway. He brushed his dark blonde hair back so he could see clearly. Instead of music, Cooper now heard faint cries and whispers. It sounded like...*children?* And then, screams of pain and agony. Poor Cooper's face contorted in shock. His eyes were wide, his body stiffened, and he brought his controller up close to his face. He kept progressing, just to see what would happen next.

He was in Freddy's world now. At least...he was close...oh, so very close. Freddy had waited for nightfall to arrive. By then, he was able to use the Necronomicon to its full potential. Now, he could sense Cooper slipping away from reality. And as an added bonus, he didn't have to worry about any unnecessary distractions or setbacks from that airhead Ash Williams, since Freddy could just send more Deadites out for him while he conducted his special work. Now that he had the Book of the Dead, after Freddy took the souls of one of his victims, their dead bodies wouldn't go to waste. *Just another service the book provides for me.* Freddy thought.

Cooper couldn't see, more accurately, he refused to. His eyes stared straight at the screen, meaning he was oblivious to what was lurking under the sofa. Out from under the sofa, Freddy's gloved hand emerged, his blades crawling slowly like a spider's legs. He reached closer and closer to Cooper's bare foot. Freddy was just about to grab him by the ankle and pull him under when–

Cooper put both of his feet on the cushions. He clutched his knees like a child would when watching a scary movie. "I don't wanna play anymore!" he whined.

Freddy retreated his hand. He decided to wait just a little longer. When the time was right. *Soon enough...little piggy.*

Just after Cooper had cried in fear, blood splattered on the television screen. He couldn't tell if it was coming from inside the game, or if it was really happening. Cooper shouted. "Aaah!" He turned his head away from the screen. "Evelyn!" he called.

Evelyn set her drink down on the table and walked to Cooper. "What is it?!" she worriedly asked.

His voice was shaky and he could barely manage to even get the words out. "Th-th-there's...s-something...wr-wrong...something's very wrong." he said. He pointed to the bloody screen. His breathing was uneven. "Look!"

Evelyn calmly looked at the screen, which was still covered in blood, and the sounds of tortured screaming had become so loud that it was audible through Cooper's headphones. She returned her gaze back at her boyfriend, her calm demeanor remained unchanged. She smiled and shrugged. Her look was empty, but her voice was happy. "What are you talking about?"

He felt hopeless. Cooper just shook his head and cried "No! No!" He was about to leap up and run away when, quick as a jungle cat, Freddy's hand shot out from between the sofa cushions. Cooper screamed as loud as he could. "Aaaaaaaaaaah!!!" He grabbed Cooper and pulled him in, sinking him down into the dark recesses of what laid beneath.

Chapter 18

He awoke on a wooden table. Thick, sludgy, water seeped into his clothes and hair. His head ached and every bone in his body was still buzzing. Cooper realized he still had his controller in his right hand. He figured he must've been so scared that he clutched it tighter than he thought. *Well,* Cooper thought. *at least I have a weapon...I guess.*

Cooper tried to pick himself up, but it wasn't without a struggle. He felt like his arms and legs were broken from the impact. He didn't even remember falling or landing here. He just remembered being pulled in and being consumed in darkness. He groaned in pain as he stood up.

He looked up and saw that he was inside an old, beaten-down, ramshackle. It was the exact same location as the game he and Evelyn were playing. There was termite-infested wood paneling. Moss-covered pantries on the sides, filled with rusted pots and pans. Below was mucky water, about two feet deep. His led slipped from the mossy table, sending his whole body falling in the water. He could taste the bitterness of the slimy, green water as it entered his mouth. He stood back up, his clothes now heavy from being soaked underwater. He gasped and choked trying to spit out the dirty water.

As he looked around, he couldn't believe what was surrounding him. Everything looked and felt real. He was actually roaming around inside his video game.

Cooper stepped away from table and decided to explore. *If I keep moving,* he thought. *maybe he won't find me.* He sloshed through the water, trying not to make too much noise. To his left, he was bombarded with tall cabinets with moldy panels and chipped wood. To his right, was the door that led outside. The further he went, the more he could see the night sky. It was hazy, and more he looked, he realized that the sky was a dark red. He was now out of the ramshackle, and no longer stepping into a small pool of dirty water. The path that he was on led uphill. He was afraid as to what waited for him there, so he turned a corner, circling the shack.

It was getting darker. It was as if he was walking into a dark cave. In a matter of seconds, it was pitch-black, and Cooper had to graze the side of the shack to guide him through. He whispered to himself. "I can't see shit!" He noticed a corner up ahead and turned sharply to his left.

As soon as he took his first step, he tripped. He gasped as he fell over a metal barrel that had fallen over in the middle of his path. The trip sent him landing flat on his face. He now had a mouthful of dirt. "Fucking barrels!" he whispered. He looked to his left and saw a row of barrels next to him. He rolled over and, out of anger, Cooper kicked one them, thinking it wouldn't make much of a noise. Unfortunately for him, the barrel knocked over, creating a domino effect and crashed loudly against the others. The noise was so loud, it echoed throughout.

Cooper froze and felt his heart race. *He's gonna find me now!* "Goddammit!" he hissed. He struggled to get back up, using his hands to navigate in the dark. Out of the emptiness, he heard a god-awful scraping noise against something metal.

Scrreeeechhhh!

Cooper flinched. He knew it had to be Freddy. He quickly got up while trying to get the ringing in his ear to stop. *How the fuck did this happen? I didn't fall asleep! Did I?! Please, God, I don't want to die...*

Scrreeeechhhh!

The sound came distantly from behind him. This time, Cooper turned around. He wanted to know how far Freddy was from him so he could try to lose him. He could hear the sound of Freddy's work boots, heavily and slowly, thudding against the soft ground. He felt his breathing getting faster and his sweat dripping down his forehead. He felt like his heart had shot up to the top of his throat.

Scrreeeechhhh!

Now that he was facing in front of him, he could see bright, white sparks flying as Freddy scraped his claws against a stack of pipes along the side of the shack. As he did so, it allowed Cooper to catch a glimmer of Freddy's hideous face from the light.

His face had become even more repulsive than just from the burns. It's as if the Book of the Dead was affecting him the longer he had it. Barely visible under his wool hat, his ears grown long and tapered at the ends with sharp point, almost like horns. His burned skin appeared even more red and scarred.

He also noticed...that Freddy was only about eight feet away from him. The only thing Cooper could think of was...

"Oh, fuck this!" he turned away from Freddy and bolted, not caring where he went, just as long as it was away from Krueger. He could hear Freddy's deep, cackling laugh fading from his ears as he ran away. "Ha ha ha ha ha..."

His intent was to run as far away as he could, out of the darkness and into the light, however little light there was. Even though it was against his own rules, he headed towards the woods. As he ran, he felt a metal gate slam against his body. "Come on!" He was trapped inside the confines of the video game world. He panted heavily as he turned, and ran back inside the shack.

Finally, he could see how many places there were to hide. There were small, dark corners and large cabinets to hide in. Slowly and cautiously, Cooper walked further. His eyes searched everywhere, hoping he wouldn't spot Freddy. But there were shadows at every corner, he knew that know matter careful he was, Freddy could still be lurking somewhere. He could have been right next to him the entire time.

By now, Cooper felt lost. He had turned every corner that he came across, not knowing where it would take him. It wasn't long before he spotted the large break in the wall he had just entered before. He had been going in circles. "Please, wake up..." he muttered. He was about to turn another corner.

Directly behind him, there was a slight movement in the water. A body had risen from below. It didn't just come to the surface, it continued to slowly incline upward until it stood up straight.

He heard the sound of dripping water. It sounded like it came from right behind him. His heart dropped as he turned around. Drenched in mucky water, was Freddy. He smiled creepily as he looked down at him. Cooper gasped. His eyes widened like a deer caught in the headlights. He took a huge step backward and turned in the opposite direction and ran away.

As soon as he ran back outside, Cooper ran into something. He couldn't see what it was at first, he just knew that it wasn't the wall...and it felt wooly and itchy. He looked up and saw Freddy staring at him. *How did he even do that?* Before Cooper could scream, Freddy reached out and grabbed Cooper's throat.

Freddy laughed as Cooper gasped for air. "Haaa ha ha ha ha ha ha ha ha ha!"

He grabbed Freddy's arm and managed to break away and run like he had planned. "That's not funny!" he shouted. He looked behind him and saw Freddy chasing after him. Cooper didn't know what to do. He needed to slow him down somehow. Out of panic, the only thing he could think of was to throw his controller at him. His voice cracked. "Fuck you!"

Evelyn stood by the kitchen counter, facing away from the living room. She tilted her head up, knocking back the last sip of the soda she had been drinking. She wiped her lips with her thumb and threw the bottle in the trash.

"Mhmmm...mhmmm..."

She heard a faint moaning coming from the living room. Evelyn turned around and saw Cooper with his eyes closed, twitching his fingers, and softly mumbling. She shouted as she ran over to him. "No!" She jumped onto the sofa and hovered over Cooper. She tried everything she could to wake him up. "Cooper?" she said as she repetitively smacked the side of his face. Then, she shook him. "Cooper?!" she shouted louder. "Wake up! Come on, wake up!" But, it was no use. Evelyn could feel her eyes start to water. She couldn't just sit there and do nothing. She was determined to do everything she could until Cooper woke up.

At that moment, she remembered what Ash had told her earlier that day. Frantically, she grabbed her phone from the table and reached for Ash's phone number from her front pocket. She dialed the number and whispered to herself. "Answer the phone, Ash. Come on." While she waited for him to answer, Evelyn held Cooper's hand. "Cooper, wake up! Please!"

Cooper had now escaped Freddy, and entered another dark room in the shack. It was small, eerie...and also a dead end. There was nowhere else to run. He couldn't turn back, because Freddy could be right behind him. Cooper was frantic, and at his wit's end.

Cooper, wake up! Please! his girlfriend's voice echoed throughout the room.

"Evelyn?" he called aloud. For a brief second, the corners of his mouth twitched up into a smile. Her voice had given him a small sense of hope. Hope that maybe he can escape Freddy and survive. Cooper found a large cabinet in front of the wall, and hid inside it. He darted his eyes in every direction.

From the same entrance he had just come from, Cooper could hear a tapping noise against the rotting wood.

Tap...Tap...Tap...Tap...

Tap...Tap...Tap...Tap...

And then, that awful screeching again, against the glass window.

Scrreeeechhhh!

Just then, Freddy emerged from the black shadows. The sound of his laugh made Cooper freeze. "Ha ha ha ha ha..." It sent a chill down his spine. Freddy had gotten closer to him. He could tell. He could hear Freddy's knives tap against the cabinet door.

Tap...Tap...Tap...Tap...

There was a moment of silence.

Freddy then ripped the doors off the hinges and grabbed Cooper by the ankle. He pulled him out and dragged him through the thick water.

Cooper choked as the water filled his lungs. His head shook in and out of the water, giving him only a fraction of a second to breathe again. The mucky water blinded him. He relied only on his hearing. What he heard was the sound of sloshing water and Freddy wriggling his knives.

Cooper forced himself to be strong. He flailed his legs and kicked Freddy in the arm, forcing him to let go. He stood back up and put on a brave face, trying to convince Freddy that he wasn't afraid of him anymore. He gestured to him, telling to come forward. "Come at me, bro!" he taunted.

Freddy smirked, partially showing his fanged teeth, and raised his bladed glove above his head, and launched his four razor fingers at Cooper's face.

Cooper's eyes widened and his nostrils flared in fear. In just the nick of time, Cooper jolted his body to his right, barely missing Freddy's knives. Instead, they landed on the wall, knocking against wall with a loud *snap!* noise. Cooper's voice cracked again. "No!" he shouted. "Don't come at me!"

Freddy, now angered at Cooper's escape, looked at the direction he moved to see him running away, and grabbing one of the rusted metal pipes on the wall.

The cold pipe creaked as Cooper broke it off at its curving point. He put his weight into it to break the pipe, so when it finally gave, the force caused him to fall on the floor, splashing in the water.

He quickly got back on his feet and held the three-foot long pipe like a sword. With wild-eyes, he stared at Freddy, who, by that time, had already reached slicing distance to Cooper. He swung the pipe at his knees, hoping to knock Freddy down, but he merely jumped over it, with agility and virility. Cooper backed off a few steps further, stretching the distance between him and Freddy. "Yeah, that's right." he said with false confidence. "I'll fuck you up Freddy! You ugly motherfucker!" he swung the pipe like a baseball bat to intimidate him.

"Oh, how scary!" Freddy said sarcastically. He got in his face and pointed his knives at him, causing Cooper to whimper like a child.

Cooper attempted to sound threatening, but his face wasn't showing it. "I'm serious, man!" he warned. "I'll knock your head right off!"

Freddy chuckled. It sounded like a low, animalistic growl. "Like I haven't had *that* done to me before!"

Cooper swung the pipe as hard as he possibly could, aiming it straight as Freddy's head. It made impact. He actually hit Freddy, knocking his head clean off of his shoulders. It flew and landed in the far left corner of the shack, splashing in the water. His seemingly lifeless head floated to the top. Cooper watched and waited for something to happen. He grinned wide and laughed crazily, but looked over and saw that the rest of Freddy's body was still standing, breathing, and moving.

Freddy's headless body jerked his leg up, and kicked Cooper hard in the chest, knocking him to the ground. It knocked the wind out of him. Cooper coughed and gasped for air, as he watched Freddy stride to the corner where his head rested, and pick it up.

He put his head back on his shoulders, setting it in place with a simple *crack!* of his neck. Next was his dirty brown hat, which he bent over to pick up, and return it to its rightful spot on the top of his head. "You think you have what it takes to kill me?" he said as he strode, confidently and arrogantly, back to Cooper, who managed to stand up straight again. "I am immortal. And you are a weak, little, fuck."

He gripped the pipe tightly in his right hand, and held it up again. "We'll see about that." Cooper swung the pipe again, this time aiming for his ribcage, on his left side.

Just before the pipe could make contact with him, Freddy blocked the pipe away with both hands. He gripped it and pulled Cooper in. Freddy held up the pipe and hit Cooper sharply in the stomach.

Cooper let go of it. The pain was so severe that he bent over, wrapping his arms around his stomach, and let out a small scream. "Aaah!"

But, it wasn't enough for Freddy, he wanted Cooper to suffer more. He kicked him again, knocking him into the water. He saw the boy twitching and stumbling to try to pick himself back up, so Freddy swatted the pipe on his back.

THWACK!

Cooper's screams gurgled from below the water. "AAAH!"

He hit him again, this time on his shoulder. *THWACK!*

His screams were mixed with crying. "AAAH!"

Freddy reveled in his pain. "Haaa ha ha ha ha ha ha ha ha ha!"

By then, Evelyn had already called Ash. She told him that Cooper had fallen asleep. She told him he needed to "get here now!" and was waiting for him to show up. Still hovering over Cooper, Evelyn knew there was nothing else she could do, but she refused to stand idly by while her boyfriend was in danger for his life.

She stared at his face with her tear-stained eyes, and saw him convulsing, and moaning loudly. He was in pain, and Freddy was the cause of it. He was killing him.

Just then, she saw blood dripping from the corners of his mouth, and felt his body shaking violently.

"No...No!" said Evelyn. "Cooper! COOPER! COOPER, COME BACK TO ME!" she kept trying.

Freddy watched as Cooper tried to drag himself away, whimpering in pain. This was what Freddy loved: the chase, the torture, playing with his prey, and watching them beg for mercy. He smiled, evilly.

Cooper laid on the ground and looked at Freddy. "Please." he said weakly. "Please, just no more."

"What's the matter?" he asked him. Freddy stepped closer and grabbed Cooper by the collar of his wet shirt. He lifted Cooper up until he was on his knees. "Sniveling, little, pussy." he growled.

COOPER, COME BACK TO ME!

Freddy heard Evelyn's voice coming through to his world, echoing in the boiler room. He decided to use it against the boy. He nodded his head. "Oh..." he said, slyly. He slowly walked a circle around Cooper. "Sweet, little Evelyn..." he said contemptuously. He knelt down next to Cooper close enough to whisper in his ear. His voice was low and demonic. "Did you see the love letter I wrote to her?" he said, referring to the cut on her leg. Freddy licked his lips, revealing long, slimy pointed tongue, like that of a snake's. Freddy whispered in his ear. "...I fucked her!"

Tears streamed down Cooper's face. He knew it wasn't true, that he was just trying to mess with his mind. He knew Freddy was a sick bastard. "NO!" he shouted, refusing to fall for it. Nonetheless, the torture Freddy put Evelyn, and himself, through made him cry. "Goddamn you!" he yelled.

Swiftly, Freddy got in his face. "OH?!" he shouted, challenging Cooper's threat to him.

Her heart raced, and her hope that Cooper could be saved was eventually fleeting with every bruise that appeared on his body out of thin air. Her eyes never left his face. In just a matter of minutes, the look on his face went from slight distress, to crippling fear and agony. His eyebrows would move up and down. His eyes would move rapidly under his lids. His lips would twitch, as if he was trying to communicate to Evelyn from inside the dream realm.

She inched closer to him, brushing his hair back, and cupping his face. "Can you hear me?" she asked him. "Come on, say something!" She waited until it seemed like Cooper was actually responding.

He squeezed her hand tightly. His voice was strained. When he spoke, he sounded like he had the life beaten out of him. He almost couldn't breathe. "Evelyn..." he didn't sound awake. From his tone of voice, it sounded like he was saying goodbye to her. "I love you."

Freddy tilted his head to the side. "You know what, lover boy?" he sneered, cocking his elbow back and raising his infamous glove. "You talk too much!" Before Cooper could react, Freddy launched his knives into Cooper's skull and out of the back of his head.

The long knives on Freddy's index finger and pinky shot through both of Cooper's eyes, dissecting his brain, and cracking through the back of his skull. Like a waterfall, blood poured through Cooper's eye sockets, racing down his neck, and soaking his clothes.

The blades on his middle finger and ring finger stabbed through the inside of Cooper's mouth. He slid them down further until they poked through the back of his neck. Freddy could faintly hear Cooper gagging and choking on Freddy's knives, including his own blood. He shook his body until for a moment, until he was completely still. Finally, he was dead. *I thought that little brat would never shut up.*

Evelyn remained close to Cooper's face. She kept waiting for him to say something else, to give him a sign that he was still alive. For a split second, she saw his eyes and mouth open. *He's awake!* she hoped. *He came back!*

But her hope was washed away when, instantly, her face was sprayed with her boyfriend's blood. It was like she was hit with a water balloon. Evelyn screamed bloody murder. "Aaaaaaaaaaah!!!" She jumped back as far away from him as he could. She tripped over the table in front of the couch and fell on the floor.

Freddy wasn't done with him. Not just yet. "It's time for the grand finale!" he cackled. His glove still stuck inside the front Cooper's lifeless skull, Freddy turned him around until Cooper faced away from him. Like pulling the tab on a soda can, he used his muscle power to pull his arm up, splitting Cooper's head horizontally in half.

The skin on the corners of his mouth ripped open, his jaw ripped out of its hinges, his neck cracked, snapped, and broke off. The insides of Cooper's head were now open and visible. His tongue rested just over his bottom teeth. It was long, red, and slimy. Freddy was able to see down the hole in his, now exposed, neck, and the top of his mouth, which now faced upward.

Freddy grinned in satisfaction. With his newly-acquired strength, it felt as easy as snapping a thin tree branch. He yanked his glove out of Cooper's skull and raised it to view. It was drenched in blood, muscle tissue, and a few tiny pieces of bone.

It's been far too long since I've seen this. Freddy thought. With his left hand, he reached down into the hole in Cooper's neck, grabbed his spine, and ripped it out of his body. He held it up in the air like a trophy.

With nothing to support him anymore, Cooper's mutilated body fell down, his back floating above the water.

"Oh..." said Freddy as he looked down at his dead body in fake sympathy. "I always knew you were spineless!"

As Freddy cackled maniacally, his eyes had changed, but for only a second. They changed from the regular blue color they had always been, to a pale, pupil-less, white. Freddy was absorbing Cooper's soul.

After a while, Evelyn had wiped off the blood from her face with her, now dirty, purple shirt. She had brought Cooper's lifeless body down to the middle of the floor with her. Sitting with her legs crossed on the floor, she had laid his body on her lap. She held him, tighter than she ever had before, rocking back and forth on the floor.

She sobbed quietly, refusing to accept his death. Even though it was obvious, with his bloody body and punctured eye sockets, that Cooper was gone and never coming back, Evelyn didn't want to let him go. He was the first person that came into her life and made her feel truly safe. And now, Freddy took him away from her...forever.

Her voice was soft. "Give him back to me." she begged. She hiccupped from her cries. "Please don't leave me!" She continued to cry.

As Evelyn slowly rocked back and forth, keeping her eyes closed, refusing to look at Cooper's mutilated body, she was blind as to what was happening right in front of her.

Cooper's eyelids raised all the way up, showing his empty, black, sockets. He lifted his arm, and grabbed Evelyn's neck, wringing it tightly.

Chapter 19

Cooper gripped his once-beloved Evelyn's neck tighter and tighter. The sound of her gasping for breath gave him a great, sinister, pleasure. Cooper's soul had been taken from his body, and had now been absorbed by the Springwood Slasher himself, Freddy Krueger. His pure, innocent soul served as fuel to make Freddy stronger. Not only was he back from the dead and ready kill again, but now, his dark powers were growing. Kill by kill, soul by soul, Freddy was that much closer to being able to cross from the dream realm, to the realm of the living. And with each empty vessel he left behind after the bloody fun was over, the Deadites took their place to spread even more fear. The Deadites, the dark spirits that inhabited the Necronomicon, now followed under his command. His rule. Freddy Krueger was now their king.

Evelyn felt Cooper's hand ringing around her neck. His once smooth hands had now become coarse and jagged. His fingernails, now long, sharp, and rotted black, pricked against her skin. When she felt like she was about to blackout, Evelyn felt herself being thrown onto the floor. The possessed Cooper laid on top of her, pushing her, keeping her down to the ground.

His face was only a few inches away from hers. She could see just how much his face had changed in the short time from when she mourned his dead body, to when he opened his eyes to strangle her. His skin had gone from a healthy tan to a gray color that was almost inhuman. His eyes were gone, there were only deep, black holes in the sockets, with wide lacerations tracing from the hole in his socket to his forehead. His jaw had been dislocated, and it constantly hung open. At the same time, it seemed as if his jaw line had been grossly elongated, like that of a crocodile. His teeth had rotted to a dark yellow, and his gums were black. He swung his long, thin tongue out to swipe the corner of his mouth. Cooper roared with the chorus of multiple deep, and demonic, voices.

Her eyes widened in fear. She felt her whole body shake as Cooper lowered down and growled, "Join us..." She didn't want it to be real. In the back of her mind, the wanted the past two days to simply be part of a bad dream that she could wake up from, unharmed, without Freddy Krueger to worry about. But she knew it was real. She had to accept it. She had to accept that the man she loved was dead, and his body was now a puppet for those demonic spirits. She had to accept that everyone she knew and loved was in danger, and if she didn't do something soon, and if Ash didn't show up within the next two minutes, they too, would die.

Luckily, her hands were free. She shook her head and yelled. "No!" She pushed Cooper off of her, sending him rolling across the dirty, crumb-filled carpet. She picked herself up and sprinted towards the kitchen. She pulled open the top drawer and grabbed a silver steak knife with a black handle, and then quickly detoured to the hallway.

As she ran across to the narrow hallway, she saw Cooper lifting up off the ground where she pushed him. He wasn't that far from her. She knew she had to keep running. But still, she couldn't help but notice the quick, and terrifying, way Cooper stood up. It was instant, like she blinked her eyes once, and there he was. She looked down and saw that his feet never touched the ground. He was levitating.

Although he could not see her, he could sense her fear, and allowed that to guide him. Cooper jerked his elbows up, holding up his arms so that they were parallel to his shoulders, and pointing his jagged claws at her like an old, Hollywood monster. Still hovering over the ground, he swiftly charged at Evelyn.

She kept running as fast as she could, just barely escaping him as she went into his bedroom, slamming the door shut and locking it.

He stopped in his tracks and lowered back down to the ground. He hissed in discontent. In that moment, something in the air had changed. Cooper twitched his nose and jerked his head in every direction to find where it was coming from. It smelled like burnt flesh. He could sense Freddy standing beside him, speaking to Cooper from his realm. And he could feel his horrid breath against his ear. "*Make her one of us.*" sneered Freddy.

And just like that, Freddy was gone. Cooper yelled from the top of his lungs. "EVVVEEELLLYYYNNN!!!" He banged against the door repeatedly.

Evelyn stood against the door, feeling Cooper's fist hitting against it over and over again. She looked up and saw the door coming off of its hinges. She needed to find a way to block it. She looked to her left and saw a small television stand. Evelyn grabbed it and inched it in front of the bedroom door.

The noise stopped. It was quiet. It was so quiet, that Evelyn could hear the sound of her heartbeat echoing in her eardrums. She hesitated at first, but eventually put her ear to the door to find out if he was still there. She heard the floorboards creaking, each sound getting quieter as it happened. *He's actually walking away.* she thought. *But I'm still stuck here.* Even though Cooper had left her alone for now, she was still trapped.

She breathed a sigh of relief and pushed herself away, when Cooper's hands busted through the door, making a small hole in the center. Evelyn shrieked. "Aaah!" He grabbed her head, tilting it so that she faced the front of the door and saw Cooper on the other side. Long ribbons of saliva dropped down from his open mouth.

Still gripping the knife, Evelyn held it up and sliced Cooper's fingers until he finally let go. Evelyn backed away as far as she could, but Cooper had busted the door completely off of its hinges, and threw it aside. He leaped over the television stand and ran to Evelyn.

She acted quickly. She ducked down and ran past Cooper, and jumped over the stand. Evelyn ran back into the living room and prepared to open the front door when she heard–

"Evelyn, wait!" It sounded like Cooper's voice. His real, true self, was calling to her.

Evelyn spun around and saw Cooper, looking alive, and without a spot of blood on him. He stood at the end of the hall. He looked shaken. "Don't leave me." he said, meekly.

She still kept her hand on the doorknob, shaking her head in disbelief. She ordered him, her voice cracking as she spoke "Get away from me." She gripped the knife even tighter, causing the bones in her hand to cramp. "You're not Cooper."

"No!" he tried to convince her. "You don't understand. I found a way to come back. Freddy thought he had me, but I slipped away from him, somehow." A tear came down his face as he took slow steps closer to Evelyn. "I mean, it *did* die, but it was only for a minute. You believe me, right?." His voice was filled with desperation. "Please... please, Evelyn." he begged. "You have to believe me. I'm alright now." A tear streamed down his face. "I'm so sorry I hurt you, Evelyn. I love you. Just, please!"

Evelyn refused to fall for it. She kept shaking her head and muttered, "No...no...get away from me..." under her breath.

He walked closer to her. "Do you remember the first day we met?" he asked. "I woke up late for work, so I was in a big hurry. I passed by you in the parking lot and tripped on my shoelaces. My face smacked right on the ground. I remember, everyone else laughed at me, but you didn't. Do you remember that?"

Evelyn loosened her grip on the doorknob and gazed at him. She answered him. "Yes..." whispered. "Of course, I remember that."

He now stood a few feet away from her. "Evelyn, I love you. Please, don't leave me. I need you."

She slowly took her hand off the doorknob as Cooper walked towards her. He wrapped his arms around her. She slowly returned his hug, feeling safe in his arms again. She kissed him. She thought she would never have the chance to do that again. "I thought I lost you." she said.

"I'll never let that happen again, I promise." He held her tightly and whispered in her ear. He smiled. "You know what I'd really like right now?"

She answered his question with a question. "To get out of here?"

"No." He shook his head. "What I *really, really* want to do..." He squeezed her ribs tightly. "...right now..." he tilted her head up to face him. "...is to..."

Evelyn immediately felt that something was not right. Not only was Cooper holding her too tight, but she couldn't feel the ground beneath her. *NO!!!*

Cooper's face morphed back into is evil Deadite form, instantly. He bellowed with that demonic voice. "RIP OUT YOUR SOUL!!!"

Evelyn screamed, kicking and punching Cooper, hoping he would loosen his grip. But he was too strong. She felt betrayed and foolish. Above all else, she thought she was going to die.

Evelyn heard a loud crash. The front door burst wide open. She averted her gaze away from Cooper to see Ash standing below them. He kicked the door behind him, slamming it shut. He had changed from his blood-soaked white shirt to a dark blue one.

Ash looked surprisingly calm and clean-cut. At least, compared to Evelyn, he was calm. He looked straight at the monstrous Deadite known formally as Cooper. "Let her go!" he ordered.

He didn't hesitate to drop Evelyn to the ground. Why would he waste energy gathering that measly soul when the Chosen One was in right in front of him for the taking? Cooper lowered to the ground as well, and set his sights on Ash.

Evelyn got up and stood by Ash. "You okay?" he asked her, not breaking eye-contact with the demon.

She didn't answer. She noticed how Cooper prepared to charge at him. If anything happened to Ash, Evelyn wouldn't know what to do. She would be left to fight Freddy alone. As she stepped closer to him, she felt a gun hidden inside his leather jacket. Without a second thought, she stole Ash's 9mm pistol and pointed straight at Cooper.

She hesitated for a second before pulling the trigger. It's one thing to lose the love of your life. But, to be the one to actually kill him? She didn't want to do it.

"What are you waiting for!" Ash shouted. "Kill him!"

Cooper began to charge at them quickly, raising his long fingernails above his head. He screeched like a banshee in that petrifying voice.

Evelyn squeezed the trigger.

BLAM!

A large, gaping hole appeared in the center of Cooper's face. His blood and brains sprayed in the bullet's direction, splattering on the wall behind him, leaving a large, red splash on the wall, his television, and the stack of games next to it.

Mimicking the high-"C" that still rang in her ear from the blast, Evelyn screamed at the top of her lungs, which seamlessly turned into sobbing.

Cooper, the Deadite, was finally dead. He dropped to his knees, and then landed face-first on the floor, completely silent and still.

Tears ran down her face. She couldn't stop herself from crying. Her knees went rubbery. They shook and no longer supported her. She dropped to ground while Ash lowered with her.

He took the gun away from her shaking hand and put it back in his holster. He held her and patted her head to console her. "I know." he muttered. "I know." he related to her. "It'll be alright." He wasn't absolutely sure about that last remark. It had been so many years since Linda had succumbed to Deadites, but he still never fully got over her death.

For the both of them, it felt like they had been sitting there in the same spot for hours, even though only a couple of seconds had passed by. Reality struck them hard when they heard the sound of police sirens coming from outside the building.

They both poked their heads up at the same time, realizing what they were hearing. Evelyn thought about it for a moment and realized the neighbors must have heard her and Cooper screaming earlier. And the gun blast only added to the worry. She felt her entire body stiffen. The last thing she wanted was for the police to discover what happened and get locked up for the rest of her life.

Ash and Evelyn looked at each other and realized they had to get out of there as soon as possible. "C'mon," Ash grabbed her arms. "we gotta go!" He helped her up until she stood on her own two feet.

Evelyn detached her gaze from Ash and back to Cooper's corpse. *What about Cooper?* she pondered. *We can't just leave everything like this.* She looked back at Ash and pointed at Cooper's dead body. "No! Ash, wait!" she protested. "They're gonna know something's wrong if we just leave him like that."

There was no time left. There was too much of a mess in that apartment to try to cover anything up. The police were on their way and could burst through that door at any second.

He shook his head defiantly. Ash pushed Evelyn, leading her to the window in the living room. "There's no time." he told her. "We gotta leave *now*!" Ash pulled the curtains back and opened the window, while Evelyn briefly stared at the front door. She could already hear footsteps shuffling up to the entrance.

As soon as he lifted the window pane up, a gust of wind blew in his face, along with little droplets of rain. A storm had blown in just before Ash had arrived. He let Evelyn go first onto the metal stairwell that descending to the bottom floor of the building. He followed behind her. They raced down the flight of metal stairs as quickly as they could. As Ash descended, he could already hear the police banging on the front door.

BANG! BANG! BANG! BANG! BANG! BANG!

"Police! Open up!"

That guy sounds familiar. Ash thought as he walked down the last flight of stairs. *Was that...Officer What's-his-face?*

A loud crash of thunder and a bright flash of white light lit up the area as they descended, all the while being drenched in the rain.

The front door busted open, and three police officers swarmed in, pointing guns and looking all over the apartment. Lagging right behind them was Officer Harris and Lt. Moore.

Officer Harris walked slowly into the living room. He stopped as soon as he heard a *crunch* beneath his shoe. He looked down, and saw what he thought was the most revolting, mangled body he had ever come across in his career. It was Cooper. He had never seen anything like that. He nearly gagged from the sight of him. *This kid was shot. His eyes are cut out. His jaw's been ripped, and his skin's all...*he didn't want to look at him anymore. "Jesus!" he exclaimed.

Lt. Moore appeared right behind him, catching a glimpse of the rotting Deadite. Unlike his partner, who looked absolutely disgusted and wanted to throw up, a mere look of confusion came upon Harold's face. "We just missed him." he said to Officer Harris. "Damn it!"

He responded. "So far, that makes nineteen of these kinds of murders."

One of the policemen came up to Officer Harris. "The place is all clear, sir." he looked down at the body, and his face contorted in disgust. "Holy shit!"

Harold looked at the officer. "You and the rest of the squad go out and see if our killer's still out there."

He nodded as he and the remaining officers left the room.

Nathan lead him away, while Lt. Moore walked to the other side of the living room once he noticed the open window. The cold wind blew through the room, making the thick curtains flutter uncontrollably. He stuck his head out the window. Through the darkness and the rainfall, he saw Ash and Evelyn climbing down the ladder. *Well, I'll be damned.* he thought. *If it isn't Ash Williams.*

From the moment he first saw Ash, he had a gut feeling he was involved in this mess. And now, seeing him and Evelyn fleeing from what obviously was a murder scene, only sealed the deal for him. It's enough that he and the entire Springwood PD tries to keep the whole Freddy Krueger ordeal under wraps, he doesn't need anyone else coming in and tearing it all apart. *The last thing we need is someone else to create fear in this town.*

If only he knew the truth...

Lt. Moore brushed his wet, blonde hair away from his face, and turned to Officer Harris. "Harris, get over here."

Officer Harris immediately followed his command, and walked towards the window where he was standing. "Yes, sir?" he asked respectfully.

He pointed outside. "I think we just found our murderer."

Officer Harris poked his head outside and saw Ash and Evelyn. "Ash?" he said with confusion. "What's *he* doing here?" Harris knew Ash was a little strange, but didn't initially peg him as a murderer. A weirdo? Yes. But, not a killer. If anything, considering where Ash lived, he thought the only reason he was acting odd because he knew about Freddy. "And isn't that one of the kids we interviewed earlier? Evelyn Marshall?" Officer Harris looked back at Lt. Moore, expecting him to give an order.

"That's it." said Lt. Moore. "I want that son of a bitch arrested. As for her," he referred to Evelyn, who was about to make a run for it. "Take her, and anyone she's come in contact with in the last forty-eight hours up to Westin Hills. That's an order."

"I'm on it." he replied.

Both of them ran down the alley, making tiny splashes in the puddles with each step they took. Ash's Oldsmobile was just across the street. As long as they could make it across without any trouble, they would be in the clear.

Ash was lagging far behind Evelyn, he found it hard to run as fast as she was. His breathing had become strained, and his heart was beating out of his chest. *Are you kidding me?!* he thought. *Why can't this ever happen when I'm not being chased?!*

The tone in her voice was hurried. "Ash, come on!" yelled Evelyn. "They're going to catch us!"

Ash could hear the sound of multiple footsteps gaining on him. He looked behind him and saw three police officers running after both of them.

"Freeze!" one of them yelled.

He tried to pick up the pace, but he couldn't move fast enough. He knew Evelyn would be able to escape them, but Ash already knew he was done for. He dug out his car keys from his front pocket and gripped them in his left hand. He called out to her. "Evelyn!"

She her turned her head back and slowed down.

"Think fast!" Ash threw his car keys at her.

Evelyn watched where they flew in the air and caught the keys with both hands.

"Go!" he told her.

Another burst of thunder and lightning filled the sky.

Anguish struck across her face. She didn't want to leave him. She wouldn't know what to do next. But she knew it was the right thing... the only thing...to do. She spun back around and sprinted to Ash's car, narrowly escaping the police. Evelyn opened the door, got in, turned the ignition, and peeled out in matter of seconds. She looked out in the rearview mirror and saw Ash being cuffed by Officer Harris.

He cuffed Ash's wrists tightly...a little too tightly. Officer Harris adjusted his thin-rimmed glasses and led Ash to the squad car, reading him his Miranda Rights as he did so.

"Ash Williams, you are under arrest for murder. Anything you say can and will be used against you in a court of law. If you do not have an attorney, one will be provided for you. Do you understand these rights as I've read them to you?"

As he was being lead to the squad car, Ash just stared off into the distance, feeling the rain run down from the top of his head, to his nose, and his jaw line. His anxiety level rose the closer he got to the car. He knew that the longer he would sit in that cell, the less there was for him to do about Freddy. Time was running out, and there was nothing he could do.

There was no smooth-talking his way out of this one.

Chapter 20

WHEN SHE LOOKED IN THE rearview mirror, flashes of red and blue lights came into view. The police were chasing her as well. Evelyn pressed her foot heavily on the gas, speeding down the glistening streets. Raindrops pattered against the windshield. The wipers smoothed across it every few seconds. After making a few sharp turns at the end of each block, Evelyn was relieved to find that they had lost track of her.

The first place she was headed to was Jill and Steven's house. At the same time, she knew the police would probably suspect that she would go there, so there was no time to linger.

Evelyn took one hand off of the steering wheel and reached in her back pocket for her cell phone. She slid down in her seat for a moment so she could reach it. The gap between the seat and the pedals were already so far apart, that when Evelyn ducked down, she lost sight of the road ahead of her, causing her to almost hit the curb. "Jeez!" she muttered. As soon as she took the phone from her pocket, she sat straight up and adjusted herself.

It was ironic when she thought about it. "Let's see," she said to herself. "I've been chased and stabbed by Freddy Krueger, attacked by my demon-possessed boyfriend, but what *nearly* killed me was crashing in Ash's car." She reached down and adjusted the seat closer to the steering wheel. "How does he even drive like this?"

She dialed Jill's number, keeping her eyes on the road. She put her phone to her ear and waited, becoming more and more frustrated with each ring. "Come on, Jill." she groaned. "Pick up." She anxiously awaited to hear the sound of Jill's voice, but all that came was–

ring......ring......ring......

Evelyn disconnected and slammed the phone down on her seat. "Damn it!"

The alarm on Jill's nightstand read 9:43 PM. Right beside it was her cell phone, which buzzed loudly. The name on the Caller ID screen read: "Evelyn". She had been trying to call Jill, but to no avail. No matter how loud the volume was on her phone, it couldn't compete with the stereo playing at full blast in Steven's room, just across the hall.

Jill had been standing outside in the hallway for the past few minutes, leaning against the neatly painted red wall, her arms crossed over each other. Since she had returned home, Jill had changed out of her tattered shirt and jeans, and threw on a baggy gray t-shirt and black leggings, and tied her hair with a rubber band. She didn't want anything from the night before to remain on her person. Touching her skin. Constantly reminding her of the horrors she had become witness to.

She waited for her mother to emerge from her bedroom at the end of the hall. It would be the first time she saw her mother since that morning when Ash dropped her off. For most of the day, her parents had been absent from their home. Jill was used to them being gone long hours of the day. But she figured that, since her house was a crime scene the night before, they would at least be home to comfort them.

At first, when she overheard Evelyn talking about kids being admitted to Westin Hills for having nightmares, she couldn't believe it. But after listening to Ash and seeing what Freddy could do, it all made sense. *It's how they kept Freddy away all these years.* By taking away all of the kids Freddy chased after, and keeping them isolated, the fear couldn't spread, and he would have nowhere to go. She could imagine her own parents in the middle of all of it. She wondered if they knew at all about this, or if they were involved in any way. *I can't believe this is happening to us.*

She felt her eyelids become heavy and start to droop. Suddenly, all she saw was a screen of black. All she was doing was resting her eyes. She could feel herself sinking down to the floor. She knew she shouldn't do it. She felt herself slipping away, but she didn't care, she was so tired.

It sounded like a faint echo in her mind.

Jill...

She heard someone calling her name. Jill winced, twitching her eyes and nose. She didn't know who's voice was, but whoever it was, it sounded dark.

Then, she felt a hand grabbing her forearm. And she also felt something else touching her skin. Something cold and sharp. Like a knife.

JILL! Freddy yelled.

Jill gasped, twitching her arms and opened her eyes wide. She saw the hand that grabbed her arm. It was a woman's, with perfectly manicured nails and a diamond ring around one finger. When she looked up, Sharon Gordon, her mother, was in front of her face. Beneath her false eyelashes and painted, red lips, she looked distraught, waiting for her daughter to say something.

Her tone was surprised. "Mom." she said, relieved that it was her who brought her back to consciousness.

Sharon had dark brown hair, just like her son's, brown eyes, and the same heart-shaped face identical to Jill's. "Honey," she said, sounding both angry and worried at the same time. "how many times do I have to remind you not to fall asleep without taking your medication?"

Jill steadied herself. "It fine, Mom." she said. "I was just resting my eyes."

"It is not 'fine'!" she immediately heard herself and lowered her voice. "You know you and your brother have a condition. And if don't take your pills, then–"

Jill took her mother's hand and brushed it away from her arm. "You know, Mom," she said, still tired. "You and Dad have made me take them for years, but you've never told me what they're called. I've never even seen the bottle they came from."

Sharon brushed her hand across her long-sleeve, dark blue dress, sweeping away any wrinkles. She took the purse that she had slung across her shoulder and held it in front of her. "You and Steven have a..." she searched for the right word as she dug around in her purse. "... very common disorder. If you don't take these before bed…well…" she took out a prescription bottle and held it in front of Jill. "If you don't take these, you're vulnerable to certain things when you're asleep." Sharon was about to open the cap, when Jill took it from her.

She held it in her hand. It was a prescription pill bottle. She turned it to look at the label. It read: Hypnocil. "Mom, what exactly do we do that requires us to take a pill every time we sleep. You've never been specific about that. Not even the doctor. Is there something you and Dad aren't telling us?"

Her mother slung the purse around her shoulder snatched the bottle away. The opened the cap. "You know what, I don't have time for this." She held the little white pill in-between her fingers and offered it to her. "It's late, just take it."

At first, Jill was hesitant to grab the Hypnocil from her mother. She knew that all they were trying to do for her and Steven was protect them. But, the fact that they had to lie to both of them to do it made her feel betrayed.

"Take it!" her mother yelled.

Her eyes still on her mother, Jill took the Hypnocil from her hand, placed it on her tongue, and swallowed it. It was routine for her. The same drug since she was at least eight years old, and always right before she went to sleep. And for all those years since, never once did she have dreams.

Sharon breathed a sigh of relief and put the bottle back in her purse. "Your father and I are going out–"

"Again?" Jill asked, her tone was judgmental. It would be the third time that week that her and Steven would be alone in the house. She thought she would be used to it by now, her parents were rarely home, day or night.

"Yes, again." she answered. "So, check the locks on all the doors," she gazed at Steven's room at the end of the hall, noticing the door rattling from the volume of his stereo. "God knows your brother won't do it." She placed her hand under her daughter's chin, tilting her head up and criticizing the dark circles that had accumulated under her eyes. "And get some rest, you look a little unkempt. You should be fine now that you've taken your medicine."

"I will." she told her. But in her head, she was thinking, *Screw that. I'll stay up for a week, if I have to.* Jill reached out to her mother to give her a hug goodbye, but she had already turned away and started to walk off.

The sound of her heels landing on the hard wood floor faded as her mother descended down the stairs. She stared down at the floor, completely unaware that her daughter needed comfort from her mother.

Jill let her arms fall down to her sides. She took a few steps forward and placed one hand on the doorknob that led to the bathroom. She hadn't showered all day, and hoped that maybe standing under the hot water for a few minutes would calm her down.

She placed her hand on the door before she pushed it open, and muttered under her breath. "You're never around, anyway." her tone was empty. "I'm pretty much living alone here."

When she stopped speaking, she noticed her brother had turned up the volume on whatever thrash album he was listening to. *Damn it, I hate it when he plays that stupid...Alice Cooper? White Zombie? Slipknot? Whatever the hell it is.* She turned the knob and yelled at Steven from across the hall. "Steven!" she shouted. "That's really annoying!"

She could hear his voice muffled from behind the closed door. "Is Mom gone?" he asked.

She expected him to know that already. "Yeah!" she said.

"Then shut the hell up!"

She lifted her middle finger, holding it up in front of his door even though he couldn't see her. "You can't see me, but I'm flipping you off right now!"

He replied. "You can't see me, but not a single fuck was given!"

"Love you!" yelled Jill.

"Love you!" he replied.

Jill opened the door and, as she entered, muttered, "Well, I'm not completely alone..." She shut the door until the lock clicked in place. She pulled the scrunchie from her hair and threw it on the mess of perfume and lotion bottles that was on the sink to her right. She tousled her blonde hair and leaned over to turn on the hot water in the shower.

She grabbed a washcloth from the sink, ran water over it, and scrubbed the makeup off of her face. When she lowered the cloth to see her face, she saw long, black streaks running down from her eyes. *Why is mascara always such a bitch to take off?* she thought. Her cheeks were red from scrubbing her face. Her once clear, glowing face was now back to its normal, pale and dull state, with blemishes visible on her forehead, chin and nose.

Jill dropped the washcloth and turned away from the mirror. She took off her black leggings and gray shirt, opened the glass panel and stepped into the steaming shower. She hoped that maybe for just twenty minutes, she could just forget about everything that happened today.

She didn't even want to stand up anymore. Jill sat down on the white, marble, tile on the floor, feeling the droplets of hot water hit her back as she sat there motionless, wrapping her arms her legs and laying her head down on her knees.

But Jill knew she still had to be careful. She made sure not to close her eyes for more than a few seconds. She didn't want to give Freddy any chance to let him get into her dreams. Jill had just taken the Hypnocil, she figured she should be okay for awhile, but still, she worried. After hearing Ash talk about how Freddy would only get stronger, she wondered how long the pill was going to work. "Next time I see them," she muttered. "I'll give everybody my stash of the Hypnocil. We can all ration it. Maybe then, we won't have to worry about dreaming. Yeah, that sounds good."

Jill leaned her head back against the dark orange tile on the wall, and felt the water patter against her face. For the first time in the entire day, she felt relaxed. She stood up and grabbed her razor from the shower caddy, and began shaving her legs.

By then, she felt the tile vibrating behind her. It was rhythmic, synchronized to the drums and bass that came through Steven's speakers in his room.

She let out a frustrated sigh. "Figures," she muttered. "I can't get one minute of quiet with that little dumb-ass here." The music was so loud, it didn't matter that there was a thick wall between the rooms. She could here it very clearly. The drums were so loud, it sounded like a cannon blast. The guitar was distorted and muddy, while the bass was just as thick. What stood out to her the most were the vocals. *The guy sounds like he's puking his guts out.* After listening to her little brother's personal collection for years, she had grown used to hearing it. But just once, at least for tonight, she wanted peace and quiet.

She balled her hand into a fist, and banged on the wall a few times. "Steven!" she yelled, hoping her voice would carry through. "Could you shut the vomit metal off for two minutes?!"

Jill traced her razor up from her ankle to her knee, listening to the quiet *shhh* that came when she glided the razor through the thick coat of soap. She held the razor up and shook the excess soap away. She anticipated Steven turning off his music within the next few seconds.

But still, he persisted. Jill leaned in close to the tile, squinting her eyes and listening closely. "Did he just turn that up?" she inquired. Jill banged against the wall once more. "Steven, I swear to God, if you don't shut that off, I'm gonna kick your ass!" And just like that, the noise ceased. It was peaceful again. "That's what I thought." she said.

When she dragged the razor again, she cut the middle of her leg. She had been preoccupied yelling at her brother, that she barely noticed until she felt that slight sting on her leg. She muttered under her breath, "Ow." Jill was used to getting nicked when she shaved, so it didn't bother her.

It didn't take very long until Jill started to hear the noise again. It was even louder this time. *The nerve!* she thought. Jill was just about to tell off her brother when the noise stopped abruptly. It was silent for about three seconds before it came back on. Then off. Then on again. "What the hell is he doing?"

By then, the music started to speed up and the sound became higher and warbled, like a cassette deck spitting a tape out. Soon, the music itself was replaced by sounds of high-pitched squealing.

Jill shut her eyes and plugged her ears. It was incredibly loud, and soon became unbearable to hear. The sound made her paranoid, and the more she heard it, her anxiety rose.

The noise quickly transitioned to what sounded like metal scraping against metal.

SCREEEEEEEEEEEE!!!

It made Jill's ears sting from hearing it. Alongside the scraping noise was the unbearable sound of children crying in pain, as if they were being tortured. "Make it stop!" she cried.

Still hunched over, Jill opened her eyes and looked down at her leg. From the knee down, her left leg was covered in blood. Some of it was being washed away from the pouring water above, leaving a red stream on the tile below. Her eyes widened in shock, and she was left speechless. With her hands, she wiped the blood from her leg. She knew that she wasn't paying attention when she was shaving her leg, but she didn't feel herself get cut again. Certainly not enough to amass that much blood.

As she nervously ran her hands down her leg, she felt her skin coming off. Soon enough, her skin and muscle tissue had unwrapped from her leg just as easy as when she took of her black leggings.

In a matter of seconds, her left leg was reduced to nothing but bare bone. From the knee down, she looked like a skeleton. Jill stared down at her leg in horror and shock. She felt like she was going to pass out. She couldn't help but scream. "Aaaaaaah!"

When she lifted her gaze from her leg to the glass panel, she saw that it too was dripping blood from top to bottom. But there was something written on the glass, like someone had dragged their finger across the foggy glass when she wasn't looking. Scrawled on the shower panel was: *I've got a bone to pick with you!*

She opened her eyes and felt her entire body awake with a jolt. Jill was back on the clean, marble tile, sitting under the hot water. *It was just a dream. The first dream I've had in ten years.* she thought. *He didn't get to me. Thank God...* The floor was clean. The only thing on the glass was steam from the shower. And it was quiet.

Jill looked down to see her leg intact, skin and all. She noticed she still had her razor in her hand. As soon as she laid eyes on it, she grimaced and threw it on the floor. *You know what? I think I'll wax from now on...*

Clutching her knees and trembling, Jill stared all around her with wild-eyed fear as she summoned the courage to stand back up. She reached out above her head and turned the knob, shutting the water off.

Her knees knocked against each other as she stood straight up. The glass shower panel was so dense with steam, she couldn't see the through the other side. Jill wiped the glass with her palm, and felt her heart stop racing when she confirmed that there was no one else with her. She pushed the door open, and stepped outside, grabbing a fresh towel from the rack to her left. Jill ran patted the towel against her bare body, drying her arms, chest, and legs. She flipped her hair over and wrapped the towel around her golden locks, squeezing the water out.

After carelessly rolling the towel up into a ball, Jill threw it into the hamper. She bent over to pick up her baggy gray shirt, and put it back on. The hem of her shirt ended just six inches below her hips, barely covering the rest of her.

Jill leaned over the counter and wiped the foggy mirror above the sink. The only thing she saw was herself, and the orange wall tile behind her. No one else was there. She thought it was ludicrous to go about thinking that Freddy was behind her all the time. He tried to get to her just now and failed. *I'm just being paranoid.* she thought. *I can't let him get to me. That's what he wants.* She wasn't going to allow herself to go utterly mad because of that bastard.

At the same time, she didn't another incident like that to happen again. Jill opened the medicine cabinet, searching behind the aloe vera, allergy medication, and aspirin to grab a small bottle of No-Doze. As the recent incident proved to her, the Hypnocil could only to so much at that point, so it was time to take precautionary measures.

She twisted the cap open, and poured a few pills into her palm, her fingers still pruned from the shower. At first, she was only going to take one, but at the last moment, she decided to take out another. *Just to be safe...* Jill titled her head back and swallowed both pills. She put the bottle back in the medicine cabinet and closed the door.

When she viewed her reflection again, she leaned in closer to examine her face. For almost two days, she had gone without sleep, and already it started to take a toll on her appearance. Dark circles had appeared under her eyes, making her look fatigued, and her eyes look sunken. Jill had always looked lovely and glowing, exuding beauty and happiness with a simple smile. And now it had all faded. Her face was dull and her mind was filled with fear.

There was nothing Jill could do about her fear, that one would simply take time to subside. But she knew there was an easy fix for the jaded look on her face. Jill turned away from the mirror. She unwrapped the towel from her wet hair, and swept away all of half-empty bottles of lotion, the hairdryer still plugged into the wall. She grabbed some makeup to put under her eyes. "I'm sick of seeing myself like this."

When Jill looked back into the mirror, she instantly regretted it. What she saw was not her reflection. It was still her, but perversely different. The face in the mirror had a blank white face, with fresh, red cuts covering every square inch. Her eyes were white as well, missing any sort of color, and the rims of the eyes were black. Her hair was a dark, ashy gray, different from Jill's blonde hair. The girl in the mirror had bright, red, blood pouring from her mouth as she opened it wide, and screamed like a banshee.

Jill gasped, ducked down to the ground, but kept her hands on the edge of the counter. Her whole body tensed up, she felt as if she couldn't move even if she tried. Her mouth gaped open, waiting to scream but nothing would come out. She was frozen. Her breathing became heavier, and her heart started beating out of her chest. *This isn't right.* she thought. *I woke up, I know I did.* "No." she begged while shaking her head in disbelief. "Please, please. This can't be real. It isn't." she tried to convince herself. "It isn't real. It isn't real." she breathed.

Ever so slowly, Jill stood back up. She didn't open her eyes fully, if that hideous creature was still there, she didn't want to see it again. She looked in the mirror, and saw nothing but her scared reflection. She breathed normally again. But, she was more confused than ever. Jill turned away and buried her face in her hands, she felt like crying. "God, what's happening to me?"

As Jill's reflection left the frame of the mirror, another person came into view. On the other side of the mirror, appeared a dark, shady figure. A figure with his head tilted, grinning, soaking in the torment of an innocent girl. It was none other than Freddy. Smooth and quietly, like a thief in the night, he reached out his right arm, the very one that sported his metal-plated glove. It was slow the way he extended his arm out of the mirror frame, and through the other side. Freddy reached out over the sink and towards the beautiful Jill, whose back was to him. He flicked the knife on his index finger up, and tapped her on the shoulder.

Jill felt something sharp poking her on her right shoulder. She sucked in her breath and spun around as fast as she could, causing her damp, stringy, hair to fly in her face. The first thing she saw was Freddy, with the corners of his mouth twisted into a scowl, and the blades of his glove a hair away from her face. "Freddy!" she realized. She felt like her heart had shot up to her throat. Her legs rattled and her knees knocked against each other.

Freddy swept his knife across Jill's throat, slitting it from ear to ear. Her dark blood poured out of her like a waterfall, spilling on her, and staining her body with red.

She tried clutching her throat to make the bleeding stop, but he had cut her too deep. Jill started gagging, choking on her own fluid. There was nothing she could do, except to watch him as he took pleasure in her pain.

Freddy grabbed the top of her head, and opened his mouth slightly, revealing his sharp, fanged, set of teeth. Before he killed her, Freddy's eyes transformed from its typical blue color, to a vapid, soulless white, and then back again.

"Vanity's a sin, bitch"

As soon as the words left his mouth, Freddy pulled her head forward, making her head collide with the glass. Jill's head crashed into the mirror, causing it to break into a hundred shards.

Jill's lifeless body dropped to the floor. The white tile was now stained with the pool of blood that was spreading out from around her. Large, jagged, shards of glass had become lodged into her forehead, her temple, the outer corner of her left eye, and her collar bone. Several smaller shards had been pierced all over various areas of her face.

Her blue eyes remained open, staring up into space. Absolutely no life lingered inside of her.

At least, it wouldn't for much longer.

Chapter 21

LAYING BACK ON THE HEADBOARD of his unmade bed, Steven tried, sloppily at best, to play along with the album that had been blasting through his speakers for well over an hour. He was determined to get all of the riffs and notes down exactly, even if it meant shredding his fingertips until they bled.

The walls in his room were white, but it was hard to tell from all of the posters that had been taped over nearly every square inch. A faded White Zombie poster covered the bedroom door. By his window, were posters of Dokken and Alice Cooper. The one with Alice Cooper was his favorite. He placed it right across from his bed, so he could look at it for as long as he wanted. It was an image from 1973, with Alice wearing a top hat, covering his ratty black hair, and holding a cane. Even under the dark, spider-like eyeliner, his eyes seemed to follow whoever was looking at it around the room.

The shelves above his disheveled bed, and even his computer desk were laden with all sorts of figurines and memorabilia. Ranging from something simple as a snow globe, the items on the shelf above Steven became more obscure as they went on. He had action figures from comic books, and game cartridges that were well over twenty years old. Doom and Mortal Kombat were stacked on his computer desk, collecting dust. They still worked, so in his mind, there was no reason to give up a perfectly good game.

Steven wore a black t-shirt that wrinkled as he held his guitar close to his chest. He hunched over it, getting a close look to make sure his fingers were in the right place. His guitar was dark blue with a few nicks and scratches on it, with a "V" shaped body. Steven had a small amplifier plugged into it. He had it placed next to him, to the side of his bed.

He had the song set on "Repeat". After the fifth listen, he was past the frustration of still not getting it right, and simply mumbled the lyrics to "Steven" by Alice Cooper as he fumbled over the chords. It was his favorite song. He knew his parents didn't intend to name him after a song, but he liked to think of it that way.

"You've on-ly lived a min-ute of your life..." Steven mumbled along with the song as he tried to mimic the piano arrangement on his guitar. *"I must be dreeeam-ing, please stop screeeam-ing..."* he felt relieved once the music slowed down and faded. Then, Steven felt a rush of adrenaline race through his body when the music swelled up louder into the chorus. It was his favorite part. *"STEEE-VEN!"* As he tried to play the chords that followed, he messed up. "Damn." he said quietly to himself, then resumed. *"STEEE-VEN!"* He sang a little louder. *"I hear my name/STEEE-VEN!/ Is some-one cal-ling me?/ I hear my name!"*

He was about to sing, "*STEEE-VEN!*" again, when he heard his name actually being called from outside. "Oh," Steven broke out of the little bubble in his mind. "someone really *is* calling my name." It was his sister, Jill. He felt a little embarrassed. He wondered how long she had been yelling at him before he finally realized it was her. *What does she want now?* he thought. "I'm not turning it down again, she's just gonna have to deal with it." he muttered. "STEVEN!!!" he heard her shout from behind the door. She didn't sound irritated at all. From the sound of her voice, she was screaming like someone was trying to kill her.

Without a second thought, Steven pushed the guitar away from his lap, shoving it to the edge of the bed. He practically jumped off of his bed and ran to the door, Alice's lyrics fading as he left the room, "*That ic-y breath that whis-pers screams of pain...*"

Steven slammed the door behind him. He didn't want any more noise distracting him. *Oh, God...* Steven worried. *She could've been screaming at me this whole time, and I never would have heard her.* "What if she's hurt?" he wondered. "Or worse? No, not worse. Please don't be worse. Please don't be worse."

The bathroom door was closed. Steven stood in the middle of the hallway, staring at the crack under the door, searching for Jill's shadow. "Jill?" he asked, hoping that she was alright. "You okay?" As soon as he spoke, the screaming returned. He heard his sister scream bloody murder on the other side of that door. He couldn't see her, but he could tell that she was in agonizing pain. There was no one else in there, at least, he couldn't tell if there was. But he heard loud thuds, like someone was taking Jill's head and slamming it against the wall.

"AAAAAH!!!" Jill screamed again right before a crash, it appeared to be the sound of objects falling to the floor.

It made Steven jump and wince his eyes. He was frozen in place.

"NO!" he heard Jill plead. "NOOOOO!!!" she screamed.

And then he knew that someone else was there. He heard another voice. It was low, almost like Jill's, but distorted and just...evil. "YOU WILL!!!" the voice insisted. "YOUR SOUL IS HIS NOW!!!"

Steven forced himself to move. He ran to the door and tried turning the knob, but it was locked. He rammed against it with his shoulder until he finally budged it open. The door broke open. Steven was ready to fend off whatever hideous creature that was terrorizing his sister. When he entered the room, he saw no one there other than Jill, who was lying on the floor.

Jill was absolutely still and silent. Her skin was pale and gray. She was soaking in a pool of her own blood on the bathroom floor, which was covered in broken glass. Jill's face and neck were covered in glass shards. And her eyes remained open, staring at nothing.

Steven stood above his sister's dead body. Every part of him had gone numb. His mouth gaped in shock. His heart dropped, along with his knees, to the floor. His eyes began to sting from tears. Steven tried to speak, but the sheer trauma rendered him incapable from uttering a single word. The best that he could do at that moment was to allow short, unintelligible noises to escape his mouth.

Her gray shirt was now covered in wet, red, splatters. Steven felt the warm, thick blood on his palms as he propped Jill up and wrapped his arms around her. Her head, spiked with glass, tilted all the way back as he held her. Her glassy eyes avoided his, staring in the direction of the sink beside them.

He cradled her in his arms. He propped her head up so he could look at her face once more. He patted her damp hair as he spoke to the corpse. "I'm sorry." He whimpered. "I'm so sorry."

Steven looked away from her face. He decided that he didn't want the freshest memory of his sister to be of her mutilated body. He only wanted to remember her as she was before. "You were calling for help, and I couldn't hear you." There were no words to describe the level of shame he felt for himself. "I could have saved you..." He couldn't help but remind himself that Freddy killed Jill. His sister. His best friend. "Fucking bastard." he cursed.

Even from across the hall, the music was still faintly audible. The noise flowed through his room and entered Steven's ears. Alice's words over the music resonated with him. *"I don't want to feel you die..."*

The soft, short, chords coming from the piano only elevated his grief.

"But if that's the way that God has planned you/I'll put pennies on your eyes."

He held Jill's lifeless body closer, pleading, "Please don't go."

"Aaaand it will goooo away."

Steven had had enough with the noise. Even though he knew it would do nothing, he felt the compulsion to shout. "Shut up!" He tried to shut it out. He could have just turned it off, but didn't want to leave her.

"You've on-ly lived a min-ute of your life."

Evelyn had lost track of time. She didn't know whether she had been driving for five minutes, or ten, or possibly an hour. She felt as if she was on the verge of losing her mind. Her panic level had risen for every second that Jill didn't call her back.

After circling around the block to make sure the police had not been there already, Evelyn felt it was safe enough to park by the street in front of their house.

She left the car running. The door opened wide, and as soon as her feet touched the ground, Evelyn sprinted across the lawn. She jumped over the porch steps and started pounding on the front door. "JILL!!!" she called, oblivious to her friend's fatal encounter with Freddy. "STEVEN!!!" she continued to rapidly knock on the door.

From out of the wall of silence Steven had mentally build around him, he heard someone knocking on the door downstairs. "OPEN THE DOOR!!!" he recognized Evelyn's voice.

Gently and carefully, he set Jill back down on the floor, where he had found her. Steven turned in the opposite direction as he stood back up. He hurried through the hallway, and down the stairs.

By then, the song was already starting to fade. It had become much quieter, but Steven was able to hear one last line before he entered the living room.

"I must be dreaming..."

Steven was gone. All that was left was Jill's stiffening corpse. She laid there, still. Rigid. Unmoving. Her empty blue eyes, while looking in the direction of the wall, stared at nothing.

Her eyes, her beautiful, sky blue eyes, had by then faded away. All color in her eyes had been replaced by a thick cloud of white. Only when her expression was truly empty, did her body begin to move.

Jill's soul was gone from the earth. It was currently being ripped and torn apart, in the malevolent clutches of Freddy Krueger. Her body was now inhabited by the spirits once trapped in the Book of the Dead, but now free to roam through the world of the living.

Slowly, Jill raised her left hand, bringing it closer to her face. She opened her hand and grabbed the large glass shard that had been stuck in the outer corner of her left eye. With each second that passed, her hand became bonier, her skin flakier, and her fingernails grew longer. Even her skin changed seamlessly every second. Her entire body and face turned pale, almost blue in spots, as if she had already been dead for several hours. She pulled the shard from her flesh, causing blood to expel from her wounds at an alarming rate. The color of her blood changed from dark red, to a slimy green, and back again.

The front door flew open. Evelyn was glad that she didn't have to call for him again. She knew that they couldn't waste time, and that they needed to move quickly.

She didn't know how else to break it to him that Freddy had killed Cooper, so she just came right out with it.

Steven was still in a state of shock. He saw Evelyn at the front door, and noticed she was in a panic. He figured that maybe she was on her way here and heard the noise. He decided to just tell her.

In unison, they blurted roughly the same thing.

"Cooper's dead." said Evelyn.

"Jill's dead." said Steven.

Both of them looked down, and noticed that the other was stained with blood. Steven held his palms, still covered in Jill's blood, out in front of him. Evelyn had Cooper's blood splattered on the side of her face, and a few spots on her purple shirt.

The blood on Evelyn was now dried and darkened, but she noticed that the blood on Steven's hands were still fresh. She assumed that Jill hadn't become possessed yet, but she needed to find her before she turned into a Deadite.

Evelyn stepped inside the house.

Steven followed her as she searched through the room, looking for her body. "Freddy killed them." Steven still couldn't believe it.

She turned to face him. "Where is she?" asked Evelyn.

"Upstairs." he answered. "But–" he was going to ask her why she wanted to know, but Evelyn had already turned away from him.

Evelyn headed up the stairs. She intended to make sure Jill didn't come back.

"Wait!" he opposed. "What are you doing?"

"Steven," she said sternly. "show me where she is."

"Why?" he sounded confused. "I mean, I don't think you need to see her like that."

"Because she's not dead yet!" she shouted. "Now, get up here!"

Steven led her up the stairs to show her the body. He tried not to break down as he directed her to the room where Freddy killed her. First, his sister. Now, his friend. It was too much.

They both stepped in front of the entrance to the bathroom. Jill's body was gone. All that was left was the shape of her silhouette surrounded by her blood. Steven's eyes widened and he felt shocked and frustrated at the same time. He had no idea what was going on.

He turned to Evelyn, pointing at the ground where he last saw Jill. "She was right there!" he said, panicked. "I swear to God, she was right *there*!"

Evelyn looked at Steven, and grabbed his arms to get his full attention. "Steven, listen to me!" she said. She told him in the calmest manner that she could muster. "I know you're not going to like what I have to say, but we have to kill her."

Steven's expression changed from fear to outright anger. "What?!" he thought she had become insane. "Have you lost your damn mind?!" He had laid down the line for her, adamantly refusing. "No, Evelyn. I can't do that." He ran his hands across his dark brown hair.

All Evelyn could think about was slapping him across the face. He didn't even realize the danger they were both in. "Stop being so–" She looked at Steven's face. She could tell he was confused or discomforted by something. "What is it?" she asked him, disregarding her previous remark.

Steven felt something in his hair and he touched it. He lowered his hand in front of his face to see what it was.

They both examined what was on Steven's hand. When Steven rubbed it with his fingers, he noticed how incredibly slimy it was. It was thick, red, and dripping down to the floor.

It landed on the top of his head, so it must have come from the ceiling. *Is this...blood? How could this have come from up there?* That was when he felt more of it drip down on the top of his head.

Steven and Evelyn both looked up at the same time, directing their gaze to the ceiling. What they saw was worse than what they could have imagined.

Crawling on the ceiling, on her hands and feet, her limbs bent and contorted resembling a spider, Jill hissed at them. She seemed to defy gravity as she suspended from the ceiling. Her back was facing them, but her head had been turned all the way around to look at them. Her mouth gaped open, expelling the same blood and saliva that dripped on Steven's head.

At first, they barely recognized that it was Jill. Her face had turned white as paper. Her hair was gray. She had removed the glass from her face, and was now covered in black and dark red lacerations all over. Jill's blank eyes were bloodshot, and the skin on her hands and legs had black veins all over, resembling spider webs across her body. The corners of her mouth were locked in a permanent, upward smile, and the inside of her mouth was soaking wet from the bright, red, blood.

"What's up, little brother?" She cackled. Then, in a movement so quick, the sound of her neck snapping made Steven and Evelyn cringe, Jill flipped her body over so that it was realigned with her head. She hissed and dropped down. She landed on top of Steven, causing him to fall on the floor.

She wrestled him down, making sure he could not escape. With her abnormally long and sharp fingernails, she began scratching every inch of him. The demon moved so quickly, it was but a flurry of arms flailing, and blood spraying. In that hellish voice, and with a touch of insanity, the demon laughed.

Steven tried to push her off, but she was moving too fast. Every time he thought he could block her away, she grabbed him, and cut him. His eyes widened when she lowered towards him, looking into his eyes. "Tell me," she bellowed as she continued scratching his skin. "do I look pretty?!" She laughed again. It sounded so inhuman and disturbing.

Steven saw this as his best chance to throw her off. He grabbed her by her shoulders and rolled to his left side. "Fuck, no!" he said to the Deadite. He pushed her off of him and sent her tumbling down the stairs.

Evelyn ran to him and helped him back up. "Come on." she said as she led Steven down the stairs with her to capture the demon.

Jill had rolled into the living room. Before she could have a chance to get back up, Evelyn jumped on top of her and pinned her down.

She could feel the immense power and physical strength that the demon had within her. Evelyn was able to hold her down, but not for very long. She looked up to Steven, who had just joined beside her. "Quick," she instructed him. "get me something to knock her out!"

Steven's mind was all over the place. He didn't know what to get that would knock out a Kandarian demon. "Like what?" he asked.

Evelyn grunted as she struggled to keep Jill down. She could feel the demon starting to break from her grip. "Anything!" she said angrily. "Now go!"

He ran off and disappeared into the kitchen, leaving only the sound of his clumsy footing as a sign that he was doing what he was told to do.

Jill kicked and waved her arms around to break free. Evelyn felt Jill starting to slide out from under her. Before she could give her the chance to escape, Evelyn pinned her arms down to the floor, putting her full weight on top of Jill.

Suddenly, Evelyn felt herself being launched up in the air, with Jill still beneath her. She looked down and saw the entire room below her, she figured she must have been ten feet above the ground.

Still suspended in the air, Jill swiftly flipped forward, slinging Evelyn off of her back. Rasped, and her voice layered, she howled.

Evelyn flew across the room and hit the front door, causing the small trio of glass windows on it to shatter. She fell hard on the floor, landing on her side. The fall knocked the wind out of her. Evelyn struggled for breath, gasping desperately, as she slowly stood up. She saw Jill lowering down to the ground and creeping towards her.

Her neck and shoulders started to convulse and twitch. The bones in her body made an awfully loud snapping noise. She spoke to her. Her voice was not one, but a multitude of sickening demonic voices. "He'll be so happy when we bring him your soul!"

Evelyn didn't know what she was talking about at first. "He?" Once she thought about it, the answer came to her, but she needed to say it aloud. "Freddy?"

"He's the one who freed us." she hissed. "And we serve him by delivering the souls of the innocent to him." The Deadite opened her mouth and spilled blood down her neck and onto the floor. "Oh, he has quite a torturous death in store for you! Now," Jill raised her hands and began to charge at Evelyn. "JOIN US–"

A loud bang echoed in the air. Whatever it was, it rendered Jill speechless. She fell down to the floor, unconscious.

Once she fell, Steven had been revealed to be right behind her. He was holding a cast-iron skillet in his hands, wielding it like a baseball bat. His nostrils were flaring, and eyes stared wildly at Jill's possessed vessel of a body. He waited until she dropped to the floor before he lowered the skillet. He looked at Evelyn. "What now?" he asked her.

Evelyn unlocked her gaze from Steven and looked past him. She spotted the door to the right of the staircase. She remembered that it led to the basement. Her eyes returned to Steven. She straightened her arm, and pointed to the door. "There." she said, still out of breath. "We'll put her in the basement."

By the time Steven had gotten a hold of Jill's arms, and Evelyn had secured her ankles, Jill had already woken up and started resisting. She writhed and shrieked as they both carried her to the basement.

Steven lowered her momentarily to open the door. At the same time, they both swung her body back and forth, and then threw her down the stairs. Steven slammed the door shut and turned the lock. Both of them sunk down to the floor and leaned back against the door, feeling Jill hit against it and try to break it open.

BANG! BANG! BANG! BANG! BANG! BANG! BANG! BANG!

And then, just as quickly as it happened. The noise had ceased. She was silent.

Both Steven and Evelyn felt their heart rate lower and start to relax.

"Yeah," said Steven. "I think that should keep her for a while."

Evelyn had felt like she was forgetting something. Something that was aching in the back of her mind. And then, it came to her. She continued to stare off in the distance. "Steven?" she asked dryly.

"Yeah?"

"Doesn't your basement have a door that leads outside?" she asked, hoping she was wrong.

Steven nodded his head. "Yeah." he answered. "Yeah, it does." he shrugged her comment off. "But it's locked from the outside, there's no way she can–" he stopped himself. After witnessing it for himself, he knew that yes, she could, and absolutely will.

They both looked at each other with frightened eyes.

"Steven," Evelyn warned him. "considering what we've just seen for ourselves: the crawling on the ceiling and the levitating, I don't think we should rule out breaking down a door."

"What do you suggest, then?" he asked.

"For you, something sharp and pointy." she said poignantly. "Me, I'm starting to grow fond of weapons that require bullets."

Chapter 22

STEVEN TURNED THE KNOB ON the front door, slowly and quietly, while Evelyn lifted the curtains and peeked out the window. She wanted to make sure that none of the neighbors were outside and able to see them. Steven pushed the door open, and took a wide stride forward to avoid the pile of broken glass on the patio where Evelyn had been thrown in the air and hit the door. She followed right behind him.

His hands were growing increasingly sweaty. He fought to stop his hands from shaking. He knew that he needed to stay focused, but the more he walked, the more difficult it became to overcome. He looked behind him to see Evelyn, steadily gripping the revolver with both hands and looking warily around her. Seeing her so collected only made him feel worse about himself.

"Where did you get this from, anyway?" asked Evelyn, referring to the revolver.

Steven didn't look back at her. He kept his eyes locked in front of him, in case Jill should happen to appear. "My parent's room." he responded. "Top shelf of the nightstand."

They stepped down the concrete steps, and veered of the pathway. They walked across the empty driveway in front of the garage, and headed towards the wooden gate that led to the backyard.

The bright, yellow, light bulb that lit above the front door had failed to reach them beyond that point, so they were know immersed in the dark of night. It was a full moon. The hazy gray light that shown from above dimly illuminated around them, helping to vaguely see what was in front of them.

Steven was now in front of the white picket fence that divided the front and back yard. There was a crude, rusted, latch keeping the fence closed. Steven raised his hand to unlock it, but something in the back of his mind prevented him from doing so.

All he could think about was his sister. Her happy, sweet face. How she could always make him laugh no matter how depressed or mad he was. Jill was like his best friend. And here he was, about to step through that door, and kill her. He couldn't bring himself to do it. He had realized that for the entire time he was contemplating opening the fence, he was holding his breath in. He lowered his arm, and let out a big exhale.

Evelyn stepped beside him and laid a hand on his shoulder. "Steven," she said sympathetically. "what's wrong?"

He continued to stare at the picket fence, refusing to look at her. He found himself stuttering when he first began speaking. "I–I–" he managed to compose himself. "just...don't know if I can do this." He started shaking his head, not wanted any of this to be true. "I can't—I can't go through with this. She's my sister. I'm killing my sister, Evelyn!"

Evelyn grabbed him by the shoulder and spun him around. She lifted his chin up, forcing him to look her in the eye. "Listen to me." he said sternly. "I understand *exactly* how you're feeling right now. You look at her, and what those things turned her into, and you still see just a small part of who she was before. And you want that part to still be alive. With you..." She thought about Cooper. Her eyes became foggy with tears, and her voice started to break, but she fought to keep it steady. "But, Steven, you also have to understand that that thing is not your sister anymore. You have to let her go."

Steven reluctantly nodded his head "yes." and mumbled, "Okay." Steven looked down beside the door, and spotted an axe just a few feet away from him. He bent over to pick it up and gripped the wooden handle in front of him. Steven finally put his hand on the lock. "Let's get it over with."

Steven lifted the latch and pushed the door to the fence, causing it to creak eerily as it swung open. *Yeah, that's pretty much how I feel right now...* Steven thought to himself. *Eeeeeeerrrrrrr...*

He emerged further into the yard with Evelyn following close beside him. Steven held up his axe, while Evelyn gripped the handle of the gun tighter, preparing for the Deadite to spring up at any moment. Evelyn checked behind them every few seconds, while Steven kept his gaze in front of him.

They arrived to the back entrance to the basement. Evelyn and Steven stood next to each other, and stared in fear when they notice that the bolted-down, twin doors had been busted open. They stared down the dark, almost cavernous, basement below them. It was dimly lit, but there was still no way to tell if she was still down there or not.

"She got out." Evelyn concluded.

Steven had looked all around them when they entered the backyard. As far as he could tell, they were all alone. He had no idea where she could be. "Where is she?" he asked.

Evelyn kept looking down the entrance, keeping a watchful eye. "Well, if she's still out here, I think we should stop keeping our backs turned."

Steven nodded, enthused. "Yeah, that sounds like a good idea."

They both turned around simultaneously.

The first thing that they see is Jill's pale, mutilated face uncomfortably close to theirs. Steven and Evelyn gasped and their eyes widened in shock.

Jill opened her mouth, making her shark-like set of teeth visible under the moonlight. She howled, her pitch was so high that it pierced both of Steven and Evelyn's ears.

Steven expressed his discontent. "Shit."

The demon raised her bony, gray hands and launched at both of them. Evelyn ducked and veered to her left, escaping her.

Steven was not so lucky. Jill grabbed him by the waist, tackling him and sending them both falling into the thick darkness of the basement. Steven dropped his axe on the ground as Jill sent him rolling down.

Evelyn couldn't see either of them, she could only hear what was going on. She crawled over to the entrance, and peeked over the edge, listening. She heard the loud thumping of the both of them tumbling down the wooden steps, as well as Steven shouting. His voice became quieter the further down he descended. After a few seconds, the falling ceased. At that point, all Evelyn heard was Steven straining and shouting in fear. Following that was the sound of Jill's wicked laughter.

"Steven!" Evelyn shouted. She desperately hoped that he was okay.

Immediately, she heard his voice speaking back to her. As he spoke, he sounded hurried. "Get ready!" he warned. "I'm coming up!"

Evelyn did what Steven said. She stood up and took a couple steps back from the entrance. She held the gun in front of her and aimed it, knowing Jill would follow behind him.

She heard footsteps heavily shuffling up the wooden steps. Evelyn pulled the hammer back until it clicked four times, cocking it. She held the gun steadily as she waited for both of them to emerge.

Coming up from the darkness, Steven frantically ran up the stairs with Jill following closely behind him. As soon as he stepped on the grass, Steven ducked down to the ground, thus allowing Evelyn to fully see her target.

Evelyn squeezed the trigger and shot Jill.

BLAM!

A small bullet hole appeared on Jill's collar bone. This time, a semi-thick stream of green blood pumped from her bullet would as the Deadite screamed in pain, and fell back down the basement steps.

Evelyn ran over to Steven, and knelt down to the ground where he was sitting. "Are you okay?" she asked.

Steven plugged his finger in his ear and wiggled it around in an attempt to make the ringing stop from the gun blast. "Yeah." he answered. "Is she dead?" he asked, unsure.

Evelyn turned away from Steven and looked down the basement. She listened closely. It was silent. Not even a creak echoed from down the stairs. She still held the gun securely in her hand, the barrel was still hot. Evelyn lowered further down, trying to catch a glimpse of Jill's hopefully dead body.

Evelyn felt a pair of bloody hands grab both sides of her head and squeeze tightly, pulling strands of hair from her scalp. Evelyn screamed and pushed back, dragging Jill out with her. Jill's right arm and chest was streaked with the blood that poured down from the bullet wound. The Deadite panted and made unintelligible noises as she held on to Evelyn.

Steven acted quickly. He grabbed the axe that he had dropped on the ground, lifted it above his head, and swung it down between Jill and Evelyn's heads. With one fatal blow, Steven grunted as he chopped Jill's arms off at the elbow area.

Now that she was freed, Evelyn pushed herself back up. Jill's rotting forearms remained clamped to the both sides of Evelyn's head. Jill's radius and ulna peaked through her amputated flesh, and the ends of her forearms began to bleed. With her free hand, Evelyn pried the demon's fingers from her head and threw the lifeless body parts on the ground. They landed with a soft thud on the grass.

The Deadite howled as fluid sprayed from the cut-off points in her arms. Although her eyes were blank, the look of fury was quite visible. The demon opened her mouth wide and revealed her monstrous teeth.

After unwrapping herself from the cadaver arms, Evelyn looked up and pointed the revolver at Jill. She prepared to pull the hammer back and squeeze the trigger, when she saw Steven run out in front of her. Evelyn hesitated and lowered the gun.

Steven held the axe up and ran towards Jill. He swung the axe at her legs, chopping them off and causing her to fall to the ground.

Her torso began to shake and convulse on the ground. Her mouth still gaped open, the corners pointed, forming an empty smile. She continued to taunt him in that warbled voice. "Her soul burns in Hell!" she shrieked. Her arms and legs still twitched and shook on the grass.

It all happened to him in a rush. Steven continued to mutilate her body with the now bloody axe. He wasn't even aware of how many times the axe split her skin and bones apart. It all happened to him in flashes. He saw one of her arms being chopped at the shoulder. Next was what remained of her legs. Then her stomach. Crudely and unevenly, he sliced and diced his sister's body. He felt her warm, slimy blood being sprayed on his face and on his arms. He barely noticed how the color of the blood changed from red to green to black.

Out of the corner of his eye, Steven saw his sister's decapitated head. It looked at him. Taunted him. The one thing he feared most in his life was losing his sister. Since the horrible mess between Freddy and Ash began, he tried to protect her. Even when the she became possessed, he didn't want his sister to be gone. But, as he held the bloody axe to the moonlit sky, and his sister's own blood dripped onto his face, he realized that she was already gone long before. There was no going back. Swiftly, and with a pained groan, Steven lowered the axe and split his sister's head semi-parallel down the middle of her face.

He felt Evelyn's hand touch him on his shoulder. She calmly tried to pull him away. With the handle still lodged in her head, Steven released the handle from his grip and turned away, wiping the blood from his face. Just as easily as he had succumbed to blinding rage, Steven broke down and cried on Evelyn's shoulder.

Evelyn hugged him, and couldn't help but allow tears to escape from both of her eyes. She had lost one of her best friends. She wanted to fall on the floor and sob like she did not too long ago when Cooper died, but she knew there was no time to waste. Evelyn wiped the tears from her eyes, let Steven go, and spoke to him gently. "We have to get out before the police get here." she said.

She prepared to walk away when she saw Steven still staring at Jill's chopped-up body. She wondered why he wanted to look at her like that for so long. All of her limbs were dislocated and bloody. Her ribcage was exposed and her intestines were splayed across what was left of her body.

Evelyn grabbed his arm and tried to lead him. "Steven," she said. "come on."

His tone of voice made him sound hopeless, but still with the intention of full-filling one last act for his sister. "No, not yet." he said. "We have to bury her."

"But," she sounded anxious. "we don't have a lot of time. The police are already looking for us."

He turned to her. "Then we'll do it quickly." he sniped.

"Fine." she said. Evelyn walked away to grab a shovel that was propped by the back door. She handed it to Steven, who promptly took it from her hands and planted the shovel into the dirt.

Steven had dug a hole in the ground that was about three feet deep. Both he and Evelyn gently laid Jill's body parts into the soil. Steven took the shovel and filled the hole with dirt. When it was finally filled, Steven released the shovel from his grip and dropped to his knees. He patted down the dirt firmly to flatten the surface, like he was planting flower seeds.

As Steven patted the dirt, the silver crucifix that hung around his neck had escaped from under the collar of his black t-shirt, and swung in front of his face. Having to stare at the cross as he was burying his sister was taunting. Dejecting. But, it also reminded Steven that as long as he was still alive, he would everything he could to make sure Krueger burns in Hell for what he did.

He felt Evelyn's hand on his shoulder, and noticed her staring at him out of the corner of his eye. "Let's go." she said calmly.

Steven nodded his head and wiped his dirt-covered hands his jeans. "Okay." he mumbled.

They both stood up and began walking back to the fence. As they walked past the door, Steven looked to Evelyn and asked, "Where are we going to go?"

Evelyn scanned the houses around the street, and noticed several porch lights beaming in the distance. *They must have heard the screaming.* She thought to herself. *And the gunshot.* She started to walk a little faster and noticed Steven picking up the pace as well. "We have to get Faith first." she said. "If we hurry, I think we can get to her in time."

Steven looked around and saw a few of his neighbors stepping outside of their houses, looking around, curious about the noise. He felt as if they were all staring at him, like they knew. He could already imagine what they must have thought about him: *There he his, that sick fuck who butchered his sister.* He looked back at Evelyn as they jogged to Ash's Delta 88. "And then what?" he asked.

Evelyn reached out to grab the handle and pull the door open, while Steven ran to the passenger's side. "And then," she repeated Steven's words. "we're gonna make a quick stop at the police station." she tried to say the words nonchalantly, but it didn't stop Steven from doing a double-take.

He lifted his eyes from the door. "What?!" he said as he tried to look at Evelyn, but she had already ducked inside the car and slammed the door. Steven opened the door on his side and bent over to look her in the eye. "Why are we going there?" Steven got inside the car and shut the door, not breaking eye-contact with Evelyn.

"To break Ash out of jail." she said as she put the car in gear.

"He's in jail?" he asked. At first, he wanted an explanation, but he quickly let it go. He didn't care how he got there, what concerned him was how they were going to take care of it, especially since he figured the police were already hunting them down. "How are we gonna do that?"

Evelyn became frustrated. "I don't know yet, alright?" Evelyn returned her gaze back to the road. "We'll figure it out when we get there. Let's just...take care of one thing at a time."

Steven crossed his arms and stared in the distance. “I don’t like this.”

Evelyn snapped. “Well, deal with it!” She lifted her foot from the brake and slammed on the accelerator, making the tires squeal as they sped down the road. They could already hear the police sirens as they fled the neighborhood.

The moon hovering above acted as a beacon that Evelyn drove towards. It’s bright light reflected down on them, backlighting the petrified trees on each side of the street that seemed to stretch over the night sky. Traveling in Ash’s Oldsmobile, Evelyn and Steven raced down the road, hurrying to find Faith and, hopefully, get to Ash before it was too late.

Evelyn began to drive faster with each block she drove through. Out of the corner of her eye, she drove past one house that sent chills down her spine, but she didn’t know why. She looked at what street she was on. 1400 Elm.

As she sped past 1428, she noticed a broken down home. It hadn’t been condemned. She could see furniture inside the house as she glanced through the window. But the chipped paint, dead plant life, and especially the bars on the second-story windows gave her an eerie feeling. The house seemed to have a certain presence, or atmosphere about it. It seemed to tower above, intimidating those who stood in front of it. And there was a mysterious, blue-ish glow coming from all of the windows.

Lt. Moore and Officer Harris had taken Ash down to the police department about twenty minutes after he had been arrested. This had been the first time Ash had ever run into any serious trouble with the police. Considering how many times he had come close over the last twenty years, he figured he’d had a good run.

Except this time, it was a matter of life or death. For every second he would have to spend in that cell, his chances of defeating Freddy would grow slimmer. If he didn't find a way to get out of there quick, Freddy's reign of terror would spread like wildfire. By then, there would be nothing Ash could do about it. *This might be the end for me.* he feared.

They both led him across the station and towards his cell. Officer Harris followed behind, keeping an eye on him, and making sure he wouldn't attempt to escape. Lt. Moore walked in front. They led Ash to his cell, where they planned to hold him for the next forty-eight hours before putting him on trial.

They had put Ash in handcuffs before putting him in the squad car earlier. The metal cuffs were so tight, they were starting to cut off his circulation in his left hand.

Still keeping in line with the two of them, Ash looked back at Officer Harris. "Hey, uh..." he began. "You think you could loosen those cuffs there, chief?"

Nathan cracked a sarcastic smile. "Not a chance." he replied.

"I'm just saying," said Ash. "this is starting to cut me off. It's the only hand I got left, and I'd like to keep it that way."

Harris chuckled softly. "Nice try, Ash."

Ash looked away from Officer Harris and turned to Lt. Moore. He stared straight ahead, so all he saw was the dark blonde hair falling from under his police cap. "What about you, Goldilocks?" said Ash. "Any chance you could let me go here?"

Unfazed, Moore continued to march forward and keep his gaze in front of him. "That's 'Lt. Moore' to you, scumbag." he said curtly.

Ash smirked. "'Moore' as in donuts there, tubby?" he taunted.

"Piss and moan all you want, Ash." said Harold. "You can't talk your way out of this."

"Just thought I'd have a little fun before I rot in the slammer."

After leading him down the cold, narrow hallway, they reached Ash's cell. Ash was looking at the floor at the time, when he noticed Lt. Moore's feet cease to move.

He stopped abruptly behind him, and looked up. "Well, here we are." he heard Moore say with an enthused tone that made Ash feel incredibly pissed. He saw his cell, which was about twice the size of a coat closet.

He smirked. "Cozy." he said sarcastically.

Lt. Moore unhooked the set of keys from his belt and flipped through each key until he found the one that fit the lock to Ash's cell. "Good." He said as he grabbed the right key and turned the lock, opening the door. The metal creaked as it swung open. "'Cause you're gonna be here for the next forty-eight hours." Moore cocked his head to the side, prompting Ash to step inside.

Ash was slow to move his feet. Officer Harris became impatient. He placed his hand on Ash's back and pushed him into his cell.

By the time he turned around, Lt. Moore had already slammed the door, and locked it. From behind the metal bars, Ash could see him smiling, taking joy in his imprisonment. Ash shot him an insolent look.

Moore continued to taunt him as he hooked his keys back onto his belt. "You know," he began. "I've been in this business for about 40 years now, and some days, it becomes too much for me to handle." He still leered at him. "Do you have any idea what it's like to go to work every day and deal with rotten little bastards who kill innocent people? And *you're* responsible to make sure these pieces of filth never see the light of day?"

Ash remained hunched over by the bars, pretending his eyes shot lasers and every time he blinked, Lt. Moore's head would be vaporized. He couldn't believe the irony in Lt. Moore's monologue. He decided to humor him. "It's funny you should say that–" But Moore cut him off, completely ignoring what Ash had to say.

"But whenever I see assholes like you behind bars, it reminds me while I'm still here."

"So you can lock up guys who didn't do anything wrong?" Ash retaliated.

"You've got some nerve, don't you, Williams?" Moore said, angered. "You shot that boy in the head at point blank range. Everyone in the building heard you. We caught you attempting to flee the scene of the murder." Moore raised his voice at him. "For God's sake, we've got yours and Evelyn's prints on the gun you killed him with!"

Ash yelled back. "Alright, Starsky and Hutch, listen to me! You got the wrong guy!"

Lt. Moore ignored him and turned away. He walked over to Harris. "You know what, I'll keep an eye on him." he said. "Why don't you go home and get some sleep?"

As soon as he heard the word "sleep", Ash immediately jumped and gripped the bars tighter. Even though Harris was responsible for locking him up, he couldn't just let another person die. Worriedly, Ash shouted, "No! Don't do that!"

Both of them looked at Ash like he was insane.

"And why the hell not?" said Harris.

Ash felt as if he had backed himself into a corner at that point. *Well, it was gonna come to this anyway. Might as well make a dramatic spiel about it.* Ash calmed himself down, and when he spoke, he made sure to keep his voice level. "I know why all this is happening. I know who's behind this. And I'm the only one who can stop him." he said.

"Cut the bullshit, Ash." Moore said, impatiently. "Who are you talking about?"

"The guy that Springwood seems to have a tough time getting rid of." said Ash. "Freddy Krueger."

Ash could tell by the look in their eyes, that as soon as he said Freddy's name, they didn't think of him as their killer anymore.

Chapter 23

NATHAN SNIPED AT ASH IN a hushed tone. "Are you insane?!" He looked behind him to make sure no one else was around that could have heard them.

Lt. Moore pointed a finger at Ash and looked at him angrily, but at the same time, fearful for what Ash had just admitted to them. "We don't talk about Krueger out in the open!"

Ash straightened his posture so that he was at eye-level with Moore. He leered at him and condescended him for the remark. "Yeah, well maybe that's the problem." Ash let go of the bars and opened his arms, reminding Moore and Harris that he was sitting in a cell. "And besides," he said. "it's not like I can run outside and blab this around town, now can I?"

Moore stared at Ash for a moment before saying something, examining his face. Now that he took Ash's words into consideration, it started to make sense. Now that he had seen him up close, he noticed the dark circles around his eyes. *He must have stayed awake for days.* he figured. He had seen that same look on so many faces at the scene of a crime that was inevitably caused by Freddy Krueger.

The thing Lt. Moore had felt most ashamed of, was that he had arrested Ash for a crime he didn't commit. In trying to keep the children safe from Freddy, he ended up only making the situation worse. *How did I not see this before?* he wondered. But still, one thing didn't make sense. Krueger always went after Springwood's youth, not some

50-year-old drifter passing through town. *Why this guy? And how does he even know who Freddy is?* Moore leaned in and asked Ash that very question. "Let me ask you something. Why you? What do you think Freddy went after you?"

I guess it's monologue time again. Ash dreaded this. He had just convinced the two of them that he wasn't crazy. He was afraid he was going to lose them again this time. He answered Moore's question with another question. "Are you familiar with ancient Sumerian spell books?" he asked. "The kind that can resurrect the dead and take over the living?"

Moore stepped back and looked at Ash suspiciously. "No." he said bluntly. "It's not part the job."

"Well," Ash countered. "it's a big part of *my* job."

Officer Harris stared, astounded, at Ash. He had no idea that the night would end up like this. Just twenty-four hours ago, he thought of Ash as just an odd resident of Springwood. He didn't stand out much, aside from a few strange nuances that Harris now realized was because of Freddy hunting him down. He walked closer to the bars, where Ash stood at the opposite side. "Who *are* you?" asked Harris.

Well, what is *there to say?* Ash wondered before answering him. *The truth, I guess would be a fine place to start.* "I'm the Chosen One." he said, sort of embarrassed, but he figured it was a hell of a way to start off his explanation. He noticed the shared look of confusion amongst the both of them. He didn't like it, but he knew this was going to be a long night.

Moore looked at him skeptically. "Excuse me?"

"I'll give you the CliffsNotes version." he said. "I go wherever I'm needed, snuff out all of the undead bastards crawling around in the world, and that book–the Necronomicon–is the reason why all this happens."

"What's a 'Necronomicon'?" asked Moore.

"It's this collection of burial rites, funerary incantations, and demon resurrection passages." he explained. "It's not something you want to get your hands on, trust me."

"But," Moore cut in. "you *did*, I assume."

Ash couldn't deny that. "Well, yeah–I–have come across it a few times." he admitted. "I found it back when I was in Michigan State–"

Harris interrupted him. "You went to college?" he asked in disbelief.

"Hey, who's talkin' here, four-eyes?!" he sniped. "Yeah, I found it, and like a dumb kid, I read from it. Even though the whole bound-in-human-flesh-and-inked-in-blood thing was kind of a dead giveaway that I shouldn't have." His mind brought him back to that night when it all came apart for him. "And since then," To this day, he would still think back and wonder that if he did anything differently, would it have mattered? Or, sometime down the line, would fate have caught up to him, and there was just no way to escape the hell his life had become after that? "those things just keep showing up. And I'm the one who has to protect people from them.

"Now, I–uh–guess you guys are thinking what does this have to do with Freddy." he said, guilty. "Somehow, he managed to cross over from his world back to ours."

"But," Harris added. "Freddy's been dead for years. How did this happen?"

"That's right." said Moore. "We've had this problem under control for quite some time before you strolled in." he said accusingly. "Explain that to us."

"Well you see," Ash tried to laugh it off, like it was a harmless mistake, but one look on Lt. Moore's face proved he wasn't going to take this lightly. "I've only been here a few weeks, getting rid of all the Deadites in this po-dunk little town–you're welcome for that by the way–but, that must've been enough time for Freddy to use me to get a hold of the book."

"What the hell are 'Deadites'?" asked Moore.

"Whenever the...evil...inside that book is let out, it possesses the living. Those things are what they're called." After having the past few days to think about it, he figured that in order to have such power over the book, Freddy must have been a Deadite himself. "And I think Freddy's one of them, at least, part of one anyway. I found the book buried underneath the boiler room where he used to work."

"It makes sense now–well, sort of." said Harris. "For weeks, we've been trying to figure out what those things were."

"But how was he able to get out of the dream realm through you?" Moore asked.

Officer Harris leaned in and mentioned something to him quietly so Ash couldn't hear. "I forgot to mention, sir," he said in a hushed tone. "he's the one who lives in that house."

Moore looked at him, surprised. "You don't mean the one on Elm Street, do you?" he asked.

"Yes, sir," confirmed. "*That* one."

Lt. Moore turned his gaze back to Ash, except now he looked at him like he was the most naíve man on the planet. "You've been living in that house?" He started to raise his voice. "The one Krueger used to live in? The one where most of the murders took place because he killed those kids in their dreams?" he turned back to Harris. "I thought we condemned that house years ago!"

Harris answered calmly. "We did for a while, but people thought it would arouse suspicion, so it's been put back on the market."

Out of frustration, Lt. Moore smacked his palm against his forehead. "God damn it!" he turned back to Ash. "You have to be the biggest fool I have every come across in my entire career!"

Ash raised his voice so that it was louder than Lt. Moore's. "Hey! I didn't know at the time, alright?!" he shouted. "Now, as soon as I found out about Freddy, I got the book, and I was gonna destroy it. Except..." The volume of Ash's voice lowered out of shame. "...he used it to bring himself back. Before I could do anything, he took it with him." Ash stood up straight. "And the longer I'm in here, that bastard's only gonna get stronger. Now, are you gonna stop asking questions and let me out of here, or not?"

Moore didn't say anything. He reached for the key looped around his belt and freed Ash from his cell.

Evelyn looked at Faith, who sat in the backseat of the Oldsmobile, through the rear view mirror. "I'm glad you're alive." said Evelyn.

She had driven as fast as she could to get to her, all the while thinking that she might have met the same fate Jill had. Seeing her face as she stood by the sidewalk waiting for them had given Evelyn hope that they can survive this.

Steven turned around from the passenger seat to catch a glance at Faith. "So am I." said Steven. For the first time in what seemed like forever to him, he smiled. Losing Jill was enough for him. He was going to live up to the promise that he made not to let Freddy take any more of his friends.

Faith gave him a half-smile. She still felt numb from knowing that two of her friends had been murdered. She sunk into the aged leather seats and stared at the floor. Since the last time they had met, Faith had changed into a dark gray shirt, torn black jeans, and black lace-up boots. Her blue bra was slightly visible under the thin fabric.

Steven looked into her brown, cat-like eyes. "We were afraid we wouldn't get to you in time."

She mumbled in her low, hazy voice. "Yeah, well...I wasn't gonna be a dumb-ass and just go to sleep after you told me not to, right?"

It was quiet for a moment after that. Evelyn had leaned back into her seat, while Steven nervously looked all around him.

Faith instantly felt a rush of embarrassment wash over her. She felt like slapping herself across the face. *God, I* am *a dumb-ass.* she thought. She looked at both Evelyn and Steven, who sat in front of her. She stuttered at first. "I–um–I'm sorry." she admitted.

Evelyn glanced at her through the rear view mirror. She knew what Faith meant. Evelyn was used to her saying whatever came to mind.

Sometimes, she had a filter. Other times, she just said the first thing she thought of. "It's okay." she assured her. "We know you didn't mean anything by it."

"I just...I can't believe they're gone." said Faith.

Evelyn replied. "Yeah." she said solemnly. "We know how you feel."

"Evelyn, could you slow down a bit?" Steven said. "You're driving like a maniac."

She turned to look at Steven, and shot him a dirty look, before locking her eyes back on the road. "We have to get to Ash as soon as possible, alright?"

"Well, it's gonna be kinda hard to do that if you flip this tin can over."

Faith pushed herself off from her seat and poked her head out from between the two of them, propping her elbows on both of their seats. "Guys," Faith said as she stared at the road that seemed to propel toward them. She had a tough time finding her balance at first. "I'd hate to sound really cheesy right now, but...what *is* our plan, exactly?"

Evelyn mashed her lips together, as if it were a reaction to her unwillingness to admit that she had nothing. Begrudgingly, she told them, "I don't really know right now." She didn't have to look at them to know that they were giving her the same look that she gave Steven not too long ago. "But, I know we have to find some way to get Ash out of there. We need him to get the book."

"Oh, sure." Steven sounded nonchalant, but Evelyn knew he was being overtly sarcastic. "Let me just reach in my wallet for the bail money." He got his wallet out and unfolded it. "What do you think, Evelyn? Is twenty-eight dollars gonna be enough? Maybe if I throw in a gift card. That should do it, huh?"

Faith gave him a punch in the shoulder. "Fine!" she said. "*You* come up with something!"

Steven didn't say a word. Instead, he leaned back into his seat and stared out the window. He couldn't come up with anything either, and he felt awful because of it.

Faith sat back in her seat while Evelyn spoke to them. “I’m just as angry about this as you are, but I don’t know what else there is to do.”

The entire time they had been driving, Faith couldn’t help but stare at the dirty sheet on the floor. It seemed to cover something, but she didn’t know what it was. She decided to ask Evelyn. “Hey,” she said to get her attention. “do you know what’s under this sheet?”

Evelyn had never noticed it before, so when Faith mentioned it, she was especially curious. Since yesterday, Evelyn wondered what Ash had kept hidden in the backseat. “No, I don’t.” she said. “Why don’t you check and see? I’m kind of curious.”

As Faith lifted the white sheet, which was stained with dirt and spots of dried blood, she overheard Steven continue to bug Evelyn about her driving.

“I’m just saying, I think I should drive. With the speed that you’re going, one sharp turn, and this car’s flying.”

After lifting the sheet, Faith found a large duffel bag on the floor. She grabbed it and tried to lift it, and was surprised as to how heavy it was. It felt like someone had packed a couple of bricks in it. She was able to eventually lift it up and plant it on the seat to her right.

Evelyn sniped at Steven while Faith examined the bag. “Can you please just relax, Steven? Do you know how many times I’ve driven the El Camino? This thing really isn’t any different.”

“Why would Ash drive this piece of crap anyway?” he groaned. “If he hunts demons all day, shouldn’t he be in something more high-tech?”

Faith unzipped the duffel bag and opened it wide to see what was inside.

“I don’t know.” Evelyn replied. “Why don’t you ask him when we get there?”

When she looked inside, she was baffled at what she found. In the duffel bag contained Ash’s trusty chainsaw, his Boomstick, and his newest edition, the pump-action shotgun. There were also three boxes of shotgun shells, two of which were empty.

The first thing that came out of her mouth was, "Whoa!"

Evelyn and Steven ceased their arguing to acknowledge Faith.

"What's in it?" asked Evelyn.

Still in shock, Faith exclaimed, "Ash is packin'!"

"What? You mean guns?" asked Steven. "What kind of stuff's in it?"

Faith listed each item in the bag to Evelyn and Steven. "Let's see." she said, almost giddy. "We have two shotguns, some ammo," she grinned at the last item in Ash's artillery. "and a motherfuckin' chainsaw!"

"What?" Steven whipped around to see them for himself. When he saw the double-barrel, the pump shotgun, and the chainsaw, his first reaction was, "Nice." But then he realized, *Wait. I don't know how to use either of those things.*

"Great." said Evelyn. "So what do we do with them?"

Faith joked. "Use the shotgun to blow a hole in the wall, then saw the bars to break him out?"

"Come on, Faith. I'm serious." she said. "If something happens to us, or Ash, we need to figure out how to use those weapons."

"Speaking of which," Steven added. "Do you even know where you're going?"

Evelyn was growing tiresome of Steven constantly nitpicking her every move. And she wasn't in the condition to tolerate criticism. "Yes, Steven." she said through gritted teeth. "The police station's just a few blocks away."

Steven leaned back in his seat, groaned, and rubbed his eyelids.

She became anticipatory. She knew that in less than a few minutes, they would be at the police station and they would be one step closer to finding Ash. She actually started to feel calm. The same feeling she wished Steven shared with her.

As she stared down the road, looking within the range that the headlights and streetlamps allowed her to see, she noticed something in the distance. She squinted her eyes, and leaned in to focus. It appeared to be people, and lots of them, out in the middle of the street downtown. “What are all these people doing here?” She blinked her eyes a few times, making sure that she actually saw what she thought she was seeing. Evelyn was definitely seeing people at the end of the block, probably ten of them, lined out in the middle of the street. They were blocking their path. “Hey,” she said to alert Steven and Faith. “do you guys see that?”

Evelyn began to slow down as both of them confirmed her suspicions.

“What the hell are they doing there?” asked Faith.

“There just...standing there...waiting, or something.” she observed.

Steven tapped her on the shoulder. “Get a closer look at them.” he said. “Turn on your brights.”

Evelyn pulled the handle toward her, turning on the brights. She had slowed down to about ten miles per hour by this time.

Now that they were completely visible, the three of them could see that these were not ordinary people. Each and every one of them looked disfigured, grotesque, and hungry. They were Deadites. Every last one of them. And their pale eyes, which seemed to glow in the night, were locked on the three of them.

Evelyn stopped the car completely, and felt her whole body freeze.

Faith leaned in close to the two of them, she looked mortified. “What *are* those things?”

“This is why we need Ash.” Evelyn said.

Steven grabbed Faith’s hand and held it tightly. “God,” he gasped. “there’s so many of them.” he turned to Faith. “Do we have enough bullets?”

Faith reached into the bag and found the boxes of shells. She threw out the two empty ones. “I don’t know.” she said disappointingly. “There’s only one box left.”

“Oh, come on!” yelled Steven. “Who only packs one friggin’ box!”

Faith snapped. “Just shut up and help me load this!” she handed him the double-barrel and two shells. Faith resumed loading the pump shotgun. *I would give anything to be anywhere but here right now.*

Evelyn watched them move towards the car. "They're getting closer." she said. "I'll back up, and you guys roll down your windows." Evelyn grabbed the handle and prepared to change gears.

CRASH!!!

Something landed on the hood of the Delta 88. The three of them gasped and the force of the crash almost made them fall out of their seats. It was like whatever it was had fallen from the sky.

Simultaneously, the three of them looked up and saw that the front window had been cracked jaggedly from corner to corner. The hood was dented. Crouched like a gargoyle atop the hood of Ash's Oldsmobile, was a scowling Freddy Krueger. His eyes glowed in the night, like a monster hiding in the trees. The rims of his eyes and the corners of his mouth were inky black and his burn marks had become even more red and made him appear more demonic. He showed his bloody, fanged teeth to them, which made them scream.

I just love it when they scream.

He looked intensely at Evelyn. He tilted his head, and lifted his gloved hand and bobbed the knives up and down, waving at her. Then, he flicked his tongue like a snake. A filthy, perverted, snake.

Evelyn switched the gearshift to Reverse. "Bastard!" she yelled at him as she took her foot off of the brake. She punched the accelerator and sped in reverse. Inertia caused the three of them to lean forward a few inches.

Freddy was knocked off of the hood and rolled onto the road.

Evelyn turned the car at an angle and stomped on the brakes. The side that had the rolled-down windows now faced Freddy. She turned to both of her friends. "Shoot him!" she ordered. "Now!"

They did what Evelyn told them to. Steven and Faith both stuck the shotguns out of the window and aimed at Freddy. At the same time, they both pulled the trigger. The two shotgun blasts sounded like one.

BOOM!!!

They managed to hit him. Shotgun ammo had been sprayed all over Freddy's chest. Blood sprayed from his wounds, and he bled like a waterfall. But he was still standing up, like it didn't affect him at all. He looked injured, but they were sure that the blast should have killed him, or at least knocked him down.

Evelyn turned to another street while Steven and Faith panicked.

"He's still alive." Steven announced in awe.

"What do we do now?" Faith asked.

"I'm going another way. I think we can lose them." she said, and proceeded to find an alternate route to the Springwood PD.

Freddy ran his left hand across his chest, feeling the warm blood that excreted from him. He held his wet, bloody hand up to his face and looked in disdain. *That fucking hurt like hell.* He grimaced and lowered his hand, balling it up into a fist. He watched the little brats as they drove away. After they had escaped, Freddy turned his attention to the group of Deadites wandering around, looking for fresh meat. "Ah..." Freddy said to himself. "I think I have an idea."

And just as quickly as he appeared, Freddy faded away from the waking world and returned back to the dream world, his lair, where he would plot his next move.

Chapter 24

FREDDY STROLLED DOWN THE WALKWAYS of the now cavernous boiler room. The sound of his leather work boots landing against the grate echoed, joining the atmospheric back round of the roaring fire from the furnaces, and the steam hissing from the pipes on the boilers that filled the room. The bullet wounds in his chest were still fresh. Wherever he walked, Freddy left droplets of his own blood behind him. Amongst the chorus of dissonant noises, the echoing cries of tortured, infant, children could faintly be heard.

The boiler room had expanded to more than twice the size of the demolished power plant on the edge of town. It was spacious, but at in most areas, filled with tight corners that made it easy for anyone to get lost in. The more lives Freddy took, the stronger he became, and his boiler room slowly transformed into a rusty, metal version of Hell itself.

The pipes had begun to resemble large columns that lined next to each other, spewing fire at the top ends. The grated walkways seemed to stretch for miles.

The boiler room appeared to be roughly five stories tall. A few metal chains hung down from the ceiling, but it was so high that none of them reached the floor. The flames that surrounded the room gave the entire place a reddish glow.

The nightmare killer slowly descended down each flight of stairs until he was at the very heart of his lair. A thick, gray, mist engulfed the floor. Freddy looked down to examine the shotgun wound in his chest. He had already stopped bleeding, and the bullet holes were beginning to recede. As long as Freddy was in his world, he could not be harmed, and his injuries were able to heal quickly. And now that he had the Necronomicon, even in the land of the living, his strength continued to grow. But still, two shotgun shells in the chest still hurt like a bitch.

Freddy disappeared in the corner. He ventured into a dark and shameless area that only the unlucky have seen. In the middle of this area was a cellar door that led further down. Down to a place where Freddy used to slowly cut and slice the children of Springwood. It was also where the Necronomicon was kept, buried beneath the floor.

When Freddy was alive, he had no idea the malevolent powers that was hidden beneath his own feet. Only after that fateful night when the parents of the murdered children came for him, did he discover the spirits trapped within the book, and become part of it as well. The dark spirits: not just the Deadites, but also the trio of Dream Demons that hunted for the sickest, most evil soul on earth to do their will, lived inside the pages of the Necronomicon. That was when Freddy knew of the book's wicked powers. And after years of defeat and being sent back to the dark bowers of Hell, did he decide to go to the ultimate source of evil, and become the most powerful Deadite of them all.

With a simple flick of one of the knives on Freddy's glove, the cellar door was opened by an unseen force. Freddy had become so powerful that he barely had to lift a finger to do move objects around. He descended down the steps of the cellar, and was brought deep down into an area filled with memories of torture, agony, and the theft of innocence.

In the middle of the cellar was an area similar to the boiler room, only smaller in size. In the corner was a workbench where Freddy had built his infamous glove. A few pieces of scrap metal, copper from the plating, spare steak knives, a hammer, and a rivet tool still laid out on the bench. All around the cellar were various items that once belonged to Freddy's previous victims. They were trophies of his gruesome killings.

In one corner was a small bed with white sheets and a blue cover, stained with the blood of fifteen-year-old Tina Grey. Freddy had dragged her up the wall and across the ceiling of her bedroom, all the while gutting her like a fish. Once he was done with her, he dropped her onto her bed. She splashed into a pool of her own blood. Freddy walked by the bed, noting the blood-stained wooden cross in the very center of Tina's bed that she used to hang on her wall for protection.

Next, was a pair of headphones that sat on a table next Tina's bed. The headphones were green, at least, they used to be until they were bathed in the blood of another poor victim of his, Glen Lantz. Glen made the mistake of falling asleep while in bed, so Freddy dragged him down and spit him back up. As he recalled, Glen's blood gushed out like Old Faithful.

On the wall next to the headphones, was a puppet hanging on Marionette strings. It belonged to a Westin Hills patient named Joey. Freddy sliced little Joey up and used his own nerve endings as puppet strings. He led him up to the tallest point of the hospital, and once Freddy separated his ties from him, Joey took a long fall to his death.

Another item on the table was an inhaler that belonged to a Springwood High student named Sheila. Poor Sheila had asthma, so Freddy thought he would give her the "kiss of death". The bastard literally sucked the life out of her.

And, separated from most of the items on the table, like it was given a special place of its own, was a lock of white hair from Nancy Thompson. Nancy was the daughter of Don and Marge, two of the parents who burned him. Nancy was so sweet and innocent, but Freddy doubted how tough she was. He might of been able to frighten her and kill those around her, but Nancy refused to go down without a fight, even in the end. Even though she had escaped his clutches once, she still couldn't save herself while protecting the children of Elm Street.

Finally, at the very end of the table, was a chipped off piece of a hockey mask that belonged to his most previous enemy: Jason Voorhees. A part of Jason's mask had chipped away during battle. Even though the dumb fuck is still alive, Freddy kept it anyway. It reminded him how easy it was to manipulate his victims.

In the very center of his shrine was the Book of the Dead sitting on a small bench. It seemed to stare at him, the human skin that materialized it seemed to resemble a face that expressed both evil and torment.

Freddy stood before it, grazing the book with his knives. His eyes, fixed upon the book, glowed eerily in the darkness. His voice was low and monstrous. "Let's see..." he murmured, speaking to the book. "What can I do with you?" Freddy sliced the cover of the book as he brought the gloved hand close to him and wriggled the knives. "You've given me another chance at life, even given me pawns to collect more souls for me." he said, referring to the Deadites that became of his victims. "But, what am I gonna do about Ash..." Freddy scowled and clenched his left hand into a fist. "That arrogant son of a bitch." He flicked the knife on his index finger, opening the book to the passage that contained the three Dream Demons, the ones who gave him the job in the first place.

At that moment, the pages glowed, and three serpentine spirits lifted themselves from the pages of the book and hovered before him. They appeared in a veil of glowing orange light. The demons had the bodies of a snake, skeletal heads, and soulless black eyes. The three of them floated around Freddy's face. When they spoke, it sounded like an echoing hiss.

"It's been a long time since we last saw each other, Freddy." said the demon as it wrapped itself around Freddy's glove.

Annoyed, Freddy immediately shook it off of him.

"Have you called upon our services once more?" said one demon that floated behind his head.

Freddy brushed the Dream Demons away from him. "I don't need you worms anymore!" he said. "I've found my own way back to the waking world."

The third demon slithered its way up his arm, and was an inch away from Freddy's face. "But," it teased. "you seek a way to rid yourself of the Chosen One."

The first one spoke again. "By collecting the soul of the Chosen One, you, Freddy Krueger, will have nothing standing in your way from controlling the lands of the dead and the living."

The demon wrapped around Freddy's arms spoke again. "Summon and lead a legion of evil, and Ash will not stand a chance against you."

The second Dream Demon slithered across his shoulder. "Only you can defeat him." he said. "Find what weakens him, and use that to bring Ash closer to death."

"Yes!" hissed the third demon. "The Chosen One must die!"

The second demon continued. "You must make yourself strong enough to go against him."

Freddy was sick of having those slimy bastards wrapped around him. He had already become more powerful than the Dream Demons themselves. He no longer had to do their bidding. He decided to give them a sign of resignation.

Freddy took the snake-like demon that was wrapped around his arm and pulled it off of him, squeezing the life out of it. Soon enough, the demon began to disintegrate into nothing but a pile of ash. Its scream echoed as it faded away.

The two other demons began to flee from him, retreating back to the book, but Freddy flicked his knife up and the other two were engulfed in flames, and turned into ash.

You must make yourself strong enough to go against him. Freddy smiled at the Dream Demon's previous remark. He chuckled and in his graveled voice, he answered, "Check."

Officer Harris and Lt. Moore walked side by side with Ash down the steps in front of the Springwood PD. They had their guns ready in case any Deadites should happen to attack.

Ash turned to his left to face Moore. "So, you've dealt with this guy longer than I have." he referred to Freddy. "Tell me, how did those kids get rid of him before?"

Lt. Moore was hesitant to give Ash information he was sworn not to tell out in the open, but he figured that since this is unlike any case he had ever dealt with, it was time to break a few rules. "In previous cases, when we interviewed those kids, they said they could pull Freddy out from their dream."

Ash stopped and looked at him with inquiry. "And then what?" he asked.

"Well, in one case, a young lady said she turned her back from him. She took back the energy she gave him by being afraid."

Ash scoffed. "Ignore the bully and he'll leave you alone?" *Who taught these guys how to deal with killers, my teacher from third grade?* "No wonder Scissorhands keeps coming back."

Lt. Moore leered at him. "I see you weren't paying attention during the whole right to remain silent portion of your Miranda Rights."

"I've never been one to keep my mouth shut about things." said Ash. "Especially when you give out crappy advice like that."

Officer Harris looked at Ash's metal hand and taunted him. "At least I can play the piano."

Ash snapped and pointed a finger at him. "You know what? You ain't leaving but two things right now–"

SCREEEECH!!!

Ash's was about to finish by saying, "Jack and shit. And Jack left town." when he was halted when the three of them became distracted by the sound of squealing tires coming from the end of the block. He looked in the direction it was coming from and saw his Oldsmobile racing towards the police station. The sound of the engine roaring became louder the closer it came to them.

The car stopped in front of Ash, Lt. Moore, and Officer Harris. Before Ash could try to spot the people inside, Evelyn, Steven, and Faith opened the doors and ran out.

Evelyn ran up to Ash, who was now at the bottom step. Steven and Faith followed behind. "Ash!" greeted Evelyn.

Ash examined the kids lined up in front of him, and noticed that there was one missing.

She could tell by the look on his face that he noticed Jill was not with them. "He took Jill." she said.

Ash turned to Steven. "I'm sorry."

Steven didn't feel like talking, especially after the scare he had a few minutes earlier. Instead, he looked at Ash and nodded subtly.

"So, they just let you go?" asked Evelyn.

"Yes, ma'am." answered Ash. "I'm that good." He stepped away from everyone and walked to his car. "Now, if you'll excuse me, I'll–" Once Ash got a closer look at his Oldsmobile, he finally saw the giant dent on the hood and the crack on the front window. "The hell did you do to my car?!"

"Krueger decided to pay us a visit." said Faith.

Ash turned away from his car to face the kids. "Freddy's here now?"

Evelyn nodded. "Yeah." She looked past Ash when she noticed something odd in the back ground. She tilted her head to get a better view. Her face dropped when she saw the same hoard of Deadites that they saw before had followed them to the police station. And they were running towards them. "And so are they." she said cryptically.

Ash turned in the direction that Evelyn was looking, and saw that in the middle of the intersection across from them were a hoard of Deadites. He counted ten of them, running as fast at they could towards them.

Lt. Moore shouted. "Everybody down!" He and Officer Harris drew their pistols.

Evelyn, Steven, and Faith crouched down to the ground while both of the policemen fired their weapons at the demons.

Ash, however, reached through the back window of his Delta 88 and grabbed his chainsaw and his double-barreled Remington. He also made sure to nab the shotgun holster that strapped around his back.

Moore and Harris fired a few shots at the Deadites, mostly in the chest area. It slowed them down, but it didn't kill them.

Ash forgave them for that. How were they supposed to know you had to shoot them in the head and chop them to bits?

"They won't stay down!" said Harris, fearfully.

"Call for backup!" instructed Moore.

Ash stood up and equipped his chainsaw to his right nub. "I don't think that'll be necessary." he said confidently.

He pointed the twin barrels at the Deadite second to the right. He pulled the trigger.

BOOM!!!

The demon's head burst. His neck was now gushing with thick blood. His headless body dropped down to the concrete.

Ash set his sights on the demon at the far right.

He executed this one the same way he did the last, with blood spilling on the road around his body as he fell down.

Ash put away his shotgun, resting it in his holster. He only had two bullets in his pistol, so he made sure not to waste them. He pulled out the pistol and shot two more Deadites.

Moore and Harris noticed what Ash was doing and began killing a few Deadites of their own. This time, they made sure to aim for the head.

All but three Deadites were wasted. The remaining three charged toward them at ramming speed. The foul beasts howled and hissed as they ran to Ash and the kids.

Ash hooked the pull-rope to his shoulder strap and started his chainsaw. The chainsaw rumbled loudly.

RRRRRRRRRRrrrrrrrrrRRRRRRRRRR!!!

That's what I like to hear. thought Ash. He looked at the demons as they charged and held the chainsaw up in the air. "COME AND GET IT!!!"

Two Deadites came running towards Ash. They laughed maniacally, and exposed the insides of their slimy mouths.

Ash held the chainsaw in front of him and rammed inside one of the demon's chest. The Deadite shook violently and screamed in pain. He bled heavily, causing some of it to spray in Ash's face. Ash directed the chainsaw upward, splitting the demon in half. Once he released the chainsaw from the Deadite's body, it fell to the ground.

Another demon came from behind the last one. Her scream was like nails on a chalkboard as she ran towards Ash.

He acted quickly. Gripping the handle with his right hand, Ash swung the chainsaw horizontally, cutting the demon off at the torso.

The last Deadite came charging up the stairs to attack Moore and Harris. Before it could reach them, Moore shot it between the eyes. It fell and tumbled down the concrete steps, leaving a trail of blood behind as it went down.

Evelyn, Steven, and Faith had stayed crouched to the ground during the whole attack. Once the gunfire was over, they felt safe enough to get back up.

Evelyn looked up from the ground, and saw the legless torso of one of the Deadites crawling towards her.

"I'll devour your soul!" hissed the Deadite. It then cackled as it got closer to Evelyn.

Evelyn backed away before she saw Ash walking in front of her.

Ash put his foot under the Deadite and flipped her over on her back. She flailed her arms around, trying to grab his legs, but he laid his foot on her stomach to make her still.

With his shotgun in hand, Ash blasted the Deadites head to pieces.

BOOM!!!

He put away his shotgun and helped Evelyn get back on her feet.

Moore and Harris walked down the steps to join Ash and the kids.

"We should set up roadblocks around the town." announced Moore. "That way those things can't get more people."

"I don't think that'll do any good, sir." Harris said. The tone of his voice suggested that something was off-kilter.

Moore turned to Harris, who was looking up at the night sky the whole time. "Why do you say that?"

Harris pointed up and gulped, like he was swallowing down a blood-curdling scream. "That's why."

Moore, Ash, as well as the kids all looked up at the sky, and saw horrors beyond their imagination.

The clouds in the sky seemed to swirl around, centering on the moon, which had turned red as blood. Filling the air were twenty or so winged Deadites. They were monsters that Ash had only seen once before, back when he was transported to the Medieval ages. They were roughly seven feet tall. The Deadites had the upper body and legs of a human. Their feet and hands were clawed. Their wings were fleshy and were twice the size of the rest of their bodies. Their white eyes glowed in the night, and their jaws were elongated, showing rows upon rows of rotten fangs.

All twenty-plus Deadites shrieked like banshees in the sky, piercing everyone's ears. They circled around the sky like vultures, waiting to attack.

Ash groaned. "Not these guys again."

One of the winged Deadites propelled downward, charging toward Ash. Its scream became louder as it flew down.

"Damn it!" Ash cursed. He reached for more bullets in his shirt pocket and quickly reloaded his shotgun.

The flying demon was now only twenty feet away from Ash. It opened up its claws in anticipation for Ash's capture.

Ash cocked the shotgun and pointed it straight at the demon. He pulled the trigger and blasted it in the head.

BOOM!!!

The headless winged demon fell down to the ground. The monstrous Deadite landed on the concrete and slid another fifteen feet across the streets of downtown Springwood.

All of the kids gaped in awe after having witnessed the killing of the horrible beast.

"That was fucking awesome." said Faith, matter-of-factly.

Ash smiled at her and put away his shotgun. "And it's only Thursday." he said with a cocky tone. "You should see me on the weekends." he bragged.

Before Ash could head back to his car, he immediately felt pressure on both of his shoulders. He found himself being hurled from the ground.

Another winged Deadite had sunk its claws into Ash and lifted him from the air.

"Ash!" Evelyn cried out.

Ash screamed in terror. "Aaaaah!" He knew it wouldn't make a difference, but he couldn't help but flail his arms and legs and taunt the demon. "Let go of me, you mangy bat!"

The flying demon hovered over the town for a few seconds after that, until it flew down and lowered one of its wings, and spun around in a circle. When it gained enough momentum, the Deadite released its grip on Ash, causing him to be propelled toward the front of a building.

Ash screamed, knowing he was going to be knocked against it. He smacked face-first against the brick wall and fell down to the ground. He groaned in pain before everything went black, and he fell unconscious.

Chapter 25

ASH FELT HIMSELF SLIPPING AWAY. He could hear people rushing to him, and calling his name, but it was no good. The outside world faded into darkness. The voices of those around him echoed as he fell further into the dream.

And then, everything fell silent. It was as if everything else in the world had ceased to exist. He couldn't even hear himself breathe. He had been in this place before. He couldn't count how many times he had been knocked out, but this time it felt different. He felt as if he was being physically pulled deeper into the dark, and he couldn't fight it.

After a while, Ash started to wonder if the crash had actually killed him. *Am I dead? Wait–no. If I'm asking myself that, then I can't be dead. Well, if I'm not dead, where am I? Where am I going? I should've never come to this town in the first place.*

And in that moment, Ash found himself standing on an old, dirt road at the edge of a cliff, overlooking the sunset. There was nothing else surrounding him other than the woods on either side of the road. Row after row of towering, rotund, trees, as well as bushes containing honeysuckle flowers, stretched down the road behind him as far as the eye could see.

He stood beside his Oldsmobile, which somehow appeared brand new. All of the cracks and dents it had acquired over the years were now gone. It looked exactly like it did when he first got it, back when he was in his twenties. Even the white, leather, interior was intact. Free of rips and tears.

There wasn't a spot in the area he was in that didn't look like a beautiful painting. There he stood in the mountains overlooking the lake that was miles below him. All of the trees were thick and full of life. The trees on Ash's left and right side were so abundant, that it formed a barricade, narrowing his path.

Off to the east, the sun was slowly setting down, becoming lost under the mess of clouds below it. The orange glow of the sunset filled the entire sky.

It was a breathtaking sight for anyone who had not been there before. But, Ash had visited this place long ago. It had been decades since he had been there, but it was all coming back to him the further he traveled. When he walked, he felt light as air, simply drifting closer to the edge of the cliff.

That was when the beautiful images ceased to occur. At the edge of the cliff was a bridge–at least, there was supposed to be a bridge–connecting the break in path in the mountain that was supposed to carry the traveler safely across. The metal bridge that connected the gap had been demolished. It looked like it had been torn down the middle, and the remaining scraps were left on both edges.

Ash stood just a few feet from the destroyed bridge. There were five metal support beams that were bent upward, jagged, and curved. They almost looked like fingers, constantly pointing at him.

His mouth gaped open, and the glimmer in his eyes went away as Ash realized that he had been taken right back to the cabin where it all began. He felt hopeless. "No..." He had to tell himself that this was only a dream. But, everything felt real. As if he had truly gone back in time. The smell of the fresh air, and the feeling of the wind gently blowing against his face only made it harder for him to convince himself that it wasn't really happening.

He knew it would be quite a while before he would be able to regain consciousness. He knew that between now and then, he was going to have to endure every trick Freddy had up his raggedy sleeve. He also knew that he was here with him, somewhere. "You miserable bastard!" he cursed him, wherever he was. "You took me right back, you son of a bitch!" Ash looked all around, searching for him. "Where are you?! Show yourself, you coward!" He put up his fists, showing Freddy that he was ready to fight. "You brought me here, I'm not leaving without a fight! Come on!"

But still, there was nothing. He looked around again, but there was no sign of Freddy's presence anywhere around him. Ash lowered his hands and smirked. "Thought so." he said. "It's easy goin' after little kids, but when you're up against someone full-size, you turn into a little pussy, don't ya!"

Ash felt the ground beneath him start to shake violently. The branches on the trees began to rustle. It felt like a small earthquake. Ash started to lose balance, and found it harder to stand still amid the rumbling ground below his feet.

CREAK!!!

Ash heard the sound of metal bending. He looked at the metal bridge beams above him. He saw that that they were moving, as if they had a life of their own. The five beams were bent in the middle. They flexed up and down, like fingers on a human hand.

His eyes widened in surprise, but he kept them locked on the moving metal support beams. *I guess calling him a pussy was taking it too far.* Ash managed to hold steady as he slowly stepped away from the cliff and made his way closer to his car.

The beams were changing rapidly in appearance. The tops of the beams thinned and formed into a sharp point, resembling animal-like claws. The beams became silver, and shined under the rays of the orange sun.

The support beams had now fully morphed into the blades atop Freddy's glove. The five blade broke away from the edge of the cliff and rose higher, revealing the rest of Freddy's copper-plated glove, and also showing part of his red and green striped sweater on his wrist. His hand was now raised above Ash's body, at a height of fifteen feet and a width of eight feet. Freddy targeted his blades at Ash, and began to quickly lower them down.

Ash made a 180 degree turn, and ran to his car. As Ash reached out to grab the door handle. He felt one of the blades latch onto the back of his leather jacket and pull him back.

"Oof!" Ash exclaimed as he fell hard onto the ground, landing on his back. He felt the ground move beneath him as Freddy used his blade to, slowly and smoothly, drag him closer to the edge of the cliff. He fidgeted, waving his arms and moving his shoulders up and down, but he could not release himself from Freddy's grip. He tilted his head upward and saw the edge get closer and closer.

Wait a second... Feeling like an idiot, Ash realized that all he had to do was take off the jacket. He slid the leather jacket over his head. Once he was finally free, Ash stood up and ran as fast as his feet would allow.

He opened the door to his Oldsmobile and hopped in. He slammed the door shut and panted heavily as he turned the ignition. *I swear, if this thing pulls a horror cliché on me and won't start, I'm gonna be really pissed.* Fortunately for him, his car was able to start without trouble.

He looked ahead and saw Freddy's gargantuan arm extended above the edge of the cliff. Without a second thought, Ash put the car in Reverse and stomped on the accelerator. Ash sped in reverse as Freddy pierced the ground with his steel blades, each stab marked closer to Ash.

Ash drove this way for a short distance. He nervously looked behind him to see where he was going, and in front to watch as Freddy rose up. He stood like a giant before him.

Freddy raised his hand up in the air and struck his glove down, aiming for Ash. He missed him by a hair, and momentarily got his blades stuck in the ground.

This was enough time for Ash to turn his car around, put it in Drive, and speed down the pathway that led to the cabin. At least this way, Ash would be able to get some distance between him and Krueger.

When Freddy spotted the fumbling demon slayer slip from away from him, he was filled with rage. *That tool thinks he can run away from me? I don't think so!* He clenched his fists and snarled. His fury had affected the environment around him. This was the dream realm. It did and acted however Freddy wanted it to. And when Freddy was pissed, that was when darkness fell.

The warm, beautiful, sunset had now dropped like a basketball from a clumsy kid's hands. It grew ever darker, and that frightful darkness was covering the sky like a tarp. The leaves on the trees shriveled up and fell the ground. The bark had decayed to a pale gray.

Freddy lifted his feet and chased after Ash, moving slowly, but still getting closer to him. His booming voice reverberated all throughout the woods. He taunted Ash as he moved closer. "FEE FI FO FUM, I SMELL THE BLOOD OF THE CHOSEN ONE!"

Ash lifted his gaze from the dirt road to the rear view mirror. He saw Freddy coming towards him, and getting closer as the seconds went by. "Damn it," Ash said under his breath. "He's getting closer."

Since Freddy now stood at such an incredible height, he didn't have to move quickly in order to shorten the distance between him and Ash. Wherever he went, darkness followed, and encapsulated the sky. In a matter of seconds, the entire sky had turned black. It became increasingly difficult for Ash to see in front of him.

There's a good chance I could crash and flip this thing over any second now. I could ram it against a tree and not even see it coming...like last time. Guess I should learn from my mistakes, huh? Ash turned on the headlights, and saw that the cabin was just down the hill. All he had to do was get there before Freddy could get to him.

Ash drove down the hill, narrowly weaving past the trees and brush as he descended further down. His nerves had gotten the best of him. He gripped the steering wheel tighter, his hands shook uncontrollably, and his heart started to beat rapidly. Ash worried that he wouldn't be able to make it in time. *What happens if Freddy actually wins this time? What'll happen to everyone? What'll happen to me?*

He looked back in the mirror again, and much to his surprise, Freddy was gone. It was like he just disappeared in the woods somewhere. Ash had no idea where he could have gone. Frankly, he didn't care. As long as he could get to the cabin safely, maybe–just maybe–he could steal the Necronomicon back from Freddy, and wake up in time to undo this mess.

Ash stopped the car once he was a few yards from the front of the old, wooden cabin. He didn't bother to turn the car or the lights off. *Freddy might be able to kill me here, but I don't think wasting the gas will have any effect the classic.* Ash jumped out of the car and walked towards the cabin.

It was exactly as Ash had remembered it. A small, one-story cabin, smack dab in the middle of the woods. There was one window on each side of the front door. The windows had been crudely boarded up, while the door had two holes right in the middle. The shingles were old, the wood was rotting, and the chain holding the swing on the front porch seemed like it was about to break at any second. He looked back just to make sure Freddy was nowhere to be seen.

The air was quiet. Aside from all of the dead trees and fog everywhere, it was actually calming. There was absolutely no noise, except for the light whistling coming from the wind. Ash felt safe enough to put his foot on the front porch step, and proceed to the cabin.

His ears twitched. Something was not right. Ash heard a low moan coming from the distance. It was a low, warbled hum that Ash only heard when something horrible was going to happen. It was the unseen force making its way towards him. The sound became unnervingly louder.

Ash turned back around and saw the evil. It was heading towards him at a daunting speed. Once he confirmed his suspicions, Ash ran to the cabin, opened the door and slammed it shut, stopping the evil from making contact with him.

The evil, only seen by the unlucky ones who fall prey to its demonic hold, exuded something different about it. It forced itself upon the front door, putting intense pressure on the door handles, hoping it would bust open. Its deep, dark, moan shook the entire cabin. Before retreating back into the forest, it sent Ash a warning sign. Piercing through the walls beside the front door, were the four, steel, blades belonging to Freddy's glove.

Inside, on the other side of the cabin, Ash barricaded the door by standing in front of it, holding his arms out wide to hold either side. He kept one ear to the door, listening and waiting for the evil to go away. Once the noise had stopped, Ash lowered his arms and stepped away from the door. He took a deep breath in and out to calm himself. After the commotion was over, Ash realized that he had been sweating bullets the entire time. Ash wiped the sweat from his forehead with his palm, and ran it across his black hair. He sidestepped to the window to make sure it actually gone. There was nothing out there, aside from the fog that settled at the ground.

Ash took the time he had to walk around the inside of the cabin. It was dimly lit, the only sources of light came from the few small reading lamps in the corner. The rest of the room was filled with shadows.

It was so much like how he remembered it, right down to the blood splattered walls. It was quite frightening. He turned to his right and paced around the room in a counter-clockwise pattern. He walked past the end table with the small reading lamp, the rocking chair in the corner that gave him an eerie feeling to look at it. Judging from the way that it faced him, he felt like it was staring at him. Next to that was the fireplace with the deer head mounted above. He stared at the buck for a brief moment, remembering what it did last time he was here–briefly re-animating to laugh at him and drive him further into insanity. *Good times.* He quickly brushed it off and walked past. The pale, wooden floorboards creaked with almost every step that he took around the living area of the cabin.

Before crossing to the opposite side of the room, Ash passed a faded wooden table that contained a stack of books pushed up against the corner, a green-shaded reading lamp, and an old tape recorder.

It was inside those recordings that held the phonetic pronunciations of the Necronomicon. And Ash was dumb enough to listen. *If only I hadn't pressed Play.* It was hard not to dwell on the past when those cruel reminders were now all around him. And for the time being, there was no escape.

Ash only looked at it briefly before making his way to the other side of the room.

There was an old couch with most of the upholstery faded and torn. Beside it was a grandfather clock that had stopped ticking. The hands were locked at 9:16. And on the floor was the entrance to the fruit cellar. It was simply a square cut in the floorboards with a chain wrapped around locks in each corner, keeping the entrance secure.

Being back was unnerving for him. He knew that this wasn't real, that it was just a dream, yet another of Freddy's dirty tricks. But the fact that he knew so much about the horrors he had experienced here, and that he was exploiting those fears, it made Ash feel violated. He knew that Freddy has been inside his mind. Through each and every dark corner, and knows his every fear, weakness, and anything else he can and would use to defeat him.

Ash shook it off. He kept reminding himself what his reason was for being here. He mumbled to himself as he stared down cellar entrance. "The book–right, right–I gotta find the book." Ash looked away from the cellar and gazed out the window. "Question is, where is he keeping it?"

CREAK!

Ash whipped around and looked out into the hallway, where the noise had come from. He expected Freddy to come out from the shadows. Ash was eager to blow the bastard's head off. He reached for his shotgun and aimed it, preparing for Freddy to rear his ugly head, literally.

Stepping out from the shadows, at first, was the sight of a delicate, bare foot. Hanging just a couple of inches above the ankle, was a flowing, lacy, white, nightgown. A woman fully emerged out from the dark.

Her strawberry blonde hair nestled just below her pale shoulders. Her brown eyes twinkled and her full, pink, lips curled up into a smile when she saw Ash.

"Linda..." he said, surprised.

It may have been because his last memory of her was sawing her possessed body with a chainsaw, but she appeared more beautiful than ever before. However, Ash never let his guard down. He knew exactly what this was. But, still...he had loved her so much. A part of him was just happy to see her again, this time without the lacerations and cadaver eyes.

Linda walked closer to him, smiling and holding her arms open to him. "Oh, Ash!" she said joyfully. "It's really you!"

Ash held his ground. As much as he wanted to hold her again, he knew that it wouldn't be right. The aimed the shotgun in front of Linda. "Stay back." he ordered.

Her eyes began to glisten with tears. Her lips quivered and she lowered her arms to her side. "Ash..." her voice was light and soothing. "I only came to say goodbye." Linda held her silver, looking glass necklace close to her chest. "We never got to say goodbye. Oh Ash, I've missed you so much."

His hand began to shake, and he couldn't hold the shotgun to Linda's face any longer. He put his finger off of the trigger and lowered it down to the ground. He said only what he felt to be the truth. "I've missed you too, Linda." He thought that it would be best to get closure, because it would be the only chance he would get.

Linda ran into his arms and hugged him tightly. She buried her head into his chest.

Ash put his shotgun back into his holster and returned her hug. He decided that for the time being, he would savor the moment. He knew that this would be the only way he could have the chance hold Linda close in his arms one last time.

"I love you so much." said Linda.

Ash felt a knot forming in his throat as he fought back tears. "I love you too, Linda." he said. "I never stopped loving you."

Because it wasn't the real Linda, he knew he couldn't let his guard down for very long. In this world, he didn't know what might happen. It was false closure and false comfort, but still, it was the only kind he was ever going to get. Ash closed his eyes and held her close.

Linda spoke to him. She kept her head ducked down, so her voice was slightly muffled. Her tone was seductive. "If you could just do one thing for me, Ash?" she said.

His eyes shot open, and his eyebrows scrunched in confusion. *This is gonna turn bad real quick, isn't it?* "What?" he asked, waiting for things to go sour.

There was a hint of coyness in her response. "Could you get me an aspirin?" she asked.

Ash could feel her pushing away from him. He let go of her as she stepped back and lifted her head up.

By then, her voice had become shrill and modulated. It was frightening to the core. Her skin was now white as porcelain. Her eyes were blank, bloodshot, and black at the rims. She oozed black blood from her mouth, and her teeth were thick and fang-like. "'CAUSE I HAVE A SPLITTING HEADACHE!!!". On the top of her head, just off-center, was a large, gaping, jagged, split. Skeletal fragments and brains were partially exposed, and blood constantly poured from the wound.

Ash stepped back and pulled his hands away from her. He didn't feel afraid. He wasn't shocked or surprised. He was just disappointed. For a brief moment, he thought that maybe he could live the rest of his life without having Linda's mutilated body be the last image he had of her. That opportunity was taken from him in a matter of seconds.

He reached for his shotgun and prepared to shoot Linda, when she did something very strange. Strange enough that it made Ash pause.

Linda cackled loudly and tilted her head back during her burst of insane laughter. Her head kept leaning further back, and her voice became even more strained until it was but a guttural growl, and then eventually ceased. By that point, Linda's head had disconnected from her neck completely and fell to the ground. It thudded on the hard wood floor, briefly bouncing back up. The rest of her body soon followed, falling lifeless to the ground.

Ash stared in a mixture of disgust and confusion. He was frozen in place. Ash didn't know if he should shoot her, or just leave her alone.

Then, the body started to twitch.

He tensed up. He leaned in and put his finger on the trigger.

Linda began to bend her legs and her arms, planting her hands and feet firmly on the floor. She lifted herself from the ground and crawled out of the room. Her decapitated head, on its own, rolled out. She retreated back into the darkness where she had come from.

Still gripping the shotgun tightly, Ash stared wild-eyed into the dark hallway where Linda had disappeared. *I think I'm starting to get a taste of what Freddy likes to do to his victims.*

Tap...Tap...Tap...Tap...

Ash looked around the room to spot where the tapping noise was coming from. He couldn't seem to find who was doing it, or where it was coming from.

Scrreeeechhhh!!!

It was the sound of metal blades scraping against a hard surface. The noise was ear piercing, and made Ash flinch.

Tap...Tap...Tap...Tap...

Scrreeeechhhh!!!

Ash knew that Freddy was with him, but he didn't know where. It drove him crazy.

"Ha ha ha ha ha..."

Gotcha! Ash heard Freddy laughing in the hallway. He readied his shotgun and soon heard the soft thudding of his footsteps coming closer towards him. "Come on out, Freddy!" he dared him. "I've had enough of your bullshit!"

Freddy emerged from the hallway, grinning and keeping his gloved hand held up to his side. In his left hand, Freddy carried Linda's head, grabbing a clump of her hair and swinging it back and forth.

Freddy looked different since the last time Ash had seen him. His charred skin was now even redder. His eyes were small, like a snake's. And his teeth were pointed, sharp, and shark-like. He grinned, looking back and forth between Ash and Linda. Freddy knew it pissed him off.

"You know how to pick 'em Ash." he said. "She's got a nice body, and..." Freddy held her head up in front of Ash's face. "she gives some pretty good head!" He forced Ash to stare at her lifeless face, permanently locked in a state of agony. Half of her face was split down the middle from when Ash had to kill her using his chainsaw. Freddy tilted his head to the side and taunted Ash in his graveled voice. "Love hurts, don't it?"

Rage had overcome Ash. He aimed his shot gun directly at Freddy's head. "Yeah, so do bullets!" Ash squeezed the trigger and unleashed a round of shells inside Freddy's skull.

BOOM!!! BOOM!!!

Krueger dropped to the ground and didn't speak a word. Ash couldn't see his face, but he noticed a puddle of blood growing in the spot where he landed.

Ash opened the barrels and removed the empty shells. Smoke rose from the barrels as Ash replaced them with two new ones from his shirt pocket. Once the gun was reloaded, Ash walked over to Freddy's unmoving body. He leered at him while still keeping a safe distance.

Freddy turned over and leapt back onto his feet as if nothing had happened to him. Not even a trace of the shotgun shells were visible on his charred face. Freddy stared at him with his snake-like eyes, and walked forward. With each step Freddy took, Ash took another step back. He taunted and poked Ash with the knives on his glove. "You see, *Ashley*..." he mocked. "You might have been the Chosen One in your world, but in here..." Freddy tapped his knife against his woolly sweater. "*I'm* the king."

Chapter 26

THE END WAS COMING. UNDER the moonlit sky, the swarm of Deadites hovered above the town. They circled, gradually lowering down, waiting to strike all at once. In the streets, the army of Deadites were ever-growing, and circling downtown Springwood. There were so damn many of them, and as long as Freddy continued to keep Ash in the dream realm, there was no stopping them.

Soon, the evil, under Freddy's manipulation, would take over all of Springwood. Then, his reign of terror would continue to spread, with the Deadites as his servants. All life, all youth, all innocence, would cease to exist. It would be Freddy's ultimate revenge: To rid the waking world of life and fill it with darkness. That was, unless, the mighty Chosen One were able to wake up from his dream.

Evelyn kneeled over Ash, her knees numbing from being on the concrete sidewalk. Her black hair slid from her shoulders and swung in front of her face as she tried to bring Ash back. She gently smacked her palm against his bloody cheek. "Ash, wake up!" There was no response. He was out cold. "Come on!" she yelled at his face. "Ash, please! You have to wake up!" She was careful not to shake him around too much. After getting body slammed against a brick building, getting slapped and shaken around doesn't really help much.

During her attempt to wake Ash, Evelyn heard the sound of several footsteps approaching her. She looked behind her to see Faith,

Steven, Lt. Moore, and Officer Harris running towards them. Soon, they circled around the two of them.

Faith crouched down by Evelyn and lightly grabbed her arms, pulling her away from Ash. From then, Officer Harris kneeled down and pressed two fingers on Ash's neck, checking his pulse.

He turned to Moore. "He's still breathing."

Lt. Moore didn't mean for his next remark to mean that he was disappointed, but that he was astonished. "How?" he asked.

"I don't know." Harris pointed up to one of the Deadites circling above them. "I thought that flying...whatever-that-is... would've killed him." He looked back at Moore, oddly relieved. "He's lucky."

Evelyn stood up and moved closer to the policemen. "What's gonna happen now?" she asked. "I can't wake him up, and those things are getting closer."

Faith interjected. "Yeah. What are we supposed to do? We can't just let him lie here."

"Okay, calm down." said Moore. "This is what you'll do: You three get Ash somewhere safe, and we'll fend off these...what did he call them?" Moore tried to recall what Ash called those hideous creatures. "Deadites?" he said awkwardly.

Steven chimed in. "How're we supposed to wake him up?"

"I'm not sure." said Moore. "Just do what you can."

"But," Faith said. Her tone was dark. "Freddy's gonna kill him."

Evelyn looked out to see the Deadites slowly moving in. By this time, they were a block away from the police station. They were all lined together like an undead army. Their white eyes glowed in the black of night. "No." she rebutted. "He'll want him awake to see this."

Steven bent over to lift Ash from the ground. "Okay, let's get him in the car." he put his arms under Ash's shoulders and tried to lift him.

Officer Harris helped him. "Careful with the neck." he commented while grabbing Ash's feet. "He's badly hurt."

Steven straightened his feet. He secured Ash in his arms, while still hurrying as quickly as he could to the Oldsmobile. "Yes, Sir States-the-obvious." he commented.

Lt. Moore, Evelyn, and Faith walked beside them.

"Will he be okay?" asked Evelyn.

Officer Harris replied. "He'll regain consciousness eventually." he looked at her, his expression lacking optimism. "But, it'll be awhile."

"So we have to face these things by ourselves?" asked Faith. "We're not gonna make it!"

Evelyn turned to her and cut her off. "No!" she protested. "We can do this." From her tone, what she said sounded more like a promise, instead of comforting words for Faith. "I'm not going to let Freddy win. We just have to get Ash somewhere safe, and fend them off until he wakes up."

As Steven and Officer Harris set Ash in the backseat of the car, Lt. Moore called for backup.

"Calling all units for backup." His voice was loud and commanding. "I want roadblocks set up all around town. We need cars, helicopters, every goddamn thing we have, we need out here! Now!"

Moore turned to the girls and spoke less gruff. "Get him someplace safe as quick as you can, alright? We can only handle so much, and once those things start attacking, I don't think Ash'll make it."

"Where do we take him?" asked Faith.

"I don't know." he replied. "The hospital, the schools, they're all in this area. And this place is already dangerous. He needs to get far away from here."

Evelyn mentally tackled the question herself. *Somewhere safe.* She unlocked her gaze from Moore and Faith, and began mathematically scanning the horizon. *And far away. A place with a lot of medical supplies, a lot of hiding places, stuff to barricade the doors, if need be...and a lot of weapons.* It was as if her eyes were magnetically attracted to the building on the horizon, and illuminated by a single working streetlamp next to it: S-Mart. *Of course. We'll clean him up with bandages, hide in the break room, block the doors with 2x4's, and unlock the display cases to get guns.* "Perfect." she said. She looked at Faith and Steven. "I know where to go." she announced. "Get in the car."

Evelyn ran to the driver's side, averting Faith and Steven's shared look of confusion. The three of them opened the doors. Steven sat in the passenger seat, while Faith sat in back, making sure Ash wouldn't sustain any further damage.

After slamming the door shut, Evelyn put the Oldsmobile in Drive, and stomped on the accelerator. The tires squealed and smoke rose from the back tires as she turned the car and sped away from the hoard of Deadites that were getting closer to the police station.

They were now on the same road that led to the station. Only now, they were traveling in the opposite direction.

Steven looked out the window and saw one of the foul things in the air, catching up to them. He watched it open its monstrous mouth and screech. It sounded like nails on a chalkboard. "Evelyn." he said nervously.

"What is it?" she said, swerving to avoid the other cars.

"One of them's following us." he pointed up to the sky where it remained about ten feet above them.

Evelyn looked in the side mirror and saw it. She quickly looked at the speedometer and noted that she was going about fifty miles per hour. *My God, those things are fast.* And then she remembered that on the street up to the right, there was an intersection. It gave her an idea.

"We don't have any more bullets left, Evelyn." said Steven. "And that thing's just gonna keep chasing us."

"I know, just..." She went faster and hoped that she would time it just right. "...just trust me, alright?"

"What do you mean? What are you–" Before he knew it, Steven felt himself being hurled to left and almost knocked out of his seat.

The dented, yellow, Delta 88 turned sharply to the other street and went a short distance before crossing the intersection. There were stoplights at each corner, each standing at about ten feet above the car, the same height that the Deadite hovered.

They crossed the intersection. The demon flew right into the stoplight, crashing its entire body against the light and the pole that suspended it. The demon howled and fell right onto the concrete, its wings twitched and convulsed violently. The creature never knew what hit it.

Evelyn stopped the car in front of the entrance to S-Mart. By this time, it was after midnight, so the store had been closed and locked up for a while. Evelyn would have to enter through the back of the building and turn on the power from there. She turned the ignition, shutting the car off. She, Steven, and Faith practically leapt out of the car, and ran to the front of the building.

She grabbed the keys from the back pocket of her jeans, and turned to her friends before leaving them. "I'll turn the power back on," she said, still panting from the run. "You guys stay here and watch my back."

Faith and Steven nodded as they watched Evelyn run to the back of the building. She ran to the corner of the S-Mart building, and turned, fully escaping from their view.

The dark-haired, heroine-in-training was now completely alone. *Don't slow down.* She reminded herself. *Don't look back. Just get inside as quick as you can. There could be some Deadites here already...I hope not...but still.* It was pitch black outside. That made her nervous. Every time she brushed against the trunk of a tree she thought, *Was that one of them? Just run. Just run.*

At times, Evelyn still couldn't believe that her blissfully simple life had taken a hard left turn into demonic possession, killer nightmares, and trying to stop the evil bastard responsible for it. Freddy killed her boyfriend and her best friend. Two of the closest people in her life, he had taken from her. She wasn't going to let him take anymore. Evelyn would do all that she could to make sure of that.

Finally, Evelyn reached the opposite end of the building and found the door that led inside. She poked around in the dark, frantically searching for the doorknob. She ended up stabbing the door a few times before she reached the lock. She turned the key, looking behind and all around her as she entered the building and locked the door behind her.

Steven and Faith stood outside the automatic doors, arms crossed, and eyes locked on the ground.

Faith's eyes started to graze from the ground and her mind started to wander with panicked thoughts. *Is Evelyn okay? She's been gone a long time. If Freddy took her too, I'll chop his undead dick off. Then again, what if this whole thing doesn't work out? What if he wins? I can't believe this is happening. I can't believe I'm out here, standing in front of S-Mart, about to drag in Ash, our hero, from the end of the world. And he's unconscious. This whole thing su–* Faith looked up, and to her left to Steven. She brushed her hair away from her brown eyes, and stared at the side of his face. Oddly mesmerized by his choppy hair, and his dark eyes, all of the danger and disasters that happened earlier seemed to fade away in the back of her mind.

Steven felt Faith's eyes looming on him. Keeping his head still lowered down, he quickly glanced to see Faith looking back. Before, Steven's mind was racing. He was scared beyond belief, but he knew that Ash would come through for them...at least he hoped that he would. As soon as his eyes locked on Faith, all of his worries disappeared. It filled him with a sense of newfound confidence. He saw her smile at him. It wasn't a big smile, but it was reassuring. It automatically made him smile in return. "Everything's gonna be okay." he said, both to Faith and himself.

She chuckled. "You think so?"

He nodded and spoke softly. "Yeah."

Just then, the two of them were overwhelmed with the sound of a swelling electrical surge, and bright florescent lights shining from inside S-Mart. They reacted, squinting their eyes and blinking rapidly, eventually adjusting to the change in light.

The automatic twin doors slid open. Striding outside to meet them was Evelyn, holding an axe in her left hand and a pistol in her right. She smiled confidently at them. She spoke in a tone that, to them, made her sound like a total badass. "Shop smart. Shop S-Mart."

The three of them carried Ash inside the store. Their arms strained the longer they held him up.

They managed to carry him past the registers, and slowly trudged their way to the garden department so they could sit him down on one of the chairs.

Ash started to groan and murmur. "Hmm...hmm...argh..." He began clenching his fists and shaking his head.

Faith, who was supporting the top half, along with Steven, asked, "What's happening to him?"

Evelyn, who held Ash's legs, answered, "He's having a nightmare."

"What do you think Freddy's doing to him?" she asked, not sure if she wanted to know the answer.

Evelyn thought about what had happened in her nightmare. How Freddy used every dark detail of her life against her. How he humiliated her, scared her senseless, and nearly beat her to death. "He's trying to kill him." she said cryptically. "Inside and out."

The three of them set Ash down on a display lawn chair. Evelyn propped his feet on the chair.

Steven hunched over and lifted one of his eyelids, examining the whites of Ash's eyes, which were now bloodshot at the corners. He assumed that it was from the prolonged lack of sleep, but after seeing Ash murmur and jerk up and down on his seat, it made him wonder if maybe it was mostly from the trauma of having Freddy beat the living hell out of him. Steven straightened up and stepped back beside Faith, worried that he would get hit as a result of Ash's spasms.

He pitied Ash. "He looks like he's having some kind of episode."

They all looked down at Ash, watching him suffer, collectively feeling their hearts sink because there was nothing they could do. Upon further examination, they started to see cuts and lacerations appearing on Ash's skin. They were small ones at first. A slice here and there on his forearms. They noticed Ash wincing as the cuts appeared. And then, a long, steak knife-sized cut traced along Ash's right shoulder to his collar bone.

"Aaaah!" screamed Ash. Tiny drops of blood escaped from his wound and seeped into his button-up shirt.

Faith winced as she looked at Ash writhing in pain. She whispered to herself. "Oh my God."

Steven felt queasy having to see Ash get tortured like this. He averted his eyes, and tried not to hear Ash's cries of pain.

While everyone else was trying not to indulge in Ash's pain, Evelyn couldn't look away. She began to feel restless. She was aching to do something to bring him back, but she didn't know what. "We can't just watch Freddy do this to him." she said anxiously. "We have to try to wake him up somehow."

"Like what?" asked Faith. "He's knocked out, it's not like a little shove is gonna bring him out of it."

Evelyn closed her eyes for a moment, desperately thinking back to her encounter with Freddy. The same thing that happened to her was now happening to Ash. All of the slices and bruises that he inflicted in the dream manifested outside of it. *Maybe the opposite would work too.* Evelyn turned to Faith once again. "Whatever Freddy does to us in our dreams, happens in real life too."

Faith interrupted her. "Yeah, no shit."

Evelyn continued. "What I'm saying is," she spoke snidely. "maybe it can work the other way around."

Faith looked confused and dropped the sarcastic tone. "Explain that to me."

"Look," she said. "we're in this huge warehouse store. There's medical supplies everywhere, I know there's something we can use to bring him back."

Faith begrudgingly agreed, nodding her head. "Okay." she exhaled. "What should I go look for, then?"

Evelyn gave her a mental list of supplies. “Smelling salts, stuff like that.” she looked back at Ash. “And it looks like we’ll need a lot of bandages.”

Faith nodded again. “Okay. I’ll get right on it.” She turned around and jogged through the wide aisles of S-Mart.

Evelyn turned back to Steven, who was still facing in the same direction, his face was frozen. He looked paralyzed from fear. Evelyn stepped closer to him. “Steven, what is it?”

The fear that Steven conveyed at that moment made his brown eyes even darker. The tone in his voice made him sound like what he said next would be his last words. “They’re here.” he said. “The Deadites are already here.”

Evelyn looked across the front entrance to see what looked like fifty or so Deadites, making their way to the store.

They weren’t that close yet. By this time, they were crossing the street and heading towards the parking lot.

Her heart instantly began to race, and every bone in her body started to shake. Her breathing was erratic. She heard Steven mutter under his breath.

“I’m pretty sure we’re gonna die.”

Evelyn whipped around and grabbed Steven by both shoulders. She yelled at him, angry and nervous at the same time. “No, Steven, we’re *not*!” she looked deep into his eyes. “If we block the front entrance, we can keep them out for a while.” She let go of Steven and pointed to the Housewares department. “Run over there and get some stuff to barricade the door.”

Just like Faith, Steven nodded. He agreed, but wasn’t fully confident that it would work. Steven ran over to the Housewares department.

Evelyn spoke to him, raising her voice so he could hear. “I’ll be with you in a second!” She turned her head to look at Ash. By now, he was sweating profusely and was streaked with his own blood. Evelyn walked over to him, kneeled down and grasped his left hand in both of her hands. She whispered to him. "Hang in there, Ash." and then, she added, "It's not over yet."

Evelyn let go of Ash's hand. She ran to join Steven like she promised, all the while hoping and praying that what she said to Ash would prove to be true.

Chapter 27

HE WAS IN THE BOILER room. His body was wet with blood. The remnants that didn't seep into his clothing dripped onto the floor. His arms, his chest, and his shoulders, burned and stung from the cuts that Freddy left on his body.

Ash had to escape, but he didn't know how to. After Freddy had subdued him and slashed him all over his upper body, Ash managed to run away. He didn't know how long he had been in the hellish boiler room, or how long he would continue to be trapped there, but Ash was going to do all that he could to keep Freddy from doing any further damage to him.

Ash's black work boots stomped against the metal walkway as he wandered aimlessly. He could feel his strength fleeting with every drop of blood that escaped from his body.

Ash looked at the floor the entire time he walked. Looking past the grated walkway, he noticed the incredible height he had reached. It was so dark, he couldn't even see the ground. Ash wasn't afraid of heights, but for some reason, the unsettling, grand scale of the boiler room had given him vertigo. He was starting to grow dizzy, and nauseous. *No, I can't give up now.* Ash told himself. *I've made it this far, I'm not gonna let Freddy win.*

Starting from the corners of his eyes, everything was starting to go black. At any moment, he was going to collapse to the floor. *No, I gotta keep going.* Ash took a deep breath and blinked a few times, hoping that it would keep him from blacking out.

Looking around, he saw boilers and steaming pipes everywhere. The lighting was odd. It made the entire area look gloomy, and disturbingly surreal. Everything appeared to look red for some reason. He looked up at the few florescent light fixtures above him, and saw that all of them had been splattered with bright red blood.

The more he looked, he saw that the place was enormous. Even though it was dimly lit, he couldn't help but notice the tiny corners and the multiple walkways everywhere. *It's like a maze.* He tried to find his way out of the narrow pathway he was walking in. To his left, he was bombarded with large boilers as tall as he was, and thick, rusted chains hanging from the ceiling. To his right was the railing, guarding Ash from falling to the ground.

The sound of hissing pipes and creaking metal filled the air. It was loud, boisterous. It started to give Ash a hell of a headache. He looked up, taking in the boiler room as he guided himself through its maze-like corners. The ceiling was another two stories above where Ash was standing. *God, how big is this place?*

Ash continued to wander around the room. He placed his hand on one of the boilers for support as he turned to the corner on his left. The blazing hot metal burned his palm, and a sharp *tsssss!* Was heard as his hand contacted the boiler's exterior. Clamping his mouth shut, Ash groaned as he quickly retreated his hand and shook it, hoping to cool it off.

He cursed under his breath. "Damn it."

Ash stopped beside edge of the walkway to catch his breath. He placed his hands on the guardrail for support. He took a moment to breathe, letting his heart rate go down, and his dizziness subside. He looked around, baffled by rooms appearance. There were metal stairways everywhere, seemingly going in all directions. *It's like an M.C. Escher painting.* For now, he just felt the streams of blood race down his skin.

A drop of blood escaped from the wound on his arm. It traced down his forearm and curved downward. The drop fell from his skin, leaving yet another thin, red, ribbon on Ash's body. The blood plunged down to the ground, through one of the holes on the grated walkway, and went *splat* on Freddy's forehead.

Freddy defied gravity as he clung to the metal walkway. His fingers and his claws poked through the holes in the walkway, just inches from Ash's feet. Freddy's hands and feet remained secure as he crawled across the opposite face of the walkway, like a red and green striped Spiderman. Once Freddy reached the guardrail, he pulled himself up, and smiled devilishly at Ash, who had his eyes closed.

Freddy raised his left hand. "Hey, Ash!"

Ash jumped and opened his eyes wide. Before he would flee, Freddy had already grabbed him by the collar of his shirt.

"Going down?" said Freddy. Once the words left his mouth, Freddy pulled Ash over the railing, and sent him falling down approximately ten feet before landing on a flight of metal stairs.

"Whoa!" he screamed. Ash landed on his side and began to awkwardly slide down the stairs. The chainsaw attached to his right hand clinked and banged against the rusty stairs. He wanted to scream, but the swiftness of his descent and the bumpy ride down prevented from speaking.

He had reached the end of the stairway. Ash rolled out to the middle of the floor, grunting and groaning every time his face hit the ground. "Ugh." Ash said as he tried to pick himself up.

He looked around, feeling the floor beneath his hands, surveying the tallness and the grandeur of where he was. He was now at the very heart and center of Freddy's boiler room. *How far did I fall?* he wondered. Considering how many times he hit his head against the stairs and how the room kept spinning as he tumbled down, it was hard to keep track. He knew that this was supposed to be the infamous boiler room, the same one he had found the Necronomicon in. But the more he looked around, he realized that it barely resembled the old, demolished, building he visited before.

Cavernous surroundings. Fire-spewing pillars made of iron. Steam that gathered around the bottom, giving the impression of fog. Pipes as far as the eye could see, bent and twisted like the branches of a dead tree. It was disturbing and awe-inspiring at the same time.

Ash tried to get up, but his legs were too weak to support him. As he tried to stand, his knees shook, and his legs felt numb. Ash fell to his knees. He groaned as they impacted against the hard ground. He lowered his weary head and tried to regain his strength. Sweat dripped from his hairline, down to his forehead, and fell to the floor in front of him. He thought that this was the end for him. That Freddy was going to kill him right then and there, and that it would be the end of the Chosen One. But, he remembered. *The Necronomicon. Freddy still has it.* he realized. *I bet it's still in the same place where I found it.* This filled him with newfound confidence and adrenaline. And then he heard the sound of approaching footsteps...and screeching metal-on-metal.

Scrreeeecchhhh!

As if my head wasn't already pounding. he complained.

Freddy slowly walked around Ash in circles. He watched him sink down to the ground, sweating and bleeding all around himself. "Don't tell me you're giving up now!" he said in an artificially surprised tone. He bragged, "I'm just gettin' started!"

Freddy stopped at Ash's side and curved his body downward to get a close look at Ash's wounds. He loved admiring his own work. He noticed Ash turning his head to look at Freddy.

Breathlessly, Ash spoke. "Hey," he said. "let me ask you somethin'."

Freddy grinned, predicting what Ash was going to say to him. "Ah," he nodded. "you want to know why I needed to get the book, what I'm using it for, and what I need from you." Freddy began pacing around him again. "You see, *Ashley*...The Dream Demons–the ones who gave me this job–live inside those old, wrinkled pages. And as long as I keep killing every little brat that comes my way, they allow me to live."

Freddy started to grimace. "But," he spit the words out. "every time one of those little bitches stop me, they send me back, and leave me here to rot. Not anymore!" he said with malice. "I'm tired of going away. They promised me immortality, and this time I'm going to make sure I get what I want.

"All I had to do was wait for someone to come to me. Someone stupid and weak enough to bring me my book. And now, I have the Chosen One before me, shaking and bleeding like a little pussy."

Freddy chuckled low under his breath. "Once I take *your* soul, nothing'll stop me."

Ash began to speak, but Freddy interrupted him once more.

"You really think all your years of killing rotten, little Deadites is gonna be enough to kill me?" Freddy crouched down until he was at eye-level with Ash. "Face it Ash, the Book of the Dead isn't the only thing that's old and wrinkled now, hmm? That answer your question?"

Ash lifted his head, looking at him, tough and unfazed. He stood up tall. "No." he answered. "I already knew all that. Minus your lame, little, deal with a couple of dream spirits." He waited until Freddy stood up in front of him to speak again. Even though Ash as a bit beaten, he still stood a few inches higher than Freddy. "What I wanted to know was, with all this dark, magical, voodoo power you have, why are you still running around in Bing Crosby's holiday sweater from Hell? Seems kinda fruity, if you ask me." Ash smiled, knowing that he had pissed him off. "What, do you only go after little girls 'cause women think you're a–oh, what was the word you used?–pussy? Me, I never had that problem."

His nostrils flared and his blue eyes glowed in anger. He scowled, partially exposing his rotten, jagged teeth. "Keep joking." he told him. "It'll distract you when I rip out your soul and kill–"

SMACK!!!

Ash punched Freddy square in the face. He watched as Freddy fell on his back, groaning and grasping his nose. "Boy, I get tired of hearing that."

His anger began to rise. *The prick actually punched me while I was monologuing!* He thought. *I don't tolerate insolent mortals in my realm.*

Especially jarheads like him! Freddy leapt up and lowered his upper body like a charging bull. He ran towards Ash, grabbing him and knocking him off his feet. Freddy continued to run, he then pushed Ash, and threw him against one of the large boilers that was behind him.

Ash was thrown against the boiler. The impact of his body against the thick steel rung loudly. Painful vibrations ran all through his body, especially around the back of his head and his spine.

Ash slid down to the floor, his body broken. While his head was still buzzing, he looked up to see Freddy pointing his bladed glove down at him, ready to execute the final blow. He quickly rolled away just in time. Freddy's steel blades instead launched into the boiler, making a sharp *ping!* sound as he did so.

Freddy looked over to see Ash standing up and backing away from him.

Scrreeeecchhhh!

Freddy scraped his knives along the boiler as he turned around to meet him. He shuffled toward Ash, raising his glove and preparing to slice him in two.

Ash hastily revved his chainsaw and raised it up in the air, countering Freddy. The mechanical roar of the chainsaw echoed throughout the boiler room. Ash saw Freddy swiftly lowering the glove, preparing to slash him, so he blocked him with the chainsaw. Ash's chain spinning, cutting against Freddy's knives, produced a high-pitched screech.

SCRREEEECCHHHH!!!

It sent bright sparks flying everywhere, in front of them, momentarily blinding the two.

Freddy retracted his blades, as did Ash with his chainsaw.

The chainsaw was still revved up, and Ash was ready to slice-and-dice the undead dream killer. Once the sparks fell to the ground, Ash charged towards the burnt bastard and sliced him from right to left, cutting him in half. Ash couldn't help but let a crazed laugh escape from his mouth as Freddy's blood splattered across his face. "Ha ha ha ha ha ha!" Once Ash had shredded him completely, he removed the chainsaw from Freddy's abdomen and watched as both halves of his body dropped to the ground.

Ash chuckled. "Timber."

Freddy laid flat on his back, choking on his own blood. He propped himself up with his elbows, staring at the gap in his upper body. "You asshole!" he yelled angrily. "You cut me in fucking half! You're gonna pay for this!"

Ash lowered the chainsaw and smiled arrogantly at Freddy, mocking him. "Oh yeah, what are you gonna do? Flail your limbs at me?"

"No." Freddy said. He smiled mischievously and slid his upper half towards the lower.

As soon as the two halves came in contact, Freddy's bones, muscle tissue, and skin began to reconnect. Even the threads from his ratty sweater started to weave back together. Swiftly, Freddy kicked his feet in the air and jumped up, standing straight. Freddy chuckled at Ash, and shot his middle finger at him, flipping him off.

"Oh yeah?" Ash countered. "There's more where that came from!" He raised his chainsaw, ready to slice him again. Unfortunately for him, his chainsaw cut off right then and there. "You gotta be kidding me!" said Ash. *How do you run out of fuel in a dream?* he thought. *Never mind. I don't wanna think about that, it makes my brain hurt.* "Guess it's time to bring out the Boomstick." Ash unlatched the chainsaw from his wrist and let it drop to the floor. It was dead weight now. He then reached for his shotgun just as Freddy began to launch at him. Ash pulled the front trigger and shot Freddy in the chest.

BOOM!!!

Freddy was taken aback from the impact of the shell. He stopped, trying to regain balance.

Ash then pulled the back trigger, this time aiming between Freddy's legs.

BOOM!!!

Freddy stared down at the damage Ash had caused. The front of his body was wet with fresh blood. He lifted his head and stared at Ash in disbelief.

Ash rested the twin barrels on his left shoulder as he mocked Freddy. "You gotta give me credit for that one." he said. "I've never hit a target that small before."

Freddy was growing tired of Ash's taunts. Sure, it was fun when *he* did it, but having someone doing the same to him was, as he thought, *fucking annoying*. Freddy used his powers once again to quickly heal himself. The wounds disappeared and the blood had dried in a matter of seconds. "Shooting me in the dick?" he questioned Ash. "That's low."

Ash scrunched his eyebrows together. "No pun intended?" he assumed.

"No more bullshit." he said. *This air-headed stock boy's going down.* Freddy ran towards Ash and raised his glove.

Ash acted quickly and hit Freddy in the face with the butt of his shotgun. The impact was so powerful that it knocked Freddy's head back, nearly snapping his neck. He immediately clenched his left hand into a fist and prepared to punch him square in the face just as Ash did to him.

Without a second thought, Ash grabbed Freddy's fist and pulled his arm toward the ground. Ash bent is right arm and hit Freddy in the face with his elbow. As Freddy shouted in pain, Ash backed away and used the time he had to reload his gun. But once he reached into his shirt pocket, where he always stored extra bullets, he had none. His eyebrows lifted in surprise and he felt his heart sink. *Where the hell are they? Come on!*

"Ha ha ha ha..." Freddy laughed mockingly at Ash as he fumbled for his precious bullets.

Ash looked at him, and saw Freddy carrying a hand full of shotgun shells in his left hand. He waved them in front of his face, like he was dangling treats in front of a hungry puppy. "Looking for these?"

"How the hell did you do that?" he asked. Ash didn't feel Freddy digging around in his shirt pocket while they were fighting. But then again, it all happened so quick, he wouldn't have been able to tell.

"You keep forgetting that I'm in control here." Freddy held out his gloved hand, his palm in front of Ash.

Ash felt his shotgun moving on his own. It was moving away from Ash's hand and started to slip away. It was like the shotgun was being magnetically pulled towards Freddy. His shotgun flew from his hand and into Freddy's.

Shit. This isn't gonna go well for me. Ash thought.

"Now," Freddy loaded the shotgun and closed the chamber, cocking it. "dance for me, bitch!" He unloaded the rounds near Ash's feet.

BOOM!!!

BOOM!!!

The shells pinged against the floor, dangerously near Ash's feet. It forced him to shuffle his feet in hopes to miss the bullets.

He just kept shooting at him. Once the rounds were empty, Freddy quickly reloaded, giving Ash no relief.

BOOM!!! BOOM!!!

BOOM!!! BOOM!!!

BOOM!!! BOOM!!!

Freddy was now out of bullets. Without any further use for it, he discarded the shotgun, throwing it on the ground. He kept his eyes locked on Ash, who was running in the opposite direction. He lifted his bladed index finger and waved it from left to right, expressing his disapproval. "Uh uh uuh." he said coyly.

He directed his powers towards the large boiler and mess of pipes that was a few yards in front of Ash. Freddy noticed the boiler begin to shake and come off of its hinges. He thrust his hands downward, causing the boiler and pipes to come crashing down right in front of Ash, blocking his path.

Ash stopped in his tracks and searched for another place to turn to, but there was none. He was trapped. It was just him and Freddy. Ash turned around to see Freddy standing just ten feet away from him.

"You know what they say," Freddy began. "if you love someone, set them free." He snarled. "If someone pisses you off, cripple him so he can't fucking move!" Freddy raised his hands, directing his power toward the large pipe hanging far above Ash's head.

"I don't think that's how it–"

THWACK!

A thick, heavy pipe crash landed on top of Ash. He fell to the ground and groaned in agony. Freddy had almost killed him. A throbbing, excruciating pain raced up and down Ash's spine.

He couldn't move. But he didn't need to, Freddy had grabbed the back of Ash's shirt and dragged him across the boiler room. Freddy dragged the 170 pound bag of dead weight with him across the boiler room floor, and closer to the massive furnace just thirty feet north of where they were now.

Ash felt the temperature rising. It was already hot enough to begin within that godforsaken boiler room, but now it was sweltering. His entire body warmed more and more by the second. Not long after that, his head was now drenching with sweat. When Ash thought there was nothing that could revive him, nothing that could bring him to move, he was suddenly sobered with the putrid smell of smoke, burning coal, and...freshly charred flesh.

Fighting the pain, Ash lifted his head and saw himself being brought to a rusted furnace. As soon as he came to realize what was going on, he was then lifted from the ground and brought to his feet. Before Ash, was the furnace, a few feet taller than him, and the gate was wide open. Ash was hit in the face by a burning cloud from the fire. His eyes began to sting and his hair was matted with sweat.

Before Ash could protest, Freddy grabbed the back of his head and pushed him into the fire.

Ash placed his hands outside the furnace wall, pushing back and preventing Freddy from throwing Ash into the bright, yellow flames. He fought the incredible, burning, pain on his palms coming from the furnace wall.

Freddy grunted and pushed harder. He could see Ash's arms start to shake weakly. He was losing his grip. Freddy grinned. "Time to live up to your name, *Ash*!"

Ash shouted, "Noooo!" His arms were numbing. He couldn't hold on much longer. He knew he needed to think of something...*anything*... and do it quick. Or else, there would be no more Ash, there would only be...ash.

The windows on the front side of the S-Mart building were mostly boarded up by now. Evelyn and Steven intended to use up all of the wood from the lumber aisle. A stack, consisting of only three planks of wood, remained.

Evelyn and Steven stood on opposite ends of the front entrance, making sure that their side was securely boarded and blocked from any Deadite intrusion.

Her wrists had grown strained from the constant hammering. It was a rhythmic process: grab a nail, hammer it steadily in place...

KNOCK! KNOCK! KNOCK! KNOCK! KNOCK!

...repeat the process five or six times, depending on the size of the plank. Move on to the next. Repeat.

At this point, unenthused, Evelyn hung yet another board in front of the window. After reaching for another nail from the box beside her feet, she realized she was out. Evelyn set the hammer down and moved her wrists around, un-tightening them. She let out a sigh of exhaustion. She was determined to keep the Deadites outside, but at the same time, she couldn't help but relish the thought of sitting down and taking a five-minute break.

Evelyn turned her head and looked at Steven, who was finishing up his side of the window. "Hey, Steven." she called.

He looked at her briefly before resuming his work. He kept a couple of nails stored in the corner of his mouth, with the sharp end facing away from him. "Yeah?" he said, muffled.

"Could you hand me another box?"

Without saying anything, Steven bent over to grab a new box of nails and threw it across the other side, where Evelyn was standing. He took one of the nails out of his mouth and securely boarded up the last window.

Evelyn caught it with both hands. Before opening the box, she took a couple of steps back to survey their work.

Steven joined her. He stood at arm's length next to her. "Looks pretty good to me." he said. He turned to her. "What do you think?"

She looked at him and smiled out of embarrassment. "Honestly, I'm just tired of boarding the windows."

"Yeah, I know what you mean." Steven walked to the center, where the automatic doors where supposed to be, before he and Evelyn had blocked them. "Let me just check this one, it looks a little loose." Steven knelt down touched the tilted plank. He pushed it back and forth, checking to see if it would break easily. The board was nailed tightly and wasn't going anywhere. "No, it's fine." he assured.

SNAP!

Just inches from Steven's face, on his right side, a pale and scabbed hand broke through the boards. Another hand followed immediately after, breaking the makeshift wall above Steven's head, trying to grab onto to him.

His figurative nerves exploded with shock. His heart pounded. As he leaped back and crawled away, Steven screamed a throaty scream and yelled the first thing that came to his mind. "Aaaah! 'Day of the Dead'!" He didn't know why, but the first thing that he thought of was the scene in "Day of the Dead" when a group of zombie hands burst through the wall.

Steven ran back to Evelyn's side. This time, his eyes were wide and his palms were shaking. He turned to look at Evelyn, but she was already gone.

Evelyn cursed as she walked to one of the checkout counters. "Damn it." She grabbed her axe from the table and jogged back to the boarded windows.

Evelyn held the axe above her head and swung down hard, severing one of the Deadite hands at the wrist.

The rotting hand fell to the ground and started forming a pool of green blood at the cut-off point.

Evelyn did the same to the other. Like an 18th century executioner, Evelyn lifted the axe up as high as she could and swiftly brought it down, cutting off the hand. Now that there were two holes in the barricade, Evelyn was able to hear the demonic symphony of hisses and growls coming from outside. It made her stomach churn.

Other than that, the Deadites were kept at bay. Evelyn lowered the axe and held it in her right hand. With her left, she gave Steven a feeble thumbs up. However, her face showed less optimism and more shock. "I think we got it." she said.

Steven stared at Evelyn's feet. He was frozen in place, not able to comprehend what he was seeing. All he could manage to say was, "...E-Evelyn?" He pointed at her feet.

Before she could ask what was wrong, Evelyn felt a tug on both of the pant legs on her jeans. She dropped her head down to see the severed hands crawling on their own, and up her legs. Evelyn let out a half-gasp-half-scream, and dropped her axe. She started brushing the hands from her thighs. The more she fought them off, the harder they squeezed her legs, refusing to let go. "Get them off me!" she yelled at Steven. "Hurry!"

Steven ran over to Housewares and grabbed a butcher knife from the display table. By the time he returned to Evelyn, she had already flung one of them off of her leg. Steven grabbed the other hand and pried it from Evelyn's thigh. Once the hands released its grip from

Evelyn, Steven reached for the other, and slammed both of them on the ground. Steven held the knife above the two hands that were stacked on top of one another, and stabbed them. He pushed the knife down hard, cutting through the muscles and bones.

The hands twitched their fingers back and forth. Green blood oozed from the stab wound, some of it got on Steven's hand. As Steven pushed the knife down, he swore he could hear the hands making a noise as they fell still. They seemed to squeak, like rats.

Disgusted from what he had just done, Steven took the Deadite kebob and pinned it to the wall next to the boarded windows. He turned around to look at Evelyn, expecting a reaction.

They both had the same look in their eyes: confusion, disgust, and a nonverbal "What the fuck was that?"

Evelyn finally spoke, brushing it off. "You know what?" she said, raising her hands up at shoulder height. "At this point, we should be used to this stuff."

"You know, you'd think so." said Steven. "But then, something even more fucked up happens that makes me question my own sanity."

"Hey guys!" Faith shouted from the garden department, where she was watching over Ash. "Get over here, something's wrong with Ash!"

He turned to Evelyn. "See what I meant?"

They ran to Faith and the presently unconscious Ash, who was still laying down on one of the folding lawn chairs. Steven stood next to Faith, who was at Ash's left. Evelyn knelt by Ash on his right side.

"What's happening to him?" Evelyn asked Faith.

Faith was restless. She didn't know how to explain it, mostly because of how it frightened her. "He just–started moving his arms and legs, like he was...fighting him, or something."

Steven and Evelyn could see it now. Ash started moving his head from left to right. He mumbled incoherently and started jerking his knees up and down. They looked at Ash's face more closely and began to notice dark, purple, bruises appearing on his cheek and jaw. And then, he started sweating profusely.

"I've tried, I can't wake him up." admitted Faith.

"Then we have to try harder." said Evelyn curtly.

With her eyes still locked on Ash, Faith pointed at him. "Wait, guys..." Faith said worriedly. "Look."

Evelyn and Steven looked at Ash again. This time, his face was now burning red. The tips of the hair in front of his face started to smoke. The dark hairs glowed orange, and slowly burnt off. The glowing embers fell and flew in all directions.

Freddy was going to burn him.

Evelyn reacted on instinct and did what she felt was the right thing to do. She brushed away the smoke from the ends of Ash's hair. She then cupped his face with both hands and got close to him. She screamed at the top of her lungs. "WAKE UP!" Her voice cracked. "ASH, WAKE UP!"

Her breaths became short and uneven. Her eyes were stinging and she felt a heaviness in her heart. The tone in her voice hinted at desperation, like she was not commanding, but begging. "Ash, wake up..."

Chapter 28

THE FLAMES DANCED WILDLY, BARELY kissing Ash's flesh. The bright, yellow fire illuminated his face. The heat was unbearable. Ash thought that if being burned alive wouldn't kill him first, the inevitable heat-stroke would.

He kept his hands locked firmly on the wall of the furnace, steadying himself as Freddy kept his hand on Ash's neck, pushing him into the fire. He felt his face burning, getting hotter by the second. The heat was robbing him of his strength, depleting him. It soon became difficult to breathe. His arms weakened. It took every ounce of will left inside of him to hold on, but the harder Freddy pushed, it became more real to him that his mortality, his life...his soul...was on the line. Ash pleaded. Begged for a way out. For his strength to given back to him. For him not to die. "God, please." he exhaled.

Freddy crept lower towards his ear. With one sentence, he took away the only speck of hope Ash had left in him. "God's not here, it's just you and me." A swell of adrenaline and diabolical pleasure rushed through Freddy's body as he prepared to throw Ash into the furnace.

ASH, WAKE UP!

Evelyn's cries traveled through Ash's ears and into the dream realm. Her voice was so powerful that it managed to break through the wall between dream and reality.

"Huh?" Freddy mumbled. He lifted his head, trying to locate where the voice was coming from. He couldn't pinpoint its location, as it echoed all throughout the boiler room. He couldn't believe it. Ash had been knocked out cold. He didn't think anything would be able to reach him. He had his Deadite minions throw him against a brick wall for fuck's sake, how was this possible?

But then he remembered. From all of the countless children he had come across, there was always one in the group that a special power inside of her. Something that gave her strength and the ability to stand up against him. Whether it be calling in other people into her dreams, gathering the strength from his victims after he killed them, or being able to take away the fear he had given her, there was always something that allowed them to fight back. *That bitch is messing up my plan.*

Ash felt Freddy loosen his grip when he heard Evelyn's voice. He knew that this was his only chance to break free. He had to act now or Freddy would surely kill him. Ash bent his right arm and pulled it back as hard and swift as he could.

His elbow launched into Freddy's side, breaking one of his ribs. "Ah!" Freddy groaned and placed his hand on his rib, feeling the knot that Ash left when he hit him.

But Ash wasn't done. No. He wanted Freddy to hurt, to suffer, to get his fucking ass kicked. Ash spun around, facing a now hunched over Freddy Krueger. He grabbed Freddy's right arm and twisted it all the way around, stopping when he heard a *snap.*

Ash had dislocated his shoulder. The sound of his bone popping out of place was gut-wrenching. It sounded like a twig snapping or a celery stalk being broken in half. Freddy shouted in pain. "Ah!"

Freddy attempted to catch his breath as Ash side-stepped away from him. "Pretty spry for a guy who nearly got his face melted off!" he sniped.

"Well, you'd know about that, wouldn't you?" Ash countered as he turned away and ran from Freddy.

*Not this shit again...*Freddy wasn't going to have Ash slip away from his grip yet again. His eyebrows tilted, resembling a "V" shape on his forehead. Freddy stood tall and placed his left hand on his right shoulder. He pushed on it, popping it back in place. *I'm not letting you get away, piglet.*

In a cloud of flames and glowing embers, Freddy disappeared from where he stood. At that moment, he was gone.

Ash kept running. He didn't care where it took him, as long as he got as far away from Freddy as he could. He panted, his breathing became more concentrated as he tried to run faster.

Then, in the blink of an eye, Freddy appeared before him. Out of nowhere, Freddy was just inches from Ash's face, appearing in a flurry of smoke and fire.

Ash stopped in his tracks. The inertia that built up from the running caused Ash to stumble.

Freddy tilted his head to the left, smiling devilishly. With the shark-like set of teeth, devil horn-shaped ears, and a soul piercing stare, it was hard to look more evil than he already was, but he still managed to pull it off. He raised his gloved hand up next to his face, his palm open. He waved his blades up and down and chuckled low under his breath.

Ash kept his gaze locked on Freddy's knives. Freddy was immortal in the dream world, but Ash was not. He didn't want those blades anywhere near him.

The moron's actually falling for it! While Freddy had Ash distracted with his knives, he balled his left hand into a fist and punched Ash right in the nose.

The impact caused Ash to lift his head up and clumsily step back. He covered his nose, feeling the blood start to spill from in between his fingers. "Bastard!" he shouted, muffled. "You broke my nose!"

Freddy punched him again, this time in the stomach. His knuckles whitened as Freddy tightened his grip. He launched his fist into Ash's midsection.

The blow caused Ash to double-over. It knocked the wind out of him. The only thing that could escape from his mouth was a faint groan.

Freddy couldn't help but smile, letting his rotted teeth become exposed under the bleak light of the boiler room. Freddy panted. The fight had worn him down as well. But the sight of Ash's pain gave Freddy a familiar happiness, causing his breathing to become erratic. He could barely contain his joy.

With Ash still bent over from the pain, Freddy grabbed his neck and squeezed tightly.

Ash choked and gargled on his own saliva as he felt Freddy's grimy hands on his throat.

Freddy lifted Ash up. He looked into his fearful, pathetic eyes as Freddy brought him up to eye-level. He grinned and lifted Ash higher and higher until his feet were no longer touching the ground.

Ash frantically swung his feet in all directions. He grabbed the hand that latched on his throat, trying to pry it away, but to no avail. Freddy's hands were like a vice around his neck. Ash could barely manage a faint, wheezing inhale to keep himself going.

"I almost feel sorry for you, Ash." Freddy sardonically spoke to him. "You've had to watch all the women you love die right in front of you. Must be sad for a guy like you, huh?" He chuckled under his breath. Freddy knew that, for Ash...for any man...that it would be heartbreaking to have all of the women in their life perish before them. But for Freddy, it was a joy. An absolute rush. Especially when he choked the life out of his wife, Loretta. "I had a wife once. Fucking bitch had to learn the hard way not to snoop around in my basement." Watching the twinkle fade from her eyes as he squeezed tighter and tighter around her neck...it was exhilarating. "How about I make you a deal?" Freddy asked as Ash continued to struggle for breath. "I'll kill you first, and your little whore can meet you in Hell five minutes later. Sound good?"

Ash couldn't speak. At that point, it became a struggle just to inhale.

Freddy lifted his gloved hand up next to his ear. He feigned to attempt hearing the noises coming from Ash's mouth. "I'm not hearing a "no"!" Freddy laughed and raised his knives high above his head, ready to slice Ash up and down.

Ash lifted his knees close to his stomach. He kicked both feet in front of him, hitting Freddy in the chest, sending them both falling on their backs, to the floor.

Ash wasted no time getting back on his feet and walking towards Freddy. He listened as Freddy moaned in pain. Seeing him groan and get the wind kicked out of him, it made Ash smile. It filled him with so much gratification to see him in pain. He launched his feet towards Freddy's ribs and chest, literally kicking him while he was down.

Again. *THUD!*

And again. *THUD!*

And again. *THUD!*

He verbally spit at Freddy as he brought his metal hand out from his jacket and attached it to his right arm. Ash released all of his hatred for Freddy out in the open, both physically and verbally. "You like to prey on children?" he said, feeling nauseated as the words left his mouth. "You motherfucker!" Ash kicked him again, harder than before.

He bent over towards the bloody, and beaten, Freddy. Ash grabbed him by the collar of his ratty, striped sweater and lifted him up. "You sick fuck!" With his metal hand, Ash punched Freddy in his jaw line.

"Ugh!" Freddy groaned as he tilted his head away from Ash, and spit blood from his mouth.

Ash lifted Freddy to his feet. He brought him closer to his face. "I was almost free, God damn it!" he said with a hint of desperation in his voice. "I found your book underneath that boiler room." Ash's face contorted in anger. "You had your chance right then, but no, you had to wait until I was gonna destroy the book to bring yourself back... JUST TO–" Ash rammed Freddy's head against the large lead pipe that was behind him. "–FUCK WITH ME! Didn't ya?!"

Freddy strained to lift his head up to look at Ash in the eyes. His whole body ached, and his head wouldn't stop buzzing. He was so hazy that, once he finally looked at Ash, it looked like he was seeing double-vision. Like there was two Ash's weaving in and out of focus.

But through his fuzzy vision, Freddy noticed the tortured look in Ash's eyes. His eyes were wild with anger, but at the same time, there was a hint of pain. All the years of endless killings and trauma, the souls of his loved ones being stripped away and replaced with pure evil, not to mention all of the innocent people who got in the way, it all built up in that moment. Not only did Freddy take away his chance at a normal life, he has now brought the world on the verge of complete annihilation of human existence. The Deadites would soon take over under Freddy's rule.

Freddy battled the raw pain in his ribs to laugh in Ash's face. The beating caused his laugh to lose its luster. It was low and guttural, but the constriction in his lungs resulted in a faint wheeze. "Ha ha ha ha ha..."

Ash almost exploded with anger. He was actually laughing in his face. After all the punches and kicks to the stomach, Freddy actually had the balls to keep taunting him. *Does this guy ever stop for one minute?* With his fist still gripping the collar of Freddy's sweater, Ash pulled him in close, and slammed him against the pipe hard enough to bend it where Freddy hit his head. "ANSWER ME!" he shouted.

Another mouthful of warm blood gushed in Freddy's mouth. Freddy spit the blood in Ash's face. *There's your answer.* A pocket of dark red blood splattered on the bridge of Ash's nose and traveled down to his chin.

A streak of Freddy's blood leaked from the corner of his mouth. His teeth were now stained red as he smiled and laughed. "What can I say?" His voice was laced with his signature cavalier tone. "I'm a bastard!"

Rage had overcome him. Ash gritted his teeth and practically growled as he yanked Freddy away from the lead pipe and violently swung him around in a circle. Once he had built up enough momentum, Ash let go of Freddy and watched as he fell and rolled on the ground.

As he lied there on the floor, Freddy leered at Ash, wishing he had another mouthful of blood to spit in his face. He stood back on his feet, anticipating another attack from Ash. Freddy put both hands up and gestured him to come closer. "Show me what you got, stock boy!"

Ash ran towards him. Once he was within punching distance from Freddy, he clenched his fist and socked him right on the right side of his face.

Freddy was taken aback, but not for long. He threw an uppercut that landed on his abdominals. With Ash now doubled-over, Freddy shot his knee up, and hit him in the same spot.

"Oof!" Ash groaned as Freddy kneed him in the stomach. Out of the corner of his eye, Ash saw Freddy's glove being raised from his right side. Ash fought the pain and straightened up. Just before Freddy could slash his knives across his skin, Ash jumped back, narrowly avoiding them.

Ash stepped forward and grabbed Freddy's shoulders. "Hyah!" He yelled as he pulled Freddy in and smashed the top of his head against the bridge of Freddy's nose.

Freddy shouted. "Ah!"

Now that his guard was down, Ash kicked him in the chest, putting his full weight into the kick.

His arms flailed. Freddy was knocked on his ass to the floor. Ash was about to step in and kick him the groin, when Freddy waved his glove in the air, from left to right. He used his powers to send Ash flying through the air, close to the ceiling.

"Aaaah!" Ash screamed. A large pipe suspended from the ceiling stopped Ash's ascent, and caused him to fall on one of the higher platforms of the boiler room. He landed on the topmost walkway, overlooking the entire area.

Ash picked himself up. He placed his hands on the guardrail as he leaned over to catch a glimpse of Freddy, who still stood in the same place that he saw him last. He looked no bigger than a No. 2 pencil from the height that Ash was looking from.

CREAK!!!

Ash looked up and saw that the pipe that he had crashed into was now unhinging. It swung from side to side. Steam hissed from the cracks as it broke loose from the ceiling and fell towards the walkway that Ash was standing on.

He ran as fast as his body would allow. As he reached closer to the corner, he heard a loud *CRASH!!!* and felt the ground shake below his feet.

Freddy laughed maniacally, hoping that the large pipe would crush him. "Haa ha ha ha ha ha ha ha ha ha!"

Before the metal catwalk collapsed to the ground, Ash escaped to the dark corners of the boiler room.

Damn it, he got away. Freddy looked around, surveying the top levels, trying to predict where Ash could have gone.

Tap...Tap...Creak!

Above, in the left wing of the boiler room on the fourth level, Freddy heard footsteps. He smiled faintly, and flicked the knives on his glove, anticipating the stabbing of his blades through Ash's flesh.

He disappeared in a flurry of smoke and fire, only to reappear in the exact spot where he initially heard the noise.

Freddy strolled across the walkway, the weight of his bladed glove pulled his arm down, slumping his shoulder. He wiggled his knives back and forth, growing restless the longer he waited.

Freddy was nearing a turning point in the walkway. He placed one of his knives on the guardrail and scraped it along as he prepared to turn the corner to his left.

Scrreeeechhhh!

He mumbled the wretched nursery rhyme that was all too familiar to him. "1, 2, Freddy's coming for–" Freddy turned sharply poking his head out from the corner. "–YOU!"

But Ash was not there. Freddy growled and retreated back to where he began. *Where did that jackass go?* he wondered.

Clink!

Freddy heard the sound of rustling chains. They seemed to be coming from behind where he was standing. Behind one of the boilers. Freddy turned around to see Ash swinging from one of the chains hanging from the ceiling.

Ash lifted his feet up as he propelled himself toward Freddy. Ash let out a battle cry as he swung to Freddy. "Tally ho!"

Freddy's blue eyes went wide as he saw the bottoms of Ash's work boots launching straight at him. The next thing he knew, Freddy felt Ash's boots crash against his stomach. He was knocked off his feet and hurled into the air.

Ash let go of the chain and dropped to the walkway as he watched Freddy fall four stories, landing back at the bottom floor. "That oughta slow you down!" Ash said as he traveled down the metal stairs.

Freddy shakily picked himself up. Every bone in his demonic body buzzed from the fall. He lifted his head to see Ash hovering above him.

"Hey. Tall, burnt, and ugly." Ash sneered. "Show me the way to the book, and I promise to make your death short and sweet."

Freddy stood up. He opened his arms emphatically. "I *am* the way." he echoed.

"All right," said Ash, annoyed. "I've had enough of your cryptic, psycho-babble, bullshit." Ash pointed a finger at him. "Now, unless you want me to kick your crispy ass again, I suggest you get with the program and–"

Freddy launched his bladed glove near Ash's ribcage. He slashed Ash's side from his underarm to his hip. Four, jagged, cuts appeared where Freddy attacked him. They quickly became red and wet from Ash's blood.

He couldn't speak. All Ash could do was gasp as his shirt was soaked with blood. Freddy didn't cut him deep enough to kill him, but he did tear the skin open, causing immense pain. Ash grasped his side and crouched down from the agony. He shut his eyes, wincing and moaning.

Freddy shouted in his ear. "No, *you* get with the program!" He pointed his bladed index finger at Ash's cheekbone. He kept applying pressure to it until he pierced the skin. Freddy retracted his glove, watching the stream of blood fall down Ash's face. "You actually think you still have a chance to stop me?" he said with haughty derision.

Then, in the blink of an eye, Freddy lifted Ash above his head. He held him above with seemingly superhuman strength. "You really are dumber than I thought!" he looked at Ash as he held him above. "You can't stop me! I've. Already. Won!" Freddy threw Ash down, slamming him to the ground.

Freddy underestimated his own strength. He threw Ash so hard, that the big lunk fell through the floorboards. "Huh." Freddy observed Ash clumsily fall through the underground level of the boiler room.

CRASH!!!

CRASH!!!

"Aaaaah!" Ash screamed.

THWACK!!!

CLINK!!!

"Whoa! Whoooaaahh!!!"

THUD!!!

Then, Freddy remembered. "Damn!" That was the area where he kept the Necronomicon. *I can't let him get to my book.*

Ash found himself in a very dark...very cold...area of the boiler room. There was no more fire, no more boilers, no more furnaces. Ash counted his blessings.

He rubbed the knot in his head as he pushed himself up and got back on his feet. Ash blinked his eyes, trying to adjust to the sudden change in light.

Ash touched his right side, where Freddy had slashed him. "Tsst! Ah!" he hissed. The wound was still tender to the touch, but he had noticed that, somehow, the blood flow had already stopped. The wound was starting to cauterize. *Strange...How am I healing this fast?*

He decided to set aside that thought and take care of more pressing matters. Like, for instance, *...finding that damned book.* He looked around him, feeling a strange sense of familiarity with this place.

This was the same basement where Ash had found the book in the first place. He recognized it: The low ceiling, the dirt floor, the workbench filled with scrap metal and various tools. *Yes!* The injuries he sustained weren't for naught. When he thought of it, the place wasn't much different from his own work area. Except his didn't have dried blood on the walls or old toys that once belonged to children. "This must be where he keeps the book." he whispered to himself.

Ash walked towards Freddy's dimly lit workbench strewn with bloody mementos of his past victims. He felt his entire body become pumped with adrenaline when he saw the Book of the Dead before his eyes. His eyes widened in surprise and he opened his palms to grab the book. He ran his fingers along the rough, leather surface. It was finally his.

Ash held the book close to him as he turned around from the workbench. When he lifted his gaze from the rotten, fleshy face of the Necronomicon, his eyes were met with another, equally terrifying face.

Freddy stood before him. His eyes glowed furiously in the shadows. Freddy gritted his teeth. "You just don't know when it's time to die," He raised his glove and rubbed the knives together.

SCHIIING!!!

"Do you, Ash?"

Ash was cornered. There was nowhere else to go. He figured he better just take whatever was coming to him, and hope that he lives through it. Ash stood his ground and braced for impact.

Freddy swung his metal glove from right to left, ready to rip Ash apart like a fucking paper shredder. But when he brought his blades down toward Ash, he was gone. He had disappeared in the blink of an eye. And he had taken the book with him.

Freddy realized what had happened. Evelyn and the rest of the kids, found a way to bring him back. "That fucking cunt woke him up!" He knew what he had to do next. And when he would arrive back to the waking world, he would make them pay. Ash, those little brats, and especially Evelyn.

Such a sweet little thing. He couldn't wait to defile and tear her apart. *I'll slice her up and down, and fuck her corpse.*

"Time to pay a visit to the land of the living."

Chapter 29

THE THREE OF THEM HOVERED over Ash, watching in horror as he kicked and screamed during his sleep. They wanted to look away when they saw cuts and slashes appearing on his skin, with pools of blood soon following, but their eyes were locked on him. It was a maddening, revolting, sideshow being displayed before their eyes.

Every time a fresh wound raced across his arms or face, Evelyn and Faith would mop up the blood and wrap the area with gauze or bandages. Steven would end up sprinting back and forth through the aisles to get more medical supplies.

They all wanted desperately to help him, to bring him out, but nothing seemed to work. Evelyn had eventually given up on trying to communicate with Ash through his dream. No matter how loud she shouted, or how powerful her cries were, Ash wouldn't wake up.

The only time he moved or spoke, was during fits of pained screams or uncontrollable convulsions. Ash would jerk his legs and arms, his chest would heave and lift from the chair, like he was being throttled. He would briefly flutter his eyes. Whenever they caught a glimpse, the whites of his eyes would be bloodshot. Bruises appeared beneath the surface of his skin. Dark, purple splotches were around his neck and on the side of his face.

Ash's pores would open and he would sweat profusely. His skin would glisten, and his face would burn red. He would then open his mouth and let out a spine-chilling scream. Freddy was killing him. And they would be spectators to his gruesome death.

After the screaming had subsided, they simply sat by him, watching over him. The three of them were riddled with tension, leaving them restless. But they couldn't leave Ash by himself. They would be with him, either to see him awake, or be there during his final moments. Each of them would run through cycles of twiddling their thumbs, rapidly tapping their feet against the floor, causing their knees to dance up and down, and biting their lips, leaving them red and chapped.

Faith was hunched over on her knees at Ash's left side, waving smelling salts under his nose. She had been doing this for several minutes, and her arms were growing tired. But, she kept on. Faith had a keen feeling that, judging by the way Ash was fluttering his eyes underneath his lids, he was slowly coming to.

Steven sat on a plastic chair adjacent to Faith, putting himself near Ash's feet. When he wasn't nervously scratching the back of his neck (all of the chaos that had unleashed had left Steven's nerves raw and sensitive, and made him realize how annoying it was to have all of that hair constantly tickle the back of his neck), he was holding his silver crucifix in between his thumb and index finger. He gripped his tightly, praying that Ash would wake up before it was too late.

On Ash's right side, was Evelyn. She sat down on the floor so that she was at eye-level with him. She had been sitting in that same position for several minutes. Her feet were getting numb, her legs were sore, and her back strained from being hunched over for so long, but she didn't care. Her throat had become sore from crying out to Ash in hopes of waking him, so she gave up on speaking. She kept her hand placed on his shoulder, thinking, maybe, keeping physical contact with Ash would drive him away from the dream...and away from Freddy.

She started to grow anxious and mad. Evelyn worried that, without Ash, they would have no way of stopping Freddy and his army. This drove her towards anger. How dare Freddy take her friends, her boyfriend, everything that she held dear in life? He exploited her deepest fears, and left her cold and lonely. And now, he wanted not only her life, but also the life of the only person who could save them. *How dare he?* she thought. *How dare he try to take everything away from me? Freddy might have gotten others before me, but not this time. I won't let him take me. And I'm not letting him take Ash, either. Freddy will pay for what he did to him. To me. To all of us.*

Suddenly, Ash's eyes opened. He gasped, taking a long, wheezing inhale. He jerked his upper body, sitting upright. He practically leaped from his seat when he awoke. He tried to steady his breathing, calming his breath as his shoulders heaved up and down. Ash looked down and noticed the Necronomicon was still secured in his arms. He held it as he did in his dream, clutching it tightly against his chest.

Everyone jumped. They tensed their muscles and gaped their mouths in surprise. They didn't expect Ash to wake up at all, especially not in the dramatic way that he did.

Evelyn's heart beat faster, pounding against her chest like a bass drum. Her eyebrows lifted and her green eyes twinkled when she saw Ash lucid and awake. She fought the knot in her throat when she shouted. "Ash!" She lifted herself from the floor and reached out to hug him. Her arms gently wrapped around his neck, and she rested her chin on the top of his matted, black-and-silver hair. Evelyn could barely contain her happiness. Her eyes watered, and she was okay with it, because this time, she cried tears of joy rather than sorrow. "I can't believe it!" she said. "For a while, we thought you weren't coming back."

Ash was glad to be back and far away from Freddy and that blasted boiler room. But he forgot that every encounter with Freddy left you beaten, bruised, and bloody. Even though it happened in a dream, all of the cuts and bruises he had acquired were very real. Once he awoke, his entire body was sore. The cuts on his arms and face, not to mention the large animal-like slash mark on his side, were still raw. They left a burning sensation deep in his skin.

But as he looked down, surveying his own body, he noticed that he was covered in bandages. Most of the blood had either been washed away, or dried under the wrap. The cuts were still fresh, but they were no longer throbbing like they had been in his dream.

As Evelyn hugged him, it reminded him of the tender bruises on his neck from when Freddy strangled him. He appreciated the gesture, but it hurt like hell. Ash winced. He put his hand on her arm and politely pushed her away. "Yeah, yeah." he said, strained. "Careful with the neck."

Evelyn retreated her arms and gave Ash some space. In the heat of the moment, she forgot all of the fresh injuries Ash had sustained. She still kept a hopeful smile on her face. She was just glad that he was alive.

Faith threw the smelling salts across the aisles. There was no use for them anymore. "I have to admit," she said with a half-smile. She embarrassingly admitted, "For a while, we, uh, kind of thought you were a goner."

"I almost was." he admitted. "Whatever you did, thanks."

Steven sat up and moved closer toward the three of them. His eyes were fixed on the Necronomicon that Ash still held close to his chest. It was the first time he had ever seen it. Over the past few days, he had imagined what it must have looked like. He knew that it would be dark and grim in appearance. Now that he finally laid eyes on it, he was oddly mesmerized by its course, grotesque design.

He remembered how Ash said that the book was made out of skin and was written in blood. He could easily believe that now that he saw the wrinkled, leathery cover. The more he stared at it, the more he realized that the book was staring at him. It seemed as though it had eyes and a mouth. Almost like, *...it was made out of someone's face...*He could just imagine some frightened person, having their skin ripped off and then have it be used as a book cover. *Was the person dead when they did that? Or were they...still alive?* He didn't want to think about it any further.

Steven diverted his gaze from the book and looked to Ash. "You got the book." he said. After all of the torture he had witnessed Ash go through, he was glad that he at least got what he came for. It made Steven relieved that they were one step closer to taking Freddy down.

Ash looked at Steven and nodded. His voice was still faint and weak. “Yeah. It wasn’t easy though.” he winced again from the cuts on his left side.

Evelyn took the book from Ash while he placed his hand on the slash marks, hoping to ease the pain. She barely touched the edges with her fingers. The feel of the book made her cringe. She wasn’t pleased by the feel of rotten flesh. Yet, she stared in awe of it. This book, this wrinkled, bloody, tome, was the key to saving them all. It brought forth destruction and evil, but it also contained the reversal to such damage. “So, this is what’s going to kill Freddy and send the evil back?” she asked, hoping that their was no catch.

“That’s the plan.” said Ash.

Evelyn sat the book by Ash and ran her fingers through her black hair. She was nervous about asking her next question. “About that–how are we supposed to use this?”

“Yeah,” Faith joined. “didn’t you say it was Kandarian? I mean, I barely passed Spanish, how am I supposed to understand a fucking thousand year old, ancient language?”

“You’re not.” he said bluntly. Ash then turned to Steven and pointed a finger at him. “*He* is.”

His eyes went wide. His mouth parted, like he was going to say something. He had several things she wanted to say at once, but the first thing that left his mouth was, “Did Freddy drop you on your head while you were down there?”

Ash sat up to meet his gaze. He stared at him. “As a matter of fact, he did. But, that’s not important right now.”

Steven looked up and matched his stare, trying to show him how serious he was. “I don’t know, Ash.” He looked down at the book, picturing all of the things that could go wrong. *What if I mispronounce a word? What if I start reading, and one of those things come after me?* His eyes went back to Ash. "You'd be risking a lot...and...I can't be responsible for anyone else dying around me."

"Listen, kid." he said sternly. "You're the only ones who can do this for me, and I trust you with it. Just like I trust Evelyn, and Sailor Moon over there."

From across the way, Ash could hear Faith shout at him. "Fuck you!"

Evelyn stepped forward so that she was now standing a few feet from him. "He's right." she said. "You can do this, Steven. And, you're not alone. We're here for you."

Faith moved to Ash. "Yeah, I know you were incapacitated at the time, but we handled things pretty well while you were..." Faith semi-sung the rest of her sentence to the tune of "Enter Sandman" by Metallica. "...Off in never, never land."

"Really?" Evelyn said, almost chuckling. "Metallica lyrics, is that what we're doing right now?"

"Yes, that is what we're doing right now. Will you let me finish?" she sniped. She counted all of her achievements on her fingers as she spoke them to Ash. "And Evelyn, too. While we were all going crazy, it was Evelyn's idea to come to S-Mart, board up the doors, and try to get you out of the dream."

She looked back at Evelyn. "She even wasted one of those Deadites on the way over here!"

Steven sniped under his breath. "She almost killed us with her driving, but other than that..."

Evelyn ignored his comment and turned to Ash. "I know we're not your choice to do this, but you can trust us." She then turned away, and put her hands on Steven's shoulders. "And I know you're scared. But to not be a little scared right now would be stupid. You have only one job, and it's to read a book. We'll protect you, okay?"

Steven's voice was small, almost a whisper. "Yeah, okay." he agreed.

Ash put both feet on the floor and stood up. He took the Book of the Dead from Evelyn and offered it to Steven.

Steven had reached out his hand to grab the book, when Ash pulled it back, just slightly away from Steven's reach.

"You sure about this?" he asked.

Steven leaned further and grabbed the book from Ash's hand, indicating that he meant, "Yes". "It's just reading." he said nonchalantly. "How hard can that be?"

Evelyn stood up and touched Ash on his shoulder, prompting him to turn to her. "Ash." she called. "What's going to happen when Steven reads from the book? You've done this before, right? How does it work?"

A look of uncertainty washed over his face. He knew what had to be done. The problem was that, last time Ash tried to get rid of the evil, he ended up wandering through time and space, eventually ending up in the year 1300 A.D. "Yeah, I've done this before, sort of." he answered meekly.

Steven stepped forward, eager to hear what answers Ash had for him. "How'd you do it?"

Ash turned to Steven. "Basically, you–recite the, uh–pages, and–that causes the evil to manifest itself in the flesh. Which in this case, would probably be Freddy. Judging from what we saw outside, I think that part's taken care of." Ash looked at Steven sternly as he gave him instructions. "By reading these pages, what you're gonna do is open up a rift in time and space, and send the evil back."

"Back where?" asked Steven.

"Wherever it originated, I guess." replied Ash. "With Freddy, I'm guessing that'd be right before the parents torched him."

Steven opened the book and thumbed through the thick, wrinkled pages. "Okay, so, what pages do I read from? There's a lot in here."

Ash took the book from Steven's hands. "Let me look at that." he scanned each pages, quickly turning each one. He hoped that the sight of the reversal spells would jog his memory.

Faith questioned him. "You don't know where they are?" she asked, a little doubtful.

Ash snapped. “It’s been awhile, alright?” Once he had reached the last two pages in the back of the Necronomicon, he had found the pages. “Ah, here they are.” He handed the book back to Steven, his thumb marking the spot where he should read from.

Ash began to walk off, when Evelyn joined behind him. “When was the last time you had to do something like this?”

“Thirty years, give or take.”

Steven wanted to make sure his own worries would be at rest once the whole ritual started. “And it worked?” he asked.

“Well, it’s not like I got rid of it for good, but for a while it worked, yeah.”

Evelyn glared at him and studied his face. “So, you don’t really know if this is going to work?”

“Listen,” he said. “last time I had to do this, I had no idea what the hell I was doing. I–I was careless, and...I made a few mistakes. That’s probably how I ended up here. But, I know what I’m doing now.”

Evelyn nodded. She muttered just quietly enough for Ash to hear. “Okay...”

They both went their separate ways.

Steven had kept the book open to the passage that Ash had showed him. He mouthed the pronunciations to himself, insuring that when the time comes, he wouldn’t screw up the incantation.

He looked up and saw Evelyn walking toward him. He lowered the book, giving her his full attention. “Hey.” he greeted.

“Are you nervous?” she asked.

Steven half-smiled and expressed his sympathy. “Yeah.” he said. “A lot, actually.”

“I am too.” said Evelyn. “A lot’s happened in such a short amount of time. It doesn’t really give you a chance to think and let it sink in. Although, I guess that’s a good thing, because a lot of bad things have happened lately. It’s not good to dwell on it, you know? You just have to not think about it, and keep moving.”

He admired her bravery. How, even in the most dire situation, she was able to take charge protect them all when she needed to. Even though he tried to, he wished he could instantly be like that when the situation called for it. "If it weren't for you, I don't think we would've made it this far."

Evelyn was taken by surprise by Steven's remark. It both flattered and humbled her. "Really?"

"Yeah." Steven looked back at the page he had been studying. "It looks like Freddy's gotten pretty powerful now. But, we'll get through it." Steven wondered whether he would be able to do his part, or crash and burn when the time came. He looked back at Evelyn. "Um, Evelyn? If anything happens to me," he could already see the worried look on Evelyn's face as he spoke. "I know that you'll do the right thing and take over for me."

"Nothing is going to happen to you." she said adamantly.

Steven faintly smiled again. "Just promise me that you'll be there." he lowered his head so that he was now staring at her intensely. "Just in case."

Evelyn took a deep breath to both relax and prepare herself. "I promise."

"Thank you." Before he walked off, what he said to her would linger in her mind. "You're stronger than you think."

She watched him as he left her to join Faith, who embraced him with a hug. His words still left an echo in the back of her mind. *You're stronger than you think.* She then heard Ash's voice speaking to her from behind.

"Kid's got a point, you know." said Ash.

Evelyn turned her head to look next to her, and up to see Ash's face. She couldn't help but become transfixed with his scars, his bruises, his cuts. This beaten and wounded man had placed so much trust in her. "If it weren't for me, Freddy wouldn't have hurt you so badly in the first place."

Ash shrugged it off. "I've had worse."

She kept beating herself up for things she had no control over. *Maybe if I had gotten to the police station sooner, Ash wouldn't have gotten hurt...If I hadn't traveled to the dream to see Freddy for myself, he wouldn't have hurt me. And I wouldn't have given him the fear that he feeds off of.*

She had to ask him. "Before, when you said that you trusted me." She needed to know: why was she the one everyone relied on? "Why? Why, do you trust me with all this?" Evelyn kept looking at the floor, already embarrassed at the question she had just asked him.

He thought back to the first time he met Evelyn. She was the only one who didn't treat him like the ego-centric, paranoid, freak that people made him out to be. Even when everyone else had doubted him about Freddy, she gave him a chance. He didn't meet people like that often. He saw something in her. It was the way she kept fighting, no matter what was being thrown at her. It reminded Ash of himself. "Because you trusted me."

Evelyn lifted her head to look in Ash's eyes briefly before he turned away. She couldn't quite explain it, but Ash's kind words caused her lips to curve into a smile. She felt more sure of herself, and in her mind, she started to agree with them.

No more second guesses. No more doubts. No more fear. The self-pity and insecurities had stopped there.

Ash marched, putting more distance between him and his little army of twerps. He turned around to see the three of them standing next to each other, almost in a perfect line.

There they stood: Scraped, bruised, and shaken. This was not what he expected to have fight alongside him during his battle with evil himself, Freddy Krueger. But, they were all he had.

This preparation. This anxiety. This pre-battle fear. It wasn't new to him. He had led a war against an army of the dead once before, so it wasn't like he was treading new territory.

But at least then, he had an army of over two hundred men backing him up. They were armed, well-trained, and clad head-to-toe in 14th Century armor. And who did he have now? Two eighteen year olds and a sixteen year old who didn't know a .44 Magnum from their own asses? This wasn't Lord Arthur and his brigade. Nor was it Henry the Red and his men. He knew it would be a challenge.

And this time, Ash wasn't dealing with merely a Deadite version of himself, Bad Ash, in this battle. He was up against Freddy Krueger, the ruler of nightmares, and invader of minds. Someone who actually had the powers of the Necronomicon already in his arsenal. Getting beaten to a pulp in his dream was bad enough, now Ash had to face him again with his hoard of Deadite minions.

It was time to prepare them for the fight of their lives.

Ash put his index finger and thumb in his mouth and let out an ear-piercing whistle.

Everyone stopped what they were doing and looked at Ash.

"Now that I have your undivided attention." he said, his voice commanding like a drill sergeant. "I'm gonna to tell you some stuff you might not wanna hear." Ash slowly paced around them, judging their faces to see if they would break already.

Steven lifted his head from the book and said snidely, "Oh no, 'cause up until now, everything you've said has been so cheery."

Ash leered at him, annoyed that he had interrupted him, but still amused by his sarcasm. "You back-talkin' me, boy?"

Steven laughed quietly as he resumed reading. "No sir, Sergeant Cliché."

"As I was saying," continued Ash. "There's four of us in here, and by now, probably Deadite-riddled version of Springwood out there. It doesn't look good for us right now."

Evelyn jumped in. "But what about the police?" she inquired. "I thought Lt. Moore was going to have the whole department backing us up."

"That's true." he said. "But, judging from those bats on steroids flyin' around, I'm pretty sure there won't be much of them left either."

"So, we don't have anyone to come help us?"

"Nope." Ash answered. "Just us, baby. Just us."

The look of anguish on their faces was too strong to ignore.

Come on, Ash. he reminded himself. *You're supposed to tell them, "It's gonna be alright", not "All hope is lost".* Ash changed his tone. "Look, guys." he said. "I've been where you are. I know you think this is a suicide mission. That we're gonna be trapped here while the world goes to Hell, but it's not like that. We can beat Freddy and those creatures. I know you're scared, I was too–"

CRASH!!!

One of the florescent light fixtures that suspended below the ceiling fell and shattered on the floor. It landed just a few feet behind Ash.

"Aah!" he shouted as he turned around to see what the noise was all about. He saw broken glass everywhere.

Baffled by what had happened, the four of them looked up in unison to see what had caused the light to fall.

In the middle of the ceiling, there was a glass window pane that allowed part of the sky to be visible to them.

On the other side of the skylight, was a group of winged Deadites smashing their clawed fists against the window pane. They opened their mouths and ran their slimy tongues along the glass, dirtying the window. Their muffled screeches sent chills down each of their spines. The center of the glass was already started to crack.

"Shit." muttered Ash. "It won't be long before they break through." He then turned to Evelyn. "Did you block access to the roof?"

Evelyn nodded. "No, we only had enough wood to block the front door. I didn't even think to lock it."

"Then it looks like we're gonna have to get up there and weed 'em out. Because, if they break through that glass, we're screwed."

Curiosity struck Steven. "How are we gonna do that?" he asked. "There's like a dozen of them up there."

Ash smiled faintly, and took a few steps over to the Sporting Goods department. "Maybe." he said coyly. He stopped once he reached the display of hunting rifles, shotguns, pistols, etc.

They were all locked behind glass. Each arranged by brand, model, and price. On Ash's left were rifles, to his right were shotguns, and in the counter in front of him were pistols of varying caliber.

Ash held his arms out, gesturing toward all of the weapons at their disposal. "But, we have a dozen or so of these down *here*." He could see the figurative light bulbs flicker above their heads, and the grins form on their faces. "So," he said. "who's with me?"

"How many do you need?" asked Evelyn as she walked with Ash to open the lock.

Ash replied. "One for each of us, at least."

"Okay." Evelyn mumbled. She brought out her keys from her pants pocket and searched for the one that unlocked the glass doors. "Hold on a second." she said quietly.

Ash walked behind the counter and grabbed the barstool behind the register. Gripping it with both hands, Ash swung the chair in front of the glass, breaking it.

SMASH!!!

The sound of breaking glass made Evelyn jump and lift her head. She saw Ash dropping the barstool to the floor that was now littered with glass shards. He grabbed two or three guns at a time.

"That works too." Evelyn said.

Ash crouched down to grab the appropriate box of ammunition for each gun. He then turned to place each on the counter. Soon, Ash had the entire counter laid out with guns and boxes of ammo.

He let Evelyn, Faith, and Steven pick out whatever gun they wanted, but not without telling them that they should probably go with something lightweight. "It's easier to run when you don't have a shotgun on your back, weighing you down."

Ash unwrapped most of the bandages from his arms. He then unfastened the leather shoulder straps that usually held his 9mm pistol and his double-barreled shotgun. Instead, he replaced them with two bullet belts, each crossing over his chest.

Making his way to the hardware aisle, he grabbed a 10 ft. metal chain. He laid it out on the counter and intertwined it with thin barbed wire.

In the garden department, Ash got an extra tank of fuel for his chainsaw and filled it to the rim.

Finally, he joined Evelyn, armed with the revolver she had before, Faith, with a small rifle with double over/under barrels, and Steven, with the Necronomicon in one hand and an axe in the other. They all stared at him, eagerly awaiting his signal to go to battle.

Ash grabbed both of his shotguns from the glass counter in front of him, spun them around with his thumbs and rested both of them in the holsters he had fashioned behind his back. They made an "X" shape behind his back. He then attached his chainsaw to his right nub, and pulled the rope, starting it.

RRRRRRRRRRrrrrrrrrrRRRRRRRRRRrrrrrrrrrRRRRRRR RRR!!!

He looped the barbed, metal chain around his left palm, securing it in his hand. Using it like a whip, Ash wrapped the chain around a support beam for one of the shelves. He pulled the chain hard, tipping the tall shelf to the ground. Various merchandise broke and sent glass and other scraps spreading out around the floor.

"Groovy."

Chapter 30

THEIR HOWLS FILLED THE NIGHT air. Their dirty claws scratched against the skylight looking into the inside of the Springwood S-Mart. Their slimy tongues, still fresh with the blood of the living, were used to lick the glass. They salivated in hunger. Long, thick ribbons of saliva dripped from the corners of their monstrous mouths. The rooftop of the S-Mart was littered with the foul presence of Deadites.

Thirteen winged Deadites crawled on the rooftop, waiting for fresh souls to bring to their new Master. The demons had wings made of skin, each side was six feet in length. The corners of their wings had sharp, curved talons to eviscerate the innocent people of Springwood.

The faces that belonged to these hideous creatures were inhuman. Their eyes were blank white. Eyes that were soulless, evil, glowing in the dark of night. Their brow bones were prominent, and arched into a constant expression of anger. Their jaws were elongated, revealing rows of jagged, rotting, fangs. Above were a set of ears that were pointed and elfin.

The Deadite in the center of the rooftop, amid the swarm of its winged brethren, rose up. It stood in the crowd of demonic monsters. The Deadite tilted its head, facing the clear night sky. It flapped its leathery, fleshy wings and unleashed a spine-chilling, high-pitched, screech into the air. The airborne creature was calling forth more Deadites to surround the building.

The foul creatures were starving, they had not eaten in hours. But, they knew that Ash and his band of misfits were for Freddy, their master. The souls of the children may give him strength, but the soul of the Chosen One will give him immortality. He had commanded his Deadite followers to bring Ash to him, so that he may devour his soul and truly be eternal.

Other Deadites joined in the howls, creating a chorus of unnerving, demonic sounds. They raised their claws to the sky, sticking their slimy tongues out, licking at the fresh night air.

It was not just the roof that had been run amuck with the presence of evil. On the front of the building, there were twenty Deadites and counting. They scaled the walls, hoping to reach the top of the building. They had failed in trying to bust through the front door, so they had opted for a different route.

They piled on top of each other until one had reached the bottom curve of the blue "S" in the large, florescent, "S-Mart" sign. Once the Deadite had reached that point, he pulled up more to join him. This Deadite, who had once been a teacher at Springwood High before his body was possessed (hence the button-up shirt and tie), helped another Deadite up.

His voice was raspy, like a hissing snake. "Pick up the pace!" he shouted. "We must hurry!"

Another Deadite, who was previously an auto-mechanic at the local body shop, explaining the oil-stained coveralls, replied. "I'm going as fast as I can!" His voice was slightly lower than his counterpart. "You lousy bag of bones!"

The male demon shouted again. "We must bring him to Freddy before dawn!"

There was a demon behind him, climbing over him to catch up. This demon was younger than the previous two, and female. She couldn't have been more than sixteen. Her brown hair covered most of her pale gray face. "Our Master is waiting!" she added, hitting her foot against the demon behind her as she climbed above.

The coverall-clad Deadite had a look of scorn washing over him as the young demon's foot hit his face. He hissed. "Don't hit my face, you harpy!"

The adolescent Deadite turned her head back to face him before scaling the wall. "Try to keep up, you old sack of bones!"

The male demon shook his fist at her. "Why I oughta..."

The Deadite, now at the top of the "S-Mart" sign, heard the commotion and spoke.

"We must not bicker!" he said. "It will take all of us to bring him to Freddy! Ash must die!"

The others below heard him and began chanting. "Ash must die! Ash must die!"

Behind the crowd of demons climbing to the top of the building, were even more, filling the entire parking lot. The entire lot was packed shoulder-to-shoulder with hideous demons. They all ran past each other, laughing in psychotic glee, and climbing over any Deadite that was too slow to keep up the pace.

The swarm had been outstretched to the streets. The Evil Dead ran amuck in downtown Springwood. They filled the streets. Some couldn't wait to get to S-Mart to surround Ash, while others kept a walking pace, scouring the area for other fresh souls. Freddy told them to save Ash for him, but he didn't say anything about pedestrians.

The streets, congested with the possessed bodies of Springwood residents, were soon becoming scenes of horrible wrecks. Although it was 2:00 AM at this point, there were still people driving down the streets. They had no knowledge of horrors that were ahead.

One man, who was already nodding off behind the wheel, opened his eyes to a sight beyond his imagination. In the middle of his headlights stood three Deadites staring back at him.

The man opened his eyes wide, and gasped. "Oh, shit!" He turned the wheel as hard as he could.

SQUEAL!!!

It inevitably caused his gray Chevy Malibu to swerve, and flip over in the Deadite-filled street. The car was now upside down.

The windows on each side collapsed from the pressure. Small shards of glass were now lodged in the side of the man's head. The doors were dented and the front and back bumpers were dislodged. Smoke rose from the engine as the air bags deployed.

Although almost every bone in his body had been crushed, the young man was still alive. The side of his head bled, dripping on the roof of the car as he was upside down, barely contained by his seatbelt.

The three Deadites grinned. A fresh soul was brought before them. He couldn't fight them. He couldn't push them away. All he could do was scream as they tore away at his pretty flesh.

They rushed toward him. They pulled the door off of its hinges to get to him easily. The middle Deadite ripped off his seatbelt. The man grunted as he fell to the ground. The demon grabbed him by his shoulders and dragged him out of his car and into the fresh night air.

He was a young man, in his mid-twenties. He had light brown hair and was wearing a yellow, hooded sweatshirt that was now covered in glass and stained with blood. His name was Mark, and he was a male nurse at Westin Hills psychiatric hospital, as noted by the nametag that hung from his lanyard. Mark was barely able to open his eyes, weakly fluttering them as a sign of consciousness.

The trio of Deadites hovered over his body. The middle Deadite shouted in excitement. "How sweet, fresh meat!"

Mark opened his eyes and saw only rotting skin and pale eyes. He wanted to get up and run away, but he couldn't move. The bones in his arms and legs were shattered. The pain was excruciating. All he could do was scream. "Aaah!" The terror in Mark's eyes would bring compassion to anyone, but not to the Deadites. All they wanted was to feed. "Please! No!" he pleaded. "Somebody! Please! Someone help me!"

The Deadite in the middle grabbed him by the neck, while the other two grabbed both of his limp legs. At once, they bit into his flesh, taking hunks of skin and muscle with their teeth. The middle demon tore a chunk of skin from his cheek. The other two rolled his pant legs up and bit into the fatty layer of skin behind his shins.

Mark bled profusely. As if getting into a car crash wasn't enough, now he was getting eaten alive by the Evil Dead. Mark screamed. "AAAAAHH!!!" The pain was unbearable, he just wanted to die so that he would no longer have to feel it.

After what felt like hours, but had actually just been less than a minute, Mark had already started to change. The color in his brown eyes were disappearing. It was as if a swarm of storm clouds were covering his eyes as they began to turn milky white. His skin became paler. The veins under his skin became thicker, and changed from light blue to black. They were visible in his neck and up to his face. Eventually, Mark's screams of terror and turned into a warbled and scratchy howl. Mark was now one of them.

This was not the only instance of chaos and destruction. All throughout the streets of Springwood, there were wrecks, fires, and Deadites taking the lives of ordinary people, recruiting more into their army.

The once peaceful, suburban, paradise that was Springwood was now Hell's gateway. The clean streets were overrun by Kandarian demons. The streetlamps and illuminated the sidewalks with yellow lights were now being tipped over by the filthy bastards, causing more darkness the overcome the area.

When the mongrels weren't causing destruction at every turn, they were feeding. Every block was stained with blood. Some of the Deadites would pause at the corners to drag the limp bodies of their prey, and feast on their flesh and bones until they were one of them.

Empty and wrecked cars, semi-trucks, and motorcycles were strewn in the middle of the streets. The Deadites would simply climb over them in their pursuit to find and capture Ash. Gas fires would erupt as a result of the wrecks. The night air was lighted with the bright orange flames.

It may have been because of the fires and smoke that filled the air, but something had caused the sky to change in appearance. It was no longer black with the subtle glint of the moon hovering above. Above the streets was a sky that was red as blood.

This scene of unimaginable horror stretched out for miles. It was no longer just downtown Springwood that was sullied by the presence of evil. This spread out for miles. Further away, near city limits, were more demons racing to their destination.

Beyond the horizon, there was a hill overlooking the entire town. Since Springwood was a fairly small town, it wasn't the sight of a busy metropolis. But there were a few large buildings, and plenty of lights shining out from the dark, country air.

The smell of burning gasoline and smoke was barely detectable from the distance. But, the howling battle cries of the Deadites were still loud and echoing.

It was the perfect spot to overlook all of the destruction and carnage.

At the very top of the modest hill, the ground began to open up. A three foot long split formed in the dirt and began to spread open. A bright flash of red light came forth from the opening in the ground. The ground moved, crumbling and spreading wider for what was about to emerge from beneath the earth.

From the hole in the ground, flames shot into the night sky. A wall of fire rose about six feet tall from the dirt. Glowing embers swirled around the dancing flames, eventually falling to the ground and causing all plant life that came in contact with it to wither and die.

In the midst of the roaring fire, there was something inside of it. A silhouette was visible in the center. It was in the shape of a man. His head was tilted down, putting emphasis on the fedora on the top of his head. His right shoulder was slumped down, and on his hand was the sight of long, six-inch long, finger knives.

The flames crashed down just as quickly as they had risen. It was revealed that from behind the curtain of flames was Freddy.

A hoard of Deadites came running down the hill, scattered, unorganized, and laughing with maniacal glee. Most of them had no idea where Ash's location was, they were just ready to be free and claim more innocent souls.

Freddy tapped the knife on his index finger against his right leg. He stood at the very top of the hill, watching over all of the Deadites that were so eager to do his bidding. His pale, blue, eyes leered at them, observing as they scattered about aimlessly. Their raving and imbecilic laughs annoyed him, almost as much that hockey puck Jason's blank stare of his.

Glad I don't have to deal with that fucker again. He thought.

He stared at the hundreds of Kandarian demons before him. Freddy clicked his tongue against the roof of his mouth, and shook his head in disapproval. *This just won't do. I think they need a little...incentive.*

Freddy raised his glove arm in front of him, extending it so that it was completely level and straight. He flicked his index blade up towards the sky.

As soon as he lifted his bladed finger, each and every one of the Deadites ceased to move. They no longer ran, climbed over each other, or spoke. They were completely still. It was as if they were frozen in time. But they were not.

Freddy didn't have to speak, but with that small gesture, the demons mentally heard their master calling them. Telling them to stop what they were doing immediately, and listen only to him.

The Deadites planted their feet to the dirt, and all fell silent. At once, they turned around to the opposite direction, so that they were now looking up at their ruler on the hill. They all stared, slack-jawed and salivating with hunger, eager to obey Freddy's commands.

He reveled in the sight of the many Deadites before him. All of them, obeying his every command. Staring at him, waiting to hear the next word from their master. The corners of Freddy's lips curved into a self-satisfied grin. He spoke to himself in that low, graveled voice of his. "I'm beginning to enjoy this."

Freddy scanned the army of Deadites in front of him. His eyes trailed from the front row that was thirty feet away from him, to the very back that stretched just beyond the horizon. Freddy spotted something odd in the middle of the crowd. He squinted his eyes to focus on what he was seeing.

What he saw was one of his Deadite minions, who had already captured someone. The demon was holding the man close. Holding him down. Trying to dig his nails into him, and take a chunk of his flesh to change him. They were far away, so the man's screams were but a faint whisper in the wind. The man had a look of pure terror in his eyes. He flailed his arms and writhed his body in an attempt to escape, but it was not working.

As Freddy examined more closely, he began to notice the police badge on the side of the man's shirt, and the blonde hair below his ears. A light went off in Freddy's head. It was Lt. Moore, Ash's new best friend from the Springwood Police Department. *He'll know where Ash is hiding my book.* Freddy realized.

Using his bladed hand again, Freddy pointed to the Deadite in the middle of the crowd. He called to him. "You!"

Freddy had stopped the Deadite from sinking his teeth into Lt. Moore's skin. The demon ceased his attack and looked up at Freddy. His mouth was still hanging open as he hissed at Freddy for interrupting his feast.

He ignored the Deadite's disgusting reaction, keeping his eyes locked on Moore's fear-stricken face. He waved his index blade, gesturing them to come forth. "Bring the pig over to me!"

The Deadite grabbed Moore tightly by the back of his shirt collar. He hissed his words as he replied to Freddy. "Yes, my lord!" The demon yanked Moore in Freddy's direction. He pushed him forward, causing the Lieutenant to stumble.

The Deadite restrained his arms as he led Harold to the top of the hill. After the two had reached the top and were a mere ten feet from Freddy, Moore freed himself from the demon's grip. "Let go of me, you ugly son of a bitch!" He could still hear the demon rasping behind him as it backed away.

Moore turned his head away from the Deadite, and saw Freddy's charred face staring right back at him, smiling. *Bastard.*

The first thing he thought to do was grab his gun from the holster on the side of his belt. He clicked it back, cocking it, and pointed it right in-between Freddy's eyes. His hand remained steady, and aside from the sweat dripping down his face and along his eyelids, so was his gaze. "I'll do it." he said, his voice sounding like that of a crazed murderer. "I swear to God, I'll blow your brains out right now, Krueger."

Freddy half-smiled and, with his left hand, took off the dirty, brown, fedora that usually rests on his head. He opened his arms and gestured his hands in a way to tell Lt. Moore to "go ahead". He spat his words out. "I dare you, pig." he said, putting emphasis on the word "pig". "Shoot me!"

Moore let no time pass when putting two bullets in the sucker. Moore pulled the trigger and shot Freddy twice between the eyes.

BLAM!!!

BLAM!!!

Freddy was knocked back. His head pointed to the sky from the impact of the bullets. Under the moonlight, the sight of blood spraying from his forehead was visible. He screamed in pain. "Aagh!" He then doubled over, dropping his hat to the ground and putting his hands on his bullet wound. His dark red blood spilled from between his fingers and dripped out on the grass. He continued to moan in agony.

Lt. Moore slowly lowered his gun, not sure what had just happened. His face was fixed in an expression of both victory and confusion. He was still high from adrenaline from shooting the bastard, but at the same time, he wondered how it was so easy. *This can't be right.* Moore debated to himself. *He's down, but...why would he have just let me shoot him like that? Unless...*

Freddy lifted his head so that his eyes now looked into Moore's. Freddy's blue eyes glinted with pain and agony. His breath was short and erratic.

Freddy wiped the blood from his scarred face with the sleeve of his sweater. Once he lowered his arm, Moore noticed that the small, marble-sized holes in the middle of his face stopped bleeding. Not only that, but Freddy's look of hurt and cringing pain were also gone. A slick smile crossed his lips, slivers of his sharp, rotted teeth showed. He opened his mouth. Moore thought he was about to laugh at him again, but he was wrong.

"You actually fell for that?!" Freddy kept his sly smile as he walked towards Moore. He lowered his voice so that Moore was the only one to hear his words. "How did you ever get promoted to Lieutenant?"

Moore's face had been frozen until now. He exploded in anger and shouted in Freddy's face. "Rot in Hell, you bastard!"

"Been there already." said Freddy. He shortened the distance between himself and Moore. "Now, enough small talk." He was now inches from Moore's face. Freddy grabbed his by the front of his shirt, clenching the fabric with his fist. "Where is Ash?" he sneered.

Moore kept a straight face. He knew that they were all holding themselves up inside S-Mart, but he would be damned if he was going to give that information to Krueger. "I swear I don't know where he is." he said, trying to sound desperate.

Freddy thrashed him around and shouted in his face. "YOU KNOW DAMN WELL WHERE HE IS! NOW TELL ME!" Freddy lowered his voice and felt his nostrils flaring, and the corners of his lips moving up. "Or..." Freddy raised his right hand, and let the knives on his fingers dance in front of Lt. Moore's face. "...do you need some motivation, hmm?"

The blades were inches from Moore's face, moving around, shining under the light of the moon. He saw how sharp they were, how they could easily cut through his skin without Freddy having to put much effort into it. There were still speckles of blood on the silver blades. He felt his heart begin to pound against his chest. He looked around, but there was no escape. Moore was surrounded by Deadites.

"Why do you need Ash, anyway?" said Moore in an attempt to deflect the current situation. "You got what you came for."

Freddy's snide expression turned into that of scorn. "That jarhead has my book." he explained. "He could actually do some damage to me..." Freddy laughed quietly to himself. "...*if* he figures out how to use it. Plus, the soul of the Chosen One would ensure that no one," Freddy emphasized every word that followed. "Ever. Gets. Rid. Of. Me. Again."

Moore spoke again. "So, that's what you're after? His soul?"

Freddy nodded his head "yes". "Mmm hmm." He could picture it now: Ash cowering on the cold ground, broken and sliced, begging for life. Just like so many of his victims before him. And then, when Ash has had every fabric of his dignity torn from him, Freddy sinks his glove into his body. Over. And over. And over. When his intestines have been spilled out of his body, and that last shred of life into his eyes fades away, Ash's soul will escape from his body and become absorbed by Freddy. He will have won. Not just the battle, but dominion over the dream world and the waking world.

The sound of emerging footsteps broke Freddy's bloody fantasy. One of his Deadite followers approached behind him. The demon had been traveling a long way, which explained his shortness of breath as he spoke to him. His voice was raspy and he felt himself catching his breath in between words. "My lord." He addressed Freddy as such.

Freddy didn't bother to turn around to look his minion in the eye. The Deadite had interrupted his interrogation. He scowled, continuing to stare at his knives as he twiddled them under the moonlight. His tone was curt. "What?" he asked, his voice was even lower and more demonic than the Deadite's.

What the demon said next sparked Freddy's interest. "I've come a long way. I know where Ash is keeping your book."

As soon as the demon finished speaking, Freddy ceased to play with his glove. His eyes widened in interest. He shifted his body slightly to the right to look the demon in the eye. His tone was much calmer now. "Go on." he instructed.

The demon did as he was told. "He and the others are hiding inside the S-Mart," the Deadite pointed his finger in the downtown area. "just a few miles north of here. There are already dozens of us there trying to break through."

"Oh." Freddy grinned mischievously as he looked in the direction where the Deadite was pointing. He glanced back at the demon. "Well?" he sneered. "What are you waiting for, huh? Get out back out there, and break the fucking doors down!"

The Deadite kept a calm face. He lowered his head. "Yes, my lord." He then ran back down the hill, disappearing among the crowd of demons.

Freddy turned back to Moore, who was still sweating and still had a look of fear in his eyes. Freddy twitched his face into an evil smile. "I'd do it myself, but uh, without my book, I'm not as powerful as I am in the dream realm." He raised his blade up in front of Moore's face again. "I suppose you're lucky." he said. "In the dream, I could bash your brains in with just a flick of my blade." He traced his knives ever so close by Moore's skin, watching them move.

Despite being in a stranglehold by Krueger, Moore's words managed to come out clearly. "You're gonna kill Ash, and then what? Just keep killing until there's no one left?"

Freddy lifted his gaze to look at Moore. "That's right." he said. "And you know what? I think it's time I get an early start!" Freddy bent his arm and cocked his elbow back. Before he could even execute the kill, he could hear Moore's defiant cries.

"No!" he screamed. "No! Don't!"

Fast and swift, Freddy shot his arm out in front of him. Through his glove, he could feel the blades break through Lt. Moore's ribcage.

CRUNCH!!!

He felt Moore's body tense up as he forced the knives further into his ribs, feeling the gelatinous texture of his organs as he moved the blades around inside his chest.

Moore cried out in pain. "AAAAAH!!" He clenched his teeth to prevent further screams from escaping his mouth. He could feel himself slowly slip away, but the excruciating pain of having Freddy's knives jammed inside his body was not subsiding. He felt his uniform getting wet from the blood that was gushing from the four holes in his chest. Some of his blood was building in his throat. He began choking on it, spitting up thick, red, mouthfuls that stained his chin, and dripped onto the sleeve of Freddy's sweater. His screams were replaced by wet, gargled, choking noises.

Freddy was almost sad that the screaming had ceased. It his favorite sound. It was music to his ears. It was what he lived for. Freddy's laughed was crazed, dark, and warbled. "Aha-hahahahahahahahahaha!"

After his demented laugh had ceased, Lt. Moore was dead. Freddy retracted his gloves from his chest and let his lifeless corpse drop beneath his feet. He watched Moore bleed out on the grass, his eyes were now empty and his face was now fixed in a permanent state of terror. Freddy felt Moore's soul escaping from his body and emerge in his own. His eyes became pale white and glowed for a moment, before returning to its original pale blue color.

"That's what I'm talkin' about." He growled. "I already feel stronger, now." Freddy turned back to face his army of the undead. He raised his gloved hand, pointing his index blade towards the direction where he now knew Ash was hiding. "I want all of you slimy sons of bitches to get out there, and bring Ash to me! Kill the innocent, and possess the living! Go!"

As soon as he gave them the word, the Deadites turned around and ran towards the city. Each and every one of them laughed in a demented fashion, screaming and screeching as the headed to downtown Springwood.

Freddy watched as the last batch was slowly disappearing in the horizon. He lowered his arm, tapping his blade against the side of his leg. By the fourth tap, Freddy was immersed into a wall of flames just as he was before. The fire stood tall for a second or two before dropping back under the earth. Freddy was gone along with it. The only trace of his presence there was the dead body of Lt. Moore, lying on the top of the hill.

Just as it did on the top of the hill on the edge of Springwood, the wall of flames appeared again, this time on the roof of a building that was a few blocks away from the S-Mart downtown. Freddy appeared in view as the fire lowered and went away.

He walked to the edge of the building and kneeled down, overlooking all of the chaos that was unfolding. He watched as over three hundred Deadites ran through the streets, causing fires, destruction of the town, and feasting on the souls of the living as they passed by.

Freddy trailed his gaze, following the mass of Deadites as they all gravitated towards one destination. They clogged the street as they ran past, through the parking lot, and finally reaching S-Mart. They were making progress, it seemed. The demons had the entire building surrounded. There was no escape.

Freddy's time was coming. But, judging from how well they had boarded the place up, it would take a little more time before he was able to make his grand entrance. "I'll join them soon enough." he said to himself. Freddy stood back up and took a few steps back. "But for now,"

A cloud of smoke and embers formed just three feet behind him. The whispers of black smoke whirled around, as if it was forming some sort of shape.

Freddy bent his knees, as if to sit down. Once he finally lowered himself, the dark cloud of smoke went away, and was replaced by a chair. But it wasn't just a chair, it was a large and articulated throne. The throne was tall, the top extended well above Freddy's head. It had large, wide armrests which Freddy placed both hands upon. The sides were pointed and gray. The edges were made out of small, human, bones. The rest of the throne, such as the seat itself, reflected various colors, most of them pale, some darker than others. But, the interior had an odd texture to it. It wasn't leathery or wrinkled, but it was certainly rotted. The main frame of the throne appeared to have faint traces of tortured faces on it. It had been fabricated by the flesh and bones of young children.

Freddy sat back comfortably on his demonic throne. "I think I'll enjoy the show." He lifted his feet up until another cloud of black smoke appeared, this time forming a footrest made entirely out of bones. He planted his dirty work boots on it. He laughed softly to himself. "Ha ha ha ha ha...That's right my little piggies, do the work for Uncle Freddy."

Chapter 31

THE WALLS SEEMED TO CLOSE in as they ascended up the stairs toward the roof. The stairway was so narrow that the four of them had to move in a single file line. Ash led the way, while Evelyn, Faith, and Steven followed. They each moved at a slow pace, barely lifting their feet to reach the first step, and clutching their weapons so tightly that the palms of their hands began to sweat.

Only a faint light came forth from the single bulb that was suspended from the ceiling. The light bulb hung from a thin rope. It swung from side to side, like a pendulum. The white light was growing dim, the bulb was about to give out, each brief flicker was longer than the one that came before it. It was usually standard policy to make sure that all of the exits were well lit, but no one had ever needed to come up to the roof until now. Plus, Ash was too preoccupied with hunting Deadites, and figuring out how to get rid of Krueger, to make sure that all of the exits were up to code.

As the dim light flickered and swung, it caused the four of them to fall victim to the blinding darkness every few seconds. The preparation speech that Ash had given them a few minutes before had given them confidence, but that adrenaline was slowly waning the further they walked up the stairs. They had seen the horrible creatures on the roof, looking at them from through the glass. The closer they approached the door, the more their fear had escalated.

Ash clutched his ten foot long chain tightly in his left hand. He stared at the door as he slowly crept closer toward it. The further he walked, he more clearly he could hear the howls and screeches coming from the mouths of the wretched Deadites behind the door. He felt his hand start to shake, making the chain rattle and clink as he dragged it along the steps. His ears twitched as he could faintly hear the kids whispering behind him.

He could hear Faith's voice. "I'm scared out of my mind right now."

And Evelyn's hushed tone. "So am I. My hands are shaking."

Faith whispered again. "Promise you won't let those things get to me."

Ash assumed she was talking to Steven, as he was the next one to speak. "I'm not gonna let anything happen to you."

And then Faith. "Me neither."

He couldn't help but let his anxiety come to the surface. Ash had never gone against so many Deadites before. And not only that, he didn't have much of an army to back him up this time. It was the four of them against the entire population of Springwood.

Ash was just one step away from the roof entrance. He placed his hand on his door handle, but stopped himself. He couldn't bring himself to open the door. Over the course of the long, treacherous night, Ash had grown fond of these kids. He realized that they weren't the obnoxious, air-headed brats that he thought they were.

These kids, they were barely eighteen, and they were ready to go to battle without a second thought. They were willing to risk their lives, their immortal souls, to make sure that Freddy goes back to Hell where he belongs. In a way, Ash was proud of them and admired their bravery. He was their age when he unwittingly unleashed the damn things in the first place. And now, almost thirty years later, he's created a new generation of demon slayers. But these kids weren't as experienced as he was. *I've had my whole life to be ready for this. How long have they had? A few hours? I don't know if I could live with myself if I just sent them out there to die.*

He remembered the unfortunate perks that came with being the Chosen One. All of the people that Ash was close to. Everyone that he ever cared for, loved, or tried to protect, eventually fell victim to the dark spirits. *I tried to save my friends. I tried to save Linda...and Sheila... but the damned things took them, too. I don't know if I'll even be able to save* myself *this time.*

After returning from the slideshow of memories that went by in his mind, Ash looked down and realized that his hand had been shaking from squeezing the door handle so tightly. He wasn't going to send them out just yet. Ash let out a frustrated sigh, and let go of the door handle.

Evelyn looked over his shoulder, noticing the worried look on Ash's face as he whipped around to face the three of them. She looked up into his eyes, still anxiously gripping the revolver in her right hand and the axe in her left. "Ash, is something wrong?" she asked. "I thought we were going to go out there and kill those things."

"Are you guys positive about heading out there?"

Evelyn squinted her eyes, and almost looked offended by Ash's question. "Well, we're not 'positive' about it, but we're ready."

Ash stumbled on his own words. "I–I just–don't know if it'd be right to send you out there. I've seen this kind of thing before, and it's no picnic, believe me."

Evelyn was dead serious and the look on her face conveyed it. She took a wide step toward Ash, leaving only inches between them. She looked up at his scarred face. Her tone in her voice was calm and relaxed. "Ash, you've prepared us well enough for this. I understand that you feel a little odd about sending us to fight with you..." By then, her tone had altered, becoming almost demanding. "...but you are *not* going out there alone. We aren't letting you."

Steven stared at the ground as he muttered to himself. He kept his voice quiet, so he assumed they wouldn't hear him. "I don't know, I wouldn't mind hanging back in the break room for a few minutes while Ash does his thing."

To Steven's surprise, Evelyn heard every word. He saw the look of scorn on her face as she quickly turned around to face him, her black hair swung in front of her face. "Shut up, Steven!" she sniped.

Steven looked at her and shook his head in confusion. *It was just a joke, what's the big deal?* he thought. "Jeez, Evelyn. When did you grow balls all of a sudden?"

Evelyn ignored his comment and slowly turned her head back to face Ash. She lowered her voice back to a steady tone again. "This is our fight, too." she said. "We've all lost someone close to us because of Freddy...so, you can understand why we're not going just sit this out, can't you?"

Ash couldn't help but twitch the corners of his mouth into a smile. He admired Evelyn's confidence. "Yeah." he answered. "I guess I underestimated you, kid."

She had grown tired of Ash constantly calling her "kid". Evelyn smiled back at him, her eyes where steady and exuded bravery. "Again. My name is Evelyn."

They stared into each other's eyes for a while. Evelyn felt like it was too long. She couldn't help but notice the way Ash was staring at her. She couldn't quite figure out what he was thinking behind those brown eyes of his. Ash just continued to look into her eyes, smiling the entire time. *Was he being derisive, like he usually is? Was he distracted by other thoughts, and he was just looking through me? Or was he looking at me in a different way?*

Evelyn leered at him, and chuckled softly at how Ash never broke eye contact with her. The awkwardness from their prolonged stare almost made her forget about the Deadites, scratching and howling on the other side of the door. "Um, Ash?" she asked.

Ash shook his head and cleared his throat in an attempt to appear nonchalant. "What's that?" he asked. He didn't know what had come over him. Although it was just for a few seconds, his mind was completely taken away from Freddy, the Deadites, everything. Over the past few days, that was the only thing he had been thinking about.

Ash had been completely intoxicated by Evelyn, staring deep into her dark green eyes.

Was it because of the way she returned his smile back at him? Was it because of the transformation she had undergone in that time? When he first met her, she was meek and quiet. And now, she was standing before him, stained in blood, with an axe in one hand and a gun in the other, ready to fight alongside him. He realized that the reason he had become so beguiled with Evelyn, was because she was becoming more like him.

Evelyn held her voice steady as she ordered him. "Open the door already." she said.

Ash lifted his scarred chin and nodded. "Gotcha." He turned his back to her and placed his left hand on the door handle. He pushed on the handle, but it wouldn't budge. No one had come up to the rooftop in so long that the hinges had rusted.

He turned to his side and leaned his right shoulder against the door, while still gripping the handle. Ash pulled back, leaving twelve inches between him and the door. He slammed into it.

BANG!

The hinges on the corners started to creak and break off of the door. Ash slammed into it again.

BANG!

Ash leaned back even further, putting his full weight into the last budge. He grunted as he slammed his body against the door. "Argh!" This time, the rusted hinges broke free.

BANG!

The door flew wide open, and the force that Ash put into breaking the door down had caused him to side-step several feet outside, putting him in the midst of all of the Deadite horror. Ash heard shuffling footsteps approaching from behind him. As he straightened his back, he looked to see that Evelyn, Faith, and Steven had run outside the door to join him.

Evelyn stood by Ash's left side, while Faith and Steven took the right side. Evelyn gripped her axe tightly in her hand, her eyes widened in caution and her hands shook, but the rest of her body was still.

Steven stood just a few feet beside Ash. He held the Necronomicon tightly, clutching it by his chest with his left hand. He too had an axe, which he slowly raised up to his head in defense. His breathing became erratic as he eyed all thirteen Deadites staring at them in hunger.

Faith stood next to Steven, at the furthest corner of the rooftop. She wiped the sweat from her left hand onto her black jeans as she held the stock with of her rifle with her right hand. She positioned her rifle, placing the stock against her right shoulder, her finger barely touching the trigger. Faith pulled the hammer back until it clicked, insuring that her weapon was locked and loaded. She tried to remember what Ash had told her about proper stance. She briefly looked down to the ground to make sure that her left leg was in front of her, with her foot pointing straight, and that she put most of her balance on her right leg, with her right foot pointed to her right. After mentally checking off everything on her list, Faith closed her left eye, keeping her sight locked on her target, which was the winged Deadite closest to her. It looked at her intently, with its slimy tongue hanging out, rasping at hissing at her.

Ash stood in the middle of them. His chiseled face was still, and his dark brown eyes surveyed the mess of Deadites from left to right to left again. All thirteen of them paused, their inhuman bodies were completely still.

They stared at them, their elongated mouth hung open, allowing bloody saliva to drip from down to the ground in long ribbons. Their teeth were visible under the red night sky. The gums attached to their fanged teeth were rotted black. The winged creatures hissed and growled just audible enough to send chills down the their spines.

The cool breeze came forth through the night air, causing Ash's dark, matted, hair to dry, and the sweat on his brow to disappear. He lifted his chainsaw arm, causing the pull rope to swing and catch on the holster straps that crossed his chest. Ash then dropped his arm down, causing his chainsaw to roar.

RRRRRRRRRRrrrrrrrrrRRRRRRRRRRrrrrrrrrrRRRRRRRRRR!!!

Ash laughed under his breath, taking joy in the fact that the oversized bats were already fearing him. He cocked his thick eyebrow, smiled, and parted his lips to speak. "Come get some, you mangy bags of flesh!"

As the words left his mouth, one of the Deadites shrieked like a banshee, piercing Ash and the kids' ears. The bat-like monstrosity ran towards Ash on all fours, like an animal. It began to flap its large wings, lifting its body off the ground. The demon let out a high-pitched squeal as it leapt toward Ash.

Ash put one foot behind him and tensed his knees, steadying himself. His chainsaw still humming, Ash lifted his right arm and shot it through the Deadite's chest, and out its back.

The chainsaw roared from inside the Deadite's body. The demon convulsed violently as the blades speedily cut through its organs, slicing them away. Blood sprayed both from the demon's back and through its chest. The sound of bones breaking and sawing were heard above the hum of Ash's chainsaw. The Deadite lowered its wings, as it was on the brink of death.

Ash then dropped his barbed chain to the ground and reached behind his back for his trusty Boomstick. He grabbed his shotgun by the stock and slipped his finger through the trigger and brought it out. He aimed the double-barrels in front of the Deadite's dark, leathery face. Ash pulled the trigger.

BOOM!!!

The shotgun shell exploded in the Deadite's face. It's skull was littered with shrapnel. Speckles of blood, and gray matter shot in Ash's face as the Deadites head was blown clean off of its shoulders.

Ash lifted his left leg and placed it against the lifeless Deadite's body. He pushed, causing the creature to slip out of Ash's chainsaw and fall limp to the ground. He spun his shotgun around once, suspending it with his thumb, before placing it back in his holster.

Out of the corner of his eye, Ash spotted another foul creature charging at him at a quickening pace. An ungodly screech left the demon's mouth as it ran to Ash, raising its talons up to the sky, preparing to rip his skin.

Ash bent down to quickly pick up his barbed chain. He grabbed the end and rotated his wrist, wrapping the chain around his hand. Ash stood up and lifted the chain high above his head.

Evelyn noticed the spiked chain swinging dangerously close to her face. She widened her eyes in surprise, and quickly stepped out of the way.

The chain spun around in the air. As the demon quickly shortened the distance between it and Ash, he lowered his left arm, directing the chain toward the Deadite. The chain acted as a whip, clinking in the night air as it wrapped all the way around the Deadite's neck. While the metal chain was constricting the demon's airways, choking and suffocating it, the barbed wire intertwining it was stabbing the Deadite's neck.

The demon stopped in its tracks and dropped to its knees. It screeched once again, this time in agony. The barbed wire cut through the demon's skin, causing blood to pour from its neck. The demon grabbed the chain and used its talons in attempt to break free from the tight hold, but the chain was wrapped so tightly that freedom was impossible.

Once more, Ash wrapped the chain around his hand, giving him a stronger grip. He pulled his arm back quickly and yanked the chain hard. The chain squeezed the Deadite's neck even tighter. Blood began spraying from the Deadite's neck, staining Ash's silver chain to a gooey red. Ash grunted as he pulled the chain one last time.

The Deadite's screams ceased. Its head rolled back, facing up to the red sky, and then further back so that it was now looking at the eleven demons behind it. The sound of bones snapping could be heard as the demon's neck broke.

SNAP!

And then, the wet, squishy sound of the demon's muscles and skin splitting came forth. As Ash continued to pull on the chain, the demon's head had been completely ripped off from its neck.

The head dropped to the ground and rolled on the rooftop. It left a trail of blood seeping from its neck as it traveled. The head finally stopped once it was in front of Ash's work boots. Ash, satisfied by his own kill, shouted, "Whoo! Damn, I'm good!"

The disembodied head still continued to howl and hiss at Ash, causing him to look down and look at it in the eye. He took a moment stare at its ugly features up close: Dark, rotted flesh. Sharp, sinister bone structure. An elongated jaw line, home to rows of fanged teeth. A bald head with long, pointed ears curving up, past the top of the head, resembling horns.

Ash placed his left foot on the top of the Deadite's head, and rolled it around for a second before bending his foot back. Ash then launched his foot forward, kicking his head, sending it flying into the crowd of Deadites.

Ash dropped the chain to the ground. He lifted both arms up straight into the air. His right arm was bent slightly due to the weight of his chainsaw, but he still managed to lift it up. Ash shouted, "GOOOAAAL!"

Angered at the death of two of their brethren, the remaining eleven Deadites simultaneously charged at Ash, Evelyn, Faith, and Steven at full speed. The shouted in their warbled, high-pitched tone, flapping their wings and raising their talons.

Evelyn steadied herself, pointing her revolver at the Deadite that was heading toward her. She bent her arm and raised her axe so that it was parallel to her left shoulder.

Ash reached for his Boomstick and spun it around with his thumb. The shotgun rotated halfway, stopping when the barrel was pointed toward the crowd of Deadites. He then raised his idling chainsaw, pointing the blades forward.

Steven tightened his grip on the Necronomicon with his left hand, making sure that it would not slip from his hands during battle. He spun his the handle of his axe with his right hand, turning the position of the blade so that it was facing forward.

Faith repositioned her stance. She looked through the sight of her rifle, locking on her, now moving, targets.

Two Deadites ran, side by side, toward Ash. They were determined to mutilate Ash from head to toe, and bring him to their Master as they promised.

Ash pointed his shotgun at the Deadite duo. He placed his hand on the trigger. He let them know that this would be their first and last attempt at trying to capture him. Coyly, Ash said, "Bye bye!" and squeezed the trigger.

BOOM!!! BOOM!!!

The heads of the Deadites on Ash's left and right exploded from the impact of the shotgun shells. They bled from the fresh holes in their necks, and fell dead on the ground.

Only nine winged Deadites remained.

One demon that had come from the far edge of the rooftop was now running towards Evelyn. It stood on two feet, standing upright as it charged at her. The demon's tongue hung outside its mouth. The slimy piece of muscle swung from side to side.

Evelyn pulled the hammer back, clicking it four times. It was now ready for action. Evelyn placed her index finger on the trigger and squeezed it.

BLAM!

The winged demon had stopped running. Its head whipped back, facing the sky. When the demon lowered its head, it was revealed that the bullet had merely grazed along the left side of its scalp. While there were large chunks of bone and muscle tissue missing, it was not enough to kill the monster.

Evelyn flared her nostrils and cursed herself for not hitting her target. "Damn it!" she sniped. She still needed some practice. She saw that the Deadite had picked ip where it had left off. The creature began running to her again.

Out of pure impulse, Evelyn raised her axe and began charging toward the Deadite. She screamed, as if letting out a battle cry. "Aaaah!" The dark-haired warrior-in-training swiftly lowered the axe. The quick motion had ceased once Evelyn's axe impacted against the Deadite's face.

The axe sliced across the demon's forehead. The blade cut through the skull and pierced its rotting brain. The Deadite screeched and dropped to its knees. Blood began pouring from the wound, spraying from the slash mark. The blood stained Evelyn's knuckles. The demon eventually fell to the ground, laying on its back.

Evelyn placed her left foot on the Deadite's chest. She pushed down and she attempted to pull the axe from the demon's skull. She grunted as the blade finally broke free. She took her blood-stained sneakers off of the Deadite and stepped back. She raised her revolver and aimed it in-between the demon's eyes, and squeezed the trigger.

BLAM!

More blood gushed from the Deadite's face. It was now dead. Evelyn felt a smile form on her lips. She shook the blood from her axe, feeling proud of herself for having killed her first Deadite.

Eight Deadites remained.

Over on the far side of the building, on Ash's right, Faith felt her arms begin to tense up as she spotted another demon charging toward them. She felt the palms of her hands begin to sweat. She hoped that her rifle wouldn't slip from her fingers as she looked through the sight and moved followed her target.

The winged menace began to flap its wings up and down. Soon after, the creature was lifted from the ground and propelled itself toward Ash. The demon raised its talons, preparing to sink its claws into Ash and take him with it.

Ash looked up and notice the Deadite was hovering above him. He quickly dropped down to grab his barbed chain. He stood up and swung the chain around above his head. Ash aimed the chain at the Deadite's neck.

The chain wrapped around the demon's neck, just as Ash had hoped it would. The demon howled in pain, but it did not accept defeat. The Deadite flew over Ash and curved its body to the side, turning counter-clockwise. It now flew away from them.

The demon was flying at such a high speed, that it began to drag Ash with him, as he was still holding on to the chain. Ash felt a brute force pulling him forward. His eyes widened and his brows lifted. He screamed, "Wh-Whoa!" as the Deadite flew across the sky. Ash felt the tips of his work boots getting hot due to the friction.

Steven shouted. "Oh my God!" He pointed to the sky there the demon was dragging Ash with his own chain.

Faith felt her heartbeat increasing, and her clammy sweat mixed with the cool night air on her forehead. She knew she had to act quickly, or the Deadites would kidnap Ash. She pointed her gun, aiming it at the demon's head. She couldn't get a clear shot, the Deadite's flying pattern was too uneven to for her to aim properly.

She heard Steven's voice in her ear. "Faith, do something, they're gonna kill him!"

And then she remembered something that she learned from every shooter game that she had ever played. *Every time there's a moving target, shoot where they're going to be, not where they are.* Faith aimed it just an inch ahead of the Deadite and pulled the trigger.

BLAM!

The rooftop rained blood from the Deadite's neck as it fell lifeless to the ground. The demon's body dropped in the middle of the crowd. The rest of them had parted, forming a circle of space as the corpse crushed to the ground. Its bones shattered and it organs collapsed. A pool of blood formed around the body.

Inertia had caused Ash to nearly fall on his face when the demon had stopped dragging him. Ash fell on his hands and knees. When he looked up, he noticed the remaining seven Deadites looking down at him in hunger. Ash let go of his chain and stood up.

His chainsaw still idled. The low hum was still audible over the rasps and hisses of the winged demons. Smoke came forth from the chainsaw as Ash raised it up. He leered at the Deadite that stood a couple of feet in front of him.

"What're you looking at?" Ash grabbed the handle with his left hand and rammed the chainsaw into the stomach of the Deadite in front of him. His chainsaw roared loudly as it sliced through the demon's ribcage and burst through its back. Ash could faintly hear the demon screaming in agony over the powerful roar of his chainsaw.

The demon's blood dripped down to the ground, staining the rooftop with a thick puddle of red. Ash directed his chainsaw upward, cutting the creature vertically. The saw sliced its ribs, to its neck, and to the top of its head. From its midsection, the demon had been cut in half. The two halves of its upper body were now separating, revealing the creature's inner organs, skull, and brain. The Deadite fell beside Ash's feet, dead.

Ash wasted no time in killing the next Deadite that was closest to him. Using a motion similar to swinging a baseball bat, Ash swung his chainsaw from right to left, cutting another demon at the hip area.

The monster's bones snapped and crushed at the touch of Ash's blades. It shook and convulsed uncontrollably as it was being sliced in two. Thick, dark, blood drenched from its lower body. Its legs were now red and wet from its own blood. The demon began to choke and spit up mouthfuls of blood, dripping down from its mouth to its chest.

Ash had finally sawed the demon in half, like the trunk of a tree. Once his chainsaw had come forth from the other side of the demon's body, Ash lowered his arm and reached for his pump shotgun. He pulled it from his holster, held it by the pump, and shook it down, loading it. He then held it properly, with his finger on the trigger, pointed it at the demon's head, and shot it.

BLAM!

The demon's head exploded as its upper half slid off from the lower half of its body. The upper half landed on the ground, its intestines and organs spilled out on the ground. As for the lower half of the body, the demon's legs bent, dropping to its knees, finally landing on the ground. The air was now foul with the smell of rotting Deadite flesh amid the night air.

"Yeah." Ash said coolly as he put his shotgun back in the holster. "That's what I thought."

Five Deadites were left.

Two winged Deadites in the far corner charged at Steven and Faith. The one that ran toward Steven was on all fours, while the one charging Faith was standing on its back legs. The both released a powerfully loud screech.

Faith and Steven noticed the attack, and began running in different directions. Faith ran to the other side of the roof, joining Evelyn. Steven side-stepped just a few feet in front of the door where they had entered.

Steven shakily raised his axe above his head. Fear had washed over his face. He began sweating profusely, and could barely breathe. Steven held in his breath as he saw one of the ugly creatures running faster toward him. *Oh God, I'm gonna die! I'm gonna die! I'm gonna die!* He was frozen in place. He knew he should do something, but his body wouldn't let him move. He was paralyzed by fear. He couldn't bring himself to kill something so big and menacing. He truly thought that he was going to die horribly at that moment. All Steven could do was whimper, "Oooohhh..." and shut his eyes, not wanting to see the monster up close when it killed him. He heard the demon screech loudly, and then–

BLAM!

Steven opened his eyes to find a bloodied demon standing four feet from him. There was a hole about one inch in diameter on both the left and right side of its head. The demon was not moving, only letting quiet hisses leave its mouth.

He looked to his left, to see smoke coming from the barrel of a rifle. His eyes grazed along the length of the barrel, and at the very end, saw Faith lifting her head and smiling at him. Steven laughed awkwardly, "Ha ha ha ha..." and smiled back at her.

Faith lowered her rifle, pointing the barrel to the ground. "Steven!" she shouted at him. "It's not moving, kill it now!" She pointed at the demon.

Out of the corner of her eye, Faith saw the Deadite that was running toward her, getting closer. Without hesitation, Faith raised her rifle again, and squeezed the trigger in a hurry.

BLAM!

She hit the winged monster in the chest. The demon was halted, but not dead. Faith reached in her pants pocket for another bullet. She hastily grabbed one, reloaded it, and pulled the hammer back. Faith aimed more accurately and shot the Deadite in the head.

BLAM!

The monster was now dead and fell lifeless to the ground. It left a pool of blood, forming from the gunshot wounds on its chest and forehead.

Faith lowered her rifle again and turned to Evelyn. They smiled at each other and shared a high-five.

Steven was so lost in Faith's cat-like eyes, that for a moment, he had forgotten that they were fighting a Deadite army. He turned his head back to face the Deadite. Now filled with confidence, Steven raised his axe and hit it across the demon's head. He spilt the skull open. Steven lifted the axe again as the demon fell to the ground, screaming. He lowered the axe, again and again. The Deadite's blood splattered on Steven's jeans, his black shirt, and his face. Steven finally stood up straight once he saw that the demon was now thoroughly chopped and dismembered. He wiped the blood from the top of his lip, and laughed again, this time in relief. "Ha ha ha ha!"

Three Deadites remained.

Evelyn was busy reloading her revolver when she noticed another Deadite charging at her. She lifted her head to see that it was approximately twenty feet from her. Evelyn gasped and inserted the last bullet in her gun, closed the chamber, and pulled the hammer back all the way. When Evelyn looked back up, the demon was now only seven feet away from her. *Oh God, no...*

Faith stepped in between them. Faith grunted, "Ugh!" and hit the demon hard with the butt of her rifle. The demon was halted. Faith stepped out of the way and smiled at Evelyn. "He's all yours."

Evelyn chuckled and smiled. "Thanks." She raised her revolver, aiming it at the Deadite's head. She shot it three times: in the forehead, in-between the eyes, and the mouth.

BLAM! BLAM! BLAM!

Blood and brain matter sprayed from the back of the demon's head as it fell to the ground. It landed with a loud thud, finally dead.

Evelyn lowered her revolver, pointing the barrel to the ground. She looked over to her right, and saw Faith, with her back to her. She had her rifle laid down to the ground. Evelyn leaned over so she could see what was in front of Faith. She had her arms wrapped around Steven. He had dropped his axe to the ground, but kept the book in his hand. He returned her hug.

They were both so happy to be alive, and with each other. Both Faith and Steven were smiling from ear to ear and hugging each other so tight, it looked like they were trying to squeeze the life out of each other. Steven picked her up off of her feet and began spinning her around. Evelyn could hear them talking to each other.

Evelyn smiled meekly for them, trying to be as happy as they were. But she couldn't. Seeing them together reminded her of Cooper. She remembered how happy she was when she was with him. He would meet her at work every morning and greet her with a hug not unlike the one Steven and Faith were sharing. They spent most of the day together, whether it be at work on the weekdays, or playing video games and watching movies on the weekends.

And then Freddy took him away from her. The bastard killed the only man she ever really loved. She will never have those precious moments with Cooper ever again, because of *him.*

Evelyn felt her eyes begin to strain from emerging tears. She fought them back as hard as she could. She didn't want tears clouding her vision at a time like this.

And at that moment, Evelyn heard that ear-piercing screech again. She looked up to see another winged Deadite flying in the air, hovering above Steven and Faith. It was propelling toward them. "Guys, move!" shouted Evelyn.

Faith and Steven simultaneously lifted their heads up to see the demon flying over them. Their hug was broken and they both backed up as far as they could.

The demon closed in on Steven and lifted its clawed hands above its head. The demon used its talons to grab a hold of Steven's shoulders, and then flapped its wings, lifting him off of the ground.

Steven screamed at the top of his lungs. He wondered why the Deadite was trying to capture him. *I thought these guys wanted Ash. Why me?* And then he remembered. He was still holding the book. Freddy wanted the Necronomicon more than anything.

He could hear Faith shouting. "Steven, no!"

Steven began to whimper again, when he felt a hand grab him by his ankle. "Wha–?" Steven muttered. He looked down below him to see Ash holding on to Steven's ankle.

"I got ya!" shouted Ash.

Steven looked back up at the Deadite holding him captive. The demon was straining to keep flapping its wings. The weight of having both Steven and Ash to carry was too much for it. It began to slow its flight and lower down.

Ash pulled out his Boomstick from the holster across his back. He shouted at Steven. "Don't move!" Ash aimed the double-barrels at the demon's head, and squeezed the trigger.

BLAM!

The demon's head exploded from the close range of the shotgun shells. Its body, along with Steven and Ash, fell on the ground.

They both fell on their backs, landing on the rooftop. Their bodies were sore and their bones were vibrating from the fall. Faith ran over to Steven and held her hand out, offering to lift Steven up.

"Steven!" she shouted as Steven took her hand. She helped him back on his feet.

Ash groaned in pain. He hadn't taken a fall like that in quite a long time. He hoped that he hadn't broken any bones. *Well, I guess I'll find out now, huh?* Ash prepared to pick himself up from the ground. He opened his eyes to find Evelyn's hand in front of him, offering to help him up. Ash smiled and took Evelyn's hand. She immediately pulled him back on his feet.

Ash stood back up and looked into Evelyn's emerald eyes. She smiled back at him.

"Are you okay?" she asked.

Ash played it off with his usual charm. "Yeah, I've had worse falls."

Evelyn chuckled. "I believe you." She looked down to see that Ash was still clutching her hand. She smirked at him playfully and retracted her hand.

Only one Deadite was left.

The four of them turned their heads to see a single Deadite standing on the far edge of the roof. They readied themselves, waiting for its attack.

The Deadite scanned the four of them with its blank eyes. The creature howled and flapped its wings. It flew across the sky, but not toward them. No, the creature flew in the other direction and fled downtown to join the others.

The four of them were baffled for a moment. They figured that, after seeing twelve of them get slaughtered by Ash and his crew, the creature chose not to push its luck.

Faith shook her fist in the air. "That's right!" she shouted. "Fly away, you little pussy!"

All four of them began to laugh. Even Ash began to crack up.

Ash turned around, heading for the door. "All right, let's head back." He heard everyone's footsteps begin to follow him. "We can restock, reload, and get ready for round two later."

"JOOOIIIN USSSSSS!!!"

All four of them turned around to see twenty or so Deadites climbing on top of the building. The same Deadites that had been scaling the walls had now reached the top, and were ready to bring Ash to their Master, Freddy. They all chanted, "Join us! Join us!"

As Ash reached for his Boomstick, he shouted, "Aw, gimme a break!"

Chapter 32

"GET BACK IN POSITION!" ASH called as he walked away from the roof entrance. He held up two fingers, signaling Evelyn, Faith, and Steven to follow him. His face remained steady, but inside, his heart was racing and he felt his bones shaking. He had only two bullets left in his Boomstick and his pump shotgun.

As he looked across the rooftop, observing all of the Deadites that were making their way up, he realized that there was just too many of them. There would be no way that they would be able to stay up there and battle it out with so many Deadites, and come out alive. Ash's fear began to take over, but he would be damned if he was going to let it be known.

Ash placed his hand over his shirt pocket, feeling around for any spare bullets. At this point, he would need all that he could get. As he ran his hand over his pocket, he could only feel four extra bullets inside his pocket. "Damn." he muttered.

Evelyn stood at his right, with her revolver in her right hand and her axe in her left. She heard Ash cursing under his breath. She turned her head to him and leaned over to speak to him. As she spoke to him, her eyes never left the emerging hoard of Deadites. "What is it?" she asked.

Ash looked at her briefly as he replied. "I'm a little low on ammo." he said. "I've only got four on me now."

"It's okay." Evelyn said, hoping to offer comfort. "I'll cover for you. I still have six more in my revolver."

Ash nodded his head, but his face was still stone cold, masking his ever-growing fear. "Sounds good."

Faith and Steven stood at Ash's left side. Faith stood at the end of the rooftop, just a few feet away from the edge. She held her rifle a little carelessly this time. Instead of resting the stock against her shoulder, she held the rifle beside her hips. Just like Ash, she knew that trying to fend off as many Deadites as this would be useless.

She felt Steven's breath next to her ear as he spoke to her. "How many bullets you got?"

She didn't have to look at his face to sense his worry, it was all in his voice. She broke her gaze from the Deadites to look at Steven's face, which was inches from hers. "I can't remember." she said. "But, it's not much."

"Oh..." said Steven, disappointingly. His tone was riddled with sarcasm. "That's good to hear."

Evelyn stepped closer to Ash and asked him another question. She got his attention first. "Ash?"

He answered. "Yeah, what?"

Her eyes were locked on the Deadites that were scaling the walls. She couldn't believe that they used to be people at one point. Each of them were so mangled and rotted, that they were unrecognizable to their own pure selves. Their skin was gray, their eyes were blank, and their bones protruded from beneath their decaying skin. She hoped that she would never become one of them. "How many of them do you think there are?" she asked.

Ash scanned the edge of the roof, estimating at how many Deadites were approaching. "Twenty, maybe." he answered. "But from the looks of it, there's more of them coming our way."

Faith's voice was heard amid the Deadite growls. "Oh my God..."

Ash, Evelyn, and Steven turned their heads to the left to look at what Faith was marveling at. When they turned, they saw Faith, standing on the ledge on the left side of the S-Mart building.

She leaned over slightly so that she could face the north side of the building, observing the parking lot. She had her rifle lowered, with the barrel pointed down to the ground. Her light brown hair danced in the calm wind as she looked onward. The pupils inside her brown eyes became small. Her lips parted slightly, as if she was staring in awe.

"What is it?" asked Evelyn.

She, Steven, and Ash took a few steps toward her, trying to see what she was seeing. Each of them lowered their weapons, for the moment.

Faith raised her left arm so that it was parallel to the ground. "Look." she said cryptically. She pointed to the parking lot on the north side with her index finger.

Evelyn raised her foot and stepped on the ledge, joining Faith. She was standing in front of Faith. She raised her chin to look over the edge of the building.

Ash and Steven took a few steps forward, and looking where Faith was pointing.

What the four of them saw, were Deadites filling their entire S-Mart parking lot. Aside from the crowd of possessed vessels scaling the walls and climbing to the top of the building, there were hundreds of them running and piling on top of each other, trying to get to Ash.

Faith spoke again. Her tone was laced with desperation and hopelessness. "They're *everywhere.*"

Ash's eyes grazed along the parking lot, seeing all of the undead bastards coming for them. His gaze trailed past, and onto the streets, where it was a scene of debauchery and absolute madness.

There were Deadites walking the streets of Springwood, taking the souls of the living, and causing mayhem and destruction wherever they went. There were auto wrecks, fires, and blood staining the streets.

Ash looked further past, and saw that there were even more. He looked on the horizon, to see that the Deadites just kept coming their way. It was as if the entire population of Springwood was possessed by evil and was making their way to S-Mart. "Wow..." muttered Ash. When he spoke again, his voice was loud enough for the rest of them to hear. "I don't think we have enough bullets for this."

Evelyn nodded her head from side to side, agreeing with Ash's statement. She looked at Ash, who was facing away from her. "So, what are you thinking? Retreat?"

"For right now, yeah." he answered. "I think the best thing to do would be to go back inside, and fend off as many as we can until dawn." Ash turned his head to look at them, further explaining his last remark. "Deadites can't survive during the day."

Just then, Faith felt something tighten around her left ankle. Before she could even look down, she was being pulled off the ledge. Faith raised her arms and screamed at the top of her lungs. "Aaaaaah!"

Everyone turned around to look at Faith again. By the time they had turned to her, she had already been dragged down from the building. A male Deadite had grabbed her by the ankle and dragged her down to be captured by the others who were piled on top of each other.

She had dropped her rifle to the ground when she had been yanked from the building. The impact had caused the rifle to go off on its own.

BLAM!

A single bullet shot out from the barrel. Since Steven had been standing adjacent to her, the rifle had been facing him. The bullet landed in Steven's left arm, just inches above his elbow.

Steven screamed. "Aaah!" He dropped his axe and the Necronomicon, allowing it to drop to the ground. He then gritted his teeth, muffling further screams. He bent over as he grabbed his arm with his right hand, hoping to stop the blood flow. He felt his palm get wet as his blood seeped through the sleeve of his black shirt. His dark, red blood streamed down his arm and through his fingers.

The pain was excruciating. The hot bullet was now lodged in his arm, and he could no longer move it. A feeling of numbing agony raced up and down his left arm. He could still feel the bullet inside him. It broke through his skin and muscle tissue, and it hit the bone. He couldn't help but let out a helpless cry. "Aaagh! Aaaaah! Fuck!"

Meanwhile, Faith was being dragged down by the hoard of Deadites, who had scaled the west side of the building. She locked her hands on the ledge, using every ounce of strength within her to keep herself up. But, the more she held on, the harder the foul things pulled.

Some held her by her ankles, while others were trying to climb on top of her. The feel of their slimy, decaying skin touching hers made her want to vomit. But, she fought that feeling and focused on hanging on to the ledge. She grunted as she tried to pull herself up. "Ugh! Get off me!"

She could feel their rough hands sliding up and down her legs, caressing her inner thighs. The male and female Deadites were hissing, moaning, and laughing evilly as they groped Faith. *What the hell?* she thought. She felt more hands touching and squeezing her backside.

Faith could then feel jagged nails reaching up her shirt, and scratching her stomach. Those same hands began to slide up and grab the cups of her bra. Faith's eyes began to widen and her face contorted in anger. She turned her head around, pulling her knee towards her, freeing her ankle. She then turned back and lowered her head at the male Deadite that was groping her.

Faith launched her knee toward the Deadite's head. He retreated his blistered hands. "I said," Faith turned her head to face the Deadites behind her. "GET THE FUCK OFF ME!" She kicked as many of the demons as she could with her foot.

But there was too many of them. Soon, they began to overpower her. The vile monsters began to climb on top of her, clawing at her with their long, dirty nails. "You shouldn't fight back, Faith!" one of them said in that wretched voice. "It only hurts worse when you do!"

Faith turned back to look at Steven, who was looking at her in horror. She screamed for help. "STEVEN!" She felt her hands start to slip from the ledge. It wouldn't be long before the Deadites would be able to capture her and turn her into one of them. "HELP ME!" she pleaded.

Steven felt a surge of adrenaline run through his body. He wasn't going to let anyone else he cared about become a vessel for those foul creatures. He saw Faith's eyes glisten in fear, she reached her arms out for help. He ignored the pulsating pain running through his arm. Steven picked up his axe with his right hand and began to run as fast as he could toward Faith.

He made his way past Evelyn and Ash, and raised his axe. There was a Deadite on top of Faith's back, trying to hold her down. It was a male demon. His hair was short and dark. His skin was pale and gray. His face was sunken, showing his cheekbones, which were poking through his skin. Also, the lower half of his jaw was missing. All that remained was his long, slimy tongue.

The demon was also very thin and scrawny, which made Steven even more relieved about fighting him. He lowered his axe just as the Deadite raised his head to look at him in the eye. The axe landed on the demon's face, between his white eyes. His skull split open, and green blood oozed from his face and down to his neck.

He screamed. "Aaaaaah!" as he released his grip from Faith and put his hands on his face in attempt to pull the axe from his skull. Steven's axe was lodged far too deep into his head. There was no breaking free.

Steven let go of the handle of his axe and reached his hands down to grab Faith's. "Quick, grab my hand!" he shouted.

Faith climbed over the mountain of Deadites beneath her. She kicked any of the demons who tried to pull her back down again. She grabbed both of Steven's hands. She held them as tightly as she could, ensuring that she would never fall back down again.

Steven gripped both of her hands tightly in his. He leaned back and pulled Faith back up to the rooftop. Once she was halfway up, Steven moved his hands up her arms, and began pulling her up by her upper arms.

Faith kept her eyes locked on Steven's as he held onto him. She stepped on the heads of the Deadites below her, helping her climb up faster. She felt the bottom of her foot finally touch the ledge. She pushed herself up as hard as she could, feeling Steven's hands grab a hold of her shoulders, pulling her in. Once her feet had touched the concrete of the rooftop, both she and Steven dropped to their knees.

They both sat on the concrete. Steven immediately wrapped his arms around Faith, and she did the same. Their hug was as tight as a vice grip. Steven rested his sweaty, bloodied head on Faith's shoulder. He rubbed her back and ran his hand through her hair.

Faith pulled him in, feeling the wetness of his blood seeping through his shirt. She felt Steven begin to flinch from her touching his bullet wound, so she drew back her arm.

Steven released the hug and held her face in the palms of his hands. "I told you I wouldn't let them get to you." He stroked her cheek with his thumbs and pulled her in to kiss her. They could taste each other's blood and sweat from the kiss, but they were happy just to be alive, that they ignored the metallic taste of the blood. Steven then pulled back and looked into her eyes.

Faith laughed softly, showing her teeth from behind her thin, pinkish lips. She playfully punched him in the stomach, and teased him. "You're so sappy!"

Steven laughed along with her. He held her hand, intertwining his fingers with hers. He didn't think that he would be able to save Faith. When he saw her being pulled under by those demons, he thought he had already lost her. But something within him told him to keep fighting. He wasn't going to let Freddy or his Deadite followers take another life on his watch. And he cared about Faith. He loved her humor and her vivacious personality, and he wanted both of them to live through this.

Their moment was cut short when they heard Ash's boots stepping on the concrete beside them. He leaned over, his chain wrapped around his fist and his chainsaw still idling. "Rule number one: No hanky-panky when there's a town of Deadites who want to eat our souls." he said bluntly. "Got it?"

Both Steven and Faith got up to their feet. Faith reached over to grab her rifle as she stood back up. Steven quickly leaned over a few feet to his left to grab his axe, and to his right to get the Necronomicon. They stood straight, looking at Ash.

"Good." he said. Ash waved his hand toward the roof entrance. "Now, let's head back." He saw the three of them turn around and walk to the door. He stared at the back of their heads as he followed behind.

Just then, Ash felt hot breath on his neck. Following that, was the smell of dead flesh. Before he could react, he heard a rough, warbled voice hissing at him. "Where are you going, Ash?" the female voice rasped at him.

Ash whipped his head, looking at the rotted Deadite who was inches from his face. The demon's skin was rotted, almost green in coloration. She had blisters and sinews of flesh hanging from every inch of her body. She was small, looking up at Ash's face. She looked so young, like she couldn't have been older than fifteen. She had short, light brown hair. The decaying girl was wearing a white, bloodied, sleep shirt. The hem was four inches above her knees. There was a graphic on the shirt, but Ash couldn't tell what it was, because it had been stained with her blood. There was also four long slash marks on across her chest, running down to her stomach. They were parallel and jagged, just like the cuts on Ash's side.

This girl had been a recent victim of Freddy's. Ash figured that he must have taken her in her sleep shortly after Ash had woken up. After he killed her, the dark spirits took over her already mutilated body. She crawled out of her own home in the middle of the night, and joined the rest of the Deadites to rampage through the city.

She spoke again. "Let me take you to him! It's so much easier when you don't fight back!"

Ash's eyes trailed down her shirt and looked at her hands which rested beside her slender hips. Her hands were covered in blood. Her fingernails, which had been painted purple, were dirty. In her hands, which were balled up into fists, she held clumps of hair. In one hand was light brown, much like hers. In the other was blonde hair. Small slivers of bone on her knuckles were exposed. His gaze went up as he saw her raise her hands next to her retched face.

"You noticed my souvenirs." the demon said. She smiled and laughed wickedly. "Once Freddy was done with her, we took over her body. What you're seeing here are the scalps of her mother and father after we bashed their brains in! Ha ha ha ha ha!"

The Deadite opened her hands. Her high-pitched laughter was then replaced with a shrieking battle cry. Her eyebrows lowered, and she scowled. The demon dug her bloodied nails into Ash's shoulders and tried to push him over the edge of the building.

Ash acted quickly. As he felt his feet touch the ledge, he turned in the opposite direction, putting her towards the edge of the building.

She had been swung with such brutality, that she had been lifted off of her feet. The young possessed girl was hurled into the air, and fell down to the parking lot, where the rest of the Deadites continued to scatter.

The girl landed on the roof of a Pontiac Firebird. The roof as well as the doors collapsed from the impact of her body. The windows shattered, sending glass flying in all directions. Then came the sound of metal bending, glass shattering, and bones crushing echoed to the rooftop where Ash stood, watching. Her bones shattered and her skull had split wide open. The Deadite bled from all over her body, spilling over the car like a waterfall. Her mouth hung open, and her arms and legs were spread out on the roof of the car. The young girl was finally dead.

Ash felt transfixed by the scene that he had caused. For the first time in years, Ash had actually felt bad about killing a demon. *I mean, sure, she was nothing but a filthy Deadite, but still...she was just a kid.* If it had been anyone else, he wouldn't have just shrugged it off with a smart-ass quip, but this one was different. This girl didn't just become possessed by ancient spirits, she had to have her mind, her body, and her soul, tortured by Freddy before it happened. Judging from the slash marks on her chest, Ash could only imagine the vile things he did to the girl before he killed her. Ash felt his heart become heavy. This was the reason why Freddy had to die. This was the reason why the Necronomicon had to be destroyed. No longer would the world be consumed by the likes of him.

He felt a hand grip his arm. Ash turned around to see that it was Evelyn. He could see in her eyes that she was worried about him. He returned back to reality as she spoke to him.

"Ash?" said Evelyn in a troubled voice.

"Huh? What?"

Evelyn pointed in the direction of the Deadite hoard that had been scaling the walls. They had now reached the roof and were running towards the four of them, all at once.

Ash pulled out his pump shotgun and began to back up quickly. "Okay, we gotta split!" Ash turned around to run. He saw Faith and Steven already heading down the stairs. He heard Evelyn's footsteps running alongside him. Among those noises, were the sounds of dozens of Deadites screaming and taunting them as they run behind them. Their distorted voices became increasingly louder.

Ash pumped his shotgun and quickly spun around to unload a round into the skull of the Deadite closest to him. He spotted one that was a mere eight feet behind him. Ash squeezed the trigger.

BOOM!!!

The demon fell dead, bleeding out on the concrete.

Evelyn pulled back the hammer of her revolver. She turned around briefly to shoot another demon.

BLAM!

Ash and Evelyn continued to waste at least three more Deadites as they headed downstairs.

The two of them raced down the narrow stairway. The laughs and cries of "Join us! Join us!" only became louder in the enclosed area. They finally reached the door that would bring them back inside. Evelyn entered first, pushing on the handle and opening the door wide.

She continued to hold on to the door handle until Ash ran through. Once Ash had entered back inside the store, Evelyn slammed the door as hard and as fast as she could. As soon as door closed, Ash held it closed as he turned the lock beside the knob, locking it shut.

The Deadites continued to bang on the door, rasping and shouting at them. A few of them tried to reach under the door, poking their decaying fingers through the crack between the door and the floor.

Annoyed by their persistence, Evelyn kneeled down to the floor, raised her axe, and lowered it. She chopped their Deadite fingers in half. Blood poured from the cut-off point in the knuckles. The demons finally retreated their hands and began to quiet down. "God, that was getting annoying." Evelyn sighed.

"Hey, look at that!" shouted Steven.

When she looked back down at the floor, she saw the fingers that she had just butchered, begin to move on their own.

Eight Deadite fingers moved around on the marble tile, slithering like worms. They moved in all directions.

Evelyn immediately stood back up. "How can they do that?" She remembered what happened last time one of those filthy appendages came after her. Before she could think of something to do to get rid of them, she saw Ash's work boot come down on them and smash them to a pulp.

Once every wiggling finger had been thoroughly smashed, Ash looked back up at them and cleared his throat. "Yeah, that happens sometimes." He said while he put his shotgun back in his holster. He turned to Steven and led him down to the medical supply aisle. "Alright, Steven. Let's get you bandaged up."

Steven nodded. He mumbled, "Okay." and followed Ash.

Ash looked at his pale face. He looked as if he had gotten two shades paler since the last time he saw him. "You lost so much blood, you look deader than those things up there."

"Do I?" asked Steven. As the both of them walked by, they strolled past a display filled with sunglasses. Steven stopped for a moment to look into the mirror that was at the top of the display. He looked up into the mirror, touching the side of his face. *Wow, he wasn't kidding.* he said to himself. Aside from the streaks of red and green blood on his forehead, Steven's face was a sickly white. "Huh, you're right." he said to Ash. "I look like a piece of paper."

Before he could turn his head away from the mirror, he saw Ash holding a box of tourniquets in his hand. He presented them to Steven, waiting for him to take it from him. "Here." said Ash. "Wrap yourself up with this."

Steven took the box from his hand, and peeled away the plastic wrapping.

Approximately fifteen minutes had passed by. By that time, Steven's wound had been properly cleaned and dressed. The bullet, however, was still lodged in his arm, but there wasn't enough time to try to take it out. Also, judging from Steven's appearance, he couldn't afford to lose any more blood from amateur surgery.

Steven sat down on folding table, which used to display two dollar DVD's, but had since been cleared, not counting their weapons. Faith stood on Steven's left side, holding a wet cloth and blotting the excess blood that had escaped from the bandage.

All of them, including Ash, had set their weapons down for now. Ash's chainsaw, two shotguns were on the far left. Evelyn's revolver and axe were beside his weapons.

Steven's axe and Faith's rifle were laid out on Steven's left side. He rested the Book of the Dead on his lap, never leaving it out of sight.

He felt better knowing that the bleeding had stopped, but he still felt a stinging pain from having the bullet still lodged in his arm. He winced as Faith applied a little more pressure than usual while wiping away the dried blood. "Tsst! Ow!"

Faith pulled back her arm and looked up at him. "Oh, sorry."

"It's okay, it's just still feels a little raw." he said. Steven turned his head to look at Ash. He stood a few feet away from him, with his arms crossed. Since he had taken his chainsaw off temporarily, he hadn't put his metal hand back on. This was the first time Steven had seen Ash's nub. It was strange to look at, but he tried not to stare as he spoke to him. "Ash, this hurts like hell. How come I have to leave the bullet in?" He felt another throb of pain race down his arm. "I know S-Mart has stuff you can use to cut a bullet out of me."

Ash firmly turned him down for the second time. "Because I said no."

"Come on, Ash. This thing's touching the bone, it fucking hurts."

"For the last time," he pointed a finger at Steven. "it's too risky. You've lost too much blood already. I can't have you passing out when it's time to open the rift."

Steven begrudgingly accepted defeat. He leaned his head back and closed his eyes. "Fuuuuuck..." When Steven opened his eyes, he spotted something that made him repeat his previous statement. "Oh, fuck!" Steven twitched his legs and jumped off of the table.

Faith looked at him in confusion. "What? What's wrong?"

"Yeah kid, have you lost your mind?" yelled Ash.

Steven stood in the middle of the circle that Faith, Evelyn, and Ash had formed around him. He pointed his finger to the sky. "Up there! Look!"

They all looked up at once. Steven had been pointing at the skylight. On the other side of the glass, was the last remaining winged Deadite that had flew away previously. It had been hitting and banging on the glass, causing it to crack. A large, spider web-like pattern of cracks had formed on the glass.

"The little bastard came back." noted Ash.

After repeatedly smashing on the glass with no avail, the demon jumped and flew upward about thirty feet, like a rocket. The four of them continued to stare, their nerves began to rise.

After a few seconds, the demon flew straight down, plunging itself into the skylight. The demon broke through.

CRASH!!!

Thousands of glass shards dropped down upon them like rain.

Ash shouted. "Get down!" The four of them lowered down and covered their heads. Once the glass had stopped falling, they looked up to see that the demon had quickly turned itself up, no longer falling down.

The undead menace flew at such a speed, that it was but a blur. The winged Deadite flapped its bat-like wings as it flew toward the front of the store. It shrieked, the high-pitched noise echoed throughout the store. It propelled itself into the barricade that blocked off the entrance to S-Mart. The foul thing launched itself through, bursting through the other side.

CRASH!!! CRUNCH!!! SNAP!!!

The dozens of 2x4's that had been used to keep the Deadites out, had now been snapped into pieces. There was now a gaping hole in the wall.

Ash, Evelyn, Faith, and Steven uncovered their heads, and stood straight up. They looked in crippling fear as they saw that the only thing keeping the Deadites at bay, had now been destroyed. They all shared the same symptoms of anxiety: Their hands began to shake. Every bone in their body felt stiff. They could hardly bring themselves to breathe in. Their eyebrows lifted and their mouths gaped in shock. They had finally found a way to keep themselves safe, and now...Hell had been brought to them.

The Deadites began pouring in the store like a bad flood. The decaying, rotted messes all ran through the large, jagged hole in the wall. Each of them, laughing and sprinting inside, claiming the building as their own. Some of them screamed out of excitement. It was like an undead, demonic, Beatle mania was taking place.

Ash stepped forward as he suddenly noticed a figure standing in the middle of them all. This one was the only one not moving. As all of the Deadites went into a frenzy, this one simply stood at the entrance, taking it all in.

Once most of the demons had made their way in, and the crowd had slowed down, the figure became visible. There at the entrance, stood Freddy Krueger. He had his head lowered slightly, his fedora titled down, almost hiding is blue eyes. His shoulders had been slumped to the side. His right arm hung lower than the left, as the weight of his glove pulled him down. He twiddled the blades on his glove. It made a sleek, metal on metal noise.

Swish! Swish! Swish! Swish! Swish!

Freddy laughed just loudly enough to be heard over the commotion of the Deadites running rampant. "Ha ha ha ha ha ha..." He raised his gloved hand, flicking up his index blade. It was this blade that he used to touch the brim of his hat, and tilt it up. His entire wretched face was now out in the open. The burns and sinews of flesh that peeled away from his skin were now even more horrifying under the florescent lighting. His eyes, were mere slits, like the eyes of a snake. His brows were arched narrowly, locked in a permanent expression of twisted deviancy. As he smiled, his shark-like teeth were exposed.

Once he lifted his hat, Freddy then brought his blades to his face, and slowly licked the wet blood from his knives one by one. It was the young girl's blood. The one from the roof. Her blood was still fresh, and he was saving this spectacle for Ash's eyes only. Freddy swallowed down the girl's thick, bitter blood. He locked eyes on Ash, and said in his guttural voice...

"Miss me?"

Chapter 33

S-MART. ONLY YESTERDAY, IT HAD been nothing more than a simple warehouse store in the middle of Springwood. Now, it had become the very center of Hell on Earth. In fact, all of Springwood began to look like the dark bowels of Hell itself. By this time, the entire population of the small Ohio town, all fifteen thousand of them, minus the four living souls held captive inside the store, were now hosts to Kandarian demons.

Every shop, every suburban home, every street was filled with the decayed masses of the Deadites. They rampaged the town, running amuck and causing death and destruction everywhere they went. But, no matter where they came from, each of them were headed to the same location. They blindly followed the orders of their Master, Freddy. They were his servants in darkness. They sought after the Chosen One.

Ash was the bane of their existence. It was his purpose in life to rid the world of evil. And it was their purpose in death to take him to Freddy, and end his. Then they would live again. No longer would they be dead by dawn. Under the rule of their new leader, every waking moment would be consumed by darkness. All light, all life, all hope would cease to exist.

The Deadites surrounded every corner of the S-Mart building, both inside and outside. There was no place to run or hide without being attacked by one of them. They all stood side-by-side behind the wall, like suspects in a line-up. Faint hisses and murmurs could be heard throughout the store. In their dark, sinister voices, they whispered amongst each other.

"Her soul will be mine..." A female Deadite said as she looked at Evelyn.

"Not if I get it first!" The male demon next to her rasped.

"Ash has no chance against Freddy." One said from the far corner.

The one beside it agreed. *"Yes, our lord shall make it rain blood on all the mortals!"*

The florescent light fixtures on the ceiling began to flicker. Everything would be bright, almost unsettlingly crisp to the eyes. But every few seconds, the store would be under the cloak of darkness, as if they were out into the night again. Although, considering all of the horribly disfigured faces lurking in every corner, being blinded temporarily wasn't something to complain about.

While the entire area had become a scene of chaos, there was only one thing that had everyone's undivided attention. Everyone inside the store, whether it be the Deadites, or the kids, all had their eyes locked on two figures: Freddy and Ash.

Freddy Krueger: The gatekeeper of nightmares. The man every child feared. And now, he was the wielder of dark powers beyond anyone's comprehension.

Ash Williams: Clerk by day. Demon slayer by night. He is the man that no Deadite has been able to claim. He is the one chosen by God to rid the world of evil.

Ash and Freddy took slow strides across the store toward each other. The distance between them shortened step by step. All sentient beings inside the building fell silent as they watched the two of them walk.

Ash's face was frozen, locked in place. His eyebrows were narrowed. His lips were pursed slightly. He seemed to show nothing but pure anger towards Freddy, but the truth was in his eyes. Behind his brown eyes, glistening under the florescent lights, showed not only rage, but also fear. Despite Ash's skills, his artillery, and knowledge of all things demonic, Freddy had proven to be something different than what he had faced before. His powers may have come from the Necronomicon, but Freddy Krueger was no mere Deadite. He wasn't just some demonic entity harboring inside the body of a person. Freddy had powers that were completely his own. He lived in people's nightmares. He festered inside their minds, raiding through the deepest, darkest areas of their subconscious, and used it against them. And no matter how many times, no matter how many people have tried, no matter how many times he died and went to Hell, Freddy always came back. Ash was afraid that, this time, he had come across a demon he couldn't kill.

Freddy looked at Ash, relishing the fear in his eyes. He kept his charred, left hand resting inside his pants pocket. His right shoulder was slumped. He had bent his right arm, lifting it high enough so that his forearm was parallel to the ground. His palm was facing the ceiling. His steel blades, spotted with the blood of his previous victim, lifted up and down, starting from his pinky to his index finger. His walk was cool and relaxed, as if he was merely gliding off the tile. While Freddy kept his signature cocky smile and intimidating look in his eyes, inside he wasn't as confident as he was with his usual victims. That was because, Ash wasn't like his usual victims. Sure, Freddy had come across a few headstrong young girls, not to mention the towering lunk that was Jason Voorhees, but Ash was different. Ash never tried to run away from him when he spotted him in a dark corner. He never simply stood in front of him, dumb and silent. Ash always had a smartass comment on hand. That in particular annoyed the hell out of Freddy. That was *his* thing. Most of all, Ash was mortal, and yet he had survived every encounter with Freddy. There was something about him. It was what made his soul to most valuable to obtain. Ash was powerful in his own human way. His soul was pure.

Freddy ignored his own fears about Ash, and kept it cool. He sneered as he looked at the bloodied demon slayer. "So Ash," he said derisively. "ready for round two?"

Ash kept his face still as a rock as he would stride closer towards his enemy. He was determined not to let Freddy's words get to him. From here on out, Ash's only goal was to kill Freddy Krueger. No more resurrections. No more Deadites. No more nightmares. He was about to say something to him, letting him know he wasn't intimidated, when he heard quickening footsteps emerging from behind him.

Unbeknownst to Ash, Evelyn had been following behind him the entire time. She didn't know what had come over her, it was as if her legs had a mind of their own. She felt herself drawn towards Freddy. All she could see were flashbacks of the horrible things he had done to the people she loved.

She saw the bloodied mess in the bedroom where he had raped and killed her friend, Meg. Her lifeless body, laying on the tattered sheets. Her eyes, listless and empty. Every inch of her body, cut open and stained with blood. And the others kids he had slaughtered in the hallway. She couldn't get the image of their blood splattered on the walls out of her head.

And then there was Cooper's mutilated body, laying limp in her arms. His eyes, slashed. His mouth, gaping as if trying to plead for help, but help never came. As if having the love of her life taken from her wasn't tragic enough to bear, he also became possessed and tried to kill her. She'll never forget the look of absolute evil that spread across his face. She'll never forget looking at him through the sights of a gun before she put a bullet between his eyes. That would be the very last image she would have of him. Dead. Bleeding. Brains and skull fragments spread out across his face. Rotting and decaying on the floor of his apartment.

And lastly, there was Jill. Her best friend. The person who was by her side and made her feel safe when she first left home. And she too was taken. Possessed by the evil. In her mind, she saw flashes of her demonic form. It bore no resemblance to the bright and happy face that belonged to her friend. Evelyn kept seeing her, crawling on the ceiling, defying gravity. She saw her bend in a way that made a contortionist in a carnival sideshow appear boring. And then there was her death. Watching Steven dismember her body with an axe, and bury her, limb by limb, in the backyard.

Freddy had caused all of this. He was the reason why everyone she loved was dead. Not only dead, but had their souls ripped from their bodies and have them be absorbed by him. They were tortured and used for as long as he was alive and breathing.

She knew it was dangerous and irresponsible, but she kept walking slowly behind Ash. She wanted nothing more at that moment, than to bring him as much pain and suffering as he had caused her and her friends.

Evelyn felt a hand in front of her stomach, barricading her movement. She looked down to see that it was Ash. She stared at his blood spotted shirt sleeve, her eyes trailing down, fixating on his nub. Her head snapped up, looking into his eyes. He looked at her, almost angrily, and spoke curtly to her.

"No." he said. "You stay back."

Her nostrils flared as she let out a frustrated exhale. She understood why he didn't want her out there. She knew that he understood her abhorrence toward Freddy, how lonely she felt right then, but she just wished that he would let her put an axe between his eyes and watch him bleed.

She heard Freddy's voice. "Oh..." he said inquisitively. Evelyn turned her head to look at him. He had his head tilted to the side. He was smiling deviously. When he spoke her name, he drew it out, savoring every syllable in her name. "...Evelyyynnn..."

He kept walking slowly. His gaze had been taken off Ash and was now directed towards her. "Being the little woman warrior, are you, hmm?" He cocked his nonexistent eyebrows. His tone was demeaning and taunting. "You couldn't save your boyfriend, what makes you think you can save him, huh?"

She didn't know what had come over her. The only thing she felt at that moment was pure rage filling her body. Her head had been clouded, all she saw was red. All she wanted to see, was his blood on the floor. Evelyn tried to run for him, but was blocked by Ash. She felt her feet lift off the ground and her arms reached for him, even though he was twenty feet away from her. She screamed. "I'll kill you, Freddy!" Her voice cracked. "You're dead, you bastard!"

Freddy took his left hand out of his pocket. He put both hands in front of him and waved his fingers back and forth. He called her forth. Beckoning her. Daring her. "Come and get it, bitch!"

Ash's ears had twitched as soon as he heard the word "bitch" escape Freddy's blistered mouth. While still holding Evelyn back, he turned his head and snapped at him. "You leave her out of this!"

Evelyn stepped back, not wanting to cause any more trouble.

Freddy stopped moving. His legs were just outside of his hips. His shoulder was slumped. His head was tilted down slightly. He laughed faintly and smirked. "It's too bad you're all going to die here, tonight. You won't get to see my reign of terror all over the waking world."

Ash lifted his chin and looked at him, derogatively. His tone was cool and confident. "In your dreams, scars and stripes."

Freddy's devious smile down turned into an angry sneer. His sharp teeth were partially visible behind his charred mouth. A powerful, malevolent growl emerged from inside him. It was trembling. If Ash had closed his eyes, he would have mistaken it for that of a wild tiger's.

In the blink of an eye, Freddy raised his gloved arm and shot it out, shadowboxing it in front of them. He used his newly found powers against them.

In that instant, a concentrated, invisible force engulfed the entire store. A low, ominous hum echoed as the force emerged. It moved forward, starting from where Freddy was standing, all the way to the back of the store. Everything except the Deadites were affected by it.

All of the racks, all of the tables, and every item that sat upon it, were lifted off of the ground. They shot out, like a cannonball, to the far end of the store. Ash, Evelyn, Steven, and Faith, were also knocked off of their feet.

The evil force sent them hurling into the air. All four of their screams filled the building. It sent in different areas of the store, separating them.

Steven felt himself start to fall downward. He closed his eyes, not wanting to see the carnage that may occur as a result. It felt like the kind of dream where he's not quite asleep, but somehow feels himself falling into a bottomless pit of darkness. It was terrifying, yet it filled him with adrenaline. His landing was abrupt. He was now in what used to be outdoor aisle, as there were folding chairs and tables all over. He felt his back land against a hard surface. He fell onto one of the folding tables, which quickly toppled over as soon as he made contact with it. He then opened his eyes to see himself on the floor, amongst the debris.

Faith had fallen a couple of aisles across from where Steven was. She landed on her side, causing excruciating pain in her right arm and her hip. She groaned in pain. "Oh...ugh..." She sat up, supporting herself on her knees. She looked around, noticing that the aisle she was in had not been tipped over. Judging from all of the butcher knives, steak knives, and other utensils, she knew she was in the kitchen aisle. *Thank God this one didn't tip over, or I'd be impaled in fifty different places right now.* she thought.

Evelyn braced herself for impact as she saw the ground getting closer to her. Once she landed, her body began to roll on the tile until she hit the wall in the very back of the building. Her back hit the wall, stopping her motion. She grunted. "Ugh!" She let her face rest on the floor, waiting for the rest of her body to stop ringing from the impact. She looked around. There was debris and merchandise everywhere. She had no idea what area of the store she was in. All she knew was that it was somewhere in the very back.

"Whoa!" Ash screamed as he was knocked off of his feet. He flew in the air for a short amount of time. His body tilted upward. He was able to look at the gaping hole in the skylight as he was being forced back. Ash finally landed on his back, only fifteen feet away from where he was originally standing. Once his body landed on the floor, Ash slid back on the sleek tile floor another ten feet away from Freddy. His legs went up over his head for the duration of the slide and then quickly dropped down. His back and shoulders ached from the fall, a wave of pain raced up and down his spine.

Once the damage had been done, Freddy lowered his arm down beside his hip. He scanned the store, taking in all of the destruction. It looked as if a tornado had made its way into S-Mart. Everything inside had been moved, knocked over, or destroyed. Knowing that Ash and his band of brats had been separated, Freddy sent the Deadites to do what they do best. He barely parted his lips to speak. When he did, his voice was warbled and low, almost to a whisper. "Go."

They followed his command. As soon as he spoke the word, the demons no longer remained still. They practically pushed themselves from the wall and ran across the store. They shrieked and laughed in perverted glee.

Once Ash heard the parade of Deadites howling their way through the store, he picked his head up to see Freddy, taking long strides towards him. He looked over to his left, and saw, in the middle of scattered glass shards a few yards away from him, was his chainsaw and his Boomstick. He acted quickly. Ash fought the pain in his upper body and picked himself up as hastily as he could.

He ran over to grab his weapons, hoping that the broken glass wouldn't cut through his boots. When he reached down to grab his chainsaw, he felt a pair of decayed hands grab him by his shoulders. They were rough, blistered, and had long fingernails that poked through his work shirt. Not long after that, the figure behind him jumped onto his back and held on tightly. Ash knew that this was a Deadite, judging from its warbled screams.

Ash grunted. "Ugh! Argh!" And turned around sharply in attempt to get the demon off of his back. "Get the fuck off of me!" But the demon simply wouldn't let go.

He knew that this tactic was going nowhere, so he acted on pure impulse. "Hyah!" Ash shouted as he jumped and fell back hard on the glass. He body slammed the Deadite down to the floor to be pierced with hundreds of glass shards. Ash rolled back to his feet, carefully avoiding the glass. When he stood back up, what he saw was a pale faced, convulsing demon laying in a pool of her own blood. She was tall, thin, and wearing a yellow tank top and flannel pajama shorts. Her skin was dark brown in comparison to her wretched, much paler face. She had dark, black circles beneath her white eyes. She had slash marks on each corner of her mouth that reached up to her ears. When she opened her mouth to howl, the entire inside of her mouth was visible.

His eyes grazed a few inches to his left. Luckily, his shotgun was now by his feet. Ash bent over to pick it up. He pointed the barrels in front of the demon's face. "Didn't anyone ever tell you," he said as he clicked the safety off. "to stay away from broken glass?" Ash pulled the trigger.

BOOM!!!

The Deadite's head exploded from the impact of the shell. Blood, skull fragments, and pieces of scalp had spread all over the area. The glass was stained with red, and lying in the middle of all the shards, was the headless body of a female Deadite.

Ash rested his shotgun on his shoulder. The smoke slowly drifted up from the barrels. He stared at the Deadite's unmoving body. Aside from her face, the rest of her looked absolutely normal. *I guess this chick had just turned, and didn't have enough time for the rest of her to look like the living undead.* he figured. "Too bad..." he said to the unresponsive corpse. "You looked good from the neck down."

Ash bent down to grab his chainsaw. As he stood up, he put his Boomstick back in his holster. He then latched the chainsaw back on his right arm. He was now ready for action.

He looked across the absolute mess that had become of S-Mart. He couldn't see the kids right off. He mumbled to himself. "They must've gone pretty far." He knew he needed to get to them as quick as possible. They were smart kids. And resilient. But still, he worried about how they would survive (or wouldn't survive) being alone and with that many demons. He scanned the store from left to right. "All I gotta do now is find you guys." he took in all of the damage that had been done to the store. "You spend seven hours a day stocking shelves, and then it all goes to shit."

Ash took one step forward when he felt someone lightly touch his shoulder. He turned his head, hoping that it was one of the kids, and that they found their way back to him. When he whipped his head to his left, he didn't see either Evelyn, Faith, nor Steven's face.

It was Freddy. He had his gloved hand resting on Ash's shoulder. His left hand was balled up into a fist. His arm was bent and pulled back by his ear.

He only saw his scowling face for a brief second before Freddy launched his fist. He punched him. Hard. And square in the face. Freddy had hit him right on the bridge of his nose. Ash closed his eyes and could have sworn that he saw stars. A deep, throbbing pain made its way from Ash's nose and across the top of his head. He heard a crunching or a snapping noise when Freddy socked him in the face. Blood poured from both of his nostrils.

That son of a bitch broke my nose!

Chapter 34

PLEASE LET THIS ALL HAVE been just a bad dream...just a horrible, horrible nightmare. Please let me wake up from this. Evelyn lifted her eyelids to find herself lying on the cold, hard, floor of S-Mart. The building was close to being in ruins. Shelves had been tipped over. Light fixtures were broken. Broken glass was scattered across the floor. It was not a dream. It was a living, waking nightmare. *...Damn...*

Evelyn felt a ribbon of warm blood slowly drip down from her scalp, along the bridge of her nose, and across her full lips. She got a taste of it as she wiped it away. She was laying on her stomach, feeling every bone in her body ring from the fall. *I can't just lay here all night. I have to keep moving, or I'll die.*

Evelyn moved her arms and placed the palms of her hands beside her, in a push-up position, and tried to get back on her feet. Once she began to push, a numbing pain throbbed in her left shoulder. She let out a surprised gasp as she retreated her left arm from she ground. She used her right arm to support herself. Once she was brought to her knees, Evelyn looked around and noticed all of the stoves and refrigerators on display. *I guess this is the Kitchen department, or what's left of it anyway.*

She stood on her own two feet, slumped and broken. Her shoulder was drooping down. It had been dislocated and was simply hanging there, limp and useless. The pain was unbearable. Plus, it felt so strange to have her own arm hang there by her side, like a meaty piece of string. *I'm going to have to force it back in the socket.* She looked around to find something that she could use.

Ten feet in front of her, was a line of fifteen different refrigerators on display. How they survived the powerful force that blew them away, she didn't know. *I think I can use this.* The raven-haired girl limped over to the fridge that was closest to her, the one right in the middle. She positioned herself on the left side, and propped her left elbow on the wall of the fridge. She gripped the stainless steel handle with her operable arm, and spoke to herself softly. "This'll hurt. But that's okay, because it'll only be a second. I can do this. I have to."

Evelyn moved to find the right angle to lock her arm back in place. She kept muttering to herself that everything will be– "Okay, okay. One...Two..." She took a sharp breath in, and pulled the handle. She practically jumped forward, forcing her shoulder back in the socket. She heard a loud *snap* as her bones reconnected. Her muscles began to tear, and a mind-numbingly painful wave of pain raced through her left arm. The pain was more brutal than having her joints separated in the first place.

She pursed her lips shut to keep from screaming, but she couldn't help but allow pained moans reverberate in her throat. "Mmmm! Nnnng!" Evelyn rested her forehead on the wall of the fridge as she let go of the handle. Slowly but steadily, she slid down to her knees, and panted heavily. She pain was subsiding, but it couldn't have gone away quickly enough. Her eyes began to burn with tears. She closed her eyelids, forcing a single tear to race down her cheek and fall to the floor. *It's over now. The hard part's over.*

Hiiiiisssssssssss! Hiiiiiissssssssssss!

"...Ha ha ha ha ha!"

Evelyn lifted her head and looked to her left, where the noise was coming from. Looking in between the rows of stoves and other appliances, Evelyn saw a lone female Deadite. She was a few aisles away, but from the direction that she was walking, she was heading for Evelyn. Her hair was bleached blonde and stringy. Her skin was pale, almost white, with black veins visible under her face and arms. Dark, red, blood splatters surrounded both of her opaque eyes. Her lips were so cracked and dry, they appeared to be red.

Evelyn's eyes widened, and she quickly leapt up. Every bone in her body rattled out of fear. *I don't have a weapon, I'll have to hide somewhere.* She looked around, searching for an adequate hiding spot. Her gaze was automatically directed to the object that was three feet in front of her: The refrigerator. She breathed a sigh of relief and muttered quietly to herself. "It'll have to do."

She grabbed the handle with both hands, slowly and quietly opening the door. As she looked inside, she realized that she wouldn't be able to fit because of all of the shelves. She looked ahead and noticed that the Deadite was getting closer. She hadn't spotted her just yet, but it was only a matter of time before she would. Evelyn acted quickly and slid both of the racks out of the fridge and set them on the floor. *It's small, but I think I can fit. It's too late to run now.*

Evelyn crept inside and quietly shut the door. She now sat, hunched and cramped, in the enclosed space. Surrounded by darkness. It was so quiet, that the only sound she could hear was her own breathing. She then realized that she should probably steady her breathing so that the demon wouldn't be able to hear her. She whispered her own advice to herself. "Shh...Calm down. How many movies have we seen where the girl's breathing *so* loud, it sounds like they're having an asthma attack?" She then took a calming inhale and exhale. *I wonder how long I'll have to hide in here.*

The she-demon crept closer towards the ruins of the kitchen aisle. She knew there was someone there. She could practically smell the fear. Her evil senses led her to the row of display refrigerators. The Deadite had a feeling that someone was hiding in that area.

She grinned perversely and quickened her pace towards the display. She slowed down once she was behind the last fridge from the right. She ran her decrepit hands over each and every one. She trilled in her warbled, almost child-like voice. "Ready or not...Ha ha ha ha ha..." She then sang her next words.

"We're gon-na get you,
We're gon-na get you,
Not another pe-ep,
Time to go to sle-ep!"

The Deadite walked to the other side and made her trip again. This time, she would search inside for fresh souls. She stopped once she was in front of the fridge in the middle of the row. She looked down to the ground and noticed two racks that had been tossed aside. She smiled. "Found you!"

She pushed it down to the ground. The demon stood over the one that contained Evelyn inside. She gripped the handle and shouted with glee, "Lunchtime! Let's see what's good!" The door flew open, almost coming off of its hinges.

The Deadite bent over to get a look of the fresh soul that was inside. She was immediately met with a sharp kick. Evelyn's right leg shot out from the fridge and made contact with the demon's jaw.

The demon cried as her head was forced to look up to the sky. "Aak!" She had lost her footing, and took a few steps back, away from Evelyn.

Evelyn wasted no time jumping over the fridge and running towards the Deadite. While the demon was taken aback, Evelyn pounced on her, knocking her to the ground. The back of the demon's head was slammed hard on the ground, making her grunt. Evelyn pinned the Deadite's arms down to keep her from attacking. *I don't know where to go from here. How am I supposed to kill her like this?*

Before she could think of an answer, she felt a powerful force hurling her to the ground. Evelyn's back was now on the floor, and the grinning Deadite was on top of her, restraining her. She felt the hideous monstrosity let go of her wrists and raise her hands up.

The demon opened her palms, revealing her long, dirty fingernails. "I'll ruin that pretty face of yours!" Before Evelyn could react, she felt her face sting from small scratches from the demon's nails. The let out a high-pitched laugh "Ha ha ha ha ha!" as she slashed away at Evelyn's smooth skin, her neck, and her collar bone.

Evelyn screamed in pain. "Aaaah!" But she repressed her pain, knowing that her screams would only attract more of the foul things. She felt her face throb and burn in agony. Her face and neck were damp with her blood.

She looked into the blank, soulless eyes of her attacker. She looked at the blood that ringed around them. In that brief moment, she was reminded that she promised to fight. She promised not to become one of them. She promised not to be a victim.

Evelyn's face contorted in anger. She did the first thing that came to mind. Evelyn balled her right hand into a fist and punched the demon in the cheek. She punched with all of the strength that she could bring out, and it worked.

Her neck whipped in the direction of Evelyn's punch. She retreated her vein-y, rotting hands to touch the side of her face.

Evelyn pushed the demon off of her. The Deadite rolled to the ground. Evelyn got up as quickly as she could, and ran far enough to find something...*anything*...that could be used as a weapon. She didn't have to look far. Just a few feet from where she was standing, there were a display of window panes that had been dropped to the floor. *I could use the glass to stab her.* They were still intact and unbroken. *Not for long.* Evelyn smiled as she turned one hundred and eighty degrees to see the she-demon standing in front of her, this time with a fresh purple bruise on her left cheek.

Evelyn didn't want a repeat from last time, so she launched her knee into the demon's stomach, causing her to double over. She then grabbed her by the nape of her neck and brought the demon down to her knees. Her head was only a foot or so away from the window pane. Evelyn hunched down, grabbed the Deadite by the back of her blonde hair with her left hand, and the back of her jeans with her right hand and shoved her into the glass with all of her strength. The glass shattered.

CRASH!

Dozens of large shards fell out of the front of the window pane. One in particular caught Evelyn's eye. It was a large, jagged shard, at least seven inches in length. It almost looked like a knife blade.

The demon was still on her knees, choking on her own blood, feeling pointed glass poke through her skull and her neck. She felt warm blood escape from her veins and run across her pale skin like a river.

Evelyn walked to the other side to grab the shard. She gripped the edged glass with her right hand, not minding that the sides were slicing her palm and fingers. She walked back to the other side, now standing at the demon's right side. She grabbed the wooden frame of the pane, and violently yanked it away. The demon was now free of the glass pillory. Now streaming with blood, the she-demon stood up to face Evelyn, still determined to devour her soul. She grinned evilly and hissed.

Evelyn's face was cold. Unlike the demon, she showed no sign of joy in what she was about to do. Her eyebrows narrowed and her lips frowned. She lifted up the glass shard, preparing to launch in straight into the demon's head. Her arm shot straight out at the demon's face.

The thin glass sliced through the demon's skull like a knife through butter. In between her eyes was a long, jagged, bloody piece of glass. Blood of varying colors poured down her face. First it was the standard red color, but then it changed to black, and then green, and then red again.

The demon's mouth gaped open, trying to form words, but words never came. The only thing that escaped the Deadite's wretched mouth her audible, incoherent, moans. "...Ah...Ah–Aaah...Uhhh..." The demons dropped to her knees. Her upper body then fell forward. Her head was unable to touch the ground at first, as the glass shard held her head up like a tee holding up a golf ball, then quickly slice through her brains and poked out of the other side. The clear glass was now red.

Evelyn's voice was steady and low. "Try to swallow my soul now, bitch."

She stared at the lifeless corpse for a moment before venturing forward. She wanted to be absolutely sure that it was dead. She was finally able to breathe normally. Her gaze lifted from the Deadite and across the store. *Where's everybody else?* Her plan was to quietly search around the store until she found Faith, Steven, or Ash without being spotted by another Deadite. As she looked onward, she saw another three making eye contact with her.

It was three males. One pointed at her, looking behind to his Deadite brethren, and back to her. Evelyn could hear him shouting. "There! In the back! Kill the mortal!"

That plan was shot down quickly. she thought. Evelyn jumped over the Deadite corpse and ran in the opposite direction of the other three demons.

As Evelyn was doing her best to run from the Deadite's on the left side of the store, on the other side, Steven had finally gathered the strength to pick himself up and walk around. His bones and muscles ached, especially his back. Landing on a folding table from twenty feet in the air does not do the body well.

Steven brushed his dark, choppy hair out of his face as he cautiously trekked through the ruins of S-Mart. Fallen merchandise had formed into piles across the floor. Some were so tall that they resembled small hills. Aside from his concern over his friends' well-being, the danger surrounding Freddy and his Deadite army, and his own aching body, Steven was amazed at how different the store had looked now because of the damage.

He wandered around aimlessly. He was careful not to step on anything that would break, or cause any sort of noise, as he was afraid that a lone Deadite or a crowd of them would be able to find and kill him.

His walk had sparked something in his brain. He remembered something that made his stomach churn and his hands shake. Steven's eyes widened and he nervously, but quietly, said to himself, "The book!" he said. "I lost the book!"

Steven whipped around and retraced his steps to the original spot where he fell. He jumped over the rubble to go back to the tipped over table surrounded by merchandise where he had landed. "Oh God, oh God, oh God..." he kept repeating to himself. He started crawling on his hands and knees, hoping that the book slid somewhere on the floor. "I had *one* job, and I screwed it up!"

Steven then got the idea to return to the exact spot where he fell and guess where the book had gone away to. He crawled back to the same spot on the cold hard floor. He laid down in the exact position he was in before. He lifted up his hand to the ceiling and drew an imaginary line with his index finger where he flew. "Let's see." he muttered. "If I fell like this, then the book probably slipped away right before I landed...I think." He traced his finger further ahead, past where he landed. Steven flipped over on his stomach. "That means the book should be somewhere over..." Steven took a guess, hoping that he picked the right area. He pointed just a few yards behind him, near the cutlery aisle. "...There."

Just then, Steven could faintly hear the demonic laughter of the Deadites coming from the distance. "I gotta hurry." he said as he pushed himself up and sprinted towards the area where he hoped the book would be.

He looked down at the floor as he walked, keeping a close eye for the leathery face of the Necronomicon. So far, the only things his eyes detected were broken merchandise. "Come on..." Steven found himself on the top of a small hill of busted merchandise that gathered on top of each other during the mayhem.

Steven dropped to his hands and knees and started taking items away one by one, trying to reach the bottom. "Come on, damn it! Where are you?" The more he removed items out of his way, the more desperate he became.

Finally, as he brushed away crumpled air conditioning filter, he noticed something peeking through the rubble. It was the corner edge of something dark and dry in appearance. There were wrinkled pages between them. Steven felt his heart race as he quickly brushed items out of the way and pulled it out. At last, the evil face of the Necronomicon was staring back at him, and was secure in his arms again.

Steven never thought he would be glad to see that face again, or touch its fleshy cover, but he was. He held his close to him and jumped back on the ground. He looked onward, his eyes locked on the cutlery aisle just a few yards away. *I bet I could find a knife or something to use. Right now, it would be kind of stupid to walk around in this place unarmed.* Steven quietly walked towards the aisle, keeping a watchful eye on Deadites as he did so.

Faith walked her way through the cutlery aisle. She was amazed that this, among maybe two others next to it, was the only aisle that had not been destroyed. Considering that she fell into an aisle filled with forks and butcher knives, she was thankful for that. Occasionally, she would see a knife or two on the tile floor, but comparing it to the damage that had been done to the rest of the store, it wasn't so bad.

As Faith neared the end of the aisle, she could see two Deadites across the way. They had not seen her, as they were facing the opposite direction. But still, she was unarmed. She couldn't go against them without some kind of weapon.

She felt her eyes trail away from the Deadites and to the shelf next to her, which carried a vast array of kitchen knives. Without pause, her arm extended to the shelf second to the top. She reached out and grabbed the largest knife on the shelf. The blade was roughly ten inches long with a thin, wooden handle. She gripped it tightly in her hand as she eyed the Deadites that were, thankfully, still far away. *It's not a rifle, but it'll do I guess.*

Faith then exited the aisle and found herself in the Sporting Goods department. Most of that area of the store was still intact. Aisles lined with bicycles, heavy bags, boxing gloves, footballs, baseballs, and bats were unharmed. But, as Faith slowly walked through each aisle, searching for somewhere safe to hide, she noticed something. Something that chilled her bones and pissed her off at the same time. "Where are all the guns?" she said, louder than she intended.

As Faith looked over to the aisle that originally held all of the guns and ammunition in S-Mart, she soon discovered that it had been destroyed. Shelves had been knocked over, and merchandise had either been broken or thrown to different areas of the building, just like everything else in the store. Faith slammed her fist against the shelf she had been leaning against. "Damn it!" she hissed.

When Faith had punched the side of the shelf, it caused something to fall and roll onto the floor, making itself visible to her. She looked down and saw that it was an aluminum baseball bat. Faith bent her knees and picked it up. She examined it, holding the handle and the kitchen knife in her left hand. At that moment, Faith had an epiphany. *Well, I can't blow their brains out...but maybe I can crush their bones and slice their guts.* Faith stood up and smiled. *I just need something to hold them together.*

She looked behind her to see a rack holding a dozen rolls of duct tape. "Huh..." Faith said to herself. "how serendipitous." Faith took one step forward and grabbed a roll of tape.

She sat on the floor, leaning against the shelf as she took the tape out of the packaging. Once she finally got it open, Faith took her knife and connected it to the end of her bat. Taking a strip of tape, Faith wrapped the tape around the bat about five times before cutting the tape. She threw the roll away and made sure that the knife was held securely. Proud of her creation, Faith smiled and almost chuckled. "Ha ha ha..."

CRASH!

Faith heard items knocking over on the shelf she was leaning against. Before she could even look to see where the noise was coming from, she felt a pair of rotted hands grip her neck tighter and tighter.

Faith couldn't breathe. She could only gulp and choke. "(gasp) (gurgle) Eck!" She flailed her arms and legs, but it only caused the Deadite behind her to grasp tighter. She moved her torso forward as she tried to unclasp the fingers around her neck. Only caused more pain to her throat.

She could hear the demon's crazed laugh. "Ha ha ha ha ha!" And then his chant. "Join us, Faith! Join us!"

By now, she had come to loathe the sound of their warbled voices. It made her go blind with rage. As the demon began to pull her in through the other side, Faith gripped the bat with both hands and launched the knife end through the other side of the shelf.

She heard the cracking noise, which she assumed meant that she had pierced the skull. She felt the demon's grip loosen around her neck. Still gripping the bat, Faith slid out from the shelf and brushed the merchandise aside to see the face of the Deadite. She indeed had struck the bladed end into the demon's skull, killing it. Blood still dripped from the knife would. She gazed at his open-mouthed stare, blank and listless. "Don't you get it?" she said to the corpse. "'No' means 'No'!" Faith yanked the knife out, causing more blood the pour. The demon fell on his side, never to get back up.

"I swear, if I have to hear 'Join us' one more time, I'm going to flip shit." Faith got back up on her feet. The muscles in her throat were still sore from the Deadite's grip. She had already forgotten how strong they were.

SMACK!

Another demon came up from behind her and hit her in the back of the head. "Ugh!" Faith groaned as she fell on her hands and knees on the cold floor. She heard the demon hiss from behind her. She instantly flipped over to look at it.

Another male Deadite was charging at her at lightning speed. Before she could react, he jumped in the air, trying to jump on top of her. Faith's body reacted before her mind could even process what was happening. Her legs bent, and her knees were brought to her stomach.

As the demon jumped on top of her, Faith kicked him in the chest. She shot her legs out with all of the strength that she had, pushing the demon away. She grunted. "Ugh!" Faith stood up and grabbed her bat before the demon could have a chance to attack her again. She ran to the Deadite.

Faith hit the demon in the stomach yet again, this time with the knife end of her bat. She felt the steel blade burst through the meat, bones, and vital organs. Out of pure sadistic pleasure, Faith twisted the bat around, causing an even bigger hole in the Deadite's stomach. The demon cried out in pain. "Aaaaah!" Faith yanked the knife away. The demon had bent over, putting his hands over his stomach in an attempt to keep his intestines from falling out.

As soon as the demon lifted his head, he was met with the sight of Faith swinging her bladed bat at his head, as if he was nothing but a fleshy baseball. The bat impacted against his forehead. His skull cracked. The demon fell on his back to the tile floor. When the demon opened his eyes, he saw Faith standing over him, with the bat over her head. She lowered it once more, swinging at his face, pulverizing his skull.

She held her bat differently this time. She kept the bladed end pointing down to the ground. She gripped the handle, with one hand over the other. As hard and as fast as she could, Faith plunged the knife into the Deadite's skull. And his eyes. And his chest. And his bleeding stomach. Over. And over again.

Once a pool of blood formed around the corpse, Faith realized it was time to stop. She breathed a sigh of relief. "Phew..." She relaxed her arms. Looking down at them, she realized that speckles of blood had sprayed on her body. She felt her cheek, it too was wet with blood. *I got a little carried away, didn't I?*

She felt it was time to get out of this department and start looking for her friends. *There's gonna be Deadites everywhere, but at least we'll be together. Safety in numbers, right?*

Faith held the bat up as she walked to the edge of the aisle. She wasn't certain that there were Deadites around every corner, but the last thing she wanted to do was risk getting attacked again. Faith neared the end of the aisle. From the other side, she could hear rasped, heavy breathing. *Oh, come on! More?* she thought. She got ready to slay another Deadite. Faith turned to the corner and swung her bat blindly. It made contact.

She immediately heard Steven's voice as he cried out in pain. "Ow!" Steven doubled over, clutching his stomach as he whimpered.

Once she heard his tortured cry, Faith lowered her bat to the ground and put her hand on Steven's back. Her voice cracked. Her eyes glistened in regret and embarrassment. "Oh, Steven! I'm so sorry!"

Still bent over and looking down at the ground, Steven finally spoke. His voice was loud enough to hear, but it was strained. When he spoke to Faith, it almost sounded like a wheeze. "I'm fine." he lied. "I forgot how good you are with a bat."

She helped Steven stand up straight. She patted his back and playfully tousled his hair. She chuckled, trying to break the tension. "I guess those two years of softball actually came in handy, huh?"

Steven smiled faintly and nodded in agreement. "Mmm hmm." His eyes trailed down Faith's arm to take a look at the bat. His gaze descended from the handle and stopped once he noticed the large kitchen knife duct taped to the end of the bat. His eyes widened in shock and he felt ice down his spine. He jumped back and pointed at the knife. "Oh crap, what the hell?!"

Faith leered at him for shouting so loudly. "What?" She looked down to where he was pointing. She raised her bat, pointing the bladed end to the ceiling. "You mean this? It's just a knife."

Steven rolled his eyes. "I know it's a knife, Faith. It's just–"

Before he could finish his thought, Faith waved the knifed end of the bat proudly in his face, like a pendulum swinging from left to right. "Yeah, I made it into a bayonet."

She smiled proudly. "Do you like it?"

Steven was baffled at that moment. He searched for the right words to speak next, but at first, he fumbled around his words. When he did speak, he raised his voice and his words seemed to run together. "You almost killed me! You could've eviscerated me with that thing!"

While Steven's face was a look of shock and offense, Faith's smile reverted to the same, serious grimace she had when she launched the knife into the Deadite's skull. "Yeah, I know. I almost did."

Steven took her scowl as a sign to calm down. He stopped shouting and spoke clearly this time. "Well, I'm glad you spared me."

Faith smiled. "Me too." She winked at him and turned around. She led him out of the aisle and tried to find their way back to Ash and Evelyn.

After walking a short distance, Steven stopped next to her and bent down to pick something up. "Hey, look at this." He picked up a matte black Beretta M9 handgun. On the shelf next to it was a box of ammunition. "It's my lucky day." he glimmered.

Faith looked next to her and noticed the handgun and box of ammo in Steven's hands. "Ooh!" she marveled.

Steven swiveled his upper body away from her and spoke like a child who refused to share his toys. "Nuh uh! It's mine now." He looked at Faith's makeshift bayonet. "You already got something. You need to stop being so greedy." He smirked at her.

Faith looked into his eyes and laughed. She took one hand off of the handle and playfully pushed his shoulder. She felt Steven push her back.

By an act of pure coincidence, Evelyn, Faith, and Steven met with one other as they found their way back to the front of the store. Evelyn and Faith made eye contact and ran towards each other.

"Evelyn!" shouted Faith.

"Faith!" replied Evelyn.

Faith dropped her bat, and the two of them smiled and hugged as if they had not seen each other in years.

"I didn't think I was going to find you!" said Evelyn with tears welling up in her eyes.

"Me neither!" said Faith. She pulled back from the hug and noticed all of the scratches on Evelyn's face. "You're all cut up, what happened to you?"

She answered bluntly. "Some of those Deadites have really sharp nails."

Faith nodded in disapproval. "That bitch..."

Evelyn gleamed and smiled widely. "That's what I said!"

"Really?!" The two of them laughed, completely ignoring all of the commotion around them.

It was Steven who broke their reunion. He tapped both of them on the shoulder and pointed outside the store, towards the parking lot. "Guuuuuys?" he said, slightly annoyed by their sudden cavalier attitude about their situation. "Look outside." he instructed.

The three of them turned their heads to look outside. They noticed that all of the Deadites had fled the store and were now circled around the lot. Barely visible inside the circle were Ash and Freddy. Both of them had blood on their faces. They looked at each other with such malice and pure loathing, that the only thing that could vent their hate, was to beat the living hell out of each other.

Chapter 35

Ash and Freddy looked at each other with such hatred, it seemed that both of their eyes, not just Krueger's, glowed in the night. Both of them were in their fighting stances, ready to kill one another.

Ash had his right arm bent, blocking himself by holding his chainsaw blade in front of him. His square jaw was covered by the ever-moving blades, but the rest of his face was visible. His bushy, black eyebrow was cocked, while his brown eyes looked at his enemy with both caution and malice. Gray smoke from the chainsaw rose up in the air, creating an atmospheric mist around both him and Freddy.

Freddy's back was hunched, like a gargoyle atop the edge of a roof. He kept both elbows bent, with his gloved hand out in front. The knives slowly fell up and down, one by one, like a subtle wave. The parts of his blades that weren't stained with blood were shining under the moonlight. When his four blades came up, they partially hid his charred face.

Ash's black boots and Freddy's brown boots both scuffed beneath the concrete as they slowly circled each other, waiting for the other to strike at any moment. There they both stood, ready to fight it out in the middle of the circle of Deadites in the S-Mart parking lot. Aside from the blood and horrid sight of the undead running amuck at every corner, the image was synonymous with two grade school bullies ready to fight in the school parking lot, while the other students have gathered round as spectators.

So it's come to this? Ash thought. *Beating the bat crap out of each other in the parking lot? Well, I have to admit, it's better than being dragged to my death by a bunch of Deadites and wait for Freddy to plunge those fuckin' knives into my skull.* His head still throbbed from when the bastard sucker-punched him...again. He still had a hard time wrapping the rules of the dream realm around his head. As if getting his nose busted in the dream wasn't bad enough, Freddy just had to pour salt on his wounds. He felt a thick, warm, ribbon of blood fall from his right nostril. It traveled from his nostril, down to his upper and lower lip and down to his scarred chin.

Freddy caught sight of Ash's bloody nose and couldn't help but laugh derisively. His laugh was low, graveled, and taunting. "Ha ha ha ha ha..." Freddy wiggled his knives emphatically.

Ash leered at Freddy, lowering his chainsaw just enough to reveal his full face. He tilted his chin upward, raising his voice over the hum of his chainsaw. "What're you laughin' at?"

"What I'm laughing at," Freddy said as he pointed a bladed finger at Ash's bleeding nose. "is your little nosebleed." Freddy smirked. "Poor Ash, you're a weak, old, dog that needs to be put down. You know what happens to old dogs." He flicked his knives up next to his face. "Time to get euthanized!"

Ash was unfazed by Freddy's attempts to scare him. All Freddy was to him was a Deadite that never shut up. "Why don't you take that prissy glove of yours and shove it up your ass!"

Freddy snarled at him. He had no problem dishing out one-liners, but it pissed him off to no end when someone else did it. "Look at yourself. You can barely hold up that fuckin' chainsaw, let alone kill me with it. You're getting weak and you know it."

He kept his tone cool and calm. "I'm still here, ain't I?"

Freddy twitched the corners of his lips into an evil smile. "Not for long." The two of them continued to circle around each other as Freddy resumed his monologue. "Face it, Ashley: You're mortal. Just one stab by my blades, and you're soul is mine. No matter how tough you think you are with that chainsaw or that 'Boomstick', you can't do a thing to me.

I've used the Necronomicon, and it's given me powers you can't even imagine. And try as you may to blow my head off, or spill my guts to the ground, just look around you. You're surrounded. All it takes is a snap of my fingers and they come running."

Ash smirked at him, unfazed by Freddy's words. "Please." he scoffed. "I've been killing these demonic bastards about as long as you've been creeping little kids in their beds at night. I've gone up against some of the ugliest things that book had to throw at me. Hell, I've even turned into one of them myself and came out of it alright. I've fought against an entire army, for Christ's sake. And I've lived through all of it. What usually sends *you* back, huh? A couple of smart-ass kids? You're nothing, Freddy. You're shit.

Plus, I know you're little secret. When you're in the dream realm, you're all tough. But once someone brings you out, you're no stronger than I am. And without that book of yours, you can't really do much except try to attack me with that flimsy glove you got there. What's that thing made out of, anyway? A couple of nuts and bolts, and whatever was layin' around in your kitchen?"

Freddy spat venomously at him with his words. "At least I still got both of my hands."

"You're goin' down, Freddy!" yelled Ash. "Without the book, you ain't got a chance against me!"

Freddy relaxed his shoulders and brought his left hand up next to his face. "You think so? Guess we'll have to put it to the test, then." Freddy snapped his fingers.

(snap)

Two Deadites that stood behind Freddy's left and right side lifted their feet from the ground, and charged at Ash by the snap of his fingers. They ran to Ash, pounding their feet against the concrete like a heard of buffalo. Their white eyes became bigger the closer they got to him.

The Deadite that charged from Ash left side was utterly gruesome. He was over six feet and five inches, just a few inches taller than Ash. He was muscular, like some sort of bodyguard or weight lifter. His skin was already showing signs of decomposition, as the skin was blue-ish in appearance. The demon had no mouth. The only thing that remained were black gums and rotted teeth.

The Deadite that came towards Ash's right was also a large male with a muscular build. His skin was dark, with scars and scabs across every inch of his face and bare arms. His jaw was elongated, stretching down to his chin. The corners of his mouth had been sliced, curving up all the way to his ears. When he opened his mouth, rows of jagged teeth were visible.

Ash's eyes darted left and right at the two of them. He thought about which one to take down first. He didn't have much time to strategize, but it wasn't like this scene was new to him. He raised his chainsaw and prepared to slay some Deadites.

Ash lifted his knee and kicked the one on his right. His boot launched towards the demon's chest and broke his ribs. As the large Deadite tumbled on the concrete, falling on his back, Ash reached for his shotgun and reached for his last two bullets in his front shirt pocket. In record time, Ash reloaded his Boomstick.

By this time, Ash could tell by the increasing sound of snarls and demonic laughter that the Deadite behind him was getting closer. He knew he didn't have time to turn all the way around and shoot the bastard, as he was already right behind him. Ash merely twisted his upper body, raising his arms, lifting his shotgun by his head. Bluntly, Ash smacked the demon with the butt of his shotgun.

While the demon behind him was knocked back, Ash turned back, facing frontward.

The first thing that he saw was the Deadite to his right charging at him. Ash straightened his arm and pointed the twin barrels at the mouth-less demon. Ash pulled the trigger.

BOOM!!!

He shot the demon in the head, unleashing the shell into his skull. Bits and pieces of the Deadite's head had blown away. Blood sprayed out of his head like a broken water balloon. The parts that remained had now been littered with shrapnel and was bleeding profusely. His head had been forced back from the impact of the bullet. The Deadite fell down, landing on the bloody concrete, dead.

Yeah, I'm good. Ash thought to himself. Now filled with self-assuredness and utter bravado, didn't even turn to face the last of the two Deadites. He bent his arm and rested the barrels on his left shoulder. Ash pulled the trigger, releasing his last shell.

BOOM!!!

Over his shoulder, Ash shot the Deadite, unleashing his last shotgun shell into his throat. It left behind a bloody, gaping hole. Some of it, however, made its way to the demon's face and chest, peppering him with shrapnel. The Deadite's head was knocked back to the sky from the force. Black and red blood poured from the dozens of bullet holes in his body. He hissed his final, raspy breath.

Ash kept his back to the demon. His shotgun was still resting over his shoulder. He looked down to the ground. He lifted his index finger up, unwrapping it from the handle of his shotgun. As the demon fought to keep his body upright, Ash kept his finger up, predicting when the demon would fall dead. He cocked his eyebrows and lifted his finger, nonverbally telling the Deadite, "No, no. Not yet."

As soon as Ash lowered his finger, he immediately heard the sound of a body dropping down onto the hard concrete. A confident smirk fell upon Ash's face. He chuckled softly, his laughter was deep and reverberated behind his throat. Ash placed his shotgun in the holster that strapped to his back.

He then turned to Freddy and started his chainsaw. Ash ran to him just as fast as his Deadite lap dogs had come running for him. He let out a battle cry, "Hyah!" and rammed the chainsaw inside Freddy's chest.

The chainsaw busted through Freddy's ribcage, sliced through his internal organs, and burst through his back. The whirring blades shredded through his body. The powerful force caused Freddy to shake along with the chainsaw. Blood sprayed in both directions: Out from Freddy's chest and back. The silver chainsaw blade was now stained with a deep red. The blades moved at such a speed, that they were merely a blur, slinging blood in every direction as the blades sawed their way through the dream demon's body.

Ash could feel his warm, almost boiling hot, blood lightly spray on his face and his shirt. He could see Freddy shaking. He could hear him as he yelled out in pain. Once he felt that he had enough, Ash pulled the chainsaw from his chest. He let the chainsaw idle, for the time being, while he reveled in Freddy's own misery.

The dream-walking killer clutched his chest with both hands and doubled over, allowing what seemed to be gallons of blood to pour from his chest and stomach. Freddy moaned in pain. "Ugh...Argh..." His breathing became strained. He inhaled only in short burst, like a fish that had been dragged out of water.

Ash wiped the blood and sweat from his forehead, pushing his black and gray-streaked hair from his brown eyes. "Yeah." he said, coolly. "Hurts, doesn't it?" He stood over Freddy, towering over him. He watched the concrete as a pool of dark blood formed around Freddy's feet. The red stripes on his sweater became even an even deeper shade of crimson from the slash on his back. Ash stared at the large gash.

His sweater frayed from the blades of his saw. Blood was dripping down his back in long, thin ribbons. His skin and muscle had been split wide open, partially revealing his insides. Parts of his spine and ribcage emerged from the hole in his sweater. *This'll be easier than I thought.* Ash said to himself.

Ash began to hear bones snapping.

SNAP! SNAP! CRACK! CRACK!

His attention was brought again to Freddy. He looked down to see his spine and ribs moving on their own. The bones jerked their way back inside. They began to sink down inside Freddy's body, in their original positions. His bones made an unsettling cracking sound as they positioned themselves back into place. The bleeding had also stopped. He no longer heard the thick dripping of Freddy's blood pattering on the concrete. It was like a faucet had been turned off.

Ash stared in disbelief as he saw Freddy slowly straighten up in front of him. As Freddy stood tall, he unwrapped his arms from his stomach and let them fall to his sides. Ash was now able to see the hole in his chest. For a moment, he could see a long slice, beginning from his stomach and ending just below his collar bone. His sweater had been ripped, showing his burnt flesh, glistening with blood. Behind his skin were wet sinews of muscle dangling over his ribs. After looking at it for only a few seconds did the ribs begin pull themselves together. Even the bleeding stopped. All that was left were the rips in his ratty sweater, and shredded muscle tissue on his chest and back.

Freddy shook the blood from his hands and looked at Ash. The look in his eyes went from agonizing torture to a self-gratified confidence. "I have to hand it to ya, Ash..." he said. His voice was once again steady and booming. "That one actually hurt."

Ash kept his chainsaw up in a defensive position. His tone was that of pure shock and confusion. "Alright, what the hell's goin' on?!" he shouted. "I thought you couldn't do that out here!"

"That's true, I'm more vulnerable out here than I am in the dream realm. But what you didn't consider was how strong I am when I've collected so many souls. You're right, earlier that would have killed me..." he said as he pointed to the large scar on his chest. "That was when I'd only gotten a few souls. But you see, I now have all of Springwood right in here." He placed his left hand on his chest. "And it's gonna take a lot more than a chainsaw to slow me down."

No matter what, Ash was determined to keep his usual sly demeanor. He lifted his chainsaw, preparing to start it up again. "Well then," he said, confidently. "I guess I'm just gonna have to wear you down until you're weak enough, huh?"

"You'll be dead before that happens." he stated, matter-of-factly.

"I don't think so, skin rash." quipped Ash. "I can go all night." Ash brought his chainsaw down, pulling the rope in attempt to get it started.

rrrrrrrrr...

What? Ash raised it up and lowered it again. *I knew I should've picked up a new one before this happened.*

rrrrrrrrr...

His eyes widened and he felt a mixture of fear and embarrassment. *The damn thing ran out of gas.* He figured, out of all of the times for his chainsaw to run out of fuel, or course it had to be right then. He muttered to himself. "Really? You pick right now to run outta damn fuel?" He looked at Freddy, who was twiddling his blades a few inches from his own face. He was ready to kill.

He laughed at Ash, grinning self-righteously. "That sort of thing happens when you get older, doesn't it?"

"Ah, screw it." Ash said. *If there's one thing I'm good at, it's how to improvise.* Ash raised the saw over his head, like he was wielding an axe.

Freddy looked above, seeing Ash's face several inches above his own. His face had a look of pure rage. His eyebrows were narrowed, his teeth were gritted, and he could almost hear him snarling like a wild boar. He looked up and noticed the saw blade glimmer under the moonlight. It came towards him in the blink of an eye. Ash slammed the blade of the chainsaw against the top of Freddy's head.

The metal smashed and scraped against his skull. He shouted in reaction to the impact. "Aaah!" His entire skull vibrated and the top of his head throbbed in pain.

Ash lowered the chainsaw and punched Freddy with his left fist. He gave him an uppercut to the chin that lifted him off of his feet and sent him hurling to the ground.

Freddy landed with a hard *thud* on the concrete. A shock wave of pain raced up and down his back, throbbing at his sides. He groaned, "Ugh...Agh..." as he writhed in pain.

While Freddy was on the ground, Ash unlocked his chainsaw from his arm. He unhooked the latches that connected the base of the chainsaw to his forearm. Once the last latch was unlocked, it fell to the ground. All that was left now was his right nub, and the metal cup-link that surrounded his wrist that connected him to both his chainsaw and his metal hand.

When Ash lifted his head to look at Freddy, he was gone. He expected him to see Freddy struggling to get up from the ground, aching and bitching about the pain he was in, but that was not the case. He simply had vanished. All that remained were the puddles of blood that expelled from his body from the saw blade. Ash, in a flurry of movement, looked off to the distance, left to right; hell, even up to the sky, but did not see Krueger. All that was around him were the circle of Deadites.

Out of nowhere, a hole in the concrete instantly appeared behind Ash's feet. Inside the hole was a vision that looked like Hell itself: Fire-y, dark, with smoke entering its way to the outside.

Freddy leapt like he had been shot out of a cannon. For a split-second, he hovered, suspended in the air with his legs bent and his arms out, "Crouching Tiger Hidden Dragon"-style. He was right, his powers in the real world were almost matched to his powers in the dream realm.

The hole disappeared from underneath him as his boots touched the ground. Freddy pulled back his right arm and prepared to launch his blades deep into Ash's spine.

Ash heard the sound of Freddy's boots landing on the concrete behind him. His reflexes took over, causing Ash to quickly whip around to see Freddy, aiming his knifed fingers towards him.

He acted quickly. Ash leapt to his left, narrowly missing Freddy's knives. While he still had his arm extended, Ash grabbed him by his forearm and twisted it toward his back. His bone snapped.

"Ah!" shouted Freddy. Ash had him bent over, the back of his gloved hand touching his scapula. He felt Ash pushing and twisting his arm. Freddy bent his left arm and hit Ash in the throat with his elbow.

Ash yelled. "Ow!" He let go of Freddy's arm and rubbed his throat with his left hand, feeling the tender spot where Freddy's pointy elbow had hit him.

Freddy used the opportunity to attack Ash again. He lifted his leg and kicked Ash hard in the stomach. He watched as Ash fell back into the circle of Deadites.

His fall was caught by a group of Deadites. He was trapped, like a fly in a spider's web. Two Deadites lowered down to the ground to restrain his feet, keeping him from escaping. Another two held his arms back to keep him from attacking them or Freddy.

As he looked closer, he came to realize that the two demons holding his arms were Buck and Anthony. He had to look close to recognize them, as their features were now heavily distorted, and their skin was a sickly gray color.

Another one, who stood directly behind Ash, grabbed both sides of his face and forced him to watch as Freddy neared him, aiming his blades at him.

Evelyn, Faith, and Steven all stood at the front of the store in awe. For only mere minutes, they watched, motionless, feeling as if they couldn't do anything to help Ash.

Once they saw the Deadites take Ash captive, holding him down while Freddy came ever closer with his blades pointed at him, they instantly felt a surge of adrenaline rush through them.

Evelyn put her hand on Faith's shoulder and practically screamed in her ear. "Go get him some ammo!"

"Gotcha!" Faith left Evelyn's side and ran to the other side of the store to grab boxes of ammo from the fallen shelves.

"Hurry!" Evelyn instructed before Faith had gone too far. She then took a few extra steps forward to talk to Steven. She grabbed his arm to get his attention. "Steven, I want you to go get his–"

Steven interrupted her before she could finish her instruction. "I know, I know, the hand. I'm on it." Steven ran over to the pile of glass on the east side of the store to grab Ash's metal hand.

Evelyn sprinted over to the Garden department to grab more fuel for Ash's chainsaw. She found herself having to hurdle over debris and avoiding glass as she made her way across.

After only less than a minute had passed, the three of them met up and ran out of the store, carrying everything Ash would need. Evelyn carried four bottles of fuel, two in each arm, along with his barbed chain. Faith carried about five boxes of shells and bullets in one arm, and Ash's pump shotgun and 9mm pistol in the other. Steven held Ash's metal appendage in his right hand, and the Book of the Dead cradled in his left arm.

"He's gonna kill him!" Faith said hopelessly. "We have to stop him somehow!"

Evelyn dropped everything in her arms, leaving it to fall to the ground. "Here," she said as she grabbed Ash's 9mm away from Faith. "Is it loaded?" she asked.

"Yeah, but the safety's on." replied Faith.

Evelyn clicked the safety off. "No problem." she said. She then closed one eye and looked through the sights.

Faith warned her. "Careful, don't shoot Ash!"

Evelyn took a few steps to the side, making sure that her angle was precise and that her target was exactly where she wanted it to be. "I won't." she said intently. She squeezed the trigger.

BLAM!

The bullet left the barrel of Ash's 9mm pistol, and grazed the scalp of the Deadite to Ash's right, holding him down. The bullet then traveled onward, finally stopping once it hit Freddy's skull.

The bullet hit Freddy straight it his left eye just as he was about to launch his four blades into Ash's stomach. The impact caused Freddy's left eye to explode. His head tilted back as thick, dark, blood sprayed out of his eye socket. The gooey texture of his eyeball against the hard metal of the bullet sounded like a TV dinner exploding in the microwave.

"Argh!" Freddy shouted as he covered his eye with his left hand. Half of his face was drenched with his own blood. The bullet went straight through his socket and was now lodged right in his temporal lobe. The bullet was still hot in his skull and the pain was unbearable. Freddy stepped back and retracted his glove away from Ash.

Steven gripped the metal hand tightly in his. He held his arm back, ready to throw it as far as he could. "Ash!" he yelled hoping that he would be able to hear him.

With one less demon holding him captive, Ash was able to turn around and see Steven about to throw his metal hand back to him.

"Catch!" warned Steven. He catapulted the metal hand across the parking lot, hoping that it would reach far enough to land in Ash's direction.

The metal appendage soared past the sea of Deadites that had packed themselves in the S-Mart parking lot. As it started to fall, it was just out of reach from the pack of demons that circled themselves around Ash and Freddy.

A single hand reached up amid the crowd of Kandarian demons. The metal appendage smacked against Ash's palm as he caught it. He lowered his arm down, elbowing random Deadites behind him that tried to take the hand away. Ash locked his replacement hand back onto his wrist and began to use it to its full extent.

He bent his metal fingers, forming his hand into a fist. He whipped around and sucker-punched one of the demons that had been holding his arm down. He then shifted his body and launched his elbow into the face of another Deadite that had tried to grab him.

Once he finally broke through the wall of undead that had blocked him in, he ran over to trio of young warriors, both delighted and relieved to see them carrying the weapons he left behind. He pointed to Faith, who was carrying Ash's pump shotgun, as well as the ammo that went along with them. "Quick. Ammo" he ordered.

Faith held a box of shotgun shells in front of him as he brought out his double barrel.

Ash grabbed a handful of shells and stuffed a few inside his shirt pocket as well as the bullet belt strapped across his chest. He then took two more and used them to load his shotgun. He cocked his gun, hearing a *click* as the twin barrels locked in place. He waved his fingers at her, gesturing for her to hand him the other weapon. "Gun!" he ordered bluntly. He put the shotgun back in the holster and proceeded to grab the remaining gun that Faith held in her hand.

He put his pump shotgun in the other holster behind his back. The two shotguns were positioned in opposite directions, the stocks pointed upward and the barrels downward, forming an X-shape behind his back.

Evelyn offered Ash's 9mm pistol and his barbed chain to him. "Here." she said as he returned them.

"Thanks." Ash said as he grabbed the pistol, the barrel was still hot to touch. He placed it back in the holster that Ash kept tucked away at his right side. He took the chain and wrapped securely around his wrist. He looked up at the kids and ordered them further. "Now you guys go get something to protect yourself with, it's too dangerous out here."

The three of them nodded in agreement. Faith replied, "Okay." as they hastily made their way back to find weapons of their own.

Before he had a chance to get away, Ash touched Steven on the shoulder and forced him to turn around to look at him. "Steven." Ash called.

Steven looked up at him, wondering what it was that he had to say.

He looked into his eyes intensely. His tone of voice was utterly serious. "I think now's the time to read out those incantations. If you don't do it now, you won't have another chance, you got me?"

Steven nodded. "Yes, sir."

Ash smiled. "Good." He let go of Steven's shoulder. "Now, if you'll excuse me..." In the blink of an eye, Ash had turned all the way around, hurling his barbed chain at a random Deadite that had tried to sneak up behind him. The chain wrapped around the demon's waist and brought him to his knees. Blood sprayed all around him, staining the concrete with dark, red, puddles. Ash grabbed his pistol and brought it out from the holster. He pulled the trigger, shooting the demon in the head. Before Ash walked over to the lifeless demon to retrieve his chain, he turned back to Steven, repeating his instruction. "Go on, move it!"

Steven's eyes went wide. "Oh–Okay!" He turned around and headed back inside the store.

Ash walked over to the corpse and unwrapped the bloody chain from its body. He looked over, noticing that the circle of Deadites had been broken. They were all scattering aimlessly. One thing that stood out the most, was that Freddy was no longer there. Only a minute ago, he was standing about forty feet away, covering his eye and screaming in pain. And now, he was nowhere to be seen. "...Where'd he go?" he mumbled to himself.

Steven had opened the Necronomicon to the section he had previously bookmarked with his thumb. The top corner of the page still had a small indent where his finger had been. He spoke aloud the words from the Book of the Dead as he jogged back to the store. His eyes never left the wrinkled, blood-sprawled pages as he nonchalantly jumped over the corpses of Deadites on his way back inside.

His eyebrows scrunched and he slowly spoke each word, and awkwardly mispronouncing each syllable. "Nos...fe..rah...tos." He spoke aloud, hoping that by speaking loud enough, it would make up for his gross mispronunciation. "Al...le...memnon..." He jumped over another body and was now only twenty feet away from the destroyed barricade that covered the automatic doors. "K–Kan...?"

At that moment, when his left foot had touched the ground, Steven felt something wrap around his ankle. Whatever it was, it was tightening around him, squeezing him like a python. Before he even had a chance to look down to see what it was, he felt it pulling him away, violently.

Steven was thrown off of his feet and fell to the ground. He shouted the last syllable of the first section of the incantation, mixing it with his surprised screams. "Daaah!" The back of his head smacked against the concrete, almost knocking him unconscious. He then felt himself being dragged along the hard, rough concrete. He was being pulled so fast that everything moving past him appeared to be a blur. The friction of it caused him to burn through his clothes. His shirt rode up, leaving his back exposed to the moving ground. The skin was being ripped off like a band-aid. Every inch of his back was now being scraped and scratched. It burned like fire on his skin. "Aaaah!" he cried in agony. Steven looked ahead of him, seeing what holding onto his ankle.

It was a tree branch. Although the branch was no thicker than his index finger, It was strong enough to trap him and pull him away from his friends. From the store. From safety. Steven's gaze quickly leapt upward, anxious to know where the sentient branch was taking him.

He saw an image of a large tree. It's image was getting bigger by the second to his eyes as Steven got closer to it. The trunk was larger than any tree he had seen before. It must have been six or seven feet wide; wide enough to seem like two trees combined. He also noticed another odd thing about it: Aside from the other trees beside it, this one seemed to be staring at him. As if it had a face. He could see it now, the bark on its base was moving, it was contorted to form a vile face. He recognized it. It looked very similar to Freddy's. It was like the burnt flesh that made up his face was now replaced with aged tree bark.

Steven's eyes watered and he allowed himself to scream helplessly as the tree pulled him in, accepting that at within a matter of seconds, he would be splattered to death.

Chapter 36

"AAAAAAAAAAH!!!" WAS THE ONLY THING that could escape Steven's mouth as he was dragged closer towards the base of the tree. His mind couldn't make sense of it all. He had never been so afraid in his entire life. The fastest roller coaster didn't compare to the shock that he was experiencing.

His entire back felt like it was on fire. He couldn't stand the feeling of being dragged along the concrete at what felt like thirty miles per hour. He could feel pieces of gravel becoming lodged in his back, stuck in his muscle tissue, as no traces of skin existed on that area anymore. He wasn't quite sure, since he couldn't see behind him, but he felt as if the only thing touching the concrete now were his muscles and bare spine. It vibrated along the hard surface. The friction of it filed down the bone. The only thing Steven wanted was for the pain to stop. *I don't care if I die anymore. Just, please God, make it stop! Make it stop!*

At that moment, during his desperate plea with his maker, he felt the transition between the rough, unforgiving concrete, to the soft grass. Freddy had now been dragging Steven into the area just off to the side of the S-Mart building. It was the area that surrounded the parking lot, encapsulated by tall trees and shrubbery. It was meant to give the building an image of serenity. What better captures the image of a happy suburban town better than perfectly trimmed shrubs and blooming flowers?

Only now, the decorations that should ensure for a peaceful image have now become the instruments for something hellish. The tall oak trees had now become alive, controlled by a demonic presence. Their thick branches undulated like the tentacles of an octopus. The bark was broken and gray, as if it had clearly been dead for several years. As the trees moved, the sound of their creaking branches and rustling leaves caused an unsettling moan in the night air.

Steven opened his eyes and saw the base of the tree only ten feet from him. He could see Freddy. His hideous face looked only more menacing now likened inside the trunk of the oak tree. The image wasn't flat. His features were prominent, extending past the flat surface of the wood. It was three-dimensional. He could see Freddy's ears on the side of the tree. Sharp pieces of wood peeled off of the base to form his jagged teeth. The creases in the bark arched to resemble his brow bones. And then he saw what seemed to be his eyes. There were two dark holes cut in the base of the tree that formed the shape of Freddy's eyes. They were blank and vapid, showing nothing but utter darkness.

Just then, Steven's body was lifted up from the ground. It was so sudden that he didn't even have time to react. The branch that wrapped around his ankle had pulled him with suck force, that it almost dislocated the bones. He felt his body being thrown around as he was being lifted up. He was now suspended, upside down. Steven briefly viewed the parking lot at the top of his gaze. Scattered along the lot and in the streets were dozens of demons, also upside-down in his view. Before being turned away, Steven's eyes trailed up, looking at the strip of concrete that he was being dragged along. He could see a faint but long trail of blood beginning from the front of the store to directly below his head.

He was then coldly reminded of the scrapes and burns along his back as the gentle breeze hit him. Although the wind was soft and calm that night, it felt like a harsh rubbing alcohol against his fresh wounds. He felt raw and exposed with his back to Freddy. He knew that he was looking at what he had done to Steven. Admiring his work. *Fucking bastard...* Steven started to bleed again. He felt a warm stream of blood trail up his back, to his neck, and disappeared into his brown hair.

Freddy turned him around so that he could see his scared, weeping face. The bark that made up his filthy mouth moved in an unreal fashion as he laughed. "Ha ha ha ha ha!" The echoes of his laughter mixed in with the moans and creaks of the moving branches.

The branch that wrapped around Steven's ankle, the only thing keeping him from falling on his head and snapping his neck, began to tighten. He could feel the bark tearing into his skin, cutting off the circulation in his foot.

Steven felt the wind against his side as Freddy jerked him around like a rag doll. His body lifted upward, towards the sky. The first thing that Steven saw was a large, thick branch getting closer to him as he propelled in its direction.

SMACK!!!

His face slammed against the oak. He felt the bones in his nose shatter and blood pour from his nostrils. A wave of pain throbbed along his nose and forehead as he swung back down. Steven whimpered, feeling some of the blood rush back inside his nostrils as he suspended upside down.

Steven thought that the torture was over, until he felt the branch swing him to his left. His choppy hair covered his face, so he couldn't tell where Freddy was taking him.

SMACK!!!

His leg, hip, and shoulder crashed against the trunk of another nearby tree. Steven yelled out in pain. "Aaah!" Steven's entire left side was numb with agony.

He didn't even have another second to process the injuries he had sustained when he was hurled a second time to his right.

SMACK!!!

The pain he was experiencing on his left side was now equally matched to his right as Steven was slammed a second time. His body had hit the base of a tree, next to the one that Freddy had taken over.

Finally, the slamming, the careless tossing of his body, had ceased. Once it was all over, Steven now had time to feel everything Freddy had done to him. He felt as if he had broken every bone in his body. From his head to his toes, he buzzed from the shock, like he was a gong that had just been hit.

A mouthful of blood made its way up his throat, nearly making him choke. Steven coughed it up, spitting out the thick glob of blood. He wasn't strong enough to spit it out on the ground. The red mouthful simply left his lips and dripped from the corners of his mouth, to his cheeks, and to his eyes. Steven closed them to avoid being blinded by his own blood, allowing it to flow down his eyelids. He felt weaker by every passing second as the blood rushed to his head, making him dizzy.

He had used every ounce of strength in him to hold on to the Necronomicon. Even when Freddy was thrashing him around, he still gripped the book tightly in his hand.

Steven felt swarms of thin branches crawl on his skin, like spiders. He opened his eyes and looked down, technically up, at his feet. He counted approximately fifteen, maybe twenty, branches tangling themselves all over Steven's body.

A long, leafy branch slithered its way down Steven's arm. The wood scraped and scratched it, leaving red lines along his forearm. The branch crawled down to his wrist and to his hand. It was the same hand that securely held the Book of the Dead.

His eyes darted down to where the branch was wrapping around the book. His grip tightened and he fought the immense pain to shout. "No! No!" He moved his arms and legs in attempt to free himself, but the more he moved, the tighter they constricted around him. His voice was hoarse. "Let go!" He felt the book slipping from his hands as the branches took it from him. “No, you bastard!” he shouted. “Give it back!”

The branch coiled around the book. He took the Necronomicon from his hand. The branch hastily pulled away from Steven, giving him no time to reach for the book. “You should never take what isn’t yours, Steven.” said Freddy. “Didn’t your mommy and daddy tell you not to steal?”

The many branches that touched Steven’s body were now wrapping themselves tighter around him. From all directions, pieces of the tree lowered down upon him to constrict his body. To trap him even further. To suffocate him.

His arms, chest, and legs were now covered in tree branches. Each of them were long, thin, and jagged, like the pointed finger of an old woman. They were wrapped around his skin tighter than a small rubber band. He could feel his limbs growing numb and cold.

Just then, Steven was turned right side up again. He was held up solely by the mercy of the frail branches. His head swirled as the blood returned back to the rest of his body. He could now see Freddy’s wretched, wooden face. *Why couldn’t he have just covered my eyes with branches, too?* he wondered.

Freddy roared in his face with his booming voice. “Guess you’re gonna have to learn the hard way!” He used his powers even further to squeeze the boy even tighter until he could see the agony in his face.

He was being squeezed to tightly, he could hardly speak. To do so would cause his chest to expand, which would break his ribs from the pressure. Instead of screaming for help, like he wanted to do, he simply let out a feigned gasp. “Ack...Ack...”

Relief washed over him as Freddy loosened his grip. He could finally breathe. Steven inhaled deeply, thankful for the air that was given to him.

He felt small branches touch the side of his face. His heart began to pound as he feared the worst. The thin wood cut into his face and slid under the skin. One of them went into his mouth, grazing his gums and the back of his throat.

Steven's muffled screams went unheard as more branches went inside his body. The twigs cut him and made their way under his skin, like IV tubes. So far, there were five branches inside his left arm, and six in his right. Approximately a dozen branches each had crawled up his pant legs. They tore through the denim. The twigs sliced through his skin and muscle and crawled inside his knees and thighs. He looked down and could see spots of blood forming in his jeans.

Three extra branches, approximately two centimeters in diameter, slithered their way up his legs, scratching the surface of his skin. His bloodied legs stiffened and twitched once they crawled under his boxers. Steven tried to scream, but it only caused his throat to hurt even worse.

Freddy's echoing voice felt like fire to his ears. "What's the matter, Steven?" he taunted. "Can't handle a little morning wood?! Haaa ha ha ha ha ha ha ha ha!" The sharp-ended twigs quickly sliced away at his inner thighs and then his penis. The branches crawled to the other side, tearing the top layer of his skin as they did so. Steven shouted purely out of reaction. "Annng!" The pain was excruciating. The entire lower half of his body was now wet with his own blood.

More branches crawled up his shirt, ripping through the thin, black fabric. The pointed tips gently caressed his skin before cutting through it. Steven shouted in protest, but his cries were muffled from the branches already down his throat. "Mmmm! Mmmm!" But his cries were useless, the twigs easily sliced through his ribs and stomach as if they were scalpels.

As the wood cut through the muscle tissue, and wrapped themselves around his many rib bones, Steven felt pain beyond his own comprehension. He screamed so loud, that it was almost clear despite the twigs in his mouth. "Aaaannng!" Tears streamed down the corners of his eyes. He started to hyperventilate, which mixed in with his crying. He hadn't cried this powerfully since he was a child.

By this time, every inch of his body had been cut, scraped, and stabbed. Dozens of wooden branches were under his skin, slicing through the muscle, wrapped around his bones. He had gotten an acupuncture treatment, with the Freddy Krueger touch to it. From head to toe, from back to front, the inside of his body was filled with tree bark.

There was no relief from pain. No area left untouched. His entire being had been violated. He felt like an empty vessel, barely clinging to life. He had one job to do, and he failed. *Why didn't I run faster? Why couldn't I have just looked where I was going? Why did I have to get sucked into this whole thing? Maybe if I'd just did one thing differently...maybe...* Steven blamed himself for his misfortunes. He desperately wanted to be anywhere else than where he was now. Even if it meant death. He pleaded. "I don't want to hurt anymore." *Please, take my soul. Just don't let it become his.*

When he saw another thin branch slithering up his stomach, he prayed that it would be the one to bring him death, swiftly and quickly. The tree branch crawled ever so slowly from his stomach to his chest, Steven knew that Freddy was making it so slow only to tease him. To prolong his suffering. To see just how much lower he could go.

He watched it meticulously as it moved up, stopping at his collar bone. His eyes never strayed from it. The branch tickled his skin as it reached under the collar of his shirt. It intertwined with the chain of his necklace, the chain that supported his silver cross. *What is he doing?* Steven wondered. The branch pulled back from his neck, bringing out the crucifix from under his t-shirt. It moved faster away from Steven, bringing the necklace with it.

Freddy spoke, his voice was unnaturally boisterous. His tone was smooth and taunting. "Five, six, grab your crucifix..."

Steven felt a tug on the back of his neck as the chain snapped. He gasped once he realized that his necklace was now gone from his person.

The glimmering cross fell to the ground, disappearing in the grass. The silver chain, still looped to the cross, followed behind it. The chain shined in the moonlight before becoming lost in the dirt.

His cross, his sign of protection, the item that he always kept close to his heart at all times, was now gone from him. Hanging in the air, suspended by tree branches, filled with immense agony, without the one thing that gave him comfort, Steven felt alone. His breathing became heavy and uneven. His eyes darted in all directions. He knew that the pain would only heighten from this point. He did the only thing that he was physically capable of doing: crying out for help. He spit out the moving twig in his mouth and screamed for dear life. "HELP ME!" He shouted at the top of his already wounded lungs. "PLEASE! SOMEBODY HELP ME! PLEEEAAASE!"

But when Steven looked around for his friends, no one was around to hear his cries. In fact, upon turning his head to look to his left and right, he noticed something that made his heart drop.

Everything was gone. His friends were nowhere in sight. Ash was not around. The Deadites had all disappeared. The parking lot. The S-Mart building. The rest of the town that had previously been within his view. All of it was gone. It was as if everything, except Freddy and Steven, ceased to exist. All that surrounded them was complete and utter darkness.

"No one can help you now, Steven." said Freddy.

Steven shook his head adamantly from left to right. "No! No!" He kept looking around, hoping that Ash and his friends would come into view. "Ash?!" he shouted. The sound of his humming chainsaw was completely gone. "Faith?!" He begged and pleaded to find his beautiful Faith coming to save him from Freddy's clutches, but she too was absent. "Evelyn?!" The rock in their group. The one who kept them going when everything seemed bleak, was gone. "PLEASE HELP ME!"

Freddy soon cut off his screams by filling his mouth with tree bark. Three branches darted into his screaming mouth. His eyes went wide as he soon discovered that he had a mouthful of twigs. The sharp edges of the wood cut into his throat. The taste of his blood was bitter as it slid down his tongue and fell down his esophagus. He choked and gagged on both the blood and the wood.

He thought that all hope was gone. Freddy now had the Necronomicon, and there was no stopping him now. Even the promise of a quick end to his life was out of the question as he could feel himself slowly bleed to death. Being pulled apart, inch by inch, by those wretched branches. He closed his eyes and cried, waiting for Freddy to do his worst and get it over with already.

SCHIIING!!!

Wait–What? Steven opened his eyes and looked at Freddy's stiffened face. He could tell that he was angry, as his brows were arched upward and the bark that made up his lips were scowling. The branches that wrapped around him like boa constrictors were now loosening their grip. *What's going on, what is he looking at?*

"Ugh!" Steven heard a familiar voice. He knew it had to be Faith.

He looked off to the side of the trunk and saw Faith hacking away at the trunk with an axe. Steven smiled and his eyes glimmered.

The axe was stuck inside the trunk. Faith put her hands on the metal handle and pulled back, dislodging the blade from the bark. The sweat from her brow fell down, cascading down her pale cheek as she raised the axe above her head. She gritted her teeth and yelled at the Freddy-tree angrily. "Let him go!" She plunged the axe into the base of the tree again. This time, when she pulled the blade out again, large pieces of bark came out along with it. "I'll chop you the fuck down!" she threatened as she raised the axe again, holding it like a bat. As soon as the blade hit, she insulted him again, each syllable that left her mouth was matched with an axe hit to the trunk. "You cock sucking–" Faith pulled the axe out and swung again. "mother–" She pulled the axe back as far as she could to ensure that her next swing would be the one to release Steven. "fucker!"

SMACK!!!

Before the axe could even make contact with the trunk, Freddy lowered one of his branches and used it to knock Faith out of his way. It sent her flying though the air.

"Ack!" Faith cried as she crashed against the wall. Her entire body was being crushed as she was caught between the wall and the enormous branch. Her nose had been broken. A few of her ribs had been cracked as her rib cage continued to be caved in from the compression. Although it continued for only mere seconds, it felt like hours to her.

Once Freddy retracted the branch, he allowed Faith to land on her feet, falling on the grass. She dropped the axe to the ground and curled up in the fetal position. She soon discovered that she had the wind knocked out of her lungs and could not breathe. Faith rolled over and got up to her hands and knees. She desperately gasped and gulped as she fought for breath. "Eck! (hiccup) Ugh!" Faith dropped the axe to the ground and rubbed her throat, reaching for air.

Freddy watched her the entire time. Once she was finally vulnerable, he slithered one of his many branches through the grass. It made its way towards her axe and coiled around the handle.

Oh my God! Evelyn's eyelids opened wider and her knees buckled. Her feet stomped on the ground as she charged toward Faith. "Faith!" she yelled, hoping to get her attention. "Look out!"

Faith caught her breath just in time to tilt her head up and see the axe blade aimed at her face. The sight of the shining blade under the moonlit sky, surrounded by leafy branches was almost beautiful, until she realized that it would be the last thing she would see before her demise.

Before she could move one muscle, she felt Evelyn tackle her, moving both of them out of the way. She grunted, "Oof!" as Evelyn's body slammed against hers. Both of them rolled on the grass, narrowly missing the fatal blow of the axe.

Instead, the blade merely lodged into the wall of the store building. Freddy had no time or reason to dislodge it. He had better weapons in his arsenal.

Evelyn laid on top of Faith. By pushing her out of the way, Faith had landed hard on her side. Her shoulder dug into the ground, and

Evelyn being on top of her was only adding salt to her wounds. She immediately got up and grabbed Faith's hand to assist her. Both of them staggered as they regained their balance.

"Come on." Evelyn said hastily. "We can't stay here, we have to run back." She didn't let go of Faith's hand. Instead, she gripped it tighter as she led her back to the store entrance, running as fast as she could.

Faith lagged behind. She felt a rising, intense feeling in her heart. Something that made it pound and her entire body shake. Something that made her not want to get out of harm's way. "Wait!" she said, still running behind. "What about Steven? I can't leave him!"

Evelyn felt just as bad as Faith did. But, she knew that if they stayed their even a second longer, they would both be killed. There was nothing else they could do. She tried to explain without making it seem like she was trying to purposefully abandon her friend. "He's too strong." she said. "He would've killed both of us back there."

As the both of them ran back, they began to see dozens of thick branches lower down like party streamers before them. They hung down, trying to trap the two of them as they ran by.

The two girls slid past the serpentine branches as they coiled up and tried to capture them. They could feel the sentient wood as it brushed by their hips, their arms, their legs, and all over their bodies.

Soon, the grass and part of the concrete lot was littered with moving, pulsating tree bark. Faith and Evelyn found themselves having to take leaping steps to avoid the branches.

They finally reached the front entrance of the store. Luckily for them, it was too far away for Freddy's branches to reach them. They were in the clear. Only a few more running steps and they would be safe inside the store.

Faith looked behind her as she ran. Her eyes locked on Steven's bloodied face. The image of him, bound and gagged by the wooden manifestation of Freddy, kept shrinking the further she ran from them. Even though it was only thirty feet, she felt a thousand miles away from him.

What she couldn't stand, the thing that she couldn't live with, was the fact that she was leaving him there to die. She was abandoning the one she loved. *No.* she thought. Her footing began to slow down. *I can't do this. I can't do this to him. I can't do this. I can't do this.* "I can't do this." The words left her lips softly. Like a whisper.

The bottoms of her boots were planted firmly on the concrete. She and Evelyn were just outside of the front entrance.

Evelyn felt a tug on her arm, and then found herself being stopped in her tracks. She turned around to see Faith, paused, looking at Steven and the monstrous oak tree that was now Freddy. "Faith, what are you doing?!" she asked. She looked past Faith to see the hoard of Deadites not too far from them. "We can't stay out here!"

Faith whipped her head back to look into Evelyn's eyes. She gritted her teeth. Her brown eyes were alive with fury. "I'M NOT LEAVING HIM!"

Her eyes began to well up in tears. She didn't want to leave him either. But there was a choice to make: Try to save Steven and have all of her friends die, including herself; or, do whatever she could to save Faith and herself. "I don't want to lose you, too!"

"I thought you said you were going to do everything you could to make sure that asshole doesn't kill any of us!"

Her voice began to break. "But we can't save him without getting killed ourse–"

Faith unlocked her hand from Evelyn's and pushed her away. "FUCK YOU!" She turned away from Evelyn and ran back to Steven.

Faith had pushed her so hard that Evelyn fell down. She landed on the concrete, the hard surface scraping her arms and back. Her head hit the ground. The pain was unnerving, her entire skull throbbed and vibrated from the impact. She turned her head to the side, fighting the pain to open her eyes.

What she saw was Faith, running as fast as her feet would take her, back to Steven. She rolled to her side and got up to her knees. She yelled at the top of her lungs. "FAITH, NO!"

She could her Evelyn's voice. She could hear the pain and the worry in her tone. But she ignored it. Her only objective was to save Steven. *I'm not going to leave him to die. I don't care how dangerous this is. I wouldn't be able to live with myself if I didn't do everything I could to save him.* Faith dodged and darted through the slithering branches, escaping their grasp.

She could see her axe lodged into the wall. *I could pull it back out, but it would take a few tries. I'll have to be quick.*

Faith was just within running distance of the axe when one of Freddy's branches shot out at her like a whip. It coiled itself around her neck. Her body leaned back as the branch pulled her away. She put her hands on the branch, trying to free herself. But she more she fought back, the tighter Freddy squeezed.

She looked up. She was so close, and yet so far away from Steven. All she could do was stand there and watch as Freddy continued to torture him.

Steven was suspended approximately ten feet from the grass at this point. He heard Faith's voice a couple of times, elating him for a split second. But, he realized that even if Faith was successful in cutting him down, there would be no saving him. Every inch of his body had been punctured. Crusty, jagged wood melded with his tender muscle tissue. He could feel them as they slithered within him. Even his ribcage had become tangled with twigs. The pain was unimaginable. He wanted to blackout just to be relieved from it, but somehow he was being kept alive. Aware of everything that was happening to him. Everything Freddy was doing to him.

Freddy tilted Steven's body so that he was now parallel to the ground. He turned him ever so slightly, so that he could see Faith.

At first, Steven thought Freddy was doing an act of kindness by allowing him to see her face before he died. But he soon realized the malevolence behind his actions. He wanted Faith to see how mutilated Steven's face and body had become. And by doing so, allowing Steven to see the revulsion on her face as well. Freddy wanted the last images of each other to be one of horror.

Faith nearly threw up when she saw the things Freddy had done to him. Steven had been bound, gagged, stabbed, pulled apart, and drenched with his own blood. Tears streamed down her face. She knew he was too far gone by now, but she still didn't want him to go. She reached out her arm, even though he was still too far away from her grasp. She screamed, "STEVEN!"

He could feel his strength, his life, his soul, draining from his body. The corners of his vision began to darken, as if everything that he was seeing was framed with pure darkness. It would be only seconds before everything would go black, and he would no longer be able to see her face. It wouldn't be very long until he would be taken from this world, and enter someplace either free of all pain, or more torturous than the agony he was experiencing. His soul would either belong to God, or to Freddy.

A single tear ran down Steven's face. It escaped from his tear duct, and raced down his cheek, to his jaw line, and fell down to the ground. Through the twigs that had stuffed themselves in his mouth, Steven tried to speak with enough power in his voice so that Faith would hear his final words.

"I'm sorry, Faith."

As soon as the words left his mouth, the branches that wrapped themselves around Steven's ribs pulled in opposite directions. Every rib in his body had snapped from his spinal cord.

SNAP! SNAP! CRACK! CRACK!

Freddy had literally pulled him apart. Vertically, Steven's body had been pulled into two halves. His chest had been burst open and his rib cage stuck out of his body, the bones had spiked through his skin. The branches that held on to his feet also pulled him in opposite directions, splitting him in half from his groin, upward. Virtually every branch and small twig that punctured through Steven's body aided in his gruesome death, pulling on all parts of his body until it was ripped from him. His flesh tore off like a meaty band aid. His bones and muscle tissue became disconnected from him. With nothing holding his blood and guts inside anymore, it all spilled out to the ground. His intestines and other vital organs dropped to the ground, making a nauseating *splat* noise as it landed. His body burst open like a bloodied water balloon. It rained blood all over the grass and a small area of the parking lot.

Faith felt the warm rain that comprised of Steven's blood over her face as she watched him die. It happened so quickly. If she had blinked, she would not have seen him horrific demise. She wished that she had kept her eyes closed. She wished that her last and most vivid image of him wasn't of his death. She screamed again. This time, it was not in desperation, but in mourning. "STEVEN!" She choked on her own sobs as she felt the warm wetness of Steven's blood seeping into her clothes.

The smell of death was still in the air. The potent scent of blood and intestines was still fresh in their noses. Only two seconds had past since Steven's disembowelment when Freddy's image disappeared from the tree. The long, python-esque branches elevated from the ground, and slithered back up to the leaves to be unseen. The tree was no longer alive with Freddy's movements and voice. It was still. Calm. Quiet.

The branch that coiled around Faith's neck seemed to only tighten around her. She looked down and noticed that it was no longer connected to the trunk. It didn't appear to be connected anywhere. She put her hands on the trunk to try to free her airways, and noticed that what she was feeling was not ordinary tree bark at all. The surface was not wooden and rough, but soft and woolly. She looked down and only saw red and green horizontal stripes. That was when she felt his chest pressed against her back.

Freddy held her tightly. He squeezed her throat with his gloved arm, and put his other arm around her stomach, restraining her. He put his charred lips to her ear and laughed softly but deeply. His hot breath sent shivers down her spine. Hearing her scream for her life sent his blood boiling.

Evelyn saw Freddy appeared behind her. She watched in disbelief as the wooden bark morphed into his arm. Once the reality of it sunk into her mind, she realized that she had to move quickly. "NO!" She fought the throbbing pain in her skull and pounded her feet to the concrete, running as fast as she could to get to Faith.

A circle of darkness appeared at their feet. Glowing embers shot up from the ground, sprinkling Faith's skin with tiny burns. She felt herself falling, almost being violently pulled down into the black hole. Both Faith and Freddy sunk down into the unknown abyss so fast that it gave Faith motion sickness. Her senses became severely disoriented when she quickly stopped falling. Her feet touched the ground and she began to rise, only it was not back to where she was before, it was much worse.

Evelyn had been running as fast as her feet would allow to get to Faith. She didn't care that she didn't have any weapons. *I can tackle him to the ground, and get Faith before he has a chance to hurt us.* When Evelyn lowered down and prepared her legs to launch at him, they were both gone. In the blink of an eye, they had disappeared into the circle of nothingness. She landed on the hard concrete, the circle was now gone from the ground with no trace of Faith left. Anger swelled in her chest. Tears streamed down her eyes. She smashed the concrete with her fists as she yelled into the night air. "GODDAMN YOU!" She only wondered what lied ahead of Faith on the other side of the portal.

That "other side", happened to be Freddy's boiler room.

Chapter 37

HIS FOREARM PRESSED AGAINST HER neck. Choking her. He loved the feel of her thin, smooth body against his hands, especially when she squirmed. *I just love it when they try to fight back.* He thought. *Makes it more interesting.* He stood behind her, feeling her writhe and try to break free. Her short, but sharp, nails scratched through the sleeve of his ragged sweater as she tried to pull him from her.

The more she fought him and gulped for air, the more he relished the moment. He half-smiled and breathed harshly against her neck. His thick exhales both teased her for her lack of air, and also sent chills down her spine from sheer perverseness of it. Despite the immense heat radiating from the boiler room, he could feel the goose bumps coming to the surface of her arm.

If I don't do something now, I'll blackout or something. I don't know, can you blackout in a dream? Everything about him and this place is so fucked up, I don't even want to know what all the rules are. Just do something–anything. Faith gave up on trying to release his arm from her throat, so she did what she was taught on her first day of her self-defense class.

Faith let go of Freddy's sleeve and bent her left arm. Without any hesitation, she launched her elbow straight into his ribs.

Freddy yelled. "Agh!" The sharp pain caused him to only let go of her for two seconds, but it was just enough time for her to slip away. As soon as she started running, he extended his arms out in front of her, trying to reach, but she had already escaped. He also noticed that the Necronomicon had been taken from him.

The bottoms of her short, lace-up boots clinked against the grate with each running step. Her heart raced and the hairs on her body stood on edge as she ran for her life. She felt as if he was right behind her the entire time, but every time she turned to look back, he was not there. She started panting and her chest felt heavy from running so hard and so fast. Between breaths, she whispered to herself. "I gotta... hide...gotta hide...somewhere."

She turned every corner that she was taken to. Every time she spotted a flight of stairs, she raced up the steps, hoping to lose him. Each turn that was made was different every time. The last thing she wanted was to go in circles and be brought right back to him. Even if he wasn't in the same spot, she hoped that by going in different directions each time, it would disorient him. However, the only person it confused and disoriented was herself. Faith had no idea where she was going. The only thing certain in her mind was that she could never stop. She absolutely had to keep moving. She couldn't let Freddy take the book from her.

It wasn't long before the top of her head was matted with sweat. The tips of her black hair was wet. Sweat dripped like a faucet from her hair, falling onto her shoulders and face. The higher she went up, the hotter it had gotten. Once she reached on of the top levels of Freddy's hellish lair, she soon felt dizzy and weak. She fought those feelings with everything in her, and kept moving. She touched the railing on the walkway for support, only to have it burn the palm of her hand. She retracted her hand and jogged past the line of boilers at her side. They hissed, spewing mist in her face.

Tsst!

It made her whole body damp with sweat. She was growing exhausted with every stomp that landed on the metal grate. *Don't ever stop.* She reminded herself. *I have to keep moving.* "Come on." she complained quietly. "Someone get me out of here, already." She looked around as she ran across the boiler room. The sheer size, height, and overall space of it was enough to make her fear of heights resurface. The dark corners, tight spaces, and its maze-like design, however, made her feel claustrophobic at the same time. It was a very odd and very unnerving sensation. She feared how dark it was, not because she feared the dark, but who could be hiding within it.

She was about to leave the dark area. She saw another flight of stairs up ahead. But just as she was about to leave, Freddy emerged from the shadows, only a few feet behind her. His right arm was bent slightly, his gloved hand parallel to the floor. In his left hand was a thick, rusted chain. He dragged it along the grated surface.

Clink! Clink! Clink!

Freddy lifted the chain and whipped it towards Faith. The long chain gathered around her ankle. Once she had reached the length of the chain, it stiffened, tightened around her ankle, and caused her to trip onto the floor of the walkway.

Faith grunted. "Oof!" Her face, knees, and elbows smacked against the metal grate. *Fuck!* She thought. *Fuckfuckfuckfuckfuck!*

Freddy gripped the chain with both his left and his gloved hand. He pulled her closer to him. With each rough tug, Faith was getting one foot closer to him.

She tried to run away again. She refused to accept defeat. She kicked her legs behind her, trying to shake the chain from her ankle. Her body squirmed and she kept looking for something to hold on to that would halt Freddy, but everything she touched in that boiler room was blazing hot. She couldn't touch any of it for even a second without burning her skin. Even the walkway was hot against her thighs and stomach as Freddy pulled her in closer.

She felt the side of her leg touch his grimy boots. *I have to do something quick, before he can hurt me.*

Freddy dropped the chain to the floor. "Come here!" he growled.

Faith rolled over on her back, just in time to see Freddy lowering down towards her. He was ready to pounce on her and do his worst.

She brought her knees to her stomach. His face was already inches from hers. She pulled her elbow back and punched Freddy in his jaw. Then again on the side of his face. She punched him and many times as was needed for him to pull back away from her.

Once Freddy leaned back to get away from her fists, she launched her feet at him. She repeatedly kicked Freddy in the chest, stomach, and face. Her hands and feet were a flurry of kicks and sucker punches until he finally gave up and stood on his feet. Faith rolled back on her stomach and prepared to run away. She was still on her hands and knees, crawling, as she built up enough speed to race.

Only a second after Faith punched and kicked the living Hell out of him, Freddy spread his legs so that each foot was on either side of her hips. "You like to put men in their place, huh?" He lowered down and grabbed a handful of her hair, just as she was about to stand up and run away. He gripped her hair tighter and pushed her back down to her hands and knees. He gritted his teeth and his voice was menacing. "You little bitch." he called her.

Simultaneously, Freddy slithered down to his knees and brought her up just enough so that her back was pressed against his chest. He yanked her head back so that she could see the fury in his eyes. He quickly leaned in and let his lips graze her ear as he growled more. "You fucking cunt!" he yelled, putting emphasis on "cunt".

He brought his gloved hand around the front side of her body so he could trace his blades along her skin. "No matter how fast you are, I'll always find you." He barely scratched her neck when he trailed down to her collar bone, then her chest, and then traced the knives across her shirt. He made thin tears up and down the length of her shirt, exposing her bare, pale skin. Still holding a chunk of her hair in his hand, he turned her head slightly to face him.

Freddy's dry, burned lips parted ever so slightly, by just a fraction of an inch. He tugged on her hair, directing her to look up at him. He spoke to her softly, but still with a low growl and grittiness to his voice. "Ohh...Faith..." He lingered on her name, hanging on every letter in it. Very slowly, he leaned down closer to her face. "You must have a lot of it to think you could ever put a scratch on me."

Her lips smashed together as she saw his lips lining up with hers. A whimper fell in the back of her throat. She tried to pull back, but Freddy was holding her with such force that it was impossible to make any distance between them. She decided to speak before he got any closer. Her voice was strained, crippled with fear. She, along with her voice, was shaky. "Wh...Wh..."

Freddy paused. He was now only six inches from her. His eyes stared deep into hers. He feigned curiosity when he replied, "What's that?" He pulled on her hair again, bringing her up higher than he was. He then slammed her head down on the floor of the walkway. The sound of her skull hitting the metal left a ringing sound that echoed throughout.

She now lied on her stomach, her palms facing down, next to her head. She put her fingers through the little grated holes on the floor and squeezed, trying to fight back the pain. She grunted and groaned. "Agh..." She words she had meant to say forced their way out of her mouth as a result of the pain. She panted and moaned in-between words. "Why...do you e-even...want me? You're already...f-fucking p-powerful...you don't need me!"

The last thing that she said caused Freddy to tilt his head in inquiry. "Well you see," he said, beginning his explanation. "Ash did quite a number on me back there, in the parking lot." He grimaced when he remembered the bullets to his face and chainsaw swings to the chest. "That made me weaker, so I need another soul or two to take care of that." He leaned in closer to her ear. "Even though your boyfriend's fixed that little problem, I thought I'd have a little more fun with you." He chuckled deeply.

In one fell swoop, Freddy stood up tall, picking Faith up with him. He swung her and pushed her away from him. His menacing strength sent her across the walkway. In the blink of an eye, her back hit the body of a thick pipe next to the line of boilers. The pipe was thicker and wider than her own body.

"Ugh!" she shouted as she slammed against the surface. *When is he going to stop hitting my head against stuff?* Faith thought as her skull throbbed. She looked up to see Freddy standing ten feet away from her. *I bet I could lose him right now if I ran.*

Before Faith could even attempt the maneuver, Freddy lifted his index blade, summoning his demonic powers.

An assortment of thick, rusted, chains appeared from behind her. She could hear them rustling against the pipe. She was about to run for it, when she suddenly felt stiff. She couldn't move. She had no control over the movements in her own body. Her arms lifted straight up above her head, and her feet shuffled back against the pipe. As soon as her arms and legs touched the pipe, the chains tightly wrapped around them, pinching her skin. She tried to move her hands and feet, hoping to wiggle her way out. She was completely immobile. The only thing under her control was her breathing, which was heavy and erratic. Her eyes widened and glistened as she watched Freddy step closer to her.

He made his steps slow and steady. The sound of his boots landing on the ground echoed, making it the only sound heard in the whole boiler room. He wanted to savor each passing second as the fear in her eyes elevated. He enjoyed the sight of her limbs quaking, and the sound of the chain rattling as she shook.

He was now standing before her. So close, that he could smell the sweat dripping from her hair. It was the sweet extract of her terror. Even though her nostrils were flared and her teeth were gritted, she couldn't change the look behind her eyes. The rest of her face showed that she wasn't going to be fazed by him, but her eyes revealed that she was terrified for her life.

Freddy kept his gloved hand lowered to his hip, while his left hand gently touched his chest over the thick fabric of his sweater. His hand grazed the sweater. He lowered his head to look at Faith in her fearful eyes. He smirked. "His soul is in here, Faith." he said, referring to Steven. "With all of them."

Her voice lowered as she stuck her neck out to shout in his face. "Fuck you, prick!"

Freddy grabbed her throat and squeezed it tightly in his hand, keeping her from speaking further. "Get used to it, bitch." he snarled. He clenched his fist around her neck until she had to open her mouth to gasp for air. "*I'm* your boyfriend now."

He lowered his head towards her. He slowly opened his mouth, waiting until his lips were barely touching hers. Still with his dark, burnt hands around her smooth neck, he kissed her. More accurately, he violated her mouth with his. Freddy breathed into her, leaving the taste of soot and burned flesh in the back of her mouth.

The sounds that came out of her mouth were a mixture of gags and shrill gasps for air. Freddy responded by forcing her mouth open even wider so that he could stick his slimy tongue inside of it. He licked the roof of her mouth. Then her tongue. Then the tops of her teeth.

When Freddy leaned back by only three inches from her face, their was a ribbon of their shared saliva connected to both of their bottom lips. It quickly broke once Faith sealed her lips shut. She shut her eyes, allowing a tear to escape from the corner.

Her eyes opened again when she felt his blades trace down her shirt, and linger towards the zipper of her black jeans. She stared into his eyes, but he was no longer looking at her. His eyes followed where he moved his glove. She came to realize just how sharp his knives were. Even the slightest touch would cut her skin or the fabric of her clothes. That was why it especially hurt when he applied pressure on her vagina through the thin denim. He flicked his index blade upward.

Faith wanted to scream. The cut left on her stung and burned. But she knew that's what he wanted: to hear her shriek. She refused to give him the satisfaction. Instead, she pursed her lips and winced, allowing only a mere groan to vibrate in the back of her throat. She suddenly felt a thick wetness between her legs. She knew it had to be blood. When surrounded by the fires and mist in the boiler room, the blood that left her body felt cold as it soaked in her jeans.

She was relieved when Freddy pulled back his glove, away from her body, and brought it up to his face. He lowered all of his knives, except the one used to cut her. The tip of the knife was red with her blood. Before it could trail down the silver, Freddy brought it to his open mouth and let the droplet fall to his tongue. His menacing eyes trailed back to look at her face. He scanned her short hair that was now matted with sweat. Her smooth, pale skin. Her heart shaped face. Her thin, curved lips. Then, her small but mesmerizing cat-shaped, brown eyes.

Fear had risen inside her again when Freddy lowered down and started whispering in her ear. His voice was low and warbled. He sounded like he had eaten coal before he spoke to her. "You know, I'd eat you right now, but..." He smiled and spoke maliciously. "I'd just be hungry again thirty minutes later."

Faith gritted her teeth, speaking softer then Freddy, but still loud enough for him to hear. "Asshole." she remarked.

His face remained the same, unfazed by her insult. In fact, he was kind of amused that she would continue to fight back, even though she knew it would cause her more pain. He chuckled softly. "Got a dirty little mouth, don't you? You filthy whore." He leaned down and kissed her again, sullying her mouth with his putrid lips and tongue.

I can't take it anymore. Faith thought. *I'm tired of Freddy treating me like this. I don't care if this doesn't do damage to him, I want the bastard to hurt.* With his tongue twisting around hers, Faith quickly smashed her teeth together and bit his slimy tongue. She could already taste the bitterness of his warm blood running down her tongue. Her front teeth were now wet and red.

The feeling of her teeth sinking into his soft, meaty tongue was a pain he had never felt before. He let out a small scream. "Ah!" He tried to pull away, but he couldn't escape her grip. Blood streamed from the tip of Freddy's tongue. Droplets fell down to the walkway.

Freddy stopped her attacks by slapping her. He hit her so hard, it caused her to release his tongue. Not only that, her head had also whipped to her left, in the direction of Freddy's slap. The side of her face was rosy and stinging from the impact.

Immediately following that, was Freddy's index blade piercing the fatty tissue above her cheek bone. The pain made her squirm as he touched the bone, still pressing hard with his knife. She gritted her blood-stained teeth as she muffled her groans. The loudest sound that came from her, was the heaviness of her breathing.

His voice was steady and deep. "Now that I have your attention, cunt..." He pressed the knife further into her cheek bone, forcing her to face him. He made her stare directly at his burned, blistered face. The top layer of his skin was nearly gone. Sinews of flesh were dangling from all parts of his face. His muscle tissue was visible, moving underneath the areas where his unburned skin used to be. He was charred, but somehow appeared red, either by the light of the boiler room, or due to his powers. His brows were prominent, and arched into an expression of anger. The rims of his eyes and the corners of his mouth were black.

Her face was already red from the heat, and stained with tears. She had been fought, slapped, and pierced with a knife. Her friends, and the man she loved, were dead. She knew that from where she was now, that she would soon join them. She didn't like it, but she slowly learned to accept it the more she looked into his vindictive eyes. *That doesn't mean I have to take it like a bitch, though.* She thought. Before Freddy could continue with what he was saying, Faith cut him off. She scoffed in his face, making his expression change. "Go to Hell." she told him. Her voice was cold, but at the same snarky, as per her usual demeanor. "Seriously, go to Hell and go fuck yourself. Fuck you in the ear, Freddy."

Freddy didn't lash out. He didn't snarl and grab her throat. Nor did he plunge his knives into her chest as soon as the words left her mouth. Instead, he half-smiled and lowered his gloved hand to his hip. He laughed softly as his hand slowly reached out and his knives caressed her bare skin, through the rips in her shirt.

Faith squirmed. She tried with all of her strength to launch her knee into his stomach, or hit him in the face with her elbows, but the chains refused to break or loosen at all. She screamed in his face. "Stop it!"

He looked into her eyes. "You don't like it when I touch you there?"

"No, you asshole! How many times do I have to say that?!"

His blades left her midsection and dropped down to her left thigh. He barely sliced through her jeans. "How about here?" He dragged his index blade up her thigh and paused when he neared her vagina. "Or here?"

Faith screamed in his face. "I hope Ash saws your limbs off, and you burn in Hell!"

He pulled his glove back, but still had it raised slightly.

This time, there was more desperation in her voice. Although she was still angered, she warned him. "Get that fucking glove away from me."

He smiled at her, showing his bloodied, sharp teeth to her. "I don't think that's possible. I can't keep my hands off you."

Faith rested her head on the pipe behind her and stared at the ceiling briefly before shutting her eyes. She opened her mouth and screamed for help. "SOMEONE GET ME OUT OF HERE!"

"No one can hear you." said Freddy. "You're all alone." He raised his glove even higher, above his head. He writhed the blades around as he shouted, "Reach out, touch Faith!" He brought his glove down in the blink of an eye. His four blades plunged deep into her stomach.

Faith screamed until her voice gave out. "Aaaah!" Her shrieks had mixed with short gasps for air as Freddy stabbed her repeatedly. She felt the four knives move back and forth through her stomach, shredding her skin, her muscles, and her organs. She shut her eyes tightly, not wanting to see the her own body being torn apart before her eyes.

His shining, silver blades turned a thick red as soon as his wrist pulled from Faith's body. He continued to shove his razor fingers inside her, grunting and growling as he attempted to pierce the knives through her back.

By the fifth stab, the fires within the boiler room became alive with a deafening roar, shooting from the pipes and vents. The sound consumed the entire area, muffling all other noises inside. Faith's pained screams and Freddy's sickening grunts became lost within the moans of the fire.

Faith's smooth, pale skin was riddled with droplets of sweat from the heat. Bright, uncontrolled flames filled the corners of her vision. The dancing flames served as the frame, while Freddy's scowling face was in the center of it all. The longer she looked at his face, she realized that it was changing before her. His burned skin became even more enflamed, almost red. The tips of his ears were growing longer, becoming sharp at the ends, like horns. The rims of his eyes and corners of his mouth were getting darker and darker until they became black as sludge. His brow bones and cheekbones became prominent and resembled that of a Deadite. When he opened his mouth, she could see his teeth growing longer and more pointed before her very eyes. It was like looking into a shark's mouth.

Everything in her vision was starting to go black. From the corners of her eyes, everything was getting darker. She could feel herself leaving her own body. The pain was slowly numbing. Every sight, touch, and sound was gradually fading away. Her screams had withered away. She had given up on trying to fight back or move in any way. She simply stood there, hanging by the chains as Freddy eviscerated her. Her hot blood soaked into her pants and inside her shoes. If she wasn't chained to the pipe, she would've surely slipped on her own thick blood. The very last thing she felt before death, was the emptiness of her stomach as all her intestines, chunks of her bones, and blood spilled onto her feet.

When it was finally over, Faith's head lowered down, limp and lifeless. Her lids were half open, barely showing her glassy eyes. Her lips parted slightly, just enough to allow a small droplet of blood escape the center of her bottom lip and splash into the puddle of blood around her feet. Her soul was now escaping her body.

He stared down at her dead body before he collected her soul. He felt Faith's soul leaving her body and joining his. He leaned his head back to the ceiling, feeling himself grow stronger. He opened his eyes, the usual blue coloration had disappeared. For a brief moment, his eyes had transformed. They had become clouded with an opaque whiteness to them. Once her soul had been absorbed into his body, Freddy's eyes turned back to normal. His Deadite features, however, did not go away.

He flicked the blade on his index finger upward, both using his powers and tossing a drop of Faith's blood. As soon as he did, the chains around her wrists and ankles unwrapped and retreated.

Instantly, Faith's lifeless body, along with the book, dropped on the floor with a mixture with a hard *thud* from the metal walkway, and wet *splash!* from the puddle of her own blood. She landed on her side, her cold, expressionless eyes staring at Freddy's bloodied boots as he grabbed the book.

The soft wind gently hit Evelyn's side as she sat on the concrete. Her long, dark hair flowed in the direction of the wind. Her knees had grown sore from digging into the concrete, but she couldn't move away. Her eyes were locked on the spot where Faith disappeared before her eyes. She still breathed heavily from running, trying to save her from Freddy. For her, it had been only seconds since Freddy had taken Faith away.

Amid the sounds of shrieking Deadites, gunshots, and utter chaos, Evelyn almost didn't hear the pattering of footsteps approaching her. Her ears finally became alert to the sound of boots stepping on the concrete, along with something dragging behind.

Once she tilted her head to look up, she saw Freddy standing over her, dragging Faith's body behind him. He had a chunk of her hair in his left hand, using it to drag her along.

Her gaze trailed from Freddy's smiling, demonic, face, down to her friend's body. She was shredded and disemboweled. Her clothes were stained with dark red splatters. Her skin was pale, almost blue in spots. Her entire stomach and chest had been cut open and emptied. The inside of her body was void, like a hollowed out pumpkin.

From head to toe, Evelyn's body went numb. She couldn't even express her sadness with tears, she was in such shock over seeing Faith's mutilated body that her face was frozen. All she could do was gasp softly, and feel a lump form in the back of her throat.

Freddy tossed Faith's corpse aside like a bag of garbage. He left her to fall on the dirty concrete. Her skull bounced on the concrete before falling limp. Her blank, milky eyes seemed to look directly into Evelyn's.

She stared at Faith's dead, expressionless, face. She didn't want to believe that the only friend she had left was gone forever. And worse, she would see no peace in death. None of her friends would. Their souls belonged to him.

That was when her eyes trailed up to his gloved hand. Aside from the rusted copper plating and blood-stained silver knives, it was what he was holding that caught her attention. Caged within his steel claws was the Book of the Dead. *He's got the book!* Evelyn realized. *And now I'm the only one left who can open the portal.*

He pointed at her with his bloody index blade, extending his arm out to her. He scowled. "You're next, cunt."

She looked at the Necronomicon as it was now within her reach. Her eyes darted between the book and his enraged stare. She debated on whether or not to take it right then, as Freddy continued to threaten her.

"I'll fuck your soul, you little whore!"

She felt the adrenaline rush through her, and she knew that it was now or never to take the book from him. Evelyn snatched the book from his claws, giving herself a couple of tiny cuts on her fingers as she robbed him of the book. She then leapt back up to her feet, standing tall. Evelyn gripped the book tightly in her fingers and swung it upwards as hard as she could, hitting Freddy in the jaw. "Fuck yourself, bitch!"

His head tilted up to the sky as Evelyn hit him. He grunted, "Ugh!" He was taken aback for a moment before returning to his original position.

Evelyn ran as fast as she could across the parking lot. She avoided all of the Deadites in her way. Most of them ignored her, only seeing her as a distraction from pursuing Ash. Some of them noticed that she had been carrying the Necronomicon, and tried to stop her. Near the edge of the lot, she found a clear spot free of Deadites. She looked across the way and saw Ash. She called to him, "ASH!"

Deadite corpses surrounded him. Covered in sweat, dirt, and Deadite blood, Ash was already growing weary from battling demons throughout the night. He didn't know how much longer he was going to last. He heard Evelyn's voice and made his way to her. She met him halfway across the lot.

"Ash," she said breathlessly. "I got the book back from Freddy."

He squinted his brows and looked at her with confusion. *I thought Steven was taking care of that.* "Whoa, whoa, back up." he said. "What happened to Steven and–"

Evelyn interrupted him. "Freddy killed them. It's just me now. Ash, I–"

He put his hand on her shoulder and stared at her intently. "Evelyn, I need you to listen." he said. "I don't want to hear you say 'I can't do this', you got me?"

She shook her head in agreement.

"Good." said Ash. "Now, we don't have much time left, so you need to read from those pages *now.*"

"I know." she said. "I want the bastard dead as much as you do."

Ash took out his 9mm and handed it to Evelyn. "Here." he offered. "You're gonna need this. These Deadites are everywhere."

Evelyn spoke softly, feeling her nerves rise. "Thank you."

He pointed his finger at her, forcing her to listen carefully. "And don't screw it up. I don't wanna get sucked up into the Middle Ages again."

Evelyn opened the book to the correct passage as Ash turned away.

When Ash turned away from Evelyn, the first thing he saw from across the lot was Freddy, standing amid the Deadite corpses. He had his blade raised slightly, ready to fight.

Ash smirked as he casually walked closer towards Freddy. "Long time, no see, Freddy." he said. "Back for another ass-kicking?"

Evelyn backed away from the two of them, not wanting to stand in the middle of a gruesome fight to the death. She began reading the words, speaking loudly and with power in her voice. "Nosferatos!" she began. "Alememnon!" *I guess Latin class wasn't a waste of time.* she thought. "Kanda!"

It was then that she felt a pair of cracked, bloodied hands on her shoulders. She felt herself being spun around, now staring at the face of her friend, Faith. Only now, her body was merely the vessel for a Kandarian demon. Her skin was a pale blue, with purple veins pulsating under her skin. Her eyes were blank. Her brows were tilted up in a "V" shape, a permanent fixture of anger.

"You've taken our book!" said Faith, warbled and with multiple voices. "And now we'll take your life!" She slid her hands toward Evelyn's throat and opened her mouth, preparing to take a chunk of her lively flesh.

Evelyn kicked her in the stomach and launched her elbow toward her face, knocking her back. While she was still down, Evelyn pointed the gun barrel at her face. She stared at the hideous distortion that had become of her friend with a cold expression. "I'm sorry too, Faith." She pulled the trigger, putting a bullet-hole in the center of her friend's face.

BLAM!

Chapter 38

Ash was halfway across the lot from Freddy, who stood at the edge. He stared at him with a cool intensity. His demeanor remained calm, but inside, he wanted nothing more than to pump his skull full of lead.

The distance between them grew shorter as Ash continued to march on the concrete. He was out of breath, sweaty, and ammo was in short supply. But his confidence remained steady when his eyes quickly scanned the lot, observing the bodies of Deadites littered throughout.

It was a picture that Ash had not seen quite as often. Dozens upon dozens of demons, lying dead on the ground. While he was familiar with seeing a slain Deadite, it was truly a spectacle to see so many dead bodies strewn across the ground. Almost every square inch of the lot was riddled with corpses. *I'm on one hell of a kill streak tonight, aren't I?*

What seemed to be sixty bodies, lied cold and still on the ground. Their bodies were stiff, contorted in inhuman fashions. All of them had been dismembered in some way. Some had been missing their arms, others missed their legs. A few Deadites had all of their limbs, including their heads, sawed off, scattered around their un-moving torso. Under each cadaver, was a pool of blood. Each puddle varied in color. There was blood of red, black, and green coloration. The entire lot had become a watercolor painting of Deadite blood. Ash had not killed every demon in the area, but he definitely cleared the S-Mart parking lot, leaving only Freddy in his sights.

"What's the matter, Freddy?" he yelled, now only thirty feet away. "Keeping your distance 'cause I just shredded all your buddies?"

Freddy sneered at him as he began to slowly walk closer to Ash. He twiddled the knives on his glove. "At least I'm not out of breath every time I kill." He pointed to Ash's chainsaw, was on the ground a few feet away from him. "Tell me, do they make walkers for people with chainsaw arms?"

Ash retorted. "Do they make special straws for people with buckshots to the mouth?"

"Shoot me all you want, Ash." replied Freddy. "Sooner or later, you'll run out of bullets."

Ash cocked his eyebrows and subtly nodded in agreement. "Yeah, I guess you're right about that." he said to Freddy's surprise. "The thing is, it won't take me very long to get rid of your undead ass..." He looked past Freddy and saw two Deadites emerging from the streets and towards them. "...even with those bags of bones you call bodyguards over there." he added. "Hold that thought." Ash grabbed the handles of both of his shotguns from his back holsters. He pulled them out and aimed the barrels at the two Deadites, who had come running from Freddy's left and right sides. He pulled both triggers.

BOOM!!! BOOM!!!

The heads of the two demons practically exploded from the shotgun blasts. Blood sprayed from the back of their heads. There were large holes where their faces used to be, now littered with shrapnel. Their heads tilted upward and their arms flailed in the air before they fell to their death. Simultaneously, the two of them dropped dead on the concrete.

"Now that the gruesome two-some are out of the way," said Ash as he gripped his pump shotgun by the stock and shook it, reloading it. "Where were we?" He aimed both shotguns at Freddy. "Oh, that's right." He pulled both triggers again.

BOOM!!! BOOM!!!

The blast from the shotgun shells caused Freddy to step back and nearly fall on the ground. He stumbled to regain his balance. There were now small holes in his striped sweater from the bullets. Small streaks of blood raced down his chest and his legs. As he put his left palm on his chest to stop the bleeding, Freddy raised his gloved hand. "Wanna play rough, eh?" he said. "Let's see how tough you are when you play with the big boys." He flicked his index blade upward, manipulating his demonic powers to force Ash back with a powerful, invisible push.

Ash felt a presence, an unseen entity, force him back far away from Freddy. It was a violent shove across the lot. He shouted, "Wh-Whoa!" as the bottoms of his boots scraped across the concrete. He slid back twenty feet away, keeping his balance the entire time. When he finally stopped moving, Ash fell forward, his head lowered to the ground and his knees fell on the concrete.

His trusty Boomstick was out of shells, and he knew he didn't have time to open the chamber and insert two more bullets in time. He quickly slid it back inside the holster and cocked his pump shotgun, as it still had two more bullets left in the chamber. He muttered under his breath. "Alright. Let's see how you like a skull full of lead."

Ash looked up. The first thing he saw was Freddy standing over him, looking down. Less than a second after seeing his burned, scowling face, Ash was met with the sight of Freddy's knee to his chin.

Freddy kicked his leg up towards Ash's face. His knee cap crashed against his chiseled jaw. Freddy saw a look of both shock and pain in his eyes as Ash's head was forced up to the sky. Tiny drops of blood escaped the corners of his mouth and fell onto Freddy's dirty, smoke-stained pants.

Ash shook his head, reeling from the pain. He turned his head to the side to spit out a tooth that had been dislodged from the kick. Before he could give him another chance to strike, Ash held his shotgun by his hip, pointing the barrel at Freddy. He pulled the trigger.

BOOM!!!

A hole the size of a fist appeared on Freddy's stomach. Dark red blood sprayed out of Freddy's body. Droplets of his blood found its way on Ash's forehead. The dream demon was forced back from the blast of the gun.

Ash quickly got back on his feet. He turned to his side and bent his left arm, launching his elbow between Freddy's eyes.

"Argh!" Freddy squinted his eyes and grimaced. He quickly regained balance and prepared to attack Ash. He extended his gloved hand out to his side and prepared to swing from right to left, eviscerating Ash. He was about to slice him, when Freddy felt metal on his forehead, pushing him away.

Ash placed his metal hand on Freddy's head, blocking him from attacking. He looked down at Freddy as he still tried to slice him apart. His blades swung from side to side, but the only thing Ash felt was the wind from his flailing knives.

"What's the matter, short-stack?" taunted Ash. "Can't quite reach?" He took a wide step to his left, taking his hand off of Freddy's forehead. As a result, Freddy fell hard on the concrete, as if there was a magnetic pull between them.

While he was on the ground, Ash quickly ran across the lot to his chainsaw, which was laying on the concrete. He grabbed the small canister of gasoline and unscrewed the cap, refueling it. He unlocked his metal hand from his wrist and placed the appendage in the empty side holster. He lowered down to his knees to pick it up. The blade was splattered with blood, leaving ribbons connecting the saw with the concrete until Ash latched it onto his arm.

Just before Ash pulled the rope to start the chainsaw, he could faintly hear the maniacal laughs of a Deadite coming from behind him. He quickly hooked the pull rope to the bullet belt across his chest and lowered his arm, starting the saw.

He quickly spun himself around to face the demon, letting his chainsaw carry the momentum. He knew that the demon had to be right behind him. As soon as he turned, he felt his blade make contact with rotten, Deadite flesh.

He had turned with such speed that the chainsaw sliced through both of the Deadites legs, like butter. The demon's legs were sawed off by the knee. Blood gushed from all directions as the demon fell on his back. His feet and calves were sprawled on the concrete next to his knees, which poured blood to no end.

The rotted fleshed demon flailed his arms, and the bloodied nubs that were his legs, crying out in pain. His screams were monstrous and warbled, far from anything that could be considered human.

Ash came into the demon's view, stepping over his body with one foot next to his right side. He cried out, "Hyah!" as he lowered down close to the Deadite and rammed the chainsaw blade into his face.

The demon's already hideous face had become obliterated by the saw blade. The blade, moving so fast that it was but a blur, sliced and ripped through his skull and brains easily. His blood, brains and fragments of his skull shot out into the air like a sprinkler.

When it was over, the demon's head had been jaggedly sliced in half. Ash stepped back to fully take in the carnage. A pool of blood varying in color formed around his body. The demon's arms and sawed-off legs subtly twitched as he awaited death. His eyes, milk white and bloodshot, blinked rapidly.

Ash stared at the face for only a few seconds when he noticed a dirty work boot step on the demon's forehead. *Freddy...*

He stomped on the Deadite's forehead, squashing his head and killing him. When his foot lowered down on his head, the demon's left eye shot out of his socket like a cannon ball. The optic nerve was still attached to the eyeball when it flew out of its socket, making it resemble a vein-y, shooting star.

Freddy swung his gloved hand in front of the eye, piercing it with the blade on his middle finger. He lowered the remaining three blades and held up the middle one, both showing Ash the eyeball and flipping him off at the same time.

"No more dicking around, Krueger." said Ash. "Drop the eye and let's get down to business."

Freddy tossed the eyeball from his blade and scowled at Ash. “Fine,” he said. “we’ll have your way.” He raised his glove up to the sky.

Ash raised his chainsaw, gripping the handle with his left hand as he held it over his head.

They both lowered their weapons down upon each other at the same time. They both moved to the side to avoid being cut by one another. Both of their deadly blades merely grazed one another, but it was enough to send sparks flying all around them.

With his chainsaw now lowered to the ground, Ash swung it from left to right like a baseball bat.

Freddy jumped back to avoid being sliced. His attempt failed as the blade sawed through his abdomen, slicing a few inches deep into the muscle tissue. His blood spilled down his stomach. There was now a ten inch long tear across his ratty sweater, exposing his slash mark and his burnt flesh.

He looks up to see Ash running towards him to do further damage. Freddy launched his gloved hand upward from his hip, aiming at Ash’s face.

Ash quickly leaned back as far as he could without falling over. He escaped a fatal wound from Freddy’s blades, but not completely free of damage. He felt a painful sting across the left side of his face. One of his knives had sliced across Ash’s face, from his jaw to his temple. There was now a fresh, red line on his face, adding another future scar to his body. One of many.

While Ash was still leaned back, Freddy jumped forward and grabbed him by the belts across his chest. He pulled back his gloved hand, keeping his arm bent and his elbow straight. He pulled Ash in while pushing his right arm forward. Freddy launched all four of his knives just above Ash’s chest. The swift, crisp sound of his knives slicing into Ash’s body echoed into his ears.

SHHHING!

Ash gasped before feeling a knot in the back of his throat. It was pain like he had never felt before. The feeling of Freddy's razor sharp knives into his shoulder was unbearable.

Freddy rattled his knives around for a few seconds, thoroughly shredding his skin and muscle tissue. It made Ash cry out in pain. It got his blood boiling. Finally, he had the self-righteous lunk wounded and in his grasp.

Blood poured from the four stab wounds in Ash's shoulder, collar bone, and the area just above his chest. He couldn't stop bleeding. He felt like a broken faucet.

Freddy placed a hand on his chest and pushed him away. The act both released his blades from Ash's body and pushed him down to the hard concrete.

Ash rolled on the ground, groaning in agony. "Oh...Ugh...Argh..." He kicked his legs as a reaction from the pain. He put his hand over his wound, hoping to stop the bleeding. Blood seeped from between his fingers.

Step...Step...Step...Step...

Ash looked up from the ground to see Freddy standing over him, taking joy in his misfortune. He wanted to saw his legs off. To shoot him. To spit in his fucking face. But he couldn't. The pain hindered him from all of it.

"I gotta hand it to you." said Freddy in his usual graveled, but cool, voice. "For a moment, it looked like you were gonna win. You certainly looked the part with your guns and your chainsaw and your cocky little attitude." He put his boot on Ash's rib, making him wince and expel blood from the corners of his mouth. He crouched down so that his face was the only thing in Ash's line of vision. "But now I'm stronger than I've ever been, and you ever will be."

Freddy stood back up, his posture straight and his shoulders back. This time, when he spoke, his voice was even lower. It was more demonic, like it had come from the fire-y pits of Hell. "And now it's time to collect the soul of the Chosen One."

From the dark regions of Springwood, on the other side of town, the malevolent powers of the Necronomicon were summoned. They were called upon by the Springwood Slasher himself. He had become so powerful, that the dark spirits were able to roam at such a speed that they had reached downtown Springwood in a matter of seconds. By this time, they were near the police station, which had become overrun with Deadites. The entire police department were scattered around this area, firing their weapons at the demons.

Freddy stood over Ash with a look of absolute evil strewn across his face. He raised his gloved hand above his head. He flexed his knives, the parts of the metal that wasn't stained in blood shined under the moon. He continued his rant. "So I..."

The evil force made its way through the town, past the crowd of Deadites and over the wrecked cars. It moved fast and smooth, like a rollercoaster. Its low, guttural roar echoed from miles away. It was now only blocks away from S-Mart.

He watched Ash cough up mouthfuls of blood as he continued to speak. Watching him twitch and squirm was almost as good as the act of killing him. "can be..."

With almost lightning speed, the evil force raced across the parking lot, dodging and darting through the bodies of Deadites, both live and unmoving. It lowered down, mere inches from the concrete, the sound of its warbled moan grew higher and higher as it entered the body of its target: Ash Williams.

"IMMORTAL!" Freddy brought his gloved hand down upon Ash. His four, long knives stabbed through his ribs, right in the middle of his chest.

Fresh blood sprayed from the four new stab wounds on Ash's chest. His cry of unimaginable agony was infused with chokes and gasps. He convulsed on the concrete, lifting his back up and down, slamming it against the ground.

Evelyn held the Book of the Dead in her hands. She brought it close to her face, squinting her eyes to read the passages as she stood under the bright florescent lighting under the front entrance. She read the incantations from the Necronomicon to open the portal, thus sending the evil back. "Kanda. Demontos–"

Her pronunciation of the passages was interrupted by a bright flash of light. Her eyes slammed shut temporarily before slowly adjusting to it. Her gaze jumped from the pages of the book to the source of the commotion before her in, quite literally, the blink of an eye.

What she saw was Freddy crouched down beside Ash's bloody, unmoving, body. His blades were mid-way deep into Ash's chest. Blood streamed down his shirt. Surrounding both of them were a flurry of lightning strikes and fog.

Freddy's demonic features were illuminated by the flashes of lightning. He lifted his head up to the sky, opening his eyes wide. His blue eyes morphed. They looked as if thick clouds had rolled inside of them, filling them with an opaque white color. Ash's soul had become absorbed by Freddy.

Fear washed over her. She felt her entire body become numb. Her legs felt like rubber, failing to support her. Her knees gave out, slamming on the concrete, taking the rest of her down with them. A lump formed in the back of her throat and her face felt warm against the cold wind. She didn't want to believe it. *No. He can't just be gone like this. Not that easily.* Her voice was timid and cracking. "No." She spoke louder this time. "You can't die." He didn't move. Not even a twitch. *He killed him. This can't happen.* "You had doubts...that you weren't strong enough, and I didn't listen. Everyone I cared about has been stolen from me...including you. But there's one thing about me that makes us different: I refuse to accept my fate. I'm not letting Freddy win." Evelyn lifted her head and held the book tightly. She shouted at the top of her lungs. "KRUEGER!!!"

Ash's body, still as a rock since Freddy had conducted his fatal blow, moved yet again. His head rolled to the side, facing Evelyn, who couldn't believe what she had become witness to. His eyelids now lifted, baring white eyes. His facial features morphed as well. His eyes sunk, and his brow bone extended, resembling that of a caveman. The rims of his eyes darkened, the entire area was now a dark purple. His chin and cheekbones elongated and sharpened. His teeth were yellow and rotted. He bared no resemblance to his former self. Ash had now succumbed to the evil.

Freddy yanked his knives from his chest and stood up. He faced Evelyn, leering at her. Reveling in her misery.

Ash awkwardly jerked and twitched his body until he got up on his feet. He stood up, just a few feet in front of Freddy. His skin, pale, scarred, and bloody, was slightly masked by the night. From head to toe, he was splattered with blood.

While Freddy's eyes had returned to their usual blue color, and his features also back to normal, Ash's eyes and face remained like that of a Deadite. Both of their eyes, Freddy's intense blue and Ash's blank white, stared at Evelyn.

Freddy looked briefly at Ash as he gave him his command. "Fetch the bitch for me."

Ash jerked his head up and down, signaling his acceptance. His feet roughly picked up and slammed down to the ground. His limbs moved without any flow or smoothness. He walked like Frankenstein's monster on drugs. His voice was monstrous. He grunted, low and menacing, in the back of his throat. He moved towards Evelyn.

Evelyn backed away, gradually getting back on her feet as she did so. There was nowhere to run. Deadites were all over town. And no matter where she would go, Freddy would surely find her. She stared up at Ash, trying to find traces of his normal self in his face. Searching for his humanity. If even a glimmer of his true self was buried under the monstrosity, it showed no sign of emerging.

Evelyn shook her head in defiance. "No..."

Chapter 39

SHE LOOKED INTO HIS DEAD, soulless eyes. An almost unbearable sense of dread filled her senses. The only thing keeping Evelyn on her feet was the rush of adrenaline flowing through her body. Her rising fear only made her more aware of everything around her, and especially the horrendous being marching toward her.

Evelyn clutched the book against her chest tightly, crumpling the leathery cover and the wrinkled pages. She had already lost everyone. Those who gave her happiness and safety. She wasn't going to lose the only thing that would stop the evil from spreading any further.

Ash's 9mm handgun rested firmly in Evelyn's hand. She squeezed the handle and put her finger on the trigger. The barrel was aimed at Ash. Her hand never shook. Not this time. She had killed enough of those foul creatures, so she was now used to looking at their contorted faces before watching them become obliterated by the bullets.

The corners of her eyes became red and watery from tears. Her nostrils flared, and her lips were forced shut in attempt to keep herself from crying.

With every step that Ash made toward her, she matched it with another step backward. Slowly, she nodded her head as if to say "no" Her voice was laced with sorrow. "Don't make me do it." she warned. "Ash, I know you can hear me. Please listen me." She breathed deeply to avoid further tears. "Come back. Please do it now." The next time she spoke, her tone subtly moved toward anger. "Listen to what I'm saying, Ash! I don't want to kill you!" She twitched her face to keep tears from escaping her eyes. "But if you don't do what I'm telling you right now, I'll have to."

"Go ahead."

Evelyn raised her eyebrows as a voice other than her own entered the air. She recognized it as Freddy's.

He stepped out from behind Ash's shadow, showing his retched face to her. "Shoot him." he said with a sinister smile. "It just means I'll have you all to myself."

She gritted her teeth to the point where they scraped and grinded against one another. She felt her face get hot as her blood boiled in anger. "You bastard! This is all your fault!" she said. It was at that point that she realized that killing Ash didn't have to be an option. *It's still my responsibility to open the rift. Maybe that will be just enough to get rid of Freddy. It might not save Ash, but at least I won't have to be killed by either of them.*

She then switched her aim from Ash to Freddy, moving her hand only a few inches to her left. "If you won't give him back, I'll do it myself." Evelyn squeezed the trigger.

BLAM!

The bullet went past Ash and went straight through Freddy's left shoulder. His blood sprayed from the wound, almost like a mist. He let out a small scream "Aah!" as he bent down slightly from the pain. When he looked back up, Evelyn was already running away.

Evelyn raced across the parking lot, hoping to get as far away from Freddy and Ash as possible. *I can't believe Ash the one I'm running from now.* she thought. *Could this get any–No, no. Don't say that. The last thing I want to do now is jinx myself.* She noticed Ash's yellow Oldsmobile in her sights. It was abandoned, free of any demonic presence. *And I never locked it, either.* She forced herself to run faster as she extended her arm out to grab onto the door handle.

She swung the car door open and jumped inside. As soon as her legs entered the car, Evelyn swung around to slam the door shut. Without hesitation, she grabbed the lock on the side of the door and pressed down, locking it. She did the same on the passenger side. She quickly leaned over to the backseat, her knees sliding across the aged white leather interior, and locked the doors in the back.

The light of the moon illuminated sparingly on the passenger side of the car. Sitting in a crouched position, facing the passenger window, Evelyn placed the Necronomicon on the seat in front of her. She flipped the book open to the passage on opening the rift. She began the incantation for what she hoped would be the final time.

Still gripping the book, Evelyn leaned over to clearly see the words in front of her. "Nosferatos. Alememnon. Kanda." As she continued to read the remainder of the passage, she gradually calmed down from the overall silence around her. Not a single outside noise could be heard from inside the Delta 88. The only things audible to her ears were the sound of her legs sliding across the leather, and the crumpling of the thick pages as she turned them. "Kanda. Demontos. Kanda." The passage was almost complete. It was then that her anxiety rose and her nerves heightened. She was so close, she prayed that she would make it through. Out of the complete, almost stifling, silence, Evelyn spoke the final word in the passage. "Kanda."

As soon as the word escaped her full, fearfully twitching, lips, she felt a smile curl in the corners of her mouth. It was finally safe to breathe easily. She exhaled for the first time in what seemed like hours. The bones in her body rattled out of sheer excitement and anticipation. She closed the book and continued to hold it closely.

The strands of her long, and now ratted, black hair flowed in front of her face as she slowly raised up. The only sounds made were her heavy exhales, which came out in short bursts. She kept a steady and watchful eye out in front of her, monitoring the passenger window as well as the back. Aside from the parking lot, which was rife with the bodies of deceased Deadites, the area was completely empty. The only thing in her sight was the portrait of the streetlamps shining down upon the dead bodies, laying in pools of their own blood.

Okay, now what? she wondered. *Exactly how long is it before this takes effect? I'm safe in here right now, but...what if this takes all night? I might not make it by dawn.* Evelyn slowly lifted herself upright, straightening her back. There was a moment of silence, complete and utter silence. It was soothing. Peaceful.

CRASH!

The glass window behind her shattered into a hundred pieces. She felt the small shards hit her skin, like sharp, stinging drops of rain.

Before she could even react from the broken window, she felt a pair of hands ring around her neck. She felt their grimy, almost decomposed, texture as they squeezed her neck tighter and tighter.

She screamed before her airways had become so constricted that no noise could escape at all. "Aaaaah–ack!" She then heard a low, menacing growl come from outside the car. It was a sound she had come to recognize as the evil incarnation of Ash.

"JOIN USSS!" Ash bellowed. He pulled her towards him, bringing her out from the shattered car window.

Evelyn gasped and shouted as the shards on the edges of the broken window tore through her clothes and sliced her arms, sides, backside, legs, and her spine. Her skin was cut and scraped. She was strangled until she was on the brink of blacking out. Her neck was pulled, feeling like it was going to be ripped from her shoulders at any moment.

After a slow and downright torturous capture, Evelyn was swiftly yanked out from the car. She felt the back of her clothes, as well as her bare arms become raw from the cuts. Even though the long scratches across her body burned and stung, she fought the pain. She continued to try to pry herself away from Ash's now brutally strong arms. Never once did she release the book.

Evelyn yelled at him with such anger that her voice was booming. "No!" she protested. "No!"

His voice was warbled and other-worldly when he growled in her ear and nodded his head up and down. "Yes..."

Ash wrapped his arms around her waist. He pinned her arms to her sides and restrained her. The more she moved, the tighter his grip became. He forcefully dragged her away from the car, leading her back to Freddy. He had her face away from the front of the store, looking directly at Freddy.

He walked slowly to her. His expression was cold, like he had no intention of showing her even the slightest bit of mercy. “Thought you could run away, huh bitch?” He stepped closer to her, now only a few feet away. “Now you know it’s not that easy.” He looked down at her, examining her freshly cut body. The scratches that she had acquired were minor. A few cuts here and there on her arms. A couple of small rips in her shirt. Only a few spots of blood had stained her body. *I can do better than that...*

A minor gust of wind blew through the uncomfortable silence in the air. It caused the leaves to rustle for a brief moment before disappearing.

Freddy used one of his knives to brush away the dark strands of hair in front of her face. He examined her face, noticing how she glistened from sweat, and the bruise on her cheek, as well as the natural redness in her lips. He looked into her eyes, green as freshly cut grass. They looked into his with pure hatred. Her pupils were as small as a grain of sand.

He smiled deviously as he watched her continue to struggle for freedom. Even though everyone she knew and loved in this world was dead, and there showed no sign of the evil ever stopping, she kept on fighting.

There was absolute silence in the S-Mart parking lot. Not one sound was made, aside from the subtle creaks and moans coming from the trees.

His blade traced down from her face to her neck, lowering more until he lingered on her collar bone. “So was mild, little, Evelyn using my book, thinking she could get rid of me?” he asked.

She stared at him coldly. She gave him nothing that would signify fear. This time, her tone and her expression was smooth and strong.

"Why do you ask, Freddy?" She tilted her head to the side, almost matching the smile he was giving her. "Do you think I did something?" she taunted. "Are you afraid that a few pages is all it takes to undo all of this? What you've worked so hard for?"

In an instant, his face was mere inches from hers. His hot breath fell upon her. He was so close that they could hear each other breathing. "You know what, bitch?" he scowled. He cut through her shirt using his blades, leaving small slash marks above her chest. "Even if you did pull off that spell," Through the rips in her shirt, Freddy sliced the skin between her breasts, and dragged down to her stomach. He watched her closely as she winced. "that book is still mine. And nothing can hurt me now. Nothing."

In the distance, a strike of lightning briefly flashed behind the dark red clouds. It was bright white, and thin as a strand of hair.

"You sure about that?" said Evelyn, with a cocked eyebrow. "'Cause I'm starting to think all of your smartass lines are just compensation. You're actually scared of me."

Freddy grimaced, giving her an up-close view of his sharp teeth and rotted gums. He pulled his blades out from under the thin layer of skin, and stepped back. "You know what, bitch?" he asked as he raised his bladed glove up to the sky.

As soon as his arm lifted up, a subtle crash of thunder echoed. It was soft, barely heard by their ears. Next, came a strong gust of wind. Unlike the previous one, it lingered, becoming stronger as time passed.

Evelyn laughed at him.

He scrunched his eyebrows in confusion. "What are you laughing at?"

She leered at him. Her voice was low and steady. "You call me a bitch and a cunt. And you still wave those knives in front of me and expect me to be scared of you." She spoke to him with venom in her voice. "It doesn't work anymore. I've done my part, and I know where you're going. So go ahead and kill me. Because you're going to die, too."

"You know what? This one isn't for power, or to make myself stronger, it's just to hear you scream." His intention was to slice her from face to stomach. At that very second, nothing else existed but he and Evelyn, and there was nothing he wanted more than to watch her bleed to death.

As soon as the words left his charred, blistered mouth, a much louder crash of thunder entered the air. It was so loud and booming that it could have been mistaken for an explosion. The boisterous noise was matched with a lightning strike that was so close to them, it filled the dark town with a white flash, flashing like strobe lights.

Freddy brushed away the crash of thunder and white lightning. Instead, he saw it as perfect ambience for a kill that was long overdue.

Evelyn had kept her eyes half shut, flinching and turning her head in anticipation for whatever Freddy had prepared for her. Out of the small sliver of vision through her squinting eyes, she saw a massive, swirling, portal opening behind Freddy.

She stared in awe of the rift for a brief moment. She marveled at the bright blue and white lights flashing from within. It was truly a mesmerizing, but frightful sight. It was a swirl of dark, thick clouds leading to a seemingly endless black hole. To her, it looked like the image of a tornado being turned to the side.

Its sheer magnitude was intimidating. The portal had opened just on the other side of the parking lot, nearing the demon-riddled streets. Everything surrounding the rift was being pulled violently inside. It was like a powerful gust of wind was forcing everything it could inside of it. Cars that had been abandoned in the parking lot were now rolling backwards, towards the thunderous, flashing rift. The trees on the side of the lot leaned to the side as they were being drawn inside, their roots unhinged from the dirt.

Evelyn's gaze went back to Freddy in that brief moment. She saw his copper plated glove coming down upon her. Before she could anticipate the fatal blow by his knives, she felt herself being shoved away. Freddy's knives barely missed her skin, merely scratching the side of her arm.

Her vision was blurred as she was shoved to the side and felt herself sliding across the body of the Delta 88. She stumbled, but did not fall. After she quickly regained her footing, Evelyn turned back to see what it was that pushed her. Whipping her raven hair out of her face, she saw that it was Ash who had prevented her death.

Ash stepped in front of Freddy and grabbed his wrist as it lowered down. With his brute and evil strength, he squeezed and twisted Freddy's wrist until he heard his bones crack.

"Argh!" cried Freddy. His body was hunched over, trying to pull himself away from Ash's grip, but it was impossible.

As Ash had him in his clutches, his body remained still as a statue, while his face twitched and contorted. The two sides of himself, the good and the evil, were colliding. His inhuman strength and violent rage was still alive within him, but his humanity was breaking through once more. Even through his pale, glassy eyes, he emoted what appeared to be great internal confliction. Instead of a gritted scowl, his mouth gaped and his lips curled. His nose scrunched. He was slowly coming back.

Evelyn stood only ten feet away from them, clutching the book in her hands and wondering, "How is he able to do that?" She looked at Freddy, ignoring his pained state, as there was something on a much grander scale taking place before her eyes. By looking at Freddy's back, she noticed that he too was being affected by the rift. A part of himself was being pulled by the incredible force. Glowing beams of pure, white, light surfaced from his back and escaped out into the open air. They were glowing and flew with such magnificent smoothness and speed, that they resembled shooting stars. Most found their way across the lot and through the town, entering into the bodies of the Deadites that were causing chaos downtown. Some wandered aimlessly all through the town. Others were directly drawn into the portal.

She stood with her back at the door of the yellow Oldsmobile, almost in disbelief of what she was seeing. Her eyes darted back to Freddy, studying his face. Judging from his obvious struggle against Ash, it seemed as though his strength was depleting. After only viewing the specs of light for a few seconds, she came to realize what they were. "The rift is tearing their souls away from him." she said. "They're going back where they came from."

The souls that entered the Deadites where those had been affected indirectly during Freddy's resurrection, not killed by him, but rather possessed by the spirits he had unleashed to consume the entire town. The ones that wandered in all directions, were those that had been killed by him. They could not return to their earthly bodies, instead they were destined for the afterlife. Those that were pulled into the rift were Freddy's previous victims from years past, the children who risked their lives to stop him, and were destined peace, once and for all.

The powerful wind blew his brown fedora off of his head. He turned to see it fly off into the rift. Freddy then saw the souls that had taken years of plotting to accomplish, all being stripped from him within seconds. With each precious soul that left his body, he felt weaker until he was ultimately powerless. "No!" he shouted. Pure, unfiltered, rage had consumed him. "NO!"

He turned back to Ash, who looked at him with a smirk on his face. He stood over him, which was easy for him considering how Freddy was slowly lowering to the ground, barely able to hold himself up.

With his soul now back in his body, Ash had a newly-found virility. He inhaled deeply. "Damn, it's good to be back." he said. He crouched down a few inches to look at Freddy in his eyes. His pained, listless eyes. "Without any soul food in you, looks like *you're* the bitch now, huh?" He twisted his wrist until it could not turn anymore, hearing the bone snap once more.

"Ah!" yelped Freddy. He breathed a sigh of relief when he felt Ash let go of him. But his relief was short-lived when he looked up to see

Ash's fist speeding towards his face. His head knocked back from the impact of the punch. Now that most of his strength had gone, the blows to the face seemed even more painful than before.

Ash made sure not to give him even a second to fight back. He hit him with everything he had. He punched him a second time in the jaw, watching blood shoot out of his mouth as his knuckles hit against his jawbone. He watched Freddy stumble and step back. This was the perfect chance for Ash to lift his chainsaw and hit the base of it against the top of Freddy's head.

Freddy dropped to the ground like a bag of sand. This time, it was him that was groaning in pain, at the mercy of someone stronger than him. He didn't like it at all. He looked up at Ash's smug, confident face, feeling his blood boil the more he had to look at him. He saw Ash lift his foot up and prepare to stomp on his head. Freddy acted quickly and rolled over, narrowly missing the boot that was about to squash his head. He got up to his feet and, without a second thought, kicked Ash in the stomach. It took a lot out of him just to exert the energy to do so.

Ash stood up, ignoring the pain in his stomach from the kick. He then moved towards him and launched his right elbow straight at Freddy's eye. He shouted in pain yet again while Ash stepped back to deliver an uppercut to his abdomen. As he bent over in pain, Ash bent his arm to launch his elbow at his head. Freddy moved away, escaping his attack.

He rushed over to grab Ash's left wrist and twisted it behind his back. He pushed harder until Ash was bent down, crying out in pain.

Evelyn watched as Freddy bent Ash's arm, not stopping until it would break. She felt something building inside her. It told her to stop standing around and being a bystander. To actually do something. To fight alongside Ash. She gripped the book tightly so it wouldn't slip from her hands. She ran to Freddy. "Let go of him!" she shouted as she jumped toward him, tackling him to the ground.

Freddy was forced to let go of Ash and was instantly met with a mouthful of gravel, feeling about one hundred and fifteen pounds of pressure on top of him. He looked up and saw Evelyn's angered face looking down at his. She delivered punch after punch straight at his jaw, nearly breaking it.

Each punch was harder than last. She looked into his pale, unfeeling eyes. They were the same eyes that served as each of her friends' dying image. Every time she hit him, she thought of Cooper. Of Steven. Of Faith. Of Ash. Everyone she cared for, and everyone she witnessed become a victim of his, she fought for them. Even when all was lost, she risked her life for them. When she prepared another, Freddy blocked her.

His palm smacked against her knuckles as he swung his bladed glove at her face. Although she backed away, the knives still cut her left cheek. The scratches were pink at first, but within seconds, they became darker until they bled.

With his gloved hand, Freddy strangled her. He then shifted his body until he was now on top of her, pinning her down. He squeezed her throat until she gagged. "You did this!" he said. He looked down and saw the Necronomicon in her left hand. *Now to take back what's mine and fix this problem.* He reached for the book and tried to take it from Evelyn's hand. It was a struggle to pry it from her hand. "Give it back!"

Freddy had pulled with such force, that as soon as the book slipped from Evelyn's fingers, he found himself lifting the book over his head. The powerful force from the portal was like a huge gust of wind, knocking the book from Freddy's hand and sending it hurdling inside. Freddy watched as the book was taken from him yet another time. He snarled as anger took over him. He could feel the pull from the vortex dragging him in. With his bladed hand still clasped around Evelyn's neck, Freddy got up to his feet just in time to see Ash running to them.

He had both barrels pointed at Freddy. "Give it up, Freddy." he ordered. His voice was tired, but steady. "Right now, you're playing footsie with the gatekeeper of Hell. Now, let her go before I splatter your brains all over the hood of my car."

His feet were now starting to drag along the concrete, closer toward the rift. He looked into the portal, knowing that the only way to get the book back was to go in after it. *Why just get the book?* he thought. *Why not kill two piggies with one stone?* Turning back to Ash, he smiled deviously. "If you want the girl so badly, then come and get her!" Freddy allowed himself to be completely consumed by the rift. Both of their feet lifted from the ground as their bodies were carried by the wind and into the rift.

Evelyn screamed and shouted as her body was flipped and spun above the ground. It was more disorienting and more frightful than any carnival ride. She cried out. "Ash!"

What made it worse was Freddy's knives digging into her back as he held her close to him, and looking into his menacing eyes that pierced into hers.

As soon as Freddy and Evelyn ventured further into the portal, it began to close off. The wind was steadily dying down, and the pull was weakening.

Time was running out for Ash. He only had one shot to enter the portal and chase after Freddy. Ash ran faster than he ever had before. His legs burned and throbbed as his feet slammed on the concrete. His breath shortened. Soon, he felt his feet no longer touch the ground as the powerful force of the rift sucked him in. Old memories came flooding in as his body flipped over and over again, making him dizzy. He yelped and shouted. "Whoa! Aaaaah!" His cries were distorted before being abruptly cut off as the rift closed and disappeared.

Chapter 40

Oh yeah, it's all coming back now. Ash thought, reluctantly. *Twirling around through time and space. Watching the cosmos zoom by. Feeling my lunch work its way back up my throat. Yeah, sign me up for this again.* Ash floated weightlessly through the empty space, watching beams of light pass him by. Once he paused to view his surroundings, it was actually a mesmerizing sight. Light of all colors rushing past him, like a fireworks show in the night sky. And then, just as he came to appreciate the beauty and serenity of being in such a vast, empty, and quiet space, there was an explosion.

Ash felt as if he had been suddenly shot out of a cannon. All he saw was a bright pale light. Then came the sound of a deafening explosion reverberating in his eardrums. He emerged from a wall of thick, gray smoke, falling through the air. The fall was short as Ash felt the back of his head slam against a hard surface. "Argh!" he shouted as he continued to fall and stumble. Judging from the images that briefly entered his vision during the fall, and from the rough, unsteady, descent, he concluded that he was tumbling down a flight of wooden stairs.

Once his fall had ended, and there was a throbbing ache growing in the back of his head, Ash found himself lying on his back, his head inches away from the last step. The wooden beam holding the rail inadvertently blocked his chainsaw blade from slicing into his skull. Ash fought the pain that had spread to his entire body and lifted himself up. He groaned and grumbled as he regained his balance and explored what, at first glance, appeared to be an ordinary basement. He slowly trekked away from the wooden staircase and ventured further into the basement. As he studied his surroundings, he realized that it was the same basement he had used to store his weapons. He was back in the house. 1428 Elm Street. "Huh..." Ash said to himself. "Guess I'm in the right place."

This time, there were no spider webs in the corners. No rust on the furnace. Not even a speck of dust on the workbench. He looked up to the small window just below the ceiling and noticed a small ray of light peeking through, illuminating on the workbench not far from where he was standing. He crept towards it, paying special attention to the shelves on the walls, which were lined with mason jars and other items. Each jar contained small body parts, preserved in dirty, greenish water. Some contained tiny, but plump, hands.

Others held locks of hair. One even contained an eyeball. The other items strewn on the shelves were children's toys; such as dolls and wooden racecars, and pieces of ripped clothing. All of these items were stained with blood. Ash tried his best to keep from vomiting as he walked up to the bench.

He placed his hand on the bench, noticing the sheets of copper lying about. Also, tools, such has hammers, metal cutters, and rivet tools strewn across. His gaze trailed up from the dirty table and paused at the calendar pinned to the wall above. The date read "December 13th, 1968" He turned away from the bench, facing the other side of the room. "And the right time." he said. "Well, at least I know I didn't screw *that* part up." As soon as he turned, he was instantly met with the sight of a rack that held about a dozen of what looked like Freddy's glove. Each was different in design: Some were made with blades that were short and curled, like the claws of a ravenous animal. Others had much longer knives, while some were made of different kinds of metal. "All right," he muttered, trying to ignore the revolting images that befell every square inch of the basement. "now I just got to find out where you're hiding."

(weeping) (hiccupping) (sniveling)

Ash's ears twitched when a new sound emerged. He turned in the direction in which it was coming from. He recognized it as Evelyn's voice, crying in the far corner of the basement. "Evelyn..." he called. He quickly walked over to the other side of the room, towards the dark corner where he assumed her to be. His footing was stopped short when Evelyn emerged from the thick, black, shadow. He watched her drag her own body across the dirty ground, pulling herself by the strength of her upper body alone, while her legs remained limp. He looked at her usually black hair, now stringy and ratted from fighting Freddy.

Then to her face, which contained bruises on her cheeks and temples. But what truly made a lasting impression on Ash were the fresh slash marks that covered her entire body. Her black jacket had been ripped from her person, leaving only her purple tank top. It exposed her arms and partially her chest. To him, she looked like a red-striped zebra. Upon looking at the cuts further, he noticed a particular pattern on every area of her body that he had his blades on. In knife wounds, the words "Freddy was here" was scrawled on her body. On her arms. Her collar bone. He had even ripped the collar of her shirt so that he could write it above her chest. The words were also on her stomach, and just above the button of her jeans.

"My God, Evelyn." he said as he ran to her. Her body collapsed just as he knelt down in front of her. He lowered down to his knees and rested her head in his arms as he stared into her fluttering eyes. "I'm sorry–I–I'm sorry I didn't get here sooner. I'm sorry that...that..."

Evelyn looked into Ash's sorrowful eyes. She ceased her crying and did her best to give him a reassuring smile. "No big deal, it's just a scratch." she said, her voice cracked and broken. "Or fifty." She laughed softly under breath, which made Ash faintly smile as well.

"I'm gonna get you out of here, kid." said Ash.

Evelyn nodded. "Okay..." she agreed softly. She winced in pain from the cut on her lower stomach. She tugged on the hem of her shirt, covering the words that were scrawled just below her belly button. She leaned her head back and closed her eyes, feeling safe enough in Ash's arms to relax herself. Once her eyes opened, she saw a pair of worn boots walking up to them. Her gaze trailed up and she saw Freddy's face. "Ash..." she warned. "Behind you."

He turned around to see that same, ugly, striped sweater standing before him. He carefully rested Evelyn on the ground and quickly stood up. He turned around to face him, only to see something he had not expected. He looked at Freddy's face. He was not the monstrosity he had come to know. His skin was not burnt, there were no scars, blisters, or pieces of charred flesh. Instead, what he saw was pale skin, thinning blonde hair, and pale blue eyes. With the exception of a few winkles, and his signature scowl, there was nothing out of the ordinary with his face. Had Ash not paid attention to the ratty sweater and bloodied glove, Krueger would have appeared to look like a normal man.

However, the look of pure evil in his eyes was the one trait that remained constant, burned alive or not. "Surprised to see me, Ash?" said Freddy. Ash's was surprised when he listened to his voice. There was nothing warbled or distorted in his tone. His voice was not as deep or as booming as Ash had come to recognize it. He simply sounded average. "Now that I've been robbed of my souls and sent back to this... hellhole...I look a little different now, don't I?"

"Well, it is an improvement." He smirked. "But face it," Ash ran his fingers along the slight scruff that had accumulated on the side of his face. "nobody even comes close to a handsome devil like me."

Freddy stifled a laugh as he readied his glove. "I see you've been hit in the head a few times too many." He twiddled his blades back and forth. "Powers or not, I'll have you fall by my blades again in no time."

"'Cause it worked so well last time?" Ash smiled confidently as he saw Freddy's snarl at him. "Maybe I need to remind you, buddy. I'm the guy with the gun." Ash grabbed his shotgun and brought it out from the holster, aiming it at Freddy. He had his finger on the trigger when

Freddy tackled him to the ground. The back of his head slammed against the basement floor. The next thing he felt was Freddy's knuckles crashing against his face again and again. He then saw Freddy raise his bladed glove, ready to strike him. Before he could fall unconscious from the punches, he revved his chainsaw and swung it towards Freddy's neck.

Freddy's ears caught the whirring of his chainsaw and quickly ducked out of the way. He rolled onto the ground, off of Ash while the moving blade scraped against the floor.

Ash rolled over and got up to his feet before Freddy did, allowing him to attack. He swung the chainsaw from right to left. When Freddy ducked out of the way, Ash felt the weight of the chainsaw take over, causing him to nearly fall.

Although he was not eviscerated, the blade did not completely miss him. The very tip of the saw managed to slice Freddy's left side, near his ribcage. Blood sprayed from the large slash mark on his side, dripping down to his pant leg. "Aaaagh!" screamed Freddy as he covered the wound with his glove to stop the bleeding. When he looked up from his wound to see two shotgun barrels pointed at him. When they touched his forehead, he heard Ash's voice.

"Say 'Goodnight', Freddy." said Ash. "'Cause now, *you're* the one who's going to sleep." He prepared to pull the trigger.

Freddy gripped both shotgun barrels and shoved them away from him just as Ash pulled the trigger. Instead of having his brains splattered on the wall, the thunderous blast merely left a ringing sensation in his ear from being so close. With the barrels still hot from the blast, Freddy pushed them forward, causing Ash to be hit in the face with the butt of the shotgun.

"Oof!" yelled Ash as his head tilted back from the impact. He fluttered his eyes, and once he regained balance, he saw Freddy running towards him. To prevent him from attacking again, Ash kicked him in the stomach, sending Freddy stumbling far across the room.

His fall was halted when his back slammed against the wall, knocking over three of the shelves that contained souvenirs from his past victims. The toys and mason jars crashed onto the floor. The sound of broken glass echoed throughout the basement.

Ash ran to the other side of the room to Freddy. He raised his chainsaw up to his face. Once he was a few feet away from him, Ash cornered Freddy and threatened him with his chainsaw. The whirring blade was brought a foot away from his neck. The gray smoke that emitted from the chainsaw hovered around them, clouding their visions and filling their lungs.

Despite the hum coming from the chainsaw, another sound entered their ears. One that came from upstairs, outside of the basement. It was the sound of a baby crying. It was strange that such a pure and innocent sound made its way into the chaos that was happening below.

Freddy smiled evilly. Even though the features that had made him frightening were gone, the look of mischievousness and pure evil could not be taken away. "You might wanna keep it down." he said. "My daughter's trying to sleep."

'My daughter...' To Ash, hearing him say those words made him cringe down to the very core of his being. He knew that Freddy had a child, but hearing him say it, and with such a devious tone, filled him with a rage he didn't even know that he had. *I'll be doing the kid a favor by killing this bastard.* he thought. Ash leaned in, pushing the saw blade closer to his neck, ready to decapitate the son of a bitch.

Freddy slid down to the ground, missing the blade. The dark basement was now briefly illuminated from the sparks coming from the saw as it scraped against the brick wall. He got up to his feet and ran as far from Ash as he could manage. As Freddy neared the stairs, he was suddenly met with Evelyn's scolding face looking up at him, and the harsh impact of four blades piercing through his stomach. He gulped as he felt the blood trickle down to his legs. He looked down and saw that he had been stabbed with his own glove, one of the many that was displayed on a rack not far from where he was standing. Freddy gasped as Evelyn quickly pulled the blades from his body. Before he had the chance to speak, Evelyn launched her elbow at Freddy's chin. "Argh!" he screamed as he stumbled backward. He looked down at her with blood dripping down the corner of his mouth. "You cu–"

Before he could complete his remark, he felt Evelyn's arms touching his shoulders. She smiled as she spun his around, facing away from her. The next thing he saw was Ash. He had both weapons raised at shoulder-level. He had one arm over the other, with his chainsaw at the bottom and his shotgun at the top.

Without pause, Ash rammed the chainsaw through Freddy's stomach and out from his back. His blood sprayed wildly, like a geyser. Both Ash and Evelyn were being sprinkled with stray droplets of his blood. Freddy's screams of pure, unbridled agony were overpowered by the roar of Ash's chainsaw. Soon his legs gave out, and he found himself slowly lowering down to the ground. Ash forced this, pushing him down until he laid flat on the ground. Ash shut off his chainsaw and aimed both barrels of his shotgun between Freddy's eyes.

Part of his ribs had been obliterated. His intestines were scrambled. Most of his vital organs had been shredded by Ash's chainsaw. He felt a pool of warm blood surrounding his body. Freddy looked up, seeing both Ash and Evelyn's blood-splattered faces. He paid most of his attention to Ash's smug, arrogant eyes staring down at him. His powers, his strength, his chances of returning from the dead, were gone. He had been defeated. Again. Once again, by some bitch who was too clever for her own good. And also, some aging smartass with a knack for slaying the undead. But what made it different this time, was that now, all of his work, all of the bloodshed, all of the nightmares, would never have existed. With one shot, the legend of Freddy Krueger would be erased from existence. So many souls would be spared. So many children would go on to live long and happy lives, and dream in peace. Freddy coughed up a mouthful of blood, spilling it onto his chin.

Ash cocked his eyebrows. "Get ready to have everything you've done over the past thirty years go right down the drain, Krueger." he said. "Once I pull this trigger, you and all your nightmares won't exist."

Freddy leered at Ash, fighting the pain to convey a look of extreme rage and malice. "I'll see you in Hell."

Ash smirked. "Tell 'em Ash sent ya!" He pulled the trigger.

BOOM!!!

Bight sparks flew in all directions as the shell exploded from the barrel. Freddy's skull was shattered into dozens of tiny pieces. His brains spread out across the, now bloody, floor, covering the area with pinkish dots. His blood streaked across the floor approximately four feet from where his head used to be. All that was left now was a jagged line marking the separation of his head from his neck, as well as the bloodied remains. He didn't re-animate. He didn't twitch. There were no dream demons roaming his body to bring him back to life. Freddy Krueger was dead.

Ash stood up tall. His voice was cool and confident. "Long live the king, baby."

He casually blew away the smoke that rose from the shotgun. He placed it back in the holster. He continued to stare at Freddy's desecrated corpse, finally feeling relaxed to know that he was truly dead. Ash then stepped away from the corpse. He went over to the workbench that harbored his tools.

He sifted through the tools and metal shavings to find the Necronomicon, hiding in the corner of the bench, engulfed in shadow. He heard faint, sloshing footsteps growing louder as they came closer to him.

He turned to see Evelyn standing behind him. He scanned her up and down, looking at the cuts and bloodstains that covered her body.

The strength in her voice was slowly returning. "Can we go home now?" she said with a faint smile.

Ash returned her smile. "Sure." he handed the book to her. She held it carefully in her hands, never breaking eye-contact with Ash.

"You better handle it, I don't have the best luck when it comes to reading from this thing."

The corners of her lips curled into a full smile. She opened the book and flipped through the pages to find the passage to send them back. "Yeah, I know." she teased. She could feel Ash's eyes on her as she placed her finger at the beginning of the page, and began reading.

It was a little after 5:00 AM. The sunrise peaked just over the horizon. The sky was filled with streaks of light pink and orange, replacing the dark blue tint of the sky. The rays of the sun lit up the clouds. The air was calm and quiet. It was a beautiful, peaceful morning in the town of Springwood.

The chaos and destruction was over. The streets were empty. The town was as clean and pristine as it was before the evil was unleashed.

The air was calm. Not a single person was outside, as it was still early in the morning. The only sounds made were the faint chirping of the birds as they flew overhead. The dim sunrise acted as a sign for a new day. A new beginning. For the first time in decades, the children of Elm Street slept peacefully.

Out of the hazy air of dawn, not far from the street sign at the end of the block that read "1400 Elm Street", a bright flash of light appeared, followed by the warbled sound of an explosion. The same rift that transported Ash and Evelyn to Freddy's time had appeared yet again, taking them back to present day. It was like cannon fire, leaving behind a cloud of thick smoke.

Ash and Evelyn were forcefully shot out of the rift. Both of them were falling from a height of nearly twenty feet from the ground. The explosion left them with soot and debris on their face and arms. Both of them painfully landed on the side walk. The force from the fall sent them rolling on the ground for a short distance. Their bodies were scraped by the concrete.

Ash had been laying still on the sidewalk when Evelyn continued to tumble closer to him. She rolled on the ground before being halted by his still body. "Oof!" she exclaimed as her left side crashed against him. She laid on her stomach, with the concrete acting as a cold, hard, pillow below her face.

The gravel from the sidewalk seeped into their open wounds, filling them with a stinging, burning sensation in their arms and faces. The blood that had spilled onto their bodies had dried into dark patches. The red blood was now oxidized, appearing in brown and black spots on the sides of their face, and thin streaks across their arms. Their bodies were weak. From head to toe, their bones ached and their muscles were worn and sore.

Ash felt like his ribcage was going to shatter like thin glass when he coughed up a mouthful of dirt and smoke. He forced himself up, slowly raising his body so that he could sit up. As soon as he was upright, his head swirled and he felt himself succumb to dizziness. Once it died down, the sensation was quickly swapped for a massive, throbbing headache. He felt like *he* had been the one who had been shot in the head.

Evelyn's arms shook weakly as she pushed herself up from the concrete. She looked down to see the same blood pattern on her face now stained on the sidewalk. She groaned softly as she sat up. She could already feel the bruises on her knees as she propped them on the ground to sit up. Once she sat up straight, she felt her lower back tighten and her muscles throb in pain. She faced in the opposite direction as Ash.

He looked at the rising sunset, breathing a sigh of relief knowing that it was all over. "It's dawn." he said, still out of breath. He looked out into the empty street. "They're all gone now. Everything's back the way it was."

Evelyn got up to her knees, preparing to stand. Her tone suggested that she was looking at something out of the ordinary. "Ash." she called.

Ash dropped his head and sighed out of annoyance. "What is it now?" he said weakly. *Like I need any more surprises right now...*

"It's the house." she explained. "It's different, look."

He turned himself around and slowly put his feet on the ground to stand up. He lifted his head to see that they were standing directly in front of 1428 Elm Street. The same house he had lived in temporarily. The same house that Freddy once lived in. It was where it all began.

Evelyn was right, it was different. The house did no longer appeared run-down or abandoned as it did when he first moved in. Instead of chipped paint and dead plants, the house was bright white, and decorated with a rose trellis that was mounted on the right side. The grass was freshly cut and glistening from morning dew.

Ash still looked in awe as Evelyn spoke. "You know, I've lived in this town my whole life, and I've never seen that house look like this before." she said, smiling faintly. "I guess since all that stuff with Freddy never happened, it never got abandoned, or condemned. It looks like every other house on the street now."

"Yeah, it does." he agreed. "Wish it looked like this when I moved in. I was getting pretty sick of having to sleep in someplace that had ghosts and demons crawling around like rats in a storm drain."

Evelyn smiled and laughed softly. As she stood up, she looked down to see Ash attempting to do the same. She responded to his pained grunts by gently grabbing his arm and helping him up to his feet. "Well, now you don't have to anymore."

The sudden shock from standing up made his bones ring. He masked his pain by gritting his teeth. "Thanks." he said.

Evelyn responded by patting his chest before slowly walking towards the door.

The blood-splattered blade dragged across the walkway as Ash paced beside Evelyn. The metal scraping along the concrete was like nails on a chalkboard, screeching through the peaceful silence of the morning.

Ash looked over to see his Oldsmobile parked in the driveway. The dents, cracks, and bloodstains from the night before were also gone. Everything seemed perfectly in place. He had never had that kind of experience before. No matter how many times he thought he had done things right, there was always something that he had ignored.

Evelyn spoke to him as she walked beside him, cutting off his daydream. "It's actually pretty now." she commented. "It's bright, and... there are no bars on the windows."

Ash smiled. "I know." he said as he trudged toward the steps. He couldn't help but think back to all of the times he thought he had gotten rid of whatever evil he had set out to kill, only to have it come back later on in his life. All because of one mistake. One mispronounced word. One demonic entity left live. *I'm not leaving anymore loose ends this time.* He reached his left hand over to his chainsaw and unlatched it from his wrist, leaving it to drop on the concrete. "Too bad it's not gonna be around much longer."

This made Evelyn stop where she was and turn to face Ash. Her eyebrows scrunched and her expression revealed only confusion. "What do you mean?"

Ash paused to face her. She looked at him like he was a madman. It was a look he was very familiar with seeing in people. "I mean I still have one more thing I got to take care of." His head lowered down as he reached for his keys. Out of the many in his key ring, he pulled out a small silver key and handed it to Evelyn. It was the key to his trunk. When she placed her fingers on it and took it from him, he instructed her. "Do me a favor and go get those cans of gasoline from my trunk."

Her eyes darted from the key to him. "You're gonna burn it down?" she said, confused. "Why?"

He looked at her intensely. "Because, I want to be absolutely sure that I'm doing things right this time. I've been dealing with Deadites and God-knows-what for the past thirty years. And now that I've wiped Freddy Krueger out of existence, I'm done. And I just want to do everything I can to make sure he can't come back."

Evelyn nodded. "Okay." she said. "Whatever you got to do..."

Despite his exhausted appearance, Ash flashed his usual charm. "I right wrongs and change history, baby."

Evelyn had grabbed four gallons of gasoline from Ash's trunk. Before soaking the house with gas, they made sure to evacuate Ash's valuables (in other words, all of his weapons) and place them inside his car. Each carried two and spilled the gasoline at opposite ends of the house.

They made sure to line each corner of every room, spilling fluid on the curtains, bed covers, and other flammable areas. The two lines of gasoline were connected at the front door, leaving a long, thin, trail ending approximately fifteen feet from the steps.

The Delta 88 was parked on the edge of the street. The trunk was now filled with all of his weapons and gear: his chainsaw, his pump shotgun, his 9mm, his holsters and straps, and his trusty Boomstick. He took another look at them all before slamming it shut. Ash and Evelyn tossed the empty gallons aside and stood beside each other, taking one last look before 1428 Elm Street would be reduced nothing but rubble and smoke-stains.

He never broke his gaze from the house when he asked Evelyn, "Got a match?"

Evelyn remembered the box of matches the took from Ash's trunk before loading his gear. "Yeah, here." she answered. "I took them from your car. You know you have an issue of *Fangoria* in there that's over twenty years old?"

"Mmm hmm." replied Ash. "Maybe now, I'll actually get around to cleaning that thing. Of course, that's about as likely as me sprouting a new hand." He turned to Evelyn. "You ready to sit by the campfire and roast some marshmallows?"

Evelyn turned to him, un-amused by his joke. "Just throw the match."

He never broke eye contact with her when he flicked the lit match from his fingertips. He turned to see it land on the wet ground, igniting a long, bright, trail of fire leading into the house.

The line of fire grew, racing towards the house. As soon as the fire grew inside, it didn't take long until the house started to burn. The curtains and furniture caught fire the quickest, taking only seconds to ignite. The glowing, orange, flames illuminated from outside the windows. Within minutes, the house was engulfed in flames.

Ash and Evelyn watched as, from bottom to top, the entire house was covered in the roaring fire. The flames danced from both inside and outside, making it appear as if the house was moving.

Ash took the Necronomicon from Evelyn's hand and stepped closer towards the burning house. "And now to do what I came here to do." He stepped closer until he was only a few feet from the monstrous fire. The bright flames illuminated under him, giving himself a dark orange glow. He gripped the rotted flesh that served as the book's cover and hurled in into the fire. The Book of the Dead disappeared from view as it flew inside. He stepped back, watching as the house started to collapse.

They both heard the creaks and moans coming from inside as the house began to crumble. First, the roof caved in. The support beams that held the house up were next, snapping in half and falling to the rubble. Soon, the entire structure of the house was reduced to a hill of flames.

"You know, I've been thinking..." said Ash as he stared at the fire. "Since everything's changed now, I bet all your friends are still alive. It's like this whole thing never–" He felt Evelyn wrap her arms around his waist. He looked down to see her hugging him, her head buried in his chest. He decided not to say anything, instead he returned her hug.

Her voice was muffled when she spoke to him. "Thank you."

"You're welcome." he said softly. "Thanks for sticking through it, and fighting with me."

She squeezed him tightly, strengthening the hug. After lingering for a few seconds, Evelyn broke away from their hug and looked up into his eyes. "I'm just sorry it couldn't do the same for you."

"Thanks for the pep talk there, Sunshine." he said with a smirk.

Evelyn quickly apologized. "I'm sorry, I'm sorry. I didn't mean it like that."

Ash smiled at her. "I know." He gave her a gentle pat on the shoulder. "You know, I'm not that worried about it anymore. That part of my life's over, and now I can finally move on...go back home."

She took one step back, away from Ash, and offered her hand out for a handshake. She smiled, her eyes glimmered as she looked at him. "Well then, have a safe trip back to Dearborn."

"I will," said Ash. "don't worry about me." He turned away and walked back to his car. The door creaked as he opened and slammed it shut.

Evelyn put her hands on the edge of the car door window, bending down just enough to look at Ash before he started the Delta 88. "I'll miss seeing you around the store."

Ash smirked as he put the key in the ignition. "Oh, I'm sure they'll find some young 'schmo' to replace me." he remarked.

Her head nodded in defiance as she smiled widely. "I don't think so." she said adamantly. "You're kind of hard to replace."

He turned his head away from the wheel and looked up at her bloodied face. He could tell by the look in her eye, and the way she shook weakly, that it was taking a lot of her strength just to stand up. "You want a ride home?"

She shook her head. "No, I can walk from here."

"You sure about that?" he said, trying to persuade her otherwise. "It's on the other side of town."

Her voice perked up. "I know. I just want to look around. See what's changed. See what hasn't changed." As an afterthought, she then added. "Plus, I think Cooper might freak out if he saw me all bloodied up and riding with you at 6:00 AM."

"So what are you going to do?" he asked. "Clean yourself up and go back to work."

"I think you'd understand if I called in sick today."

"Yeah, I would." he agreed. He looked at her kind, smiling, face one last time before leaving her. "Well, take care..."

Evelyn poked her head through the open window, and gave Ash a brief kiss on the cheek. She then pulled back and stood up tall, retreating her hands from the door.

With a smile on his face, Ash turned the key and started his Oldsmobile. He broke eye-contact with Evelyn and turned to look at the road. He immediately put his foot on the accelerator and drove away.

Evelyn watched as the distance between them grew longer. A brief gust of wind blew through her black, matted hair as she placed her hand on her other arm, feeling one of her cuts begin to excrete blood again. Once Ash's yellow Oldsmobile faded into the horizon, she turned in the other direction and slowly walked towards the ever-brightening sunrise.

The streets of Springwood were void of people as Ash cruised to survey the town. There were no Deadites. No fires. No destruction. He kept expecting to see the aftermath of the night before in the streets in front of him. He knew that it shouldn't have, but it surprised him not to see bodies of slain demons strewn about. Destructed cars toppled over, with their windows smashed and broken glass sprinkled all around. Black streaks of soot from the fires that were caused. Not even the disintegrated remains of the demons from the destruction of the Necronomicon.

The town was spotless, as much as it was when he first arrived. Just like before, the only dark and bloody element in the town was him. He now entered downtown Springwood. By this time, Ash could see the occasional car drive past him. He looked the wristwatch on his left arm. It was just after 6:30 AM, people were on their way to work. He would take a glimpse into the window on the car that was passing him by. Every time he did, he or she would look at his scarred and bloodied face in fear. As if they'd just seen a ghost, or a murderer who was on the run.

I'm not gonna miss getting those again. he thought. Ash reached into the glove compartment and grabbed a small rag. He used it to wipe the dried blood from his face as he neared the Springwood Police Department. From the distance, he spotted Lt. Moore and Officer Harris shuffling down the steps and heading for their cars. *Somebody must've called in about the fire.* Ash thought. It had been almost an hour since he had set the house ablaze. *Took 'em long enough.* As he drove by the police station, he noticed Moore and Harris turn to look at Ash's scratched and dented Oldsmobile. He shrugged it off by barely lifting his hand from the wheel and waving at them. The two policemen simply lifted their hands as a means of waving as they leered at him, confused.

Ash muttered as he drove on. "Everything's back the way it was." Tired of the silence, Ash turned on the radio. At first, he got nothing but static. His eyes darted back and forth from the road to the knob as he adjusted it, finding a clear station. The only working station at the time was one that broadcasted directly from Springwood, and it was on AM talk radio. He listed to the hosts' overly cheerful voices as they droned on about what a great morning it was and read the weather forecast. *Why are these people always so cheery all the time?* he wondered. *I don't want you to shove your perkiness down my throat until I've had at least six cups of coffee in my system.* He regretted his decision to turn on the radio and quickly shut it off.

He looked around as he left downtown Springwood. "It's a lot better now, actually." He was now on the street that he usually took to get to work. As he was driving, he wondered aloud. "I deserve a medal for this stuff." He slowed down to about 20 miles per hour as he looked out the window to see Evelyn racing across the S-Mart parking lot.

Her face and arms were no longer bloody. She had two small band aids on her cheek where Freddy had slashed her. She wore a long-sleeve shirt to cover up the gauze that she had wrapped around her arms. Her dark hair waved as she ran across the lot to meet Cooper, who had just gotten out of his El Camino.

Ash saw her mouth open, he assumed she was yelling "Cooper!". He looked at Cooper and saw his head turn in her direction and jog towards her. He only took a few steps before Evelyn crashed into him and wrapped her arms around him. Cooper broke away to talk to her.

As soon as she looked at his face, she broke down into tears, smiling from ear to ear at the same time. She hugged him again, squeezing him tightly. When she opened her eyes, she saw Ash driving by. She kept her smile and waved at him.

He whispered. "Stay safe, kid..." He waved back at her as he drove off. He picked up speed as Evelyn came out of view. Now that his sight-seeing was over, was now on the right path to exit town. It brought him joy to think about what lay ahead of him. It was what he always hoped for, but feared would never happen. The Necronomicon was destroyed. There were no more Deadites. Freddy Krueger was dead and gone. And now, he was on the road back home.

For Evelyn...

For all of Springwood...

For Ash...

The nightmare was over.

Epilogue

THE FIRE WAS SLOWLY DYING down on top of the blackened remains of 1428 Elm Street. Smoke had filled the air in a swirled pattern, forming a small, dark, cloud above the neighborhood. It could be seen from several blocks away. All that remained of the house was a large hill comprised of burned wood and other debris. Most of the materials were charred, while others were still burning in a small pit of flames.

The calm, silent, morning was interrupted by the whining sirens of the Springwood police and fire departments rushing towards the house. The harsh, revolving, red and blue lights cut through the natural illumination of the sunrise. As soon as their vehicles stopped in front of the house, firemen and police officers came rushing out. The firemen gathered their equipment, and prepared to completely put out the existing flames.

At the very top of the burning hill, was a small pit of fire. The flames danced unpredictably, crackling as glowing embers swirled beside it. The fire served as a barrier, protecting the object surrounded by the flames. At the very center of the fire, at the very top of the hill, was the Necronomicon. It was the only thing among the crumbled mess that hadn't been affected by the fire. The book was not burned.

It couldn't burn. No matter how long the Book of the Dead was being touched by the fire, not once did it blacken, crumple, or turn into ash. The wretched face of the book simply stared off into the cloudy sky, wrinkled and expressionless as the embers fell upon the cover.

Before, it lay still and motionless. Now, in a rapid motion, the leathery cover of the book opened. Each wrinkled, blood-inked page turned on its own. The pages flipped slowly, one by one. After the third page, the pace quickened and the pages were turning more rapidly, like it was being skimmed by an unseen presence.

Near the end of the book, the pages ceased to turn. The inside of the back cover was now visible, signifying the end. On what should have been the last few pages of the Necronomicon, there were only remnants of pages. That area of the book had the pages ripped from it. Two careless, jagged lines appeared near the back cover. Only small pieces of the top corners of the pages stayed connected to the book. The beginning of a passage was printed on the top of the page. In Kandarian, the introduction read, "RESURRECTION PASSAGE".

The pages flipped back in a rush, and the front cover slammed shut. Amid the echo of the thunderous slam of the book, a voice entered the air. It was carried by the wind. It was like an unsettling whisper next to one's ear, making their heart stop a beat and sending chills down their spine. It was the disembodied voice of Freddy Krueger. "Haaa ha ha ha ha ha ha ha ha ha!"

As soon as he entered the portal back to his time, he knew what Ash's plan for him would be. He knew that Ash would follow him and kill him. Before he was burned alive. Before the Dream Demons came for him. Before the nightmares began. Before Nancy, Alice, and all the others whom he had faced in the past. That was why he ripped the pages to the resurrection passage from the book before squaring off with Ash. Even though all of the children he had haunted or killed in the past were not only alive, but didn't know who he was, it didn't matter to him. He would get his revenge.

It was time for a new beginning.

It was time to start all over again.

Ash looked down at his dash, noticing that he still had half a tank of fuel left. He hoped that would be enough to at least take him out of Ohio. He looked back up at the road, carefully watching the other cars passing him by. It was going to be a long ride back to Dearborn.

The glowing, orange sunrise was replaced with a gray and dismal blanket of clouds covering the sky. A small crash of thunder rolled in from the distance.

He kept his wheel turned slightly to the left as he drove down the winding road. His gaze trailed off, taking a second to view his surroundings. For the first time, he was able to appreciate the beauty of the woods as he drove past. The thick, leafy trees were lined by the road, appearing as a green blur as he sped past. A small gust of wind flowed, blowing several brown leaves across the road in an almost beautiful motion.

His yellow Delta 88 Oldsmobile raced down the street, driving past a sign off the side of the road. The sign read, "You are now leaving Springwood."

The road was smooth, making his ride calm and easy. He had been up for over twenty-four hours. He looked in his glove compartment, in his backseat, and in the floor, searching for an energy drink or something caffeinated to keep him awake during the ride home. *Maybe after I gas up the Classic, I could check into a motel or something.* he considered. *Eh, but let's face it, I've seen enough seedy things in the last few days. I guess I'll just nap in the backseat or something.* He tried keeping himself awake by turning on the radio, but the only thing he could get was static.

A small patter came from his windshield. It was a small drop of rain. The water streamed up his window before disappearing from view.

His lack of sleep, and the smooth road, plus the soothing sounds of a quiet rain only made Ash a victim of his own senses. He felt his eyelids get heavier, lowing further down until they would shut completely.

They fluttered back open as Ash jolted awake. *Come on, I gotta stay awake. Just until the next stop.*

From deep within the woods, a dark spirit laid dormant. It started as nothing but a quiet moan against the rustling leaves that lie on the dirt. The unseen force was then moving alongside the wind, its voice was becoming deeper and more boisterous the more it traveled.

The presence moved higher off the ground until it was roaming through the trees. Sometimes, it would smoothly dodge the tall trunks, but it often busted through the trees, causing them to split in half and fall to the ground.

The spirit emitted low growl as it roamed through the woods. It was otherworldly, malevolent, and angered. The faster the presence moved, the more powerful its voice became. At it ventured out of the woods, it became louder. Guttural. Almost deafening.

It finally escaped the woods. The dark spirit moved at a quickening pace, passing all cars in front of its path. It glided gracefully as it moved, soaring over the cars and smoothly passing them.

It was then that the spirit's voice morphed into something different. It was as if it was transforming into another voice, something resembling that of a human. It was male. Only traces of the his voice could be heard. It too, was also a voice like no other. It was booming, low, and raspy. His voice echoed, fusing with the low hum of the unseen force.

His voice came in and out of the whirring of the evil presence. When he was audible, the noises that appeared were short breaths. Excited panting. Animalistic growls. All mixed with a maniacal laughter.

"Ha…Ha ha ha ha…"

"Ha ha ha ha ha ha!"

"Haa ha ha ha ha ha ha ha ha ha!"

His being melded with the dark force, infusing them together. They were one in the same. He rushed through the few cars that were in his way, and glided faster. The powerful hum only became higher. Louder.

The bumper of Ash's Oldsmobile was now in view. He caught up with it, now a few feet from the back window. He turned, now side by side with the car. He was now moving at a blinding pace, reaching the driver's side in only seconds.

Ash killed him once before. While it was a valiant effort, there are some beings that cannot stay dead. And now, his first victim, as part of his new beginning, was right in his clutches. Ash would know what it feels like to be dragged into a place of unimaginable torture. He would be trapped, never to return. Never to find salvation. There would be only pain and emptiness.

He reached the driver's side window, which was already rolled down. He drove with only his metal hand on the steering wheel. Ash's short, black, hair flowed from the breeze. He looked so...unsuspecting. In one swift motion, he launched himself towards Ash, ready to claim his soul once more.

Ash kept his metal hand on the steering wheel as his left hand came into view. In the blink of an eye, he stuck his Boomstick out of the window and fired a round of shells into his attacker.

BOOM!!!

The exploding release of the bullet had mixed in with the sharp, rising, cry of agony.

True evil may never die, but there will always be someone to fight against it.

A. S. Eggleston is an avid fan of horror movies and novels—both of which inspired her debut novel, *Freddy vs. Ash*. Currently a college student, she lives in Texas with her family.